Also by Sasha Campbell

Suspicions

Scandals

Published by Kensington Publishing Corp.

Confessions

Sasha Campbell

Kensington Publishing Corp.
http://www.kensingtonbooks.com

DAFINA BOOKS are published by

Kensington Publishing Corp.
119 West 40th Street
New York, NY 10018

All Kensington Titles, Imprints, and Distributed Lines are available at special quantity discounts for bulk purchases for sales promotion, premiums, fund-raising, and educational, or institutional use. Special book excerpts or customized printings can also be created to fit specific needs. For details, write or phone the office of the Kensington special sales manager: Kensington Publishing Corp., 119 West 40th Street, New York, NY 10018, attn: Special Sales Department, Phone: 1-800-221-2647.

Dafina and the Dafina logo Reg. U.S. Pat. & TM Off.

ISBN-13: 978-0-7582-4196-2
ISBN-10: 0-7582-4196-8

First trade paperback printing: August 2010
First mass market printing: March 2012

10 9 8 7 6 5 4 3

Printed in the United States of America

This book is dedicated to my amazing husband.
Without you, my life is incomplete.
Thank you for more than a decade of love and support.
I couldn't have done any of this without you.

ACKNOWLEDGMENTS

Shouts out to my girls T&A. Thanks for taking this hilarious roller-coaster ride with me. This story is *our* story because you were with me every step of the way. Not once did you hold your tongues. I'm going to miss seeing your faces Monday through Friday and sharing the laughs. Your friendships have meant the world to me, and you'd better keep in touch.

I have to thank my wonderful children. Even though y'all drive me crazy, you have made motherhood an experience that I will hold forever dear to my heart. I love you.

To my editor, Selena James, for giving me this chance and for believing in my work. We went around and round about the title, but I must say your decision was absolutely fitting and rings true throughout the entire story. Thanks for your opinions and for making this book possible.

I would love to hear from my readers. Please feel free to visit me at www.sasha-campbell.com.

1

Nikki

"It's ten o'clock and you're listening to Nikki Truth, the host of the most talked about radio show in the Midwest, *Truth Hurts*. As my listeners know, I don't believe in holding your hand. If you want my advice, then you better have the balls to accept the truth . . . even if it hurts. Caller, you're on the air."

"Hi, Ms. Nikki. My name is Kimberly."

Obviously, Kimberly had been listening to my show, because everyone knows if I'm not referred to as *Ms. Nikki*, I have straight attitude. "Hello, Kimberly. What can I do for you?"

"I've got a little bit of a problem."

I leaned forward on my seat, ready to hear what crazy drama was about to unfold. "I'm all ears."

"Well, Ms. Nikki, I've been married to my husband for thirteen years, but for the last year our relationship

has grown distant. I tried talking to him about it, even suggested maybe we get counseling, but he refused, saying nothing was wrong with our marriage. But I knew something wasn't right, because we haven't had sex in four months."

"Yep, that would do it. So what did you do?" I asked while adjusting my microphone.

"Well, something told me my husband was messing around."

"Something like what?"

"Like locking his cell phone, coming home at all hours of the night."

"Hmmm, those are definitely some signs."

"Well, yesterday I waited for him to get off work and followed him to this house. When I knocked on the door, guess who answered?"

"I hope for your sake it was a woman and not a man," I said with slight laughter, trying to make light of the situation.

"Oh, it was definitely a female. He came up behind her in his underwear. I confronted him. He screamed at me and acted like we've been separated for years instead of still living in the same house!"

"Okay, wait a minute. The brotha tried to pretend the two of you weren't even together?"

"Oh, yeah, and I went off!"

"Good for you, Kimberly."

"I finally asked him to choose, and he told me on her front porch in holey draws and a dingy wifebeater, he was in love with the other woman."

"Ouch! Girlfriend, say it ain't so."

Kimberly breathed heavily into the phone. *"Yep, I'm afraid it's true. I was devastated. I got back in my car and drove home."*

"Daaayum, girl! I wouldn't wish that kind of drama on anyone. So tell me, what did you do when he got home?"

There was a noticeable pause. *"Nothing."*

"Nothing?" This female was stuck on stupid.

"Ms. Nikki, that's the problem. I love my husband and I'm willing to do whatever I can to save our marriage. That's why I called. Because I need someone out there to tell me what I need to do to bring him back to me."

I shook my head and glanced through the glass at my producer, Tristan, who was shaking his head as well. There are some women out there who allow a man to get away with just about anything.

"Kimberly, honey, obviously you don't know anything about respecting yourself, 'cause if you did, instead of calling me, you would be packing his shit and burning it in the nearest Dumpster. Why in the world would you want a man who obviously doesn't want you?"

"He's the father of my kids." Don't you know she had the nerve to sound defensive?

"And that's supposed to make it right? Men can only get away with what women allow them to. He disrespected and played you in front of another woman. That's more than enough reason to dump his sorry ass." Tristan was going to have to do a whole lot of bleeping tonight.

"Hold up, Nikki. I love him, and I don't appreciate you talking negatively about my husband!"

"Excuse me, but it's *Ms.* Nikki to you, and if you love him that much, then why you even call my show? Next caller." I ended the call. Damn! I hate to say it, but women like her deserve what they get.

"Hi, Ms. Nikki. My name is Tasha, and my family thinks I need to leave my man."

Oh, Lord, not another. "Why is that?"

"Well . . . uh . . . a couple of weeks ago we were at my cousin Boo-Man's birthday party, and one thing led to another and my man hit me. I know he didn't mean it, and he swears he won't do it again."

It must be something in the air, because that night everybody was acting cuckoo for Cocoa Puffs. "Let me tell you something, Tasha. Any woman who takes a man back after he hits her, all she's doing is telling him it's okay to do it again."

"But he's going to counseling!"

"Good, he needs to. And what you need to do is find a man who respects you."

"He can't help it. His father used to abuse him."

"And that makes it right? Girlfriend, you have to respect yourself first before you can expect a man to show you respect."

"I know, but I've prayed on it and God wants me to take him back. I'm certain of it."

"Nooo, the Lord helps those who help themselves. If you go back to a man that hits you, that means you don't feel worthy of a man who won't."

"I believe everyone deserves a chance to change!"

What was up with these defensive women? "True, but are you willing to risk your life on it? What if he really hurts you next time?"

"That ain't gonna happen, I'm certain of this. He's been trying real hard to work on our relationship. In fact, last week he asked me to marry him and I accepted. So there's no way I'm letting my family or anyone else stand in the way. I just wanted to go on the air

and say that, 'cause I know my cousins Alizé and Lingerie listen to yo show."

"If you're adamant about staying with him, then all I can do is wish you the best of luck. In the meantime, do me a favor . . . take some boxing classes." I ended the call, and the phone lines lit up with callers anxious to put in their two cents. "This is Nikki and you're on the air."

"Tasha, you are pathetic. I would have taken a frying pan to his head!"

I had to laugh at that one. "I know that's right, girl."

"Trust and believe, I used to date a man who hit me. I used to think it was my fault. That maybe if I did things the way he asked me to instead of the way I wanted, maybe he would love me more and stop hitting me. But you can't change people like that. The more I tried to make him happy, the angrier he got and the beatings got worse until one day he hit me in front of my son."

"What!" I cried, adding dramatic effect. "Girlfriend, what did you do?"

"Ms. Nikki, something in me snapped. I picked up my son's baseball bat and I swung and knocked that fool hard in the arm, then I kept on swinging. I had him running out the door in his draws screaming murder!"

"Good for you." I laughed, trying to lighten the mood. "I like to hear about a woman standing up for herself."

"Humph! I might be a big girl, but I know I deserve better."

"Yes, you do. Next caller."

"Ms. Nikki, this is Petra, and I'm calling in response to the call you got from Kimberly. Yep, that was me she

was talking about. I'm the other woman, and as far as her husband is concerned, I'm the only woman in his life. Kimberly, get it in your head, daddy ain't coming home!" Click.

"Oops, there you have it! Kimberly, dear, if that don't give you a reality check, then I don't know what will." I noticed Tristan waving his arms in the air. As soon as he had my attention, he signaled for me to take line two. "Caller, you're on the air."

"Hello, Ms. Nikki."

I groaned inwardly the second I recognized the voice. If it had belonged to anyone else, I would have considered the sound sexy and soothing. Instead, I was on the line with Mr. Loser.

I looked through the glass at Tristan, who was cracking up laughing, and stuck up my middle finger high enough for him to see it. "Caller, please introduce yourself," I said as if I didn't already know.

"Ms. Nikki, you hurt my feelings. I just knew you would never forget my voice."

I rolled my eyes. "Sorry, Charlie, but I hear hundreds of voices every week. I can't remember just one."

He chuckled. *"It's me . . . Junior."*

"Hellooo, Junior!" I said, trying to sound excited to hear from him. This man was like nails on a chalkboard—annoying as hell. "Long time no hear. What's it been, a month, maybe two?"

"It's been one month, two weeks, and three days, to be exact."

"Oh, boy! I take it your newest relationship didn't work out either."

He sighed. *"No, and I don't understand it because she was perfect. I really thought she was the one."*

"If my memory serves me right, as far as you're concerned, they're all 'the one.' " Junior had gone through so many relationships it was pathetic. Nothing ever worked and it was always the woman's fault. He was what the show *The Biggest Loser* should really be about. He would have no problem winning, because he was definitely a big, fat loser.

"No, this woman was crazy."

Listen to him tell it, they all were. "Come on, Junior. Tell me what happened, even if the truth hurts."

"What's there to say? I loved her, still do, and part of me wished she'd come back to me. I just don't understand why she ended it. I was there for her, giving her everything she needed and then some, but she had the nerve to say she needed some space."

I stuck my finger down my throat. Men like Junior were sickening. "Maybe you were smothering her."

"Nope. As soon as she said she needed room, I gave it to her. I guess I just loved her too much."

"Ugh! You're turning me off. Come on, Junior. A woman likes excitement and a little mystery."

"I gave her excitement! I bought her roses, surprised her with a massage. I cut her grass, washed her clothes."

I cut him off. "Like I said, all that catering is a turnoff. That seems to be a pattern of yours."

"What do you mean?"

"I mean you can't keep a woman! I know the truth hurts, but if anyone's gonna be honest with you, it's Ms. Nikki."

He laughed. It was a soft, eerie sound. *"That's what I love most about you."*

Just like everyone else. "Junior, you call every

month to tell me how you've gotten dumped. At some point you have to realize they can't all be crazy. Maybe it's time you started looking at yourself."

"I'm a nice man."

"Didn't you get the memo? Nice guys finish last. As sad as it may sound, women don't want a man who wears his heart on his sleeve."

"I don't understand that. Women are always talking about how they want a good man, yet when they get a man who isn't trying to take their money or drive their car, they don't want him."

I sighed dramatically. "You're right, and it's a damn shame. However, we do know what we don't want, and that's a clingy man."

"I'm not smothering."

"Gotta be. You've been dumped five times in the last six months."

There was a noticeable pause. *"Wow! You've been keeping track. You obviously care more than I imagined."*

"Nah, don't get the shit twisted. I just got a good memory and you, my friend, are unforgettable."

"I'll take that as a compliment."

"Why? I wouldn't. True, there are some women out there who appreciate a good man who's also needy. Unfortunately, me and the hundred females I know don't. However, I'm gonna let the listeners be the judge. Let's see if there is one female listening tonight who'd go out with you. In fact, I'm gonna open up the phone lines and see if we can possibly make a love connection. This is Nikki Truth with *Truth Hurts,* and for any listeners who are just tuning in, I'm on the phone with Junior. Junior, say hello to the listeners."

"Hello."

I almost laughed at the way he tried to sound like Barry White somebody. "Junior is one of my faithful listeners. He is also a *good* man, who is unlucky with love. If there are any single women out there looking for a *special* kind of man, give me a call, because I'm about to hook you up." I couldn't help emphasizing *special,* because Junior was definitely a head case.

"I-I prefer picking my own women," he sputtered. I guess he was uncomfortable with me trying to help him out.

"Maybe that's the problem. You might be picking the wrong type, but I'm gonna hook you up."

"Damn, Ms. Nikki," he began with a chuckle. It was obvious I was making him nervous. *"I respect your advice, but why you always have to be so hard? In fact, why you gotta put a brotha on the spot?"*

"Hey, I'm just telling it like I see it. In the meantime, keep your head up and take my advice for a change." I depressed the button, then took a few more calls and read several e-mails, but no one phoned in interested in going out with Mr. Loser. Not that I was the least bit surprised. By midnight my head was hurting and I was anxious to wrap up the show. "This is Nikki Truth at Hot 97 WJPC, ending another evening. When things get tough, remember the truth will set you free. Until next time." I leaned back in my chair as I took off the headset. By the time I placed it on the table, the sound of Jennifer Hudson was bellowing over the air. Tristan always knew what song to play at the end of each show. Sitting back in my chair, I had to smile. Tonight had been another fulfilling night. My producer came running over to my desk.

"You did it, girl! Another fabulous night." Tristan snapped his fingers. He's sweeter than a Krispy Kreme doughnut, but he is one hell of a producer and has been one of my closest friends for years.

"Thank you, sweetie."

He blew me a kiss, then pursed his cherry lip-gloss lips as he draped a hand at his narrow waist. "After Georgia comes on to take over the quiet storm, you wanna go grab an apple martini? I bought these shoes and I'm dying to be seen. Girlfriend is looking fierce!" He struck a pose, and I couldn't do anything but laugh. One thing Tristan knew was clothes. And even better, he knew how to get them cheap. Whenever I was in the mood for shopping, I took Tristan because he knew where to find every bargain from St. Louis to Chicago.

"Nah, I got an early day tomorrow at the bookstore. I was planning to go home and take a hot bubble bath and curl up under the covers."

He pursed his lips with disapproval, then sat his narrow ass on the end of my desk in front of me. "Miss Thang, I ain't even gonna try to beat around the bush about it. You need some dick in your life." I got ready to speak but he held up a heavily jeweled hand. "Hold on. Let me finish. Nikki, girlfriend, it's been six months, girl. Enough is enough. It's time for you to move on."

Tears burned at the backs of my eyes, and I let one roll down my cheek. Tristan was one of the few people I allowed to see me this vulnerable. He was right. I needed to start facing reality, but deep down, I wasn't ready yet to admit my marriage was over. "I know. You're right."

"Of course I'm right," he said with a toss of his fabulous weave. "Let's go get our drink on. I promise just one and we're out."

Tristan and I had been friends for almost five years,

and that was long enough to know he wasn't going to give up until I agreed. I slipped into my winter coat, said good-bye to the rest of the night owls, then strolled out of the studio to my silver Lexus. Every time I saw my car it made me smile and gave me what I desperately needed—something to smile about. As I climbed behind the wheel and pulled out of the parking lot, I couldn't help but think about what Tristan had said. I needed to give up hoping and finally move on. Deep down, part of me knew my marriage was over, but a part of me still hoped and prayed we still had a chance. But I needed to do something because wondering what the future held was starting to drive me crazy. Luckily, I had my bookstore, Book Ends, and the best job in the world at WJPC radio. I still don't understand how I had been so lucky professionally.

I was already working for the station as an intern when the general manager agreed to let me liven up the first half of the quiet storm. I had this crazy idea to serve the needs of the hundreds of lonely listeners who tuned in at night by giving them the opportunity to call in and express their feelings. Hell, all the show required was common sense and my own style of bold, in-your-face advice. The crazy idea earned me thousands of loyal listeners. Even though it's part-time, I love the hell out of my job. Giving advice is something I'm good at. Instead of getting a degree in radio broadcasting, I should have majored in social work like my girl, Trinette. Nevertheless, giving advice is what I do best. I don't hold punches. But no matter what I say or, better yet, *how* I say it, the listeners love me, and the calls and letters keep pouring in. That's why I was pulling out of the parking lot in a pretty-ass silver IS 350 convertible with butter soft leather interior. The proof is in the pudding. It's a damn shame. I could give other people advice about their lives while my own was a damn mess.

My husband and I are separated, or at least we have been since Donovan's unit, 138th Engineering Battalion, was activated and sent to Iraq. Lord, please forgive me. But his being sent to war was actually a blessing. We'd been having problems for some time, and the night before Donovan left, the two of us decided that maybe time and distance would give us a chance to decide if we wanted to either stay together or file for divorce. I guess he decided on the latter, because despite all my letters and care packages, I haven't received a single call or letter, nothing but a sorry postcard the first week he was there. I know his ass is all right, because my girl Tabitha's husband is in the same unit and she makes it her business to come to the bookstore just so she can rub it in my face how often she talks to her fat-ass husband.

After six months of nothing, I need to start facing the fact that my marriage is over and has been for quite some time. Yet a part of me still was not ready to let go. I don't know if I am just being stubborn or plain stupid like half the women who call in to my show.

Tristan made a right at the next corner, and I rolled my eyes when I realized where he was headed. I thought we were going to a bar close by and having one drink. Yeah, right. I should have known he was going to take me to his favorite hangout. Straight Shoot. A gay bar. Not that I mind. Hell, I sometimes have more fun with gay men than I do with straight mothafuckas, who are too busy trying to run game.

I climbed out just as Tristan came over switching his skinny ass toward me in knee-high, red leather boots. I'm hating, because he's got a walk that's out of this world, like he's related to Ms. J from *America's Next Top Model*. He's wearing black jeans, a white blouse and a red leather jacket with a wide belt cinched tight around his small waist. Tristan's five foot ten with mile-long legs. I'm barely five six, so he definitely makes a statement walking beside me.

I frowned with annoyance. "I thought you said one drink."

"We are!" Tristan batted his eyelashes, trying to look innocent. I know there is no way he's leaving early. Thank goodness I drove my own car. "I hope you ain't using me as an excuse to hook up with Brandon tonight."

Tristan pointed his long nail in the air. "Gurlfriend, puhleeze! He's yesterday's news."

"Since when?"

He snapped his fingers. "Since I found out he was messing around. Don't you know that sneaky bastard left a message for another bitch on my damn answering machine?"

"What!" I tried not to laugh but couldn't help myself.

I could tell he didn't see anything the least bit funny. "I guess he thought he was calling that bitch's house."

I shrugged. "At least you found out early."

"You right, because I was ready to rock his mothafuckin' world." He winked and signaled for me to follow him inside.

The club was real tasteful and clean with small intimate tables and chairs and low lighting. There was a big stage in the middle. Tristan moved to a long table in the back that was occupied by friends of his. Two of them I had met before. Coco and Mercedes. Both men were prettier than me.

Mercedes glanced down at the watch on his wrist. " 'Bout time you bitches got here."

"I know that's right." Coco gave Tristan a high five as he slid in the seat next to him.

"Sorry I'm late, but if y'all weren't listening, let me tell you, the show tonight was off the hook! Matter fact, let me introduce the rest of y'all to the hostess with the mostess, Ms. Nikki Truth."

I waved and took the chair at the far end.

The other he/she I didn't know started squirming in his seat. "Oooh! Girlfriend, your show is the bomb! I never miss it."

Mercedes gave a rude snort. "She ain't lying. You've even answered her calls a few times."

I gave the one with the blond weave a long look. "Oh, yeah? When did you call?"

She looked uncomfortable. "Last month."

Mercedes filled in the details. "Girlfriend, here was Oasis. She called telling you her man insisted on the cat sleeping in the bed with them."

Laughing, I nodded my head. "Oh, yeah, I remember. I told you to tell him to get rid of the cat or you were leaving his ass."

"Yeah, and the next day he packed his shit and left," Oasis announced with disgust.

"Damn. I'm sorry."

"Wasn't your fault," she said, and made an exaggerated show of fanning herself. "I think that cat was licking a lot more than just his paws under those covers."

The table roared with laughter. Tristan signaled for a waiter and we both ordered a martini. The deejay was rocking some old school. I had gotten my drink and was having fun with the others when I felt someone tap me on the shoulder. I looked up, and it was a young slender woman with her head shaved bald and jeans hanging low on her hips.

"Yo, ma, you wanna dance?"

I looked up into the most amazing brown eyes I'd seen in a long time. Her lashes were naturally long and incredibly thick. Mascara had nothing to do with it. I would give anything to have eyes like that. I don't know how long I stared at her before I finally shook my head. "Nah, boo. I'm strictly dickly."

The look she gave me rang loud and clear. She could do anything a man could do, only better. "Yo, don't knock it till you try it."

I smiled. "Not knocking it. I just prefer my dick to be attached, not strapped on."

"A'ight, ma. If you change your mind, you know where to find me." With a nod of her head, she turned on the soles of her Air Force Ones.

I watched her walk away and had to admit she had a hell of a swagger that made my nipples tighten. Damn, had it been that long since I had some?

I raised my hand and quickly ordered another drink. Yep, Tristan was right. I needed some dick—quick!

2

Trinette

"Trinette, open the got-damn door!"

All I wanted was a tennis bracelet. Instead, I had some knucklehead banging on my bathroom door, trippin' about a photograph he shouldn't have found in the first place. I don't know what it is, but once you give a brotha some, he seems to lose his damn mind.

The evening had started off perfect. I had made a fabulous dinner of a tossed salad and Cheeseburger Macaroni Hamburger Helper. Afterward, we moved up to my bedroom, where I gave Cory a massage. The entire time I was rubbing oil all over him, I was thinking about the beautiful one-carat diamond and ruby bracelet I saw at Jared that looked gorgeous on my arm. Ready to get down to business, I flipped Cory onto his back and rode him as if he were a mechanical bull. Ms. Netta got mad skills, and I had the brotha speaking in tongues. I just knew that by the time I was finished with him there was no way he was going to deny me my bracelet. But before I could even begin hinting about jewelry, that idiot came and then had the nerve to fall asleep. I was so pissed off, I decided to treat myself to a hot bubble bath before I put his ass out, and had barely put my big toe in the water when Cory slammed his fist against the door, scaring the shit out of me. Now all I wanted was for him to get the hell out my house.

"Cory, I ain't in the mood," I warned.

"I want an answer," he demanded.

"Take your nosy ass home!"

"Yo, I ain't going nowhere till you tell me the truth!"

Damn! After reaching for my washcloth, I mopped beads of sweat from my forehead. The lukewarm water did nothing to cool my raging temper. "I already told you the truth," I mumbled.

"Then why you got this mothafucka's picture in your drawer?"

What the hell was he doing in my drawer? Didn't his mama teach him, if you go looking for trouble, you're sure to find it? Besides, it was my house. If he wasn't gone by the time I finished my bath, as soon as I dried off, I was putting his ass out.

When it comes to men, I know when to cut my losses. Well, I was there. I was tired of Cory's bullshit and his crooked dick. "I already told you. I forgot it was in there."

He snorted rudely. "You must think I'm stupid or something. I know you're still fucking him. Now open this door before I knock it down!"

Leaning forward, I turned the faucet on, adding more hot water to the tub while also trying to drown out his nagging voice. This is what I got for inviting his ass to my house. For once, I should have listened to Nikki.

Why is it after you give a brotha some coochie they think they own you? I ain't never been able to figure that shit out. There was no ring on my finger. Well . . . at least not this week. He wasn't paying my bills, yet Cory had the audacity to go through my personal belongings looking for some shit to trip about. A photograph he had no business finding in the first place.

Sinking lower into the water, I allowed my mind to wander back eight years, to the day I met Leon Montgomery. The first man I ever loved and the man I later married. He was also the man whose photograph Cory found in my drawer.

"Trinette, you hear me talking to you!" Cory banged on the door again and broke through my thoughts.

I shook my head while wondering how the hell I ended up with a psycho. I guess I had to take part of the blame. I should have been honest and told Cory I was married. My bad. I screwed up. I just didn't think that bit of information was important, considering we'd only been seeing each other two weeks and I didn't expect it to last much longer. It couldn't. There was nothing he or any other man could do for me but give me their money, buy me nice things, and lick Ms. Netta's coochie. Plain and simple. *Hmmm.* I guess this meant I wouldn't be getting that bracelet.

I don't know why I went out with Cory in the first place. It wasn't like he was my type. He's a pretty boy with gray eyes and wavy hair. I don't do pretty boys, because they spend more time in front of the mirror than I do. And I definitely can't have that. However, when I first spotted him at the gym, all I could do was stare as he used the equipment. I wasn't staring because he had muscles on top of muscles. I was staring because I had seen his face in the newspaper two months before after he had won the Missouri Lottery. $100k. While I watched, I wondered what it would take for me to get his attention. An idea finally hit me. I moved over to the deltoid machine and purposely faked ignorance. Sure enough, Cory came to my aid. It took everything I had not to run my tongue across his massive biceps. Then after a few minutes of proper instruction, he asked me out. Cory was shorter than my usual sponsors, but since his pockets were fat, I was more than willing to make an exception.

Big mistake.

"Trinette!"

I turned the water off because with him banging on the door and hollering like some damn fool, relaxing was totally out of the question. I climbed out and reached for a towel.

"Boo, why you lying to me? Huh? I want an answer!"

His whining was quickly wearing my nerves. I dried off and reached for my robe, hanging on the back of the bathroom door. "Lie to you about what?" I asked as I swung the door open. Would you believe the fool had the nerve to have tears in his eyes?

I rolled my eyes and moved over to my dresser drawer that was still sitting wide open. A colorful array of Victoria's Secret garments had been thrown every which way. Organization has never been one of my strengths, but that was beside the point.

Cory flung the photo back into the drawer. "I can't believe this shit! Everything I've done for you and this is how you treat me."

"Hold up. Everything like what?" Because he had

yet to spend any *real* money on me. I reached for the remote and turned the television off. I wanted to make sure I didn't miss a single word of what he was about to say.

"I just made breakfast for you last weekend."

I laughed as I closed the drawer and moved to take a seat on the end of my queen-size bed. "Since when is popping two Eggo waffles into the toaster considered cooking?"

His brow bunched as he spoke. "It's the thought that counts. Besides, last week we went out to dinner and a movie."

"Oooh! Big spender. You took me to Steak 'n Shake with a coupon, and the movie was a matinee." Now, I don't have a problem with cutting corners. Lord knows my broke ass does when I don't have a choice. What pissed me off was we dropped by Walmart on the way so he could stuff my purse with candy and soda. He better recognize. Ms. Netta is used to being wined and dined by a man. I didn't mind giving a brother a little coochie for monetary gain. Hell, usually at this point in the relationship, brothas are passing hundred dollar bills my way to support my insatiable shopping habit, but not this broke joke. The money stopped coming my way after the first week. I'm not gonna front. Cory bought me a pair of diamond earrings, took me on a shopping spree in Chicago the weekend before, and even gave me two thousand dollars when I lied and told him my car was about to be repossessed. But for the past several days, all he wanted to do is lie in my bed and watch television. Uh-uh, as far as I was concerned, we still had thousands of dollars to spend. Or at least that's what I thought before I picked up his pants and tossed them at him, then noticed a crumpled piece of paper on the floor. He was still going on and on about finding Leon's picture and demanding to know who the dude was when I reached down and picked the piece of paper up and stared at it.

-131.48

What the hell? It couldn't be right. There was no way in hell Cory's account was negative in less than three months. But Wachovia Bank was the name on the debit card he had been swiping all over town the past two weeks. Or at least until the previous Thursday when we'd gone to get gas and he'd acted like the strip on the back of the card was bad. It was then that I wondered why. His fake ass was broke. I couldn't believe I let him play me like that.

Cory tried to speak, but I held up a hand, silencing him. "You know what, Cory? There's a lotta things I will tolerate, but never someone going through my personal belongings. So listen to what I am about to say. It's over between us. Now leave!"

He was pacing back and forth across the length of my small room. His chest was heaving and his hands were balled by his sides. He looked hurt. A muscle twitched at his dimpled cheek. His eyes were glassy. I wished I could feel sorry for him, but he'd used up all his chances. Besides, his behavior was starting to scare me.

I rose from the bed. "Cory, I'm not gonna ask you again."

"I ain't going nowhere till you tell me who that mothafucka is!"

He moved all up in my face like he was about to beat a sistah down. I met him eye to eye. I'm no punk, but I'm no fool either. My heart was beating rapidly against my ribs. I took a step back just to be on the safe side. "Whoever he is, he obviously has more money than you have, Mr. Lottery Winner." I balled up the ATM receipt and tossed it at his head. He picked it up, uncrumpled it, and stared down at it. Busted! The embarrassed look on his face was priceless.

"You need to leave."

He moved toward me. "I said I ain't going nowhere."

"Now, listen to what I'm about to say. Koolaid's only a phone call away. So the choice is yours. Either get out or get put out," I said, with a combination of anger and fear marking my every word. Not that I needed my brother's help. With a quick left hook, I was almost certain I could get in a few good licks. However, since he knew my brother by reputation, the threat sounded much more effective.

Cory stared at me for a long moment like he was contemplating his next move, then he reached out and tried to hold me in his arms. "Why you doin' me like this? I thought you were feelin' me, boo."

"That was before I discovered your ass was broke." I jumped out of his reach, moved around my bed for the phone, and made a show of punching numbers. "I'm calling Koolaid." I was really calling time and temperature, but he didn't need to know that.

"A'ight, I'll go, but this discussion ain't over," he replied, his eyes flashing with anger. "You still ain't told me who that nigga is in the photo."

I punched END on my cordless but continued to hold it in my hand just in case I needed to clock the fool upside his head. "We don't have shit else to talk about, and the man in the photo is none of your business."

He gave me a look of disbelief. "Oh, so it's like that?"

"Yeah, it's like that."

"Fuck you, then, you gold-digging bitch!"

See, this is what I was talking about. Take a deep breath, Netta. Any other time, I would have kicked a brotha in his nuts for calling me a bitch, but since he was getting the hell out of my house, I allowed the comment to slide.

While I kept an eye on him, Cory quickly slipped into a sweatshirt lying at the end of the bed. As soon as his Jordans were back on his feet, he made a show of grabbing everything he'd left at my house over the last two weeks, which wasn't hard to do, considering I kept most of it in a small box next to the door. Cory had gotten too comfortable. I'd been telling him to take his shit back home to his mama, because I wasn't about to be washing some negro's stinky-ass draws.

Cory grabbed the box, then took his time walking to the door as if I might change my mind. Halfway down the hall, he paused and looked me directly in the eyes. "Once I walk out that door, I ain't ever steppin' up in here again."

"You promise," I mumbled, then stepping around him, I went to the door and swung it open. "Have a nice night."

Suddenly Cory wasn't the tough guy anymore. Tears were running down his face, and thick white spit was in the corners of his mouth. "Why you doin' me like this?" he whispered.

My stomach did a nosedive. Damn, I hate to see a man cry. I almost felt sorry for him. "Because I told you I wasn't looking for a serious relationship. Obviously you forgot the rules since you decided to go rummaging through my stuff."

"Yeah, a'ight." He leaned forward and tried to kiss me. I quickly backed up. I'd be damned if he was going to touch me with that foul shit near his lips.

Cory shook his head like I was making a big mistake. "You a trip," he said as he stepped out the door.

"No, you tripped!" I spat as I slammed the door and immediately locked it behind him. I then moved over to the window and watched out the corner of the blinds as he loaded the backseat of his orange Mitsubishi Eclipse. Bitch-ass car. I'd been teasing him since day one that he drove a gay-ass ride. I even refused to be caught dead riding in the passenger side, which meant most dates we rolled in my Benz.

I kept watching as he climbed behind the wheel. There was no way I was taking my eye off him. I had learned long ago to never turn your back on a brotha after you kicked him to the curb. I made that mistake once and had sugar put in my tank.

I waited until Cory had reached the corner, then sighed with relief as I made my way up to my bedroom. Once there I collapsed on the bed and stared up at the ceiling, wondering if my husband and his money would ever be enough. So far, the answer was no.

Damn! I really wanted that bracelet.

3

Nikki

"I can't believe he acted like that!" I screamed after my best friend brought me up to speed on her relationship with Cory. I was falling out my chair while Trinette didn't look the least bit amused. Well, too bad. How the hell did she expect me to react? I can't believe she really thought she was going to con Mr. Lottery out of his money. Seems to me, he might have already heard about her reputation.

Trinette rolled her eyes. "It's not funny. That nut made me think."

"Think about what? That you should stop bringing fools home? Damn, Netta, I told you before, don't shit where you sleep. One of these days your actions are gonna catch up with you." I shook my head and started laughing again. What the hell was she thinking bringing a man to her house? Hello! Did she forget she was married? Okay, maybe Leon doesn't live with her, but not only does he pay the bills, the man also has a key.

She gave me a dismissive wave. "It's not funny."

I pointed an accusing finger at her. "You're right. It's not funny. You had no business bringing that bum to your home."

Trinette frowned. "Hell, I didn't have a choice. Cory lives at home with his mother."

"Oh, my God! That's even worse. Why in the world would you be interested in someone who doesn't have his own place?"

"Girl, what can I say? He had just won a hundred grand, and I wanted some of it."

"What else is new? You thought he was your lottery ticket." If she didn't have a degree I would have sworn her ass was slow. The way she uses men sometimes is downright sickening. "The warning signs were already there. If it had been me, the first thing I would have questioned was, if Cory had all that money why didn't he get his own place?"

She rolled her eyes. "Cory told me his mom lived with him because her health wasn't the best."

"And you believed him? I bet her name pops up on the caller ID." I gave Trinette a long look. She just stared at me, neither confirming nor denying my statement until she could no longer hold a straight face and started laughing. "Goofy ass! You can be so gullible sometimes."

When she finally stopped laughing, she said, "Yeah, I know. I wasn't thinking straight with that one. How'd you know the phone was in his mama's name?"

I shifted my eyes and glared at her. "Why you think? Because that's his mama's house, not his."

Trinette gave me a long, hard look. She hates when she's wrong and I'm right. "All I know is, he better not even try to call me. I can't believe his ass is already broke. That fool can't afford to pay for me to get my nails done. You know I don't have time for a brotha if he can't provide me the lifestyle I'm accustomed to."

"Accustomed to? Trinette, you forget, you grew up in the projects just like me."

She cringed at the reminder, then had the nerve to look embarrassed as she glanced over at the table beside us to make sure the couple hadn't overheard. "That was a long time ago," she whispered. "Now quit talking so loud!"

Our waitress arrived, and while Trinette placed our order, all I could do was stare at my friend and think how stupid she can be at times. She'd been married to Leon Montgomery, a CFO for one of the largest financial institutions in America, for almost eight years. Now, he isn't all that to look at. Leon's got a serious receding hairline and is too skinny for my taste, but he has all the personality in the world to make up for it. I love him like a brother. Have for years. The only problem I have with Leon is that for the last two years, he has allowed Trinette to do whatever the hell she wants, and as a result she has absolutely no respect for him as a man.

"And bring us some more salsa and chips," Trinette tossed over her shoulder as our waitress departed with our orders. She straightened the cowl-neck of her black knit dress. As always, everything was accessorized all the way down to the diamond bracelet dangling from her wrist. I love her style. One thing about Trinette, she may be a size 16, but the chick can dress her ass off.

She has the smallest waist and big perky breasts, and she makes sure everything she wears emphasizes both. I've envied her assets for years.

"When's Leon getting home?"

Trinette pursed her magenta-painted lips in a thin line at the mention of her husband. "He'll be here Friday. I guess I better change my sheets," she added, then had the nerve to cackle. I knew it was wrong, but I couldn't help but to laugh along with her and shake my head. My girl was seriously living on the edge. Because he worked in Richmond, Trinette saw Leon one weekend a month, which allowed her ass twenty-eight days a month to pretend she was single.

I gave her a warning look. "You think that shit is funny, but as I've said to you many times before, one of these days he's gonna sneak up on your ass."

She tossed a heavily jeweled hand my way. Unfortunately, the one ring missing from her finger was a wedding band. Trinette swears up and down that yellow gold breaks her finger out. Yet it's funny how that sucker is back on her finger like clockwork the second Leon's plane lands at the Lambert–St. Louis International Airport. "Leon would never come unannounced, because he doesn't like surprises." She gave me a look of satisfaction just as her eyes traveled over toward the entrance. I followed the direction of her gaze and spotted a tall man in a gray suit who had just strolled into the restaurant . . . alone. I'll admit he was gorgeous and just the way Trinette liked them. Leon was due home and she needed to be trying to save some coochie for him, which meant keeping her attention on our side of the room. I swung the toe of my stiletto boot at her shin.

"Ouch!" She shot an accusing glare across the table at me.

"Stay focused! After Cory, a man should be the last thing on your mind."

Trinette tossed me an incredulous look. "That will never happen."

"Well, it should . . . at least for the rest of the week. You know Leon's home this weekend and he'll wanna talk about you moving to Richmond in June like you promised."

"I'll just give him some extra loving and he'll forget all about me joining him." She wagged her brow suggestively.

I took a long, deep breath, shifting my body in the chair before speaking. "Trinette, Leon's been living without you for two years. One of these days he's gonna decide enough is enough and find another woman."

She raised a finger to chastise me, then looked like she had second thoughts before she finally spoke. "And when he does, I guess it will be time for us to finally go our separate ways, but I don't see that ever happening. Leon loves me. We're already talking about going to Hawaii for Christmas this year."

Sometimes her overconfidence was enough to make me sick. I love my girl, really I do, but she can be so self-centered at times. Two years ago, Leon accepted one helluva promotion that sent him to the corporate offices in Richmond. Ever since, Trinette has been coming up with every excuse imaginable as to why she hasn't joined him yet. Last September she enrolled in a master's program at Lindenwood University just so she'd have an excuse to stick around at least another year.

The waitress returned with our frozen margaritas and chips. Mexican happy hour once a week had been a ritual of ours for years. I reached for the homemade salsa and poured some on my plate.

Trinette grabbed a chip and popped it in her mouth. "I'm thinking about buying a new car."

She had to be kidding. "Your Mercedes is less than two years old."

"You just said it. *Old.* I want that new E-550 I saw on a commercial last night."

"Oooh! I love that car." I'm sure the envy was apparent in my eyes. "What color?"

"Red, of course. I think while Leon's here I'll convince him to go over to the Mercedes dealer with me." I watched her eyes wander briefly across the room again. I snapped my fingers in front of her face, drawing her attention again.

"So in other words, you need him to buy you this new car. Have you even started working on fixing your credit yet?"

"For what? As long as I got a generous husband, who needs good credit?"

I brought my untouched drink to my lips. "If you fixed your credit you could buy stuff yourself and not have to depend on Leon or all those other men to buy you the things requiring credit to purchase. The last thing I'll ever be is dependent on a man," I replied between sips.

"Leon loves me depending on him."

"No, you love depending on him. All you have to do is work on one debt at a time and start paying off all those damn credit cards along with whatever else you have on your report."

She rolled her eyes. Trinette hates me talking about

how fucked up her credit is, but come on. She's a grown-ass woman and it's time she started standing on her own two feet and stop using men to provide all her needs. She's married to a financial executive, yet her finances are jacked up. "You need to get it together. You'll be thirty-one next month."

Her face suddenly became serious. "If it'll make you happy, I will order a copy of my credit report and start working on fixing some stuff."

"Sounds good."

You would never guess we grew up in the same neighborhood. Englewood Park housing projects. Two skinny kids with big dreams of living the good life. The path I followed took me a little longer than Trinette. Marriage. College. Years of struggling to make ends meet. Donovan opened a barber shop. A Cut Above the Rest took three years before we finally saw a profit. Then two years ago, I took the plunge and opened my bookstore. Afterward, I started my radio segment, *Truth Hurts*. Life had been a struggle, but finally I'm starting to see the light.

But things were different for Trinette. She knew what she wanted from the beginning—a man who was going to do big things, and skinny-ass Leon was her answer. They met in college. He was smart, was good with money, and had a job, Trinette's top requirements in a man. Back then he let her run over him, and ain't much changed since. However, her behavior was getting out of control. She was screwing brothers for money when she had a husband who was loaded. It wasn't because she needed the money. It was because she enjoyed the thrill of fucking around without getting caught. She also loved the control she had over other people's money.

"You heard anything from Donovan yet?"

Trinette changed the subject, which meant she was tired of me getting in her ass. I decided to play along. I waited until our waitress delivered our food—chicken quesadillas—and moved to the next table before I responded. "Nope. It's pretty clear at this point. . . . My husband isn't the least bit interested in me or our marriage anymore." I reached for my knife and fork and focused on my food.

Trinette knew she had hit a sore spot with me and gave me a sympathetic look. "Maybe it's time. You said yourself Donovan pretty much ended the marriage before he was deployed."

"I know, but I had hoped distance would have made the heart grow fonder." I gave a rude snort. "Obviously not."

We'd been having problems for some time, but I had still tried to support my husband and had hoped the time apart was all it would take to bring our marriage back together, but apparently it was all in my head. Our marriage had been dead for a long time. There was too much pain and neither of us knew how to fix it, and I no longer had the energy to keep trying.

For several seconds we ate in silence. I thought about my life a year ago and compared it to life at that point. Sadly, not much had changed.

"The Minority Business Association is having a party next weekend. You wanna go?"

Usually I don't go to social functions like that. Mostly bougie black women trying to outdress each other while acting like they're all that. But I didn't have anything else to do. Tristan said it was time for me to move on, and possibly find some dick in the process.

It'd been so long since I'd had sex, I had cobwebs between my legs. "Maybe."

"It will be fun. We can eat and sit back and talk about folks. You never know, you might meet yourself a nice *professional* man."

I frowned at Trinette. She had never considered Donovan's barbershop a true profession. "We'll see."

"Well, don't wait too long. I need to buy tickets in advance. And it's dress to impress, so we can hit the Galleria if you want."

I nodded. Shopping sounded like a fabulous idea.

After happy hour, we said our good-byes and I watched Trinette walk to her Benz while I moved to my Lexus. "Don't forget. We're going shopping Friday before Leon gets here."

"Okay," I yelled over my shoulder. I didn't have the will or the enthusiasm it was going to take for me to move on with my life. I put my key in the ignition and sat there in the parking lot warming up my car long after Trinette was gone. Only a fool sits around and waits on a man, but something kept nagging at me that my marriage just wasn't quite over yet. And as long as I had that feeling, it was going to be hard to let go.

4

Trinette

Let me just say I love my job. I really really love my job. I work because I want to, not because I have to, and I make sure everybody knows it.

I strolled in on Wednesday before eight A.M. looking fierce of course. I found a slamming burnt orange pantsuit on clearance at Nordstrom for seven hundred. I paired it with a pair of chocolate Jimmy Choos and a thick chocolate belt, showing off my narrow waist. As usual I strolled into the office carrying my morning latte. There was absolutely no other way to start my morning.

"Good morning, Trinette."

I waved at Chuck, our building security guard, before I turned the corner and stepped into our suite.

The moment I did, I looked over at our receptionist, Claudette, and I almost spilled my latte all over me. And you better believe I would have sent that chick the dry cleaning bill. I don't know what possessed that girl to get red tracks sewn in her head over the weekend. Don't she know she looked like Homey the Clown?

"Good morning, girl." I swung my fabulous three hundred dollar weave over my shoulder. Showing her how it's done. Only the best for me. Obviously she knew nothing about that.

I strutted through the office waving, being fake. I know half the hoes I work with are hating on my ass. And I'm all right with that. See, I walk with my head held high and strut like my shit don't stink, because it don't. Hell, I can't help it if I care about how I look and they don't. Most of the other case managers at the Division of Children and Family Services walk in looking like they just rolled out of bed. Not me. I get up extra early to make sure I look extra good.

"We've got a meeting at ten today," Patricia called from her chair as I moved in the cubicle across from her.

"What about?"

She shrugged her wide shoulders, then reached inside a box of Dunkin' Donuts. "Don't know. Yolanda sent out an e-mail to just the case managers."

Yolanda Webber was our director, so any time she held a meeting, it impacted our workload. We were already overworked—not that I was complaining. I probably had the largest caseload, but that was because I am good at what I do, and Yolanda recognized my dedication to the job.

"Good morning, ladies."

"Good morning," I said under my breath as Maureen Morgan sashayed by, leaving behind a cloud of her expensive, overly sweet perfume. I couldn't help noticing she was wearing a new outfit. Trust me. I know when someone is sporting something new. Maureen had on a honey brown jacket and matching skirt that showed off her slender body and extremely long legs. I would never tell her, but I would do anything to have legs like hers.

"How was everyone's weekend?" Maureen asked as she lowered herself into the chair behind her desk. She had been out of the office all week.

"Relaxing," I replied.

"Drama," Patricia said, then raised her brow. She had already given me all the details of her drama-filled weekend with that wannabe thug she was dating. Her life reminded me too much of the ghetto life I left behind.

Maureen fanned her fingers in front of her. "Well, I had a fabulous weekend. Michael and I put a contract on a new house."

Patricia rolled her chair closer. "Oooh! A new house? Where at?"

"In Webster Grove." Maureen reached inside her purse and pulled out not one but two flyers, enough for the both of us. "It's more than three thousand square feet, five bedrooms, and even has a sunroom," she announced proudly.

I stared down at the paper in my hand and the $400k price tag. "Daaayum, girl! What you need this much house for?"

"I like space."

I looked in envy and found myself wishing for a home like that. I used to have one just like that if not better. Now I'm back living in the same three-bedroom condo Leon and I bought the first year we got married. My place didn't even have enough closet space for all my clothes. Leon had traveled so much, we never stayed in either of the other homes we had bought long enough for me to fully enjoy them. And the second he was transferred due to a merger, we sold it and bought another. The only place we ever kept and used as rental property was the condo. When he was promoted to CFO and announced he would be moving to Richmond, I had returned to St. Louis during the entire transition. But I had long since grown tired of the small condo. I wanted a jetted tub like the one I saw in the picture. I wanted to sit out on a sunporch and watch the sun rise. And dammit, I was going to have it!

"I sure hope the sellers accept our offer. Michael and I are so excited."

My eyes traveled over to the ten-by-thirteen photograph Maureen kept on her desk of her darling Michael. The first time I saw him, I found myself licking my lips. He was a pork chop waiting to be sucked. Michael Morgan was a former NFL player who now owned a large car dealership. I had spotted him Monday while at happy hour with Nikki and would have gotten his attention if Nikki hadn't been with me. I love my girl, but she doesn't understand the power of the pussy. That's why her ass ain't had none in months, which didn't make sense to me. She's a sexy size 10 with a small waist and the prettiest mahogany skin. Her breasts are too small, but she has enough ass to make up for what she's lacking. Her best feature is her large brown eyes and her locks that are honey blond, long, and gorgeous. Nikki's pretty, which she'd have to be to hang with me. I'm thick, caramel, and luscious, and she's slim and sexy. Together we're a force to be reckoned. Yet instead of hanging with me, Nikki wanted to sit at home, waiting for her husband to call. Now, don't get me wrong, I love me some Donovan, but he was away, and instead

of twiddling her thumbs, Nikki could have been finding another way to pass the time. While he was serving
our country overseas, she could have been servicing
the needs of some rich men in St. Louis.

The phones started ringing, and it was time to get
to work. Even while I helped my first client, my eyes
kept traveling down to that flyer. By the end of the
morning, I was calling a realtor and made an appointment to discuss putting my place on the market. All I
had to do was convince Leon. And I knew just how to
persuade him. As soon as I hung up the phone, my private line rang.

"DFS, Trinette speaking."

"Good morning, boo."

Ugh! No, Cory was not calling me. "Didn't I tell
you not to call me no more?" Hell, I'd been telling his
ass all that week.

"I know, but I wanted a chance to show you I've
changed. I went out and got a new car to prove it."

Did he really think getting rid of that gay-ass car
was going to make a difference? "I don't care if you
got a chauffeured limousine! There is no more us, and
if your cheap ass calls my job again, I'm calling your
mama."

There was a long pause. The last thing Cory wanted
was for me to call Mommy Dearest and tell on him.

"You don't mean that," he finally said.

"Oh, don't try me. I'll even come over and show
her those doo-doo-stain draws you left under my bed!"
The phone went dead. I looked over at Patricia, who
was trying her damnedest not to laugh. "Stanky ass," I
mumbled under my breath.

She busted out laughing and I joined her. Cory had
a lot of nerve calling me after what I found under my

bed. I guess his mama had never taught him how to wipe his ass properly. Just thinking about sex with him made my stomach cringe. The things I do for money.

My nine o'clock appointment arrived. I moved into the conference room, which is separated by partitions, and down to workstation three where a chick was sitting. She could have been cute if it wasn't for the hoop earring dangling from the corner of her nose.

"Cimon Clark."

A pair of hazel eyes met mine. "Yep," she mumbled, chewing her gum like it was going out of style. "Where's Casey?" she asked. The frown on her face indicated she wasn't too happy to see me. That's just too damn bad. It was time she learned you can't always have what you want.

I gave her a saccharine smile. "Casey transferred to Iowa, so I'm your new worker."

Cimon rolled her eyes and put a crumpled piece of paper on the counter. "I got this letter saying I need to renew my food stamps."

I nodded. "Yep. You're required to do so every six months. You bring a copy of your lease and utility bills?"

"Uh-huh." She passed the documents to me.

I looked through the papers, then went through a list of standard questions. "Do you have a phone?"

She shook her head. "Nope. Can't afford it."

"Anyone else living in your house?"

"Nope, just me and my three kids. Y'all need to increase my food stamps 'cause three fifty ain't enough to feed four people." Cimon sounded disgusted.

That chick was tripping, because that sounded like enough food to me. I was typing notes in her case file when I heard Ciara's new song playing. Don't you know that hoochie reached inside her purse and pulled out a cell phone, then had the nerve to start talking.

"Whassup? Giiirrrl, I saw that! Yep. I'm running to the mall in a few."

No, she didn't. I stopped typing and stared her ass down. "Excuse me, but are you here to handle business or not?"

Cimon had the nerve to suck her teeth and roll her eyes. "Velveeta, girl . . . I'ma have to holla back." She hung up, then leaned back in her chair and crossed her arms. Velveeta? What was her mama thinking naming her after processed cheese?

I cleared my throat. "I thought you didn't have a phone?"

She had the nerve to try to look dumb. "You said a house phone."

"I said a phone. I didn't say what kind. If you don't have a job, how you pay your cell phone bill?"

"Why you all up in my business?" She rolled her neck as she spoke.

Did this bitch not know I had the upper hand? "I'm your caseworker, so you best believe I'm gonna be all in your business."

She looked like she had an attitude for a second, but she had sense enough to shut up. I was already sick of her ghetto ass.

"Do you have a car?" I asked.

"Uh . . . yeah."

I tore my eyes away from the screen long enough to look at her. "Okay. What kind of car do you have?"

She hesitated. "I'm driving a 2000 Honda Civic. It's paid for."

I entered the information in the computer. "Let me

go make copies of your documents. I'll be back." I rose
and went to the copy machine, then came back to find
Cimon sending a text message. That girl was really
pushing her luck with me. As soon as she spotted me,
she put the phone away. She better have. "All right. According to the information you provided me, we'll be
increasing your stamps to four twenty. They'll be available in two weeks."

"Thanks." Cimon grinned like she suddenly thought
of something funny.

"Is something wrong?" I couldn't keep the attitude
from my voice.

She gave it right back to me. "Nope. Nothing at
all." She stuffed her documents back in her purse, then
rose.

Oh, I wasn't done with her. "While you're here, I
need you to go to the career center next door and apply
for some jobs."

Cimon looked at me as if I told her ass to rob a
bank. "Why I need to do that?"

"Don't you wanna do something with your life
other than receiving food stamps and living on Section
8?"

"Fo' what? It cost me more to get a job and pay for
a babysitter." Another chick trying to get over on the
system. Women like her made me sick.

"You got three kids, which means you are entitled
to full education benefits. You can get a free ride. I
wish I could have gotten a degree for free. Did you
know you are eligible for child care?"

"Fo' real?" She gave me a greedy look.

"Yeah, as long as you're working or going to school."
Cimon sucked her teeth and quickly lost interest.

Ha! She really thought we were going to pay for day-care while her lazy ass lay around at home with some thug.

I pointed down at the sheet of paper on the counter. "I need you to sign here and here."

I stared at her pinch braids while she signed. They looked like she had just gotten them done. It would have cost her at least one fifty, but she didn't have money to feed her kids. Did I tell you women like her made me sick?

After she left, I went and took a bathroom break and checked my makeup on the way out, making sure I was still looking good. I was. Before going into the office, I went outside to get a newspaper from the rack out front. It was the week before the Martin Luther King holiday and cold as hell. I dug a quarter out of my pocket and was shivering as I reached for my paper. I was moving back into the building when I spotted Cimon climbing into a bad-ass midnight blue Lincoln Navigator. Before she could pull out of the parking lot, I memorized the license plate, which was easy. CIMON. That bitch thought she was slick. Just wait until she tries to swipe her EBT card and comes up short. You got to get up very early in the morning to fool me.

5

Nikki

I removed the last magazine from the rack and took a seat on the floor. Running a bookstore was hard work. But I wouldn't have had it any other way. Book Ends was open seven days a week with a different event scheduled almost every evening. That night was open mic night, which meant I wouldn't close the store until after nine. Not that I was complaining.

I looked across the store at Karen, my assistant, as she rang up another customer's order. It was buy two, get one free day, and as usual the store had been busy. I was grateful business had been good. As much as I wanted a black bookstore, the only thing black about it is the owner. I learned that catering to just my people was not a smart business move. No offense, but you know good and well we like to borrow each other's books instead of trying to support black bookstores, which is why so many have gone out of business. I'll admit, I can't compete with the prices at Walmart and some of the other online stores, but that's why I offer specials. I also make sure I have books for everyone. White, black, Chinese, religious, you name it, I try to have it in my store.

"Nikki, the mail's here," Karen cried from the front counter. As soon as the last customers left, I rose from the floor and grabbed the mail from behind the counter.

"I'm running to Popeyes. You want me to get you something?"

I looked up at her gold-toothed smile. At first glance, Karen wasn't what one would consider front desk material with her blond weave and long fake nails. But she was fresh out of business school with exceptional customer service skills. After two bad seeds, especially a thieving bitch by the name of Tiara, who I fired in November after discovering she was stealing books and selling them to her friends for a third of the price, Karen was a godsend. Trust and believe, I have a business to run, and if and when I need Karen to tone down the hair and clothes, I'll tell her. I know she's a single parent with four kids, so I don't have a problem paying for her to get her hair done if needed.

I took a moment to consider Karen's offer. I had planned to have a bag of popcorn and a diet drink, but I was sure by late afternoon I'd be hungry for some food. "Go ahead and take enough outta petty cash to cover both our lunches and grab me a two-piece white."

"Thanks, Nikki."

"No problem." I waited until after Karen left before I headed to the back. I had a camera up front, and the bell over the door was so loud, it could be heard from the Dumpster in the alley. I popped a bag of butter popcorn, grabbed a Coke from the refrigerator, and when the timer went off, I carried my food back to my desk and took a seat. While I chewed on popcorn I thumbed through the mail, leaving greasy fingerprints. Bills and magazines, and then my heart practically stopped as I stared down at an envelope that was handwritten. Oh, my goodness! I knew that writing anywhere.

Donovan.

My hands were shaking as I reached for the letter opener. I ripped the seal, then I removed the sheet of notebook paper.

> *I hope all is well with you. Nikki, you know I love you and would never do anything to intentionally hurt you, but I've got to be honest. Being here is giving me a lot of time to think and I feel it's time for us to move on. It appears over the last four years we stopped growing as a couple. Talking hasn't done us any good, neither has distance, and I can't keep living like this. It's time I start trying to figure out what is going on with my life. That does not mean I do not love you. I know you will continue to be successful, and I wish you all the luck in the world. Twelve years of marriage, you don't just wipe away. I want you to know if you need something you can always contact me. Love, Donovan.*

My stomach dropped. I had waited months for a letter from him and finally it had come, only it wasn't at all what I had expected. Donovan had just ripped my heart out. *It's time for us to move on.* Those words floated around the store like a heavy cloud only seconds away from raining down on me. Damn him! The last thing I wanted to do was cry, because I'd known our marriage was in trouble long before Donovan left for Iraq. Yet that didn't stop the tears. I couldn't help it. I started bawling like a baby. Thank goodness Karen was gone and no one was in the store so I could sit there and feel sorry for myself. I failed at my marriage. Part of me thought, hoped, distance and time would bring us back together; instead it had done the exact opposite. What had gone wrong? As far as I was concerned, our life together should have been perfect.

Donovan and I both grew up in Englewood Park housing projects, where crack was the drug of choice. A week wouldn't go by without somebody trying to kill someone else. That was just the way of life for us.

Mama struggled to raise my sister, Tamara, and me, and did everything she could working part-time as a cashier at the local drug store. Money was tight, but one thing about my mama, she knew how to make the dollar work. Clothes we got from the Salvation Army, but you'd be amazed at what she could find.

I had always been good at school and knew I wanted to be a nurse or in some other field helping people. I had big plans to have a better life, and so did Donovan.

Donovan and I didn't start dating until junior high. He was a cutie then. Redbone, five ten, with a medium build, and the sexiest smile. Donovan grew up with an alcoholic father who kicked his ass on a regular basis. Whenever his father put him out, Donovan would come over and I would sneak him in through my bedroom window. We'd spend the night holding each other and planning a better life. I didn't give him my virginity until our sophomore year, and I never regretted it. As soon as we graduated high school, we got married with my family's blessing. Both of us attended college locally—he on a track scholarship, and me with the help of financial aid. We lived in a one-bedroom apartment that was no better than the projects, but neither of us complained. We had each other, and that's all that truly mattered. I worked as a manager at Walgreens during the day and an intern at the radio station at night while Donovan opened a barbershop. When I found out I was pregnant, neither of us thought life could get any better. We were so happy. We saved everything we had and bought our first home one month before Mimi, short for Tamika, was born. It was hard juggling work and motherhood, but Donovan didn't want someone else raising our daughter, so we arranged our schedule to make sure Mimi was always with one of us.

A sob rose to my throat and tears spilled and dampened my mail. I remember being so tired, so very tired. If only I hadn't been so willing to please my husband and had insisted on a babysitter for help, maybe she . . . maybe things would have turned out differently.

I stared down at the tear-stained letter. According to its contents, it was time for me to say good-bye not to one but to two of the most important people to ever become a part of my life. Part of me still wasn't ready to let go, even though deep in my heart I knew I had lost them both years ago.

6

Trinette

I arrived at my lovely two-bedroom condo. My maid, Consuela, had come through for her weekly cleaning, and the house smelled fabulous as usual.

I stepped through the house on my beautiful mahogany wood floor. Last year Leon had a fit when I told him I planned to pull up all the carpet and replace it with wood flooring, but in the end I got my way and haven't regretted my decision yet. One of Consuela's responsibilities was cleaning the floor with Murphy Oil Soap once a month, and her hard work rang true.

I headed to my room and slipped out of my clothes and moved into the shower. It was important for me to smell fresh and look fabulous when Leon arrived. I needed a new house, and it was going to take a little extra loving to convince him. In the end I would get my way. I always did.

As I lathered my body I thought about my life with Leon. He was an excellent provider and a good man. I didn't know if I would have been where I was if it wasn't for him. I don't give him all the credit, but some just the same.

Don't get me wrong, I love my husband, but at that point in my life it had to be about me. I'd traveled around being the dutiful and supportive wife for five years while he had been transferred all over the place as a result of one bank merger after another. Every time we had to move, I smiled; said good-bye to my job, my friends, and neighbors; packed up our stuff and prepared for the next location. Five years without objections or questioning, what about me? But at thirty, I decided it was finally my time to shine. It was time for me to finally start living life for me. That's why I went back to school, and after years of starting and stopping, I finally got a degree in social work and was lucky when I landed a job at the Division of Children and Family Services. For the first time in my life it wasn't about simply earning a paycheck. I finally had my first job that held real meaning. I was able to finally do for me. I was no longer just Leon Montgomery's wife. Or the little bucktoothed girl from Englewood Park. I was finally Trinette Meyers-Montgomery. With my job as a caseworker, I had a real purpose, a career with promotion potential. And no one, not even my husband, was going to take that away from me.

Speaking of promotion, you better believe I had every intention of getting Yolanda's job when she left. I had busted my ass for two years, staying late, making sure all my case files were in order. I was better than half those lazy heffas who worked in my office. I worked hard to get where I was and I'd be damned before I let anyone take that from me. You see, people are quick to judge, but they have no idea who I am or where I came from.

I was dogged most of my life. A girl from the projects with a mother who turned tricks to supplement her welfare. Darlene wasn't even good at what she did, because all she seemed to bring home was more babies. Four brothers one after the other whom I was left to raise while dear old Mommy chased after a pipe dream. Watching her wearing her cheap perfume, coming home smelling like sex, I knew I would never allow a man to use me up the way she had. Only I got it worse. My uncle Sonny victimized me for years. Mama turned a blind eye because Sonny gave her money. He robbed me of my virginity and my dignity at twelve and kept having his way with me until I was fifteen, when I finally tried to bite his dick off. He never touched me again, yet that didn't stop him from staring, watching and wanting me. I started dating, trying to erase the shame, looking for love in all the wrong places and getting my heart broken one time too many from broke-ass niggas promising the world. Instead, all I got was a sore coochie and a wet ass. By my junior year, I started to believe I was no better than my trick-ass mama. By the time I graduated, I had come to the conclusion men weren't shit and I wasn't about to risk my heart to another. No more being used and abused. It was time for me to be on top. Determined to have more than I came from, I went to college and used every mothafucka who came up in my face trying to run game. As a result, I was the baddest female on campus. You wanted some head, it cost you. You wanted to play with my titties, it cost you. You wanted some ass, you better believe I charged the hell out of all them tired brothas. My rationale was that a female is going to give a man some anyway, so why not get paid for your time? My roommate thought I was crazy, but she was singing a different tune when she got her heart broken by one jock after another and had nothing to show for it but the baby growing in her belly. Fuck that! I kept a stash of condoms, because when I walked away, I didn't want to have to remember his name. Trust and believe, I had brothas falling all over me, but I was only interested in the size of their wallets. No one had a chance of stealing my heart. That is, until I met Leon.

He was a senior who was going places. He loved me, and I loved everything he did for me. With a degree in finance and a job offer from the largest bank in the states, I knew he could provide me the life I was intended to live. So when he asked me to marry him, I gladly dropped out of school and followed him around. With his six-figure salary, he introduced me to fine dining and vacations in the Caribbean. He bought my first house and a fancy car, and it wasn't long before I grew accustomed to my new lifestyle and I never once looked back. I came a long way from that little lost ghetto girl. After all that I went through, I deserved everything life had to offer me plus some. I never saw my mama and rarely contacted my brothers. I couldn't. They were all painful reminders of a life I no longer wanted to remember. I was now Trinette Meyers-Montgomery. Married to a CFO. Who would have ever guessed it? I was willing to do whatever it took to take my life to the next level. By any means necessary. Call me a whore.

A user. Whatever. Ms. Netta considers herself a survivor.

I climbed out the shower, reached for a plush cream bath towel and wrapped it around my body, then moved into the master suite and took a seat on the bed while I rubbed my body down with mango-scented lotion. Leon said I always smell good enough to eat. I giggled at the thought. That night, I wanted him to get his eat on for sure, because a sistah had an itch that needed to be scratched. I blew out a breath at the thought of Cory's pathetic ass. I don't know what in the world I was thinking. I'm a woman to be wined, dined and pampered. The only thing I found impressive about Cory was his lottery winnings and his crooked dick. He always managed to find my spot, but even that wasn't enough for me to take him back after his money ran out. I hoped the sex with Leon would be better this weekend. *Yeah, right.* I wasn't going to put much stock in that possibility. Our sex life lost its spark ages ago, and I just wasn't interested in putting in the extra work required to bring it back. However, that night I was on a mission.

My cell phone rang. I retrieved it from my purse and gasped when I saw the number. "What are you doing here so early?" I barked into the receiver.

"I love you too," Leon replied with a hearty chuckle. "I caught an early flight. Unlock the door. I'll be pulling up in a second."

Shit! I hung up, then put on a new white teddy I bought at the mall. I hated rushing and Leon knew it. I believed in order and things being planned out, and he had ruined the romantic mood I had intended to set.

I reached for a lighter and quickly lit the scented

candles I had positioned around the room, then pulled back the comforter and unlocked the front door just as I heard a car pull in the driveway. Leon always insisted on renting a car for the weekend. That way his wife was at home waiting when he arrived. I slid my feet into a pair of classy high-heel slippers with white fur on the top, then moved to the bedroom door and struck a pose. Within seconds the front door opened and he was standing in the living room below with that big, ugly green suitcase I hated so much. I smiled down at him. "Hey, sexy."

"Back at you," he said while staring at me as if I were a movie star. Leon came up the stairs and I met him halfway. Wrapping my arms around his neck, I kissed him. "I missed you so much," he murmured against my cheek.

"Me too." I missed him, but I was sure it was nothing like what he was feeling. I mean, I just saw Leon for both Christmas and New Year's less than two weeks ago. I don't know what it is with men, but they act like they can't go a day without lying up in some coochie. Now I know Netta's got the best stuff in town, but damn can a sistah get some air.

I took my husband's hand and led him up the stairs to our room and helped him undress. "How was your flight?" I asked, because Leon loves small talk.

"It was long. Now I'm ready to snuggle up with my wife."

Men. "I can't wait to hold you either, boo-boo." I knew exactly what my husband wanted to hear.

I unbuttoned his shirt, then brought my lips to his chest and kissed a trail from one nipple to the other just the way he liked it. He moaned and I smiled, then reached for the buckle, unzipped his pants and slipped my hand inside. My man doesn't have the biggest dick in the world, but what he got is just enough for me to take a nice, long ride. That's if he can stay hard long enough.

Leon started taking off my clothes. I pushed him back onto the bed and straddled him and began kissing him, starting at his neck and working my way down. Like clockwork, he started moaning.

"Oh, baby, that feels gooood."

Of course it did.

"I can't wait too much longer."

He never could.

"It's been too long," he moaned. "The first one's gonna be quick."

It always was.

"The next one will be longer, I promise."

I rolled my eyes. He always did.

I lowered on his length and rode him hard, and Leon was right. Before I even had a chance to come, he was crying out.

"I'm coming, baby! Oooh-weee!"

I rocked my hips and pretended to come as well, then collapsed on top of him, showering light kisses along his neck and cheek.

"I missed you so much," he said with a sigh.

"Me too, boo. Me too." I rested my head on his chest, then sighed long and heavy. "Leon, I'm almost certain I'm gonna get Yolanda's job."

"That's great," he replied around a yawn.

"I just need to be patient a little longer, and when she leaves in a few months, I am certain her job will be mine."

"Uh-huh."

I wrapped my arms around Leon and held him tight. "Boo, if I play my cards right, I'm gonna be able to transfer to the Richmond office before I know it so that we can be together. I can't wait until we're living together again."

"Me either, baby."

Okay, here we go. "Uh, Leon, sweetie, I was thinking . . . it's time to sell my condo. The rates are low right now, and I think this is as good a time as any to buy something else at a good price. That way when we move to Richmond we'll have rental property back here. You said we needed a tax write-off. I think a new house would be a good move."

"What's wrong with this condo?"

I sat up on the bed. "Leon, this neighborhood is going downhill! Folks been knocking on the door begging for money." Actually I was exaggerating. My neighborhood wasn't that bad, but he didn't need to know that.

"Uh-huh," Leon said, then rolled over and closed his eyes.

Uh-uh. Oh, hell, no. He wasn't going to sleep until we finished talking. "Boo, we need to talk about this. This is important."

"I hear you, Netta, but I'm tired."

"You got all night to sleep! I want to talk about buying a new house. If we don't sell this condo, I won't ever be able to get rid of it. We've got to start thinking about our future."

"The future is living in Richmond together."

I wrapped my arms tightly around him and started kissing his chest. When you want something, the best thing to do is to let your man know how much you need him. "I look forward to living in Richmond, but sweetheart, it's time for things to be about me. I need to finish this master's program and I need to get that director's position." I quickly added, "But that doesn't mean I don't love you."

"I love you too, Netta."

I gave him a few kisses before I continued. "Leon, I would like to sell the condo."

"Why? We're just gonna use it again as rental property."

"Haven't you been listening to anything I have been saying? I don't wanna stay in this neighborhood. There have been several break-ins recently."

Leon gave me a worried look. "Maybe I need to get you a security system on the condo."

"No, what we need to do is sell this place. The neighborhood is going down. Did I mention they're renting the condo on the end with Section 8? I really think it's a good time to sell. We've got plenty of equity in this place, and with the housing market so low I . . . I mean *we* could get a deal on another house."

"You're probably right," Leon replied, although he still didn't look totally convinced.

"Then after I get Yolanda's job, graduate and move to Richmond with you, we can decide if we wanna rent it or sell it at that point."

His head started bobbing.

"Leon, if you don't wake up! I really want this." I straddled him and allowed my mouth to travel downward as I spoke. He immediately woke up and started moaning. "Mama needs a new house," I purred.

"Hmmm, and daddy needs some head."

I gave him a hard look. "Leon, I'm serious. We've owned this condo since we first got married. It's time to let it go and invest in something else."

"You're probably right," he said, and I smiled and started kissing him again. "As soon as you pay off all those credit cards we can start looking."

"I already paid them off," I mumbled against his chest.

Leon raised my head so he could look me in the eyes with skepticism. "You have? Since when?"

"Since I promised I would pay them all off." Damn, my ass was lying. Not only had I not paid them off, I had gotten three or four more credit cards he knew nothing about.

"Well, good then. We should have some money left over this month in our joint checking."

What money? I dropped my eyes before he could see the look of panic. I spent the last of the money getting my hair and nails done. "We've got more than enough money in our savings to buy a house."

"Uh-uh. We're not touching that unless we have to."

We had close to a hundred thousand in savings that he wouldn't let me touch. Said he was saving it for a rainy day. Well, guess what? Pressure was raining on my ass to move.

"You come up with the earnest money and all our closing costs, and I'll let you use some of our savings for the down payment."

Let? I had to bite my tongue. Who did he think he was talking to? Okay, I'll admit, he contributed more than 97 percent of our savings, but so what? There's no *I* in marriage, only *us*. "Sure, sweetheart, that sounds like a plan." I just needed to figure out how to come up with the money. I wasn't about to tell Leon my personal checking account was overdrawn. I'd find the way to get the money. One thing about Trinette Meyers-Montgomery, she knows how to get what she wants.

7

Nikki

The last place I wanted to be was on the air, but I wasn't about to mess up one of the only good things I had going for me. I seriously needed this job to help keep me going, otherwise I'd spend another evening thumbing through photographs of what my life used to be while feeling sorry for myself.

I glanced over into the control room just in time to see Tristan wave his hand in the air, trying to get my attention. We were about to go back on the air in four . . . three . . . two . . . one . . .

"We're back from break, and if you missed the first half of the night, you missed a whole lotta *drama*," I sang. "But don't fret, because we're about to kick off the second half of the evening. For all of you who are just tuning in, tonight's topic is breakups. Sometimes we split up and get back together. Others just sit around hoping and waiting for that phone call saying, I'm sorry. Tonight, I wanna know what it took for you to finally know it was over. That you had been kicked to the curb. So, let's hear it, listeners. Spill your guts even if the truth hurts! Call me at 832-HURT. All the phone lines are open."

I looked down at the phone and every light was lit. Damn, the show tonight was going to be hot. After a dozen calls, the rush was over, and I finally blew out a long, hot breath. "Well, listeners, there you have it. Love can sometimes be a painful lesson to us all. This is Nikki Truth with Hot 97 WJPC. Good night."

I hit the switch, removed the headphones from my ears and leaned back in the chair. My head was pounding.

"You okay?"

I looked up at the concern in Tristan's face. I was hurting. There was no doubt about that. "Yeah, I'll be okay."

He squeezed my shoulder, trying to provide me comfort. "You know, Donovan's gonna regret his decision. You just wait and see. The second he gets back from Iraq he's gonna come begging for you to take his ass back."

"I doubt that. It's over between us, and I'm finally coming to terms with that. Just listening to all our callers tonight, talking about holding on and not letting go, made me realize I need to get on with my life. My marriage to Donovan is over."

"You okay with that?"

"I don't have a choice. But yeah, I'm fine."

I left the radio station and rode around, and realized I wasn't ready to go home yet. My phone rang. I looked down and was shocked to see it was Trinette. She should be curled up under the covers with Leon.

"Hey, I heard your show tonight. What the hell's wrong with you?"

"I'll have to tell you when I see you," I mumbled as I made a right at the next corner.

"Why don't you come over now? I'm just sitting studying for a test."

"Where's Leon?"

She clicked her tongue. "I put his ass to sleep."

I laughed, glad to be able to have something to chuckle about, because my life was far from amusing.

"Come on over. I'll get the wineglasses out."

I hung up with a smile on my face and hit the highway toward Kirkwood, where the bougie folks lived, and my girl was definitely bougie. As soon as I parked my car in the driveway, she came to the door to greet me. Thank goodness. The temperature had dropped and it was definitely cold outside. Typical Midwest January weather.

Trinette was standing there in a short pink robe and matching slippers. "Hurry up and get in here. I'll be so glad when this weather is over!"

"Me too." I followed her through the condo to the family room behind the kitchen. A couple of years ago Trinette hired an interior designer who had come in and made the place a showcase. Everything was new and state of the art. I took a seat on a rose-colored couch that looked fabulous with pinks and cream. I told her the house was too damn feminine for a married woman. Trinette was quick to point out no one lived in the condo but her, so she got to decide how it looked.

Trinette took a seat on a mauve recliner across from me. Since I was the closest to the coffee table, I reached for the bottle and poured two glasses. We both loved Moscato.

"So talk to me, Nikki. What's going on with you? You sounded like you were ready to kick somebody's ass," she said, and reached for a glass.

I took a couple of sips before answering. "Donovan sent me a letter."

Her eyes widened. "That's good, isn't it? Well, what did he say?"

It took a moment for me to put my words together. "He told me it was time for us to move on." My voice cracked at the end, and I took another drink because my throat was suddenly dry.

"Oh, no! You've got to be kidding." I hate when people say that like I would really joke about something like that.

"He sent the letter to the bookstore instead of the house. Why would he do that?" I looked at her, hoping she had an explanation.

"I have no idea," she said, looking as if she was barely able to get the words out, she was so shocked.

"Obviously, the fool forgot where we live." I reached inside my purse and handed her the letter to read. I already had it memorized.

Trinette took her time reading it, then released a heavy sigh. "You said you thought something was wrong."

"I know, but that doesn't make it any easier. Something has been wrong for a long time, even before Mimi . . ." My voice trailed off. There was no way I was about to go there.

"I can't believe he dumped you in a letter," Trinette snapped, and handed me the tear-stained paper.

"I-I guess that was the only way he knew how. We've

been having problems just talking to each other for a long time." I shrugged my shoulders. "I knew this . . . this day was coming. I just wasn't prepared. But are we ever really prepared?"

Leaning back in her chair, she shook her head in bewilderment. "Nikki . . . this is some shit. I'm so sorry, girlfriend. I used to envy the two of you."

I gave her a weird look. "Envy us?"

"Hell, yeah. The two of you have been together since junior high. You knew someday you would get married. And as far as I know he's the only man you've ever fucked. Now *that's* amazing."

"I guess for *you* it is."

Trinette started laughing, and I laughed along with her until she pressed a finger to her lips.

"Oh, shit!" I whispered. "I forgot Leon's home."

Trinette gave me a dismissive wave. "Don't worry. He's out like a light."

Maybe she wasn't worried, but I was. "Girl, my bad. The last thing I need is for Leon to hear." I looked around to make sure he wasn't about to walk in the room. "Enough about me, what did he say about buying another car?"

Her lips curved mischievously. What was her ass up to now? "I decided I want another house instead."

"What?" I gave her a weird look. Her announcement had come out of nowhere. "A new house? Uhhh, uhhh . . . I thought you wanted a new car?" I decided to play along. "Where at?"

She had a shit-eating grin on her face. "In Webster Grove."

I frowned. Bougieville USA. "How much?"

Trinette took a long sip while looking quite pleased with herself. "About four hundred."

Goodness, there was no way I could even dream of spending that much. "What about your condo?" It was hard keeping the envy out of my voice.

"I'm gonna put it on the market and try to sell it."

I nodded. "With the housing market the way it is, you might wanna do that first. I know too many people having a helluva time trying to sell their homes. Not to mention the value has dropped tremendously."

She gave me a shrug that said she wasn't worried. "I'm sure I won't have a problem selling this place."

"And what does Leon say about that?" I pressed.

"There was a little resistance . . . but I used the power of persuasion on him . . . a.k.a. Ms. Kitty." She purred, then tilted her glass to her lips.

I sat there shaking my head. "You are too much."

"Yeah . . . I know. Leon will let me take money outta the account for a down payment, but the earnest money, inspections, etcetera, all have to come outta my own pocket."

My brow rose. "And how you hope to do that?"

Trinette frowned as if she didn't have a clue what I was talking about. "What do you mean? I work."

I sat there with my arms folded against my chest. Who was Trinette trying to fool? "Yep . . . you work. I also know your entire check is spent on your credit cards and supporting your expensive shop habit."

"Not all of it," she retorted with major attitude.

"Uh-huh . . . whatever. I bet you Leon thinks you've been saving money, right?"

Trinette pursed her lips. She hates when I'm right. "True, but I can get around that."

"Really? And where are you planning to get the money?"

She stuck out her tongue. "You know I have my way."

I leaned back on the couch and shook my head. Trinette was playing a dangerous game. "I just bet you do. I ain't mad. If you can buy your dream home, then I'm happy for you."

"Now that's what I'm talking about. Everyone else is always trying to hate on my ass."

"I wonder why," I mumbled. Trinette is one of those women you either love or hate. There is no in between. I reached for the bottle and poured us both another glass, and for the longest time I just sat there sipping my wine.

"Why you need a new house if you're planning to move to Richmond?"

She gave me a hard look, then finished her drink. "I'll worry about that later."

What she was really saying was she had no intentions of moving to Richmond. Silence fell between us. Finally she changed the subject.

"Are you gonna try to contact Donovan?"

"For what? So he can stick the knife farther in my chest?"

She looked at me as if I was the one being ridiculous. "No, so you can decide if it's really something you both want."

I took a moment to think about what she said, but eventually I shook my head. "I'm not gonna lie. It's not at all what I want, but I'm not gonna beg someone to be with me when he obviously doesn't want me anymore."

Trinette actually managed to look sympathetic. "I just hate that things are ending without the two of you talking."

"Trinette, I love that man. The last thing I want is a divorce." And then I couldn't help it. I started bawling my ass off. Trinette put her glass down on the coffee table and moved over and took a seat beside me.

"Uhhh-uhhh . . . there'll be none of that." She reached for a box of tissues and handed me a few.

I wiped my eyes. "Bitch, don't try to act like you ain't never cried over a man. You know I know better."

"Shhh! And if you ever tell anybody I'm gonna deny that shit," she said with a sympathetic smile, then wrapped her arms around me and hugged me tight. I needed that.

I smiled at my crazy friend. One minute she could be a selfish bitch, the next she could be the most caring person in the world. "We've been friends for life. You know I know you better than your own mother."

She frowned. "You ain't never lied."

Trinette and her mother hadn't gotten along in years. I knew the reason why, but like I told Trinette, it's long overdue for forgive and forget. Darlene had been clean for almost three years and had given her life to Christ.

"Maybe you should try getting in touch with Donovan," she suggested.

"Donovan and I don't have anything else to talk about. He's right. It's over." I reached for the bottle and poured myself another glass. "Just last week you were saying I needed to quit sitting around and get on with my life. . . . Well . . . that's what I'm tryna do."

Trinette hesitated. "I know . . . but I hate seeing you so down. I miss you smiling and having a good time. So if you're sure this is what you wanna do . . . then don't get mad when I remind yo ass what you said tonight."

"It's over, Trinette." I held up my glass. "Let's make a toast."

She gave me a reluctant look before she reached for her glass and raised it in front of her. "What are we toasting?"

"Here's to new beginnings."

She smirked. "And *new* dick. Girl, you just don't know what you've been missing!"

I brought the glass to my lips. "Well, I guess I'm about to find out."

8

Trinette

I knew I needed to keep my behind out of the mall, but I couldn't help it. I liked to shop even though I knew I needed to be saving up money for my new house.

Anyway, I was at Saks Fifth Avenue and spotted this chocolate diamond ring I had to have. I wanted to wear it with this cream suit I was planning to wear to the Black MBA Association Ball. Unfortunately, it had a twelve hundred dollar price tag. My credit cards were maxed, and if I withdrew more than five hundred from our joint account, Leon would receive an e-mail alert. Nope. I was going to have to earn that puppy on my own. Besides, why should I spend my own money if I don't have to?

I pulled into the circle driveway in front of Smooth's. Happy hour was in effect, and with a thirty and older age minimum, kids and thugs weren't up in the house.

With live music and drinks starting at twenty dollars, only men with money were inside, and that was exactly what Ms. Netta was looking for. I needed a sponsor, to sponsor the purchase of my diamond ring. I had already tried it on, so I knew how good it looked on my finger. Folks were gonna be hating.

I climbed out and sashayed around my car and handed the keys to the valet, then went inside. I walked in and a tall, honey-colored brotha was onstage, blowing on a saxophone. Damn, I love me some jazz.

There was a light crowd. A few desperate-looking chicks were sitting at some of the tables. As soon as I walked in, heads snapped in my direction. None of them could hold a torch to me. I was looking fabulous in a short skirt and matching pink blazer. Did I mention how good I look in pink? The color makes my caramel skin glow and my hazel eyes luminous. While in my car, I undid the top two buttons of a cream blouse to give my double Ds a little breathing room, and every man in the house turned my way. I looked good, and I wasn't the only one who knew it. All eyes were on me! I sashayed into the lounge in a pair of fuchsia Manolos. Sistah girl was fierce!

I moved over to the bar and took a seat on an empty stool. Beneath my mascara lashes, I saw those heffas sitting in the corner hating on me. I simply pursed my magenta-painted lips and gave them a fabulous smile, then rolled my eyes and focused on the handsome man behind the bar. Light skinned, thick mustache, tall, hard build. Brotha was fine as hell. Unfortunately, he was standing on the wrong side of the bar. The side that said his ass was broke and definitely couldn't afford me.

"What up, sexy? What can I get you this evening?" he asked with a panty-dropping grin.

I pursed my lips and gave him a once-over. If I wasn't on a mission I might be giving him some serious consideration, but after that mess with Cory, I needed to keep reminding myself dick ain't everything. "I'll take an apple martini with Grey Goose."

"Coming right up."

I pulled my cell phone out my purse and dialed Nikki. While pretending to be making a serious call, I glanced around the club looking for a new sponsor. I needed a high roller, 'cause Ms. Netta needed a ring and a new house.

I'd been doing this a long time, and it didn't take me long to pick the perfect victim in the corner. Salt and pepper hair. Peanut butter brown. Slightly overweight. Oh, yeah. I love a man with a little extra meat on his bones, because those were the ones desperate enough to give me anything I wanted. He was perfect. And sure enough, it wasn't long before he looked my way. I met his piercing dark eyes, then looked away. The last thing I wanted was for him to think I was interested in him. One thing Ms. Netta never does is make the first move.

"Hello? Hello? Trinette?"

Damn, I forgot I called Nikki. "Hey, gurl."

"What's all that loud music? Where you at?"

"I'm at Smooth's." I stole a glance across the bar at the handsome stranger and smiled as I spoke. He followed my lips and hung on every word. Grinning, I crossed my legs, and my skirt rose up past the middle of my smooth caramel thigh. By the look on his face, he was definitely a thigh man.

"Ugh! What you doing in that stuck-up place?"

Sometimes I wonder how Nikki and I are such good

friends because we're so different. But they say opposites attract. "Girl, it's some fine men up in here. You need to go home, put on something cute and come over here." Mr. Sexy winked from across the room. I winked back.

"Nah, I just got a big shipment in and I wanna check inventory before I get outta here this evening."

"Nikki, that shit will be there tomorrow. Bring yo ass down here! Remember you said you were ready to get on with your life? . . . Well . . . it's that time."

She hesitated, then replied, "Maybe next time."

Mr. Sexy had turned in his chair and was giving me his undivided attention. Did he really think it was going to be that easy? Hell, no. I swung around on the stool and gave him my back. "Whatever you say, Nikki. I'm not even about to argue with you. We're still on for Saturday, right? You're going . . . even if I have to drag your ass out the house."

She breathed heavily in the phone. "Yeah, I'm going."

"Good. We'll talk later." I hung up and put my phone back into my purse, anxious to get back to business. I reached for my drink, and I took a sip. It was good. The lights dimmed slightly and I focused on the man onstage. As the musician performed, I hummed along and sipped my drink. I knew Mr. Sexy was still watching, and I swayed my hips on the stool, giving him something to look at. When the performance ended, I didn't have to turn around to know Mr. Sexy was on his way over to the bar. I smelled the Armani on his skin before I felt his presence by my side.

"May I buy you a drink?" he offered in a deep baritone voice.

I gave him a quick glance, then shook my head and turned away. "No, thank you."

"You mind if I take a seat?" he asked, pointing at the stool beside me.

I playfully rolled my eyes. "Sure. It's not my club. You can sit wherever you want."

He gave a deep, robust laugh. "Well, that's good to hear, considering I *am* the owner."

Owner! Hell, yes! Ms. Netta hit the lottery for real this time. I tried to hide my excitement as he lowered on the stool beside me, but I was already trying to figure out how much this man was worth. "So you're Smooth, huh?"

"Yep, that's what they call me." He slid his seat closer. "What brings a beautiful woman out all by herself?"

I sat there sizing him up, wondering how much I might be able to get before the night was over. I was going to have to put in some work, but from the stories I'd heard about Smooth, he was worth the sweat. He owned clubs from here to the east side and even had a couple of chicken and waffle joints. Yep. With this one I was going to have to give him Ms. Netta's deluxe package. "I just got off work and thought I'd drop in for a drink before heading home."

"You married?" he asked.

I gave him a piercing stare. "Aren't we all?"

Smooth chuckled, and I watched as that slick motha-afucka slipped his hands inside his pants pockets. When he put them back on the counter, his wedding ring just happened to have magically disappeared. Give me a break. Didn't he know, tricks are for kids? Maybe not, so I guess it's up to me to show him how it's really done. I leaned in close. "Let's just skip the small talk. It's obvious you like what you see."

He sucked his teeth while his eyes traveled the length of me. "I most definitely do."

I leaned in even closer and watched as his eyes dropped to my breasts. "What do you wanna do about it?"

Reluctantly, he forced his eyes back to my face. "I'd like to leave here and spend some quiet time with you alone . . . if that's possible."

I reached for my drink and spun on the barstool. "You ain't ready for me. I'm nothing like these chicken-head women up in here." I took a sip. "I have needs and wants, and I don't think . . . you can afford me."

"Let me be the judge of that. Anything worth having is worth spending my money on."

"My thoughts exactly." I let my tongue run across my bottom lip. "Let's go."

Smooth rose from the stool, then went and said good-bye to his friends at his table. While I finished my drink, I watched as some skank tried to push up on him. I saw her turn and look my way, then frown as he headed back over to the bar, where he tossed a twenty on the counter. I grinned in her direction and took his proffered hand. I don't know why she thought she had a chance. Once I walked in, I shut it down!

"Wanna ride with me?" he offered.

Immediately I shook my head. Ms. Netta was having none of that. "Nah. I don't want to leave my car down here." The last thing I need is to be waiting for someone to get around to taking me home.

"Okay, just follow me."

We waited together for the valet to bring my Benz and his brand-new emerald green Jaguar. I walked to the front of his car and took a picture of the license plate with my cell phone.

Smooth looked amused. "What you do that for?"

I gave him a serious look. "You can never be too careful. I'm sending this to my best friend. If I come up missing tomorrow, you're the first person she'll come looking for."

He chuckled, and I watched his big stomach jiggle like Jell-O. "Believe me. You're safe with me."

"That's what they all say." I turned on my heels and moved to my car. He held the door open, then shook his head as he stared down at my thighs. "Damn, you're thick."

"Boo-boo, you ain't seen nothing yet." Before the night was over I planned to have the money I needed for not only the chocolate diamond but my new house as well.

9

Nikki

I hurried through the hospital corridor to the nurse's station. "Mildred Stephenson's room, please."

The nurse looked down at the board, then pointed to the right. "Room 7B. Last door on the right."

I nodded, then turned on my heel and walked as fast as I could, knowing I was going to have to hear my mother's mouth. I knocked once, then pushed open the door. Mama looked my way and rolled her eyes.

"I'm glad you could make it." The sarcasm was obvious in her voice.

I pressed my lips together and decided to ignore my mother, considering I hadn't gotten the message she had left on my cell phone until after six. I've told her a thousand times, if it's important call me at work, not on my cell phone, which I usually put on silent while I worked.

I pretended she wasn't standing there and turned to

the woman beside her, who looked like she had aged ten years since I last saw her at Thanksgiving. "Hey, Aunt Charlotte."

She gave me a sad smile. Apparently, she had been crying. "Hi." I gave her a big hug, then moved over to the bed and stared down at the woman lying there. Big Mama was everything to me.

"What happened?" I waited for one of them to speak, and when neither did, I swung around and pierced them both with an impatient look. Mama signaled for me to step out the room and talk in private.

"She fell last night in the bathroom and was too weak to get up."

Tears stung the back of my eyes at the thought of my grandmother lying on a cold floor all night.

"I went over there this morning and was knocking with no luck. I had to call the police to come and break the lock to get us in."

"Why was she by herself last night?" I was so pissed.

My mother dropped her head, but not before I noticed the guilt in her eyes. "She insisted she be left alone. You know your grandmother. The last thing she wants is a babysitter."

"That may be so, but that's exactly what she needs." Sometimes I felt like the only adult in the family. "What's her doctor say?"

Mama released a long breath before replying, "She has congestive heart failure."

"Meaning?"

"Meaning . . ." Tears flooded her eyes. "Her heart is . . . is drowning in fluid."

I swallowed the lump in my throat, then reached over and wrapped my arms around Mama and held her for a few seconds. I released her, then stepped into the room, took a seat by the side of the bed and held onto my grandmother's hand. Touching her was comforting. The way she always felt to me.

Aunt Charlotte rose. "Since you're here, we're going down to the cafeteria."

I simply nodded. They left and I was glad to have some time alone with Big Mama. I reached up and brushed her silver hair away from her face. It was long, very fine and hanging loose on her pillow. The result of a mixed heritage. Big Mama would have a fit if she saw her hair all over her head. She was one of those who believed in always looking her best. I guess I got that from her. Although when I first decided to grow my locks, she couldn't understand why I insisted on growing that nappy stuff on my head.

"Well, if it isn't my little chickadee."

I smiled down into Big Mama's gentle brown eyes and fought back the tears. I didn't want her to see me crying. "You know good and well nothing was stopping me from coming down here to see you. I even brought you a surprise." I reached inside my purse and pulled out a Granny Smith apple.

Her eyes sparkled. "I ever tell you that's my favorite apple?"

I nodded. "Yes, you've told me." But I never grew tired of hearing the story.

"I remember I used to clean this old white woman's house. She had one of those big fancy houses on the north side with a pretty white picket fence. She loved having me work for her better than all her other maids. Ms. Ellie used to call me that pretty colored girl." She paused for a moment, lost in her thoughts. "Anyway, I was getting ready to head home one evening and I was hungry. She had a beautiful fruit bowl of apples. I asked her if I could have one of her Granny Smith apples and I would bring one in the morning to replace it. Ms. Ellie told me no . . . I couldn't have a Granny Smith . . . I could have a Jonathan apple. Humph! They all had bruises on them, and I don't care for those apples . . . never have. I took one look at Ms. Ellie, then walked over to the bowl, took me a Granny Smith and bit into it." Big Mama chuckled. "I said good night and left the house." She paused again and frowned at the IV in her arm. I moved around to her right and adjusted the surgical tape as she continued. "The next morning I came back, and when she opened the door, I handed her the prettiest Granny Smith apple I could find, and said, 'I told you I'd bring you another apple.' Ms. Ellie started laughing and said, 'Mildred, you so funny.' "

I laughed and stared down at my grandmother's smiling face. That's just the way she'd always been—a woman with a mind of her own. She didn't let anyone stand in her way. This was the woman who I could always turn to when I couldn't talk to my mother. Big Mama never judged. She simply listened, then gave her opinion whether you liked it or not. She always believed in allowing her children to live their lives, because to her the biggest lesson was finding out for yourself.

"You think when I get home I can get you to bake me one of those coconut cakes?" she asked. Big Mama was lying there, breathing heavily. I tried not to think about the fluid surrounding her heart. Talking was starting to be too much for her.

I squeezed her hand. "Sure, Big Mama. Whatever you want."

She covered my hand with hers and closed her eyes. For the longest time, I sat there listening to her breath. Loving the way she felt. Enjoying the way she smelled.

"You know I'm not going to be here forever," she finally said, breaking into the silence.

I had to swallow to remove the sob that had filled my throat. "I know, but I'm not ready for you to leave."

"Hmmm . . . that's too bad 'cause I'm ready to go . . . and be with my Lord. You know I gave my life to Jesus Christ when I was a little girl? I've been preparing my whole life to meet him."

"I know, Big Mama, but I wish you wouldn't say things like that."

She gave me a narrow look. "I don't know why not. Everybody has their time. Don't you know your mother is talking about me moving in with her? Uhhh-uhhh . . . you know I always said, I didn't wanna be a burden on any of my children."

"You could never be a burden. I would love for you to come and live with me." Even though I offered, I knew what she was talking about. It was nothing like having independence.

"That's worth considering. Only I don't wanna put anyone out." She laughed. "Could you see me living with your mother? She would drive me crazy with all that smoking! No . . . what I want . . . is to stay in my own house . . . cook my own meals . . . sleep in my own bed."

I nodded. "I understand. Just know I love you and the offer stands. All the years you took care of me, there ain't nothing I won't do for you."

"I know, chickadee . . . but baby . . . Big Mama is

tired. Getting up in the morning is becoming hard work."

I knew she wasn't getting any younger. I'd seen how slow she had become the last year, but I still didn't want to hear my grandmother talking about dying. I wasn't ready for her to go. And probably never would be. "I just wanna make your life as comfortable as possible regardless where you live."

"What would Donovan say about me . . . moving in wit y'all?"

"Big Mama, you know Donovan loves you as much as I do." I dropped my eyes, but I couldn't lie to her. "I don't know if you could tell, but he and I've been having some problems."

She took a deep breath. "I could tell something wasn't right. . . . I figured you'd talk about it . . . when you were ready."

I moved closer. "I thought maybe when he got back we would work on our relationship, but I guess not."

She gave me a stern look. "That's because you young folks don't know how to talk to each other. Marriage isn't sacred like it was while I was growing up. When I married your grandfather . . . I knew it would be forever. He was my first . . . my only. I didn't wanna spend my life with anyone but him. When he died . . . I lost a piece of myself." A single tear rolled from the corner of her eye onto the pillow. "Yes, Thaddeus was such a good man."

"I miss Grandpa."

She patted my hand. "And you were his favorite. All he wanted was for you to be happy . . . have a family of your own." Her expression grew serious. "Have you been by to visit your daughter?"

I quickly shook my head and rose. Standing in front of the window, I looked down into the crowded parking lot below. "No. Not since her birthday."

"Well . . . next time you see her . . . send her my love."

When I turned around, tears were running down my face. "I'll do just that."

10

NIKKI

10

Nikki

"You wanna dance?"

I turned around, and it took everything I had not to scream. Dude was sporting an Afro and wearing a shiny purple polyester shirt he left half buttoned, revealing his nappy chest hairs. I wished I had a comb in my purse.

"Nope. I'm still sipping my drink." I brought the glass to my mouth just to keep from laughing. One of his front teeth was gold . . . the other was missing.

"No problem. How about saving me a slow dance?"

I shrugged. "We'll see." The last thing I wanted to do was to promise him a dance, then I would never get rid of his homely ass.

He walked away looking pleased by my answer just as I spotted Trinette weaving through the crowd with two martinis in her hands. Trinette moved up to the table looking fierce in a cream pantsuit with a plunging neckline, showcasing her twins.

"What you doing with Lamont Sanford?"

I sputtered on my drink, laughing. "You're stupid."

Trinette slid onto the empty seat across from me, grinning as she shook her fresh weave. "Girl, puhleeze. He looks like Super Fly."

"You ain't neva lied."

We had been at Studio Blue for almost an hour, and I was actually having a good time. The club was crowded. The music was R&B without the hip-hop, and the men were definitely dressed to impress without their pants falling off their asses. It definitely makes a difference when a club has a thirty or older age requirement.

"Oooh! I almost forgot to tell you. I put a contract on a house," Trinette announced over the thump of the music.

"Already?" Damn, she moved fast.

Her dark, expressive eyes twinkled with excitement. "Yep. I told you I was."

"Yeah, but I didn't think it would be that soon. Where at?"

"What did I tell you the other day? Webster Grove. Four bedrooms . . . three baths . . . beautiful kitchen with granite countertops."

"For what? You don't even cook."

Trinette shrugged her shoulders. "Doesn't matter. I still want the best kitchen in town."

I brought the fresh drink to my lips. "What Leon say?"

"I haven't told him yet," she began between sips.

"But I'm sure I won't have any problems with him."
She wagged her eyebrows for a little added emphasis.

I took another sip and didn't even bother to comment. Trinette took her husband for granted, while I, on the other hand, would have given anything to have made my marriage work. Part of me was envious, because Donovan and I had planned on buying another house as soon as the bookstore started to make a profit. My accountant had just given me last quarter's numbers, and they were even better than before. I had planned to someday get up out of North County and move to an area with a better school district for Mimi that—

Nope, I wasn't going to go there. For one night, I was not going to dwell on the past. I planned to drink martinis, laugh, flirt and dance the night away.

"Are you okay?"

I blinked rapidly, then looked across the table at Trinette's worried expression. "Yeah, I'm fine."

"It looked like I lost you there for a moment."

"I'm fine," I said between sips, trying to convince myself as well.

She sipped her drink and I watched as her eyes traveled across the room. "Don't look now, but there's someone at the bar checking you out. You just might be lucky enough to get you some before the night is over."

I turned my head.

"I said don't look," Trinette mumbled quickly.

I pretended to focus on my drink. "Who is that?"

"Don't you know? Girl, that's Kenyon."

I gave her a puzzled look. "Kenyon who?"

"Kenyon Monroe. He hangs out with Jay all the time."

Discreetly, I glanced over to the direction of the bar

at the man she was referring to. Daaayum. He was a tall, dark chocolate morsel with cold, black wavy hair, dressed in charcoal slacks, a white shirt open at the chest and not a knotty hair in sight. I had seen him around for years, admiring him from afar, but I had never met him. Only heard about him. He was an insurance agent whose office I rode by almost every morning. "Yeah, I know who he is."

Trinette's gaze was riveted to the bar. "Nikki, he's a cutie."

"Yes, he is," I had to admit. "He's also a ho. He's gone through half the females in North County."

When she started laughing, I knew she had heard the rumors as well. "Well, he *is* cute."

"*And* he's married."

She shook her head. "Nope, he *was* married. Camille passed away last year from breast cancer. Jay said Kenyon was there by her side when she died."

I had to admit, I felt moved by the thought of a man being there with me until I breathed my last breath.

Between sips, I glanced over in his direction. Jay Tatum was standing next to him. He definitely had a reputation of being a ho. I knew because he and Trinette had been dipping and dabbing off and on for years. Kenyon and Jay were surrounded by all those hoochies. Clothes too tight and too damn small. Kenyon was smiling, and I had to admit he had a beautiful smile. No gold teeth, and none were missing as far as I could tell. He whispered something in a hoochie's ear that made her rest her hand against his solid chest. I couldn't help but wonder what he was saying. I don't know how long I was staring at him before he noticed me looking, and I couldn't help but to smile in his direction.

"Nikki?"

Damn! I turned around quickly and found Trinette watching me with a speculative gleam in her eyes. "You want me to call him over here?" Trinette offered.

I frowned. "No."

"Too late. Here he comes."

I brought my glass to my lips and tried to pretend I hadn't noticed.

"Whassup, ladies?"

I glanced up at Jay. "Hey." We grew up in the same hood. Even after all these years, he still had a body like a linebacker. He was too pretty for my taste. Long wavy hair. Tall. Butter pecan complexion and sexy bedroom eyes.

"Whassup, Jay?" Trinette said with a roll of her eyes. They had a long, crazy history. Their personalities were too much alike to take each other serious. Jay's mama had been killed in an auto accident involving a city street sweeper. He hired a lawyer and won a three million dollar lawsuit. Jay hadn't worked a day since. He had money and was stingy with it, but Trinette had a way of making him spend it on her.

Kenyon stopped in front of me. I had no choice but to look at him.

"Hello," he said, and smiled. I was right. His teeth were so pretty but nothing compared to his eyes. They were large, brown and amazing, surrounded by thick, long lashes. To distract myself from this cutie, I turned my attention back to my drink.

He held out his hand. "I'm Kenyon."

As I accepted his handshake, I tried not to look interested. "I know who you are."

His smile deepened and so did his dimples. "I hope you heard good things."

"Yes and no," I said, releasing his warm grip and reaching for my drink again.

"That's too bad."

"For you . . . yes, it is." I gave him a bored look and glanced over his shoulder.

"Can I buy you a drink?"

I held up my glass. "I already have one."

"Can I buy you another?" He wasn't ready yet to give up. Have to say, I liked his style.

I shrugged. It was hard acting nonchalant when you're attracted to someone. And this man definitely had my ass on fire. The sooner I got him the hell away from me, the better I would be. "Maybe later."

"Okay, then how about a dance?"

The music had slowed down. I watched Jay and Trinette move out onto the dance floor, then shook my head. "Maybe later."

"Is that your answer to everything?"

I rolled my eyes. "It is when I don't wanna be bothered." I paused and took a deep breath. I was being rude. "Look. I didn't come here tonight to be picked up. I'm just out having a good time with my girl."

Kenyon held his hands up in surrender. "No problem," he said, trying to conceal his disappointment, then turned and walked away.

Now that he was a safe distance away, I sipped my martini and watched him out of the corner of my eye. I was rude and knew it, but he was not at all what I was looking for. Not that I was looking. I had finished my drink by the time Trinette returned.

"What happened to Kenyon?"

"I sent him away," I replied.

"Why in the world would you do that?" Trinette asked, leaning back in her seat, shaking her head with bewilderment.

I frowned. "Why do you think? Because I'm not interested."

"Nikki, you haven't had any dick in months!"

I glanced over at the next table to see if the three females had heard. They gave me a crazy look, and I was quick to give them one back. "Thanks for telling everyone my business," I snapped.

Trinette sighed to show her annoyance, then shook her head again. "You said it was time to move on. What in the world is wrong with you?"

I rolled my eyes, making sure she knew I was serious. "Just because I'm horny doesn't mean I'm gonna pick up the first ho who comes my way."

Trinette hesitated as if she wanted to make sure she chose her words carefully. "You know I love you, girl, but you said so yourself, you need some. I didn't say marry the dude. Fuck him and send him on his way. Remember, you said it's time for you to move on . . . not me."

Yeah, and Donovan said the same thing. *It's time to move on.* I know . . . I know. I needed to start living again.

"You know I love you. Only you know when you're ready." She gave me a sympathetic look.

A waitress moved up beside me holding a tray. "Here you go, ladies. Compliments of the man standing at the end of the bar." She put two fresh apple martinis in front of us.

I glanced down at the end of the bar and spotted Kenyon looking at me in a way I hadn't seen in a long-ass time. I mouthed "thank you," and he nodded. I could feel my temperature rising and the spot between my thighs becoming moist as he continued to stare. I forced myself to look away. That man was not making resisting him easy at all.

"Mmm-hmm, I see you looking. You need to quit playing and go over there and talk to him," Trinette suggested with a smirk. "In the meantime let me go see who that tramp is all up in Jay's face. Trust and believe, if he's going home with anyone tonight, it's gonna be me." She sashayed away. I could tell by the way Trinette was shaking she knew she had several men staring her ass down as she passed. Trinette was definitely something else. She didn't want Jay, yet she hated to see him with anyone else.

I was sipping my drink when my hairdresser, Denise, came over and took a seat across from me. She was one of those hoochies I was talking about. Too thick and had way too many babies for the black spandex dress she was trying to wear. But she did a hell of a job on my locks.

"Whassup, girl?" she said, bracelets dangling at her wrist.

"Hey, Denise."

"Nikki. Giiirrrl . . ." she sang, then leaned in close so I could hear her over the hum of the music. "Kenyon wants to holla at you."

I sucked my teeth, then snuck a peek over in his direction and rolled my eyes. "He's tired. I'm sick of dogs tryna bark at me."

"Girl, puhleeze give my boy a bone. Don't believe everything you hear. He was good to Camille."

I gave her a curious look. "What about all the rumors of him dogging her out?"

Denise tossed a hand in the air. "They're just that . . . rumors. You know I'm not gonna lie for no nigga. He's legit."

"I'll take that into consideration."

"I will tell you, though . . ." She paused and looked around like somebody might accidently overhear. "I heard he ain't working with much, but that might just be rumor too." I looked down at her pinky finger. My eyes grew large, and she and I both started laughing.

"No, you didn't just say that!"

"Like I said . . . it's probably just a rumor. You know bitches be hating. Anyway, he's feeling yo ass, so please give him a break so I can get my drink on."

I chuckled and watched her walk away, rocking her hips to the sounds of Usher. As soon as Denise returned to her seat, I allowed my eyes to travel over to where Kenyon was standing, in the same exact spot as before, at the end of the bar with Jay. He pointed to his glass, asking me if I wanted another drink, and I nodded even though I had yet to finish the other. Hell, might as well have a good time. It wasn't like anyone was at home waiting for me. I was lonely, and it was time for me to start having some fun. I had just finished my drink by the time Kenyon swaggered in my direction carrying another.

"Thanks," I said. Yes, Lord, he smelled good.

"I was starting to think maybe something was wrong with me, so I sent my girl Denise to the rescue. You make a brotha have to beg."

I smiled. "Nah, never that. Just not interested in brothas trying to holla at me tonight."

"What changed your mind?" he asked, giving me a curious look.

I pointed my finger to the right. "Denise put in a good word for you." As well as shared another rumor. I put the rumors aside for a while.

"I'll have to make sure I thank her."

He smiled, and I'd be lying if I said it didn't do something to me. Kenyon had the most beautiful set of teeth and dimples to die for. Up close I could see how fine and wavy his hair was. He must have some Indian in him, and his skin was like a melted candy bar.

"Let's try this again." He held out his hand. "Kenyon Monroe."

I accepted his warm handshake . . . again. "Nikki Truth."

He leaned in close to me. "I know who you are. I've been watching you for a long time."

I liked the way that sounded. I also liked that his breath smelled like cinnamon Altoids. Nothing worse than a brother with funky breath. "Really. . . . You've been watching me?"

Kenyon nodded. "I even listen to your radio show."

"Oh, boy. Have a seat."

He chuckled and lowered himself on the chair beside me. "I actually enjoy it. You definitely don't hold no punches."

I shrugged my shoulders. "Hey, if the truth hurts . . ."

"I agree."

"Actually, I heard a lot about you as well," I commented between sips.

"Really? What you hear?"

I pushed my locks away from my face as I spoke.

"That you're a dog, but seeing you hanging with Jay, that part is obvious."

He smiled. "You can't believe everything you hear."

I sucked my teeth. "Then tell me something I don't know about you."

"I'm a good man who buried his wife of fifteen years last summer."

"I'm sorry to hear that." And I was.

"Thank you. Camille was a good woman. We had problems like all married couples, but I loved her. And I was with her until the end. Now I'm looking for someone special. I'll tell you, I'm not into playing games. When I see something I want I go after it." He gave me a cocky smile that made my stomach twirl and my pelvic muscles pulse.

"Is that right?"

"Yeah, and I've been feeling you for a while." He sipped his drink. It looked like Crown Royal. "So, tell me something about you."

"I'm married."

His face dropped. "No one told me that."

"Probably because my husband dumped me before he left for Iraq." I was trying to keep from getting angry all over again. It wasn't hard to do when you had a sexy man sitting across from you. I noticed that the smile returned to his face.

"That's too bad."

I shrugged. "I guess it's time for me to move on. It's a damn shame I give advice on relationships but I suck at them."

Kenyon reached across the table and took my hand. "Maybe because you keep picking the wrong guy."

I stared across at him. Maybe he did have a point.

"Come on. Let's dance."

I followed him out onto the dance floor and allowed him to wrap his arms around me. I closed my eyes. It had been six months since I'd had any kind of physical contact, and I can't begin to tell you how good it felt to be in the company of a man. He was so close, and I felt him grow hard and I started getting wet down low. Damn, I hadn't realized how horny I truly was until then. A woman should never go more than half a year without getting any.

"I would like to take you to dinner tomorrow night."

I leaned back and stared up at him and felt tightness at my stomach. Had he really just asked me out on a date? Yes, I believe he had, and it had definitely been a long time. *No looking back, remember?* Nope, I wasn't going to look back, but I wasn't going to rush things either. "I've got to work at the store the next couple of nights. How about next weekend?"

Kenyon didn't look like he liked having to wait that long, but he nodded anyway. "I'd like that."

He held me close again, and we stayed out on the dance floor for three songs before the deejay changed the music. I started to walk off the floor when Kenyon grabbed my hand. "You know how to two-step?" he asked.

"Nope."

He tugged my arm. "Come on. Follow my lead."

Kenyon was a wonderful dancer and following him was easy. I found myself spinning on cue and laughing, actually starting to really enjoy myself, and for the first time all night I was glad I had come out.

We moved back to the table where Jay and Trinette were sitting, and the four of us spent the rest of the night laughing, talking and drinking way too much. Close to midnight, I let Kenyon walk me to my car. When he took my hand I couldn't begin to tell you how good it felt strolling across the parking lot like a couple. He had my stomach all in knots. I hadn't felt that alive in a long time. And even though I said I wanted to take things slow, I was anticipating what was going to happen next.

"Can I kiss you?" he asked as soon as we reached my car.

I nodded. And before I had a chance to take a breath, Kenyon swooped in and covered my lips with his. Oh, my God! Dude practically stuck his tongue down my throat. Kissing was definitely not his thing.

"Can I follow you home?" he asked after I pulled back.

My body was screaming yes, but I knew it was way too early for that. "Nah, I'll talk to you tomorrow."

He nodded, then we exchanged numbers and I climbed into my car and drove home. I thought about the evening, and a smile was on my face. I hadn't felt that silly and alive since high school. I was glad Trinette made me come, because if she hadn't I wouldn't have met Kenyon. He seemed like something I could work with. By the time I pulled my car in the driveway my phone rang. It was Kenyon.

"Yes?"

"It's me. I just wanted to make sure you made it home safely."

"I'm pulling in now."

"Good. How about Trinette?"

I snorted rudely. "She and Jay snuck off somewhere together."

We laughed and talked a few more minutes before I said good night.

I walked in the house looking forward to our date on Saturday. One thing for sure, I was definitely going to have to teach Kenyon how to kiss.

ll

Trinette

"Come on, Netta."

I don't know why Jay was trying to act like he didn't know the rules. He'd been fucking around with me off and on for years and nothing had changed. "I wanna buy a new house, and I need for you to help a sistah out."

"Damn, Trinette, why can't you just give a nigga some on credit?"

"'Cause I ain't one of them broke hoochies you're use to fucking wit."

We were parked outside his place because after that incident with Cory I wasn't about to invite another fool to my condo, although Jay had been over several times. But no matter how many years we'd known each other and all the years he'd had my back, that was neither here nor there. This time he was gonna have to pay to play with Ms. Netta.

"If you don't want none of this, then fine. Take me back to my car."

He thought about it for a few seconds while his eyes raked the length of me. Did he really think he could pass up a night of getting some of me? Obviously not, because Jay barely wasted another second before he climbed out the car. Smiling, I followed him inside, and we started hugging and feeling on each other at the door. I don't know what it is, but I'd always had a weakness for him, yet there was no way in hell I could ever think about taking him serious. We were friends first and everything else came second. The fact that his pockets were fat definitely helped keep that spark burning for him. If he was broke, I probably would have stopped messing with him a long time ago.

We moved back to his room and I slipped off my pantsuit so he could see Victoria's big secret. Jay's eyes were bugging out his head.

"Damn, you fine."

"Of course I am. I only get better with age." By the time he pulled his clothes off, I was ready to put my work in.

We were going at it hard, licking, sucking sixty-nine style, when I heard a door slam. Jay sat up straight on the bed, causing me to land headfirst at the foot of the bed.

"Jay! Where your mothafuckin' ass at?"

"Oh, shit!" He scrambled out the bed trying to grab his boxers.

"Who's that?" I whispered. Whoever it was had him scared shitless.

"That's Veronica."

"Veronica . . . your baby mama Ronnie? What the hell she doing with a key?"

I leaped out of the bed, grabbed my clothes and hid in the closet. By the time Ronnie barged into his room, Jay was in his draws moving to the door.

"Where's the bitch I heard you was all hugged up with at the club?" From a crack in the door I watched her standing in front of him with attitude. She would want to get something done to her head. Dookey braids went out a long time ago.

"What you talking about? I wasn't hugged up wit no female."

She was trying to push her way into the room, but he blocked the door. "What you trying to hide?" she asked, looking over his shoulder.

"I ain't trying to hide shit. What the hell you doing here? Where's my son at?"

"He wit my mama. And you haven't answered my question."

"I ain't been with no one," he insisted.

"Then let me smell your dick." Before he had a second to object, she dropped to the floor, taking his boxers with her.

"A'ight . . . go ahead and smell," he said, trying to sound all bold and shit.

Ronnie wrapped her hands around his length and put her face all in his crotch, sniffing for some coochie. Next thing I know, she guided the head into her mouth and deep throated his ass.

That fool stood there moaning while she went to work on him. I guess Jay suddenly remembered I was just a few feet away, because he had sense enough to push her away. I might not want to fight Ronnie, but I had no problem grabbing one of the wire hangers and doing a little slicing and dicing of my own before I spent another minute in that closet while she sucked on a dick I had been dying all night to ride.

"Let's take this to the shower," he suggested.

She rose and took his hand as he led her into the master bathroom. Jay shut the door, but I could hear Ronnie again going off about what one of her girls told her she saw at the club. Women can be so stupid.

I reached down for my clothes and got dressed. As soon as I heard the water running, I stepped out.

I can't believe I wasted my time with him. Smooth had been blowing up my phone ever since I rocked his world Wednesday evening. He was a dead fuck, but his pockets were large. Before the evening was over, I had every bill in his wallet. He broke off the first grand before I finished my striptease and another grand after I got done making his toes curl. I think I put in my best work yet. But there was nothing attractive about him. He was overweight, belly stuck out farther than his dick, but as generous as he was with his money, Smooth could have had three toes and one eye in the center of his face and it wouldn't have mattered. It all spends the same, and I had a house to buy.

I quickly slipped into my shoes I found under the bed. I needed to catch a cab because I'd be damned if I was going to walk. Jay had tossed his pants over the chair, so I reached inside his pocket and peeled off five hundreds. Hell, the extra was for wasting my damn time. I had come here tonight not only to get paid but to spend time with someone I enjoyed being with, and look where it got me. The two of them were still arguing and going at it, and then the next I knew it grew quiet. By the time I had slipped my purse over my arm, Ronnie was moaning. Oh, no, his ass didn't. Just five minutes ago, he was getting ready to fuck me. Trifling ass. I moved back over to the chair, reached inside his pocket for his wallet again and took every last dime. Shit. It was enough to pay for my home inspection and drop by Saks Fifth Avenue tomorrow to buy myself a little something special. It was the least Jay could do for playing with my emotions.

12

Nikki

I spoke to Kenyon on the phone almost every night, and it shocked the hell out of me we had so much to talk about. By the third night, I found myself looking forward to nine o'clock. We'd talk until he or I started nodding off. I discovered we had a lot in common. Kenyon had a fabulous sense of humor and liked stupid comedy movies like *Step Brothers, Scary Movie,* and *Blades of Glory*. Kenyon also thought sweet potato French fries were the best thing since calamari. He liked his hot dogs loaded with sauerkraut and lots of mustard just like I do. But when the conversation shifted to a more personal level like, "What do you look for in a man?" I decided it was time to set some boundaries.

"Kenyon, I'm gonna be honest with you. I haven't completely ended things with my husband, so in the meantime, I'm not looking for anything serious."

"No problem," he said in that soft, seductive voice I had fallen in love with over the phone. There was something about it I found so soothing and familiar. It was one of those voices you would never want to forget. "We can take it one day at a time and just enjoy each other's company."

Right. I had a feeling he was just saying what I wanted to hear, but at the same time I could just be smelling myself. So far, Kenyon came across as the type of man who believed in being with one woman, which made the rumors of him being a ho that much harder to believe.

"I bought that new *Friday the 13th.*"

"Oh!" We also enjoyed horror movies. "How was it?" I fluffed the pillow under my head.

"I haven't watched it yet." There was a noticeable pause. "How about I come over tomorrow evening and we watch it at your place?"

I lay there in the dark curled deep in my covers as I considered his offer. I was trying to move on, but was I ready to bring another man to my house? I don't know how long I lay there considering the question.

"Baby, you still there?"

I smiled. I loved when he called me baby as if he'd been doing it for years. He really was a nice guy, and it wasn't like I was planning to screw him in the bed my husband bought me.

"Yeah. I'm here. Sure, why not? Watching the movie tomorrow sounds like fun." We talked until shortly after midnight before I mumbled good-bye and hung up the phone.

The following evening, I hurried home from work, then took my schnauzer Rudy over to Mama's. My dog is like a spoiled child and a tad bit jealous when it comes to me. I didn't want him to have to compete for my affection. Besides, Mama had been asking for me to bring him over to keep her company.

I visited Big Mama, then made it back home and changed into jeans and a Lakers sweatshirt. My locks I pulled in a neat ponytail off my neck. I loved my hair, but at times, managing my locks seemed like too much damn work.

At a little after seven Kenyon pulled up in my driveway in a silver Lincoln MKS. Damn, that's a pretty car. I watched him get out and come up the stairs, taking in his attire from head to toe. The brotha definitely had style. He was wearing gray Nike sweatpants, matching hoodie and brand new Jordans on his feet. I waited until he rang the doorbell, then took my time opening it. I stood there and smiled.

"Hey."

I couldn't stop smiling. "Hey." I stepped aside so he could enter.

He held up a bottle. "I hope you like wine."

It took everything he had to keep a straight face. "You know I do," I said, and he started laughing and I joined in. The ice had been broken and I felt instantly at ease.

"Come're." I went right into his arms and he gave me a big hug, then released me. "Damn. I needed that. Now I'm good for the rest of the night." He winked and I kept on smiling. Being pressed up against him had my nipples hard as hell. I took the bottle from one hand. He was holding the movie in the other as he stepped into the kitchen.

"Damn, baby. You got a nice crib."

"Thanks." While he admired my mosaic ceramic floor and granite countertops, I reached inside my cherry wood cabinet and retrieved a corkscrew.

"It looks like your talk show's got you living large."

I shrugged. "Between that and the bookstore I'm not doing too bad."

"I'm not mad. I love to see a beautiful black woman doing the damn thang."

"Thank you." I laughed and poured two glasses of wine and handed him one.

"I've never been much of a wine drinker, but maybe you can teach me a few things." He took a sip. "Hmmm, that's not bad."

"I told you. Moscato is my favorite wine."

He took another drink, then smiled. "I definitely can see why." He had the most beautiful eyes. I don't know how long I stood there like a fool staring at him before I forced my eyes away. I signaled for him to follow me into the family room behind the kitchen, where I knew he would be equally impressed.

"Oh, shit!"

The room had been my husband's oasis after a long day. Large wraparound leather couch. Sixty-inch flat-screen television with surround sound. Every kind of movie you could think of in a built-in wall unit as well as a PlayStation 3 and dozens of video games.

"I think I just died and gone to heaven."

I playfully slugged him in the arm and took the DVD from his hand. After I put the movie in, we both took a seat on the couch. I made sure to put a little space between us.

Before the movie even began, Kenyon turned to me. "Can I ask a question?"

"Sure," I said, then brought the flute to my lips.

"You either have a child or a dog, because there are toys all over this floor!"

Glancing around the Berber carpet I had to laugh. Rudy's toys were everywhere. Stuffed animals, balls and toys that made noise were scattered around the room. I was so used to them, I didn't even pay attention. "I have a dog."

Kenyon gave me a curious look. "Where's he at? Out back?"

I shook my head. "At my mom's. I forgot to mention I had a dog and wasn't sure if you like them or not."

"I love dogs. What kind you got?"

I crossed my legs and sat Indian style. "A schnauzer."

Kenyon brought the glass to his lips, then paused. "Is that one of those Wizard of Oz–looking dogs?"

I laughed. "Yeah, something like that."

Playfully he rolled his eyes. "I should have guessed." He broke out laughing and I giggled along with him. I liked him already. He had such a refreshing sense of humor. "Come're." Willingly, I slid over on the couch and he draped an arm across my shoulders while we watched the movie.

It was definitely a remake of the original and much better than all the sequels. I jumped off the couch shouting at the fool in the movie. "Run, stupid! Run!" Kenyon started laughing. Why was it folks always have to fall in scary movies?

By the time the movie was over we had pretty much finished the bottle of wine. I turned on some music and we listened to Hot 97 quiet storm. My girl Keisha was on the air. She definitely could hold her own.

"Isn't that your station?"

I nodded. "Yep. I only work Monday, Wednesday and Friday nights. Otherwise, I wouldn't have time to do anything."

"That means if I wanna take you out it's gotta be on a Saturday?"

"Yep." Johnny Gill was bellowing through the speakers telling some girl to put on her red dress and let her hair down.

Kenyon scooped me up and lowered me across his lap. "So, we still on for Saturday? I would like to take you to dinner."

My heart was pounding. I was sitting so close. The lights were low. Romantic music was in the background, and my body was definitely responding to being on his lap. I stared up into his beautiful chocolate face. The man definitely had some Indian in him. His hair was so pretty and wavy, and his lashes were long. Who could resist a man like this?

"Sure. Dinner sounds fabulous."

Kenyon leaned in and kissed my lips. I pulled back, stared down at him, then kissed him myself. He pushed open my mouth and started tonguing me. I learned a long time ago you have to teach a man what you like. They aren't mind readers. "Hold up. Okay, let's try that again and slower. Relax your tongue . . . slow down a little. Here, just follow my lead. . . . There you go . . . just like that."

He nodded. "All you have to do is show me what you like." He didn't get mad like some other brotha might. There were many who didn't believe in being corrected. But not Kenyon. He did just as I suggested and followed the stroke of my tongue, and it wasn't

long before he had gotten the hang of it and had deepened the kiss. By the time Dru Hill was singing "Tell
Me," my coochie was purring and my nipples were
begging to be sucked. Six months is a long time for a
woman to go without sex. But when his hand crept beneath my sweatshirt, I decided that unless I was ready
to give him some, it was probably a good time to end
the night before things got out of hand.

I pulled back and removed his creeping fingers.
"It's time to say good night."

He gave me a long look. "Okay." He didn't look
mad at all. That was a good sign. Kenyon rose with me
still on his lap and lowered me gently to my feet.
"Thanks for inviting me over." He kissed me.

"Thanks for sharing your movie."

He kissed me again. "Anytime."

I put the DVD back in the case, then took
Kenyon's hand and led him to the front door. Once
there, Kenyon pulled me back into his arms and
pushed my lips apart with his tongue. The man had
definitely caught on quick. He was good . . . real good.
I couldn't help but wonder what else he was good at.
The whole time he was kissing me, I was thinking
about him taking me back to my room and making love
to me with the same skill as his kissing. I had no doubt
it would be good. One final kiss, and he ended it.

"Thanks again, Nikki. I look forward to Saturday
night."

"Me too." I watched him until his car had turned at
the corner before I shut the door and moved back to my
room to get ready for bed. As soon as I slipped into my
gown the phone rang.

"I'm already missing you."

I was so glad to hear that. "I'm missing you too."

"I can't believe the way we have connected. It's like I've known you for years."

"Same here." I slid underneath the covers and we talked until Kenyon arrived home before we both said good night. I lay there in my bed, listening to the quiet storm, and found myself thinking about Kenyon and wondering if the rumor about him having a small dick was true. I hoped not. Right now he was so perfect. A little dick would definitely ruin everything.

13

Trinette

Something said it wasn't going to be a good day.

"Mrs. Montgomery, the only way we can approve the loan is in your husband's name."

"Why's that?"

She hesitated. "Because your credit isn't the best. You have a judgment on your account for a credit card, which would have to be paid before we could even consider you on the loan."

Damn department store card. I never wanted the credit card in the first place. The only reason I got it was because they offered interest free for one year. How was I to know the interest rate was going to be more than 20 percent? "Okay, I'll pay the judgment. What else?" I spat into the phone. How dare she judge me? She was probably jealous she didn't have a credit card with a five thousand dollar limit.

She had the nerve to sigh heavily into the phone. "There are also all the other maxed-out credit cards. You'll have to lower your debt ratio. Mrs. Montgomery, it really makes more sense to finance the new house in just your husband's name. His credit score is over seven hundred while yours is . . . uh . . . less than six. It will help get you a much better interest rate if we finance the house in just Mr. Montgomery's name. You can always try to refinance the house later. . . . That's if you, uh . . . improve your credit score."

That was not at all what I wanted to hear. Leon was going to have a fit unless of course I could persuade him it was for the best. But I had already told him I had been paying off my debts. If my name wasn't on that loan he was going to know my ass had been lying. "I think maybe *we* need to find another lender who is interested in our money, because apparently you aren't. I've never been late on my mortgage in eight years, so I think you should be doing everything you can to keep us as customers!"

She hesitated, then tried to sound sympathetic. "I'm sorry. With the economy the way it is, federal regulations have gotten stricter."

"Well, I'm gonna have to give it some thought and get back with you." I slammed down the phone. "Ain't that a bitch!"

"What's up, girl?" Patricia whipped her head around so fast I was surprised she didn't get whiplash. She was nosy, but I needed to tell someone, otherwise I was going to explode. I get like that when I'm pissed. I would have called Nikki, but I just wasn't in the mood for her saying, I told you so.

I looked around and made sure no one else was listening. Trust me, folks love being all up in my business. "The mortgage company will only finance the house in my husband's name because my credit sucks."

Patricia's eyes grew large. "Trinette, that's good!"

"Why's that good?"

"Because . . . ," she sang. "Then he's paying your mortgage and has the financial responsibility. Just think . . . if you wanted to divorce him, you could make him pay your mortgage. You know he's never gonna miss a payment, because the house is in his name. You get to live there and make him pay for your home while you continue living the lifestyle you're accustomed to."

The lifestyle I'm accustomed to. A smile curled my lips. Ain't that some shit. Patricia was smarter than I thought. Now if only she would learn how to dress.

If Leon insisted on my moving to Richmond with him, I could say no, and if he asked for a divorce, he would *still* have to pay my mortgage, because there is no way Leon is ever late on paying anything. I started chuckling uncontrollably. That bucktoothed, nondressing chick was good for something. Why hadn't I thought of that? "Hell, yeah!" We gave each other a high five. Now all I had to do was convince Leon it was for the best.

I was feeling good and was getting ready to call our lender back when Claudette buzzed me from the front desk. "Trinette, Cimon Clark is at station three."

I slammed the receiver down. I'd been waiting two weeks for this day. It took everything I had to erase the smirk from my face as I moved to the back where Cimon was sitting and yapping on the phone. As soon as she spotted me coming, she rolled her eyes.

"Meeka, I'ma have to call you back." She closed her phone, then pursed her lips and waited for me to speak. It took everything I had not to laugh at her ass.

"Cimon, what can I do for you?" I asked like I didn't have a clue. This was going to be brief, so I didn't even bother to sit down.

"My EBT card ain't working."

"Probably because I figured you didn't really need any food stamps since I saw you roll outta here in a Lincoln Navigator."

She sucked her teeth. "That's not mine!"

"Oh, really?" I sang as I reached down into a folder and removed a sheet of paper. "According to the DMV, the vehicle is registered in your name." I got friends in high places.

She shrugged. "It was a gift, so what?"

"A gift? That's funny, because there's a lien on the title with Wholesale Connection. And when I called them just to verify the car was indeed yours, they said your last automatic payment was rejected."

"Okayyy, and that's because I don't have any money."

"Well, the only way I can verify that is if I see your bank statement. You told me you didn't have a bank account, which also means you lied on your application."

"Regardless of what I said, I need my food stamps! What are my kids supposed to eat?" She snaked her neck as she spoke.

I gave her a sweet smile. "We'll issue you some emergency stamps, but that's it until you tell me how you afford to make a three hundred dollar a month car note with no job."

Cimon slammed her hand down hard on the counter

and rose. She had life twisted if she thought she put fear in my heart.

"You mess wit the wrong one, bitch."

"I got your bitch. Security!" I screamed. Chuck sat out in the hall just in case we needed him. He raced into the room. "I think you need to escort this . . . uh . . . female outta here."

Cimon rolled her eyes. "You're gonna regret messing with me."

"The only one who's gonna have regrets is you if you don't come correct," I called after her as Chuck ushered her away from the workstation. I'm not her last caseworker. That's the reason why Casey's no longer here—because she couldn't handle the pressure and was too damn nice. Not me. I grew up in the hood, so I know the game. Cimon might have pulled the do-rag over someone else's head and got away with it, but not me.

I sat down long enough to put a couple of notes in her electronic file, including her verbal threat, then I grabbed her case folder and headed back to my desk. I was moving down the hall, looking over my shoulder, trying to see if Cimon was still in the building, when I ran right smack into a man built like a ton of bricks.

"Excuse me." I stopped when I realized it was Michael. Tall and fine. "Hey, you."

"Hey, I see you're still as beautiful as ever." His hand was still at my waist and neither of us made any attempt to step away.

"Compliments will get you everywhere." I smiled up into his beautiful chocolate face. This man was every woman's dream of having an ex–NFL football player. Maybe not the ex part but definitely the player.

"What are you doing here? You come to see me?" I purred affectionately.

"I wish I was." He chuckled, but I could tell he was serious. "I'd give anything to take you somewhere private," he added in a low murmur.

"Dreams can come true." What I wanted was to drag him into the nearest closet and ride his fine ass.

A door slammed at the other end of the hall, and Michael dropped his hand from my waist. I guess I need to be ashamed of myself flirting right outside my office door.

"I'm here to pick up Maureen. We're going over to see the house again."

My tongue slipped from my mouth, and I licked my lips. He definitely was looking tasty. "I'm trying to buy a house myself. Just been a little short on coming up with the cash for the down payment."

Michael reached inside his pocket and removed a business card. "Call me. Maybe I can help you out with that."

I just bet you can. In more ways than one. "I'll do that." I turned away with the heat of his gaze on my ass. I glanced over my shoulder. Sure enough, he was looking, and it was obvious he liked everything he saw. That made two of us.

I sat down at my desk just as Maureen reached for her purse. "My boo's here. We're going to go and see my dream home again," she sang merrily, and waved to us as she met her gorgeous man standing in the doorway.

"She's so lucky."

I looked over at Patricia staring enviously at the two of them. She didn't know for sure who her baby's daddy was, so for her, I guess Maureen was lucky. But to me there was nothing Maureen had I couldn't have . . . including her man.

Speaking of men. I grabbed my own purse and headed out as well. I had a date with Smooth.

I was driving down the highway on my way to this little French restaurant he wanted to introduce me to when my cell phone rang. I didn't even bother to check to see who was calling. "Hello?"

"Netta, whassup?"

I immediately had straight attitude. It was my brother Cornbread. The only time he called was when he wanted something. "What do you want?"

"Damn, can't I just call because I wanna see how my big sis is doing?"

"No, because I know you. The only time you call me is when you want something. So whassup?"

He blew a heavy breath. It was obvious he was stalling for time. I wasn't in the mood for games. He was my youngest brother and also my favorite. I had been his mama for the first ten years of his life. If it had been one of the others, I would have probably hung up by now.

"How come you didn't make it to Mama's birthday party last month?"

I started laughing. He couldn't possibly be asking me that question. "Why you think? . . .'cause I can't stand her. What I look like coming to that woman's party?"

"Netta, you need to get over it!"

"Get over what?" I wanted so badly to scream, get over my mother leaving me alone with Uncle Sonny so he could rape me, but there was no way I was admitting that shit to Cornbread. It was bad enough Travis knew.

One night, my brother walked in with Uncle Sonny on top of me. All I could do was look over at Travis with fear in my eyes as I shook my head and signaled for him to go. I wasn't afraid for me, I was afraid what might happen to him if Uncle Sonny had spotted him standing there in the door. Hell, that drunk was too busy pumping his little dick inside of me to notice, but that was a chance I didn't want to take. Travis and I never talked about that night, and I definitely wasn't about to bring that shit up now.

"Mama's a changed woman."

"Changed how? Just because she's going to church and begged the Lord to forgive her for her sins doesn't mean I have to forgive her too."

"Netta . . ." There was a long pause, and I swear it sounded like Cornbread was crying. "Mama's in the hospital."

"For what?" I hardened my voice, trying to act like I didn't care and was angry I was the least bit curious.

"She needs a kidney. Dialysis just ain't cutting it for her anymore."

"Ohhhkay . . . there's three of you. . . . One of y'all give her a kidney."

"We tried. . . . None of us are possible donors."

"Oh, well, then I'm sure there is someone out there who will give her one. Is she on the donor list?" Not that I cared, but I had to ask.

"Yep, but her blood type is rare. None of us are AB negative but you and Murphy."

"Then I guess y'all better dig Murphy's ass up, 'cause she can't have one of mine!" I knew that was mean to say. Murphy was second to the youngest, and he and Cornbread were so close. But Murphy had been hardheaded from the beginning. Nothing I ever said to him mattered. He didn't want to listen. He dropped out of high school and started hanging with the wrong crowd. I wasn't surprised to find out he had started dealing drugs. Five years ago he was killed during a bust.

"Netta, puhleeze . . . do it for me." He was begging, and I hated him for putting me on the spot.

"No."

"Come in and at least see if you're a possible donor match," he insisted.

"What part of no don't you understand . . . the N or the O?" I blew my horn at a Camry that jumped in front of me. Cornbread had me so upset I almost had an accident.

"Listen, no matter how much you try to act like you hate her, she's still your mother, and everyone deserves a second chance."

I snorted rudely in the phone. He was wasting my time.

"For once think about someone other than yourself. Mama's dying and she needs you."

Don't you know he had the nerve to hang up on me. Nobody hangs up on me. Fuck you, Cornbread! Where was Mama when I needed her? I'll tell you where she was. She was out chasing a rock or sucking dick to get a fix. I remember trying to tell her what Uncle Sonny was doing to me. Darlene punched me in the mouth and said I needed to quit lying because if she had to choose which one of us had to leave, it definitely wouldn't be the person who was paying the rent. My own mother had turned her back on me, and that hurt. Now she needed me and I was turning my back on her. Tit for tat.

A tear had the nerve to roll down my cheek, and I brushed it away. There was no way I was going to cry over her or my lost childhood.

14

Nikki

I don't know why, but I was nervous. And I guess I had every reason to be. This would be my first date in fifteen years with someone other than Donovan, and it felt so weird. I was nervous and excited at the same time. I also wanted to look my best, which is why I asked Tristan to go shopping with me. Unfortunately, he had a date, so I had to beg Netta to come with me to what she refers to as the "po-folk's mall." I personally didn't see anything wrong with finding a bargain.

"What about this outfit?"

I looked over at the two-piece outfit with a plunging neckline and the coochie cutter shorts and turned up my nose. "You've got to be kidding."

She shrugged. "Hey, it will definitely get his attention."

"Yeah, the first thing outta his mouth will be, how much?"

"He might even reach inside his pocket for a stack of one dollar bills." She started cracking up.

"Netta, crazy ass, you know exactly what he's gonna think."

"Hey, I was trying to help you out. I know it's been a while since you had some, and there's probably cobwebs you need someone to come and clean out. He might be the man for the job, although . . ." She sucked her teeth for dramatic effect. "I heard he ain't working with much."

My head snapped to the left. She had heard the rumors too. It took everything I had to keep a straight face. "What I tell you about rumors?"

"Hey, I also heard he was a womanizer and crazy, but if you wanna go out with the dude, I am not gonna stand in the way of true love."

"You're the one who told me to give the man a chance."

"No, I said for you to get some dick. I was expecting you to take him home after we left the party. Not start a relationship."

I moved to the next rack of outfits on clearance. "I wouldn't go that far. He comes across as someone who likes having someone at home when he gets there . . . that he likes having a family."

"Yeah, someone sitting at home while he's in the streets."

"Come on, now. . . . If he was that bad, why would his wife have stayed with him as long as she had, and if he wasn't working with much, why would women be interested in messing with him?"

"Curiosity. Hell, even I'm waiting for you to come back and let me know whether the rumors are true, because inquiring minds wanna know."

I started laughing and reached for a pair of jeans and a matching jacket. "What you think of this?"

Trinette turned up her nose at the $49.99 price tag. "Nikki, that's something outta the 60s. Look at those daisies on the thighs and the bell-bottoms."

"Hey, bell-bottoms are back in."

She sucked her teeth. "Whatever." Trinette scanned the rack and reached for something more her style. "Here, go try this on."

I looked down at the black jumpsuit with long sleeves that zipped up the front. "This might work."

"I know it will, now go in the dressing room."

Just like her to act like she knows best. I went in and undressed. I just hate those four-way mirrors they put in the room. I can see my rolls and every bit of cellulite invading my thighs. I slipped into the jumpsuit and zipped it up. Turning side to side, I smiled. It had just enough spandex in it to accommodate my hips and sistah girl butt. I stepped out. "What do you think?"

"Daaayum! You're wearing the hell outta that outfit. I told you it would look good." I turned in front of the big mirror on the wall and smiled. She was right. I looked luscious.

"Now all we have to do is find you a fabulous pair of boots and you'll have that man drooling."

I stared at her reflection in the mirror and turned up my nose. "I'm not sure I want him doing that."

"No, what you want is for him to be drooling on something between your thighs."

Remembering how good his lips felt . . . that didn't sound like a bad idea.

By seven, I was standing in front of the full-length mirror in my bathroom. Trinette had complemented the black jumpsuit with red leather boots and a wide red belt. I have to admit I looked fabulous and more than ready to spend the evening with Kenyon. I retwisted my front locks, applied a little mascara and lipstick, then moved into the living room and took a seat to wait.

Ever since we watched that DVD together our relationship had grown closer. It felt so good laughing for a change and having something to look forward to every evening. In one week, he had brought so much joy to my otherwise depressing life. But even though I was having a good time, part of me felt guilty. I don't know why, but I felt as if I was cheating on my husband. And I couldn't understand that since he was the one who said it was time for us to move on. But deep in my heart, I felt like we still had some unfinished business to attend to. But maybe I was just trying to hold onto something that was no longer mine. All I know is, I was tired of going to bed feeling horny. I hadn't had a man hold me in his arms in so long, I was dying for that comforting feeling again.

I looked down at my watch, then reached inside my purse and decided to call Big Mama's room. My mother answered the phone.

"Are you coming to the hospital?"

I was so tired of going through this with her. Wasn't I just there yesterday? I didn't like seeing Big Mama in the hospital. It was hard for me. She and my aunt lived at the hospital day and night and felt that because I was Big Mama's favorite, I should be at the hospital all damn day. It's not my fault my mother doesn't have a life.

"I'll come out tomorrow morning." That seemed to shut her up. "How's Big Mama?"

"Doctor thinks she's doing better and will be ready for physical therapy in another week."

My pulse slowed. That was the news I needed to hear. I needed my grandmother. I couldn't imagine my life without her. "That's good to hear."

"Yes, it is. You wanna speak to her?"

"Please."

I heard Mama telling Big Mama it was me, then seconds later, I heard her speak in a low voice. "There's my chickadee. I was wondering if you were going to call me."

A smile curled my lips. "You know I've got to call and check on you."

"I'm doing fine, but I'd be a lot better if they'd just let an old lady go home and die happy. This food they're trying to feed me has no flavor."

Knowing what she likes, I couldn't help but laugh. "That's because it's good for you."

"No. Good food is what I cook at home in my own kitchen."

She ain't never lied. Big Mama could throw down in the kitchen, but most of the foods she prepared were high in fat, and after a stroke three years ago, that was the last thing she needed.

"Let's get you better first, then maybe I'll have Trinette make you a pot of greens."

She laughed. "Now you're really trying to kill me." I laughed along with her, then there was silence before I spoke again.

"Big Mama . . . Donovan asked for a divorce."

"Baby, I'm so sorry. He's such a good man. A shame the two of you can't stay together."

I released a heavy sigh. "We've been drifting apart

for years. I knew in my heart when he left for Iraq it was over."

"I sure hate that. Every woman needs a good man in her life. Women nowadays are too independent. . . . Men don't like that. They need to feel needed."

Big Mama took a deep breath, and I could tell by her voice she was getting tired. "Just pray on it. I hate to see you make a mistake you later regret."

"I won't."

"Well . . . thanks for calling me. I love you."

My eyes flooded with tears. "I love you too, Big Mama."

I hung up just as I heard a car pull up in the driveway. Rudy jumped in the window seat and peeked his head through the blind.

"He's here to see me. Not you."

Rudy gave me a look, then hurried to the door. I rose from the couch just as the doorbell rang. I swung it open and there Kenyon stood.

He was such a gorgeous man. He looked fabulous in dark jeans, a chocolate Enyce shirt and Timberlands on his feet. He greeted me with those amazing dimples. "Hi."

"Hi yourself, sexy," he said, slipping his arms around my waist. Instantly, I felt comfortable in his warm embrace. He released me first, thank goodness, because I wasn't sure if I ever would have let him go. I stepped aside so he could enter, and Rudy immediately started barking at him.

I smiled at the tickled look on Kenyon's face. "You have to rub him and acknowledge him as the man of the house, otherwise he won't stop."

"No problem. Hello, Rudy." Kenyon held out his hand for Rudy to sniff, then he rubbed his coat. "You're a good boy." He patted his stomach, and Rudy started wagging his tail. "I think I've won him over."

"Yep, I would agree." And if he played his cards right, he'd win mama over as well. "Let me grab my purse and we can leave." I moved down the hall and stayed in my room long enough to pop a few breath mints in my mouth and check my hair and makeup to make sure they were perfect, then grabbed my leather jacket from the closet and returned to the living room. I stopped at the end of the hallway and simply smiled. Kenyon tossed Rudy's ball across the room and waited for him to bring it back.

"I see you found his favorite game."

He shrugged. "Most dogs like to play fetch."

I let him toss the ball a couple more times, then I reached for a snack from the kitchen cabinet. "Come on, Rudy. Time to go in your kennel." He immediately raced into the family room where his kennel sat in the corner near the couch close to the television. That way he could watch Animal Planet while I was away at work.

"You lock your dog up during the day?"

"I don't have a choice. If I leave him out, he has a tendency to destroy things or cock up his legs against the couch."

Nodding, he started to chuckle. "You definitely can't have that."

I practically had to drag Rudy into his cage. He wanted to finish playing with his new friend. It was almost eight by the time I finally locked the house and headed out to Kenyon's Lincoln MKS.

"Nice ride," I complimented him while he opened the passenger door.

"Thanks. The car's a birthday present to myself. I've

never had a new car and decided at forty it was about damn time."

"I agree." The ride was sleek, and as soon as he started the engine, it purred like a tiger.

Kenyon pulled off, and I started to get excited about our evening. There was something about this man I found sexy and intriguing. Other than being fine, he seemed to be adventurous and enjoyed having a good time, and I desperately needed a little excitement in my life.

Jennifer Hudson's voice blared through the speakers, and I leaned back in my seat and closed my eyes. As far as I was concerned, the night was full of possibilities.

"You have any brothers or sisters?"

I opened my eyes and looked over at his curious face. "I have a younger sister who lives in L.A. What about you?"

Kenyon nodded. "My sisters raised me. I've got six of them and one brother. I'm the youngest."

"And probably spoiled rotten."

He laughed at that. "I'll never tell."

"Believe me, it won't be hard to find out."

Smiling, he reached over and captured my hand with his. "If there is anything you wanna know about me, please, don't hesitate to ask. I don't have anything to hide."

I smiled along with him, then got lost in the words of the song. It wasn't long before we pulled up in front of a townhouse. He turned off the car, and I looked over at him. "What are we doing here?"

"Having dinner," Kenyon replied, and he climbed out.

I frowned. His cheap ass had brought me to his

house for dinner. I knew it was his house because I'd looked his name up in the phone book and knew he lived on Chambers Avenue. Hell, I spent all that money trying to look good for nothing. I tried to hide my disappointment as I stepped out the car. He took my hand and we moved up the sidewalk to his place. *Kenyon better be one helluva cook.*

Kenyon released my hand, turned the key in the door and signaled for me to go before him. The second I stepped through the door, I heard a guitar playing. My head whipped to the side, and there were two Mexicans dressed in their native attire and even wearing sombreros. They were singing a Spanish serenade.

I turned to Kenyon, who was grinning. *"Benvenido a Mexico my amor."*

I started laughing. That was the worst attempt at Spanish I ever heard. Taking my hand, he led me into the dining room. The table had been set up with a white linen tablecloth, and a candle was burning in a hurricane vase in the center. He pointed into the other room. "That's my boy Felipe in the kitchen. He owns San Jose's, that Mexican restaurant on West Florissant?"

I nodded. "Yeah, I've seen it but never had a chance to eat there." A chubby Hispanic male waved to me from across the island in the kitchen.

"Well, you'll get your chance tonight. Please, have a seat."

I sat down and couldn't stop grinning. No one, not even Donovan, had ever done anything this romantic for me in my life. I looked down at the table and there was an envelope addressed to me.

"Go ahead and open it."

I reached for it and pulled out the card inside. *The new woman in my life. I knew the moment I saw you,*

you were going to be someone special . . . I went on to
read the lines that followed and was completely moved
by the words and emotions Kenyon had poured into it.
This wasn't courtesy of Hallmark. They were all his
words. I looked over at him. Suddenly I wanted him.
My coochie clenched just thinking about having his
beautiful body sweating on top of me. "Thank you."

"You're welcome."

The musicians moved into the room and positioned
themselves in the corner. The air smelled of grilled
meat and sautéed onions. I kept looking at Kenyon,
who was grinning at me, and found myself again wondering what Kenyon was working with. I thought,
please don't let the rumors be true, because I wanted to
end the evening with all that fine goodness plunging
between my thighs.

"I hope you're not upset we didn't go out to a restaurant. You mentioned you loved Mexican, so I thought
what better place to have a quiet romantic evening than
at my house."

"No, I love it. The only thing missing is margaritas."

"Oh, shit!" Kenyon rose and scrambled into the
kitchen, then came back holding a pitcher of frozen
lime margaritas and two glasses. "I almost forgot."

I took the glasses from his hand and set them on the
table while he poured. "Felipe made us a batch right
before we got here. You want salt?"

I frowned. "No. I don't like salt."

"Good. Neither do I."

He sat down and we snacked on homemade tortilla
chips and salsa while sipping our drinks. Everything
was good. The guitarist played another song, and I
slipped off my boots.

"Go ahead and get comfortable. I want you to feel at home."

Felipe came in carrying a tray of fajitas with chicken, shrimp and beef. There were even flour tortillas.

"Muchas gracias," I said. I knew a little Spanish—not much, but at least I didn't sound as goofy as Kenyon did.

"De nada, Señora."

The food looked good and smelled even better.

"I'll leave the two of you alone."

Kenyon rose and gave him dap. "Yo man, thanks for everything."

"No problem. I told you I owed you one. I'll clean up the kitchen and then we'll be on our way."

As soon as he left the room I leaned across the table and whispered, "Owed him one?"

Kenyon looked a little uncomfortable. "I helped his sister one weekend when Felipe was out of town. She was stranded on the side of the highway in the middle of the night. I went and picked her up."

"That sounds heroic of you."

"That could have been one of my sisters." He shrugged. "I try to think of myself as a good person. There is nothing I won't do for my friends."

I wondered what his limits were when it came to the woman in his life. I was interested in finding out. I waited until he fixed both our plates, then dug in. The food was delicious. The steak was tender. The margaritas were to die for.

"Felipe, *la comida* is wonderful!" I shouted into the other room.

He stuck his head out. *"Gracias, Señora."*

The guitarist continued to play while we ate. Kenyon and I talked about sports and the crazy Missouri weather. We ate, joked around and then somehow our discussion led to sex. Blame it on the margaritas.

"What's your favorite position?" I asked.

Kenyon gave me a strange look, and I slurped too much and got an instant brain freeze. "Ouch!"

"You okay?" he asked. I could tell he was trying his hardest not to laugh.

I held up my index finger. "Yeah . . . in a minute. . . . Okay . . . I'm fine now."

"To answer your question, I love giving it to a woman from behind. Something about slapping against her phat ass turns me on." He reached for a chip. "What about you?"

Oh, my coochie was drooling now. "I also love it doggy. I think I get a deeper penetration that way."

"I definitely agree."

We were both sitting there sipping our drinks, staring at each other like two damn fools, when Felipe stepped into the room. "All done, my friend. I think we're gonna head out."

The thought of the two of us finally being alone made my nipples hard. I rose, thanked the musicians and tried to give them a tip, but Kenyon refused, said he had already taken care of it. I watched the three of them leave. As soon as Kenyon shut the door, he pulled me into his arms and kissed me. Oh, but his lips tasted delicious, especially with the smell of tequila on his breath. I don't know if I was just horny or if Kenyon was just capable of making me feel that damn good. I clung to him and leaned my body as close as I possibly could. His hand came around to cup my breast, and when I moaned he reached for the zipper on my jumpsuit and slipped his hand inside. I practically came when his fingers started caressing my nipples.

"You are so damn sexy," he whispered close to my ear.

I moaned and reached down and started unbuckling his jeans. I was going to come on myself if I didn't have him inside me soon. I wanted to ride him hard.

"Let's take this to my room." He removed his hand and I almost screamed for him to put his fingers back inside my bra. Instead I followed him to his bedroom ready for more. I took in his king-size bed and the large, flat-screen television, then focused my attention back on the man in front of me.

Kenyon slipped off his shirt, and I gazed down at his fabulous chest and moaned. I'd never seen a six-pack looked that good.

"Come're."

Obediently I moved in front of him and allowed him to unzip my jumpsuit, then slide it off my shoulders and down around my waist. Without breaking eye contact, I unsnapped my bra and let it fall to the floor. He palmed my breasts.

"You're beautiful."

"You're not bad yourself."

I reached for his buckle, then released his zipper. Okay, here we were. The moment of truth. . . . I reached inside and . . . damn! I tried to hide my disappointment. Kenyon had length, plenty of that, but his penis was skinny. I squeezed it, hoping it would swell inside my hand, but it didn't. That sucker was already hard as a rock, which meant what you see was what my ass was going to get.

"That's your dick," he whispered against my nose.

Gee . . . thanks.

"I don't believe in sleeping with more than one woman. I've always been particular about who I mess with." He pulsed in my hand, and my coochie responded. As horny as I was, anything would do about now, even if it was no wider than a hot dog. *Girl, as long as he scratches your itch that's all that really matters.* Okay, that might not be totally true, but at least it's a start.

I stepped out of my jumpsuit and panties and watched him while he slipped off his jeans. He had some powerful legs, but they were skinny just like his dick. We moved over to the bed and he lay on top of me and started kissing me, starting at my lips and working his way down . . . all the way down. When his tongue dipped in between my thighs, I cried out. "Yessss . . . oooooh . . . that feels soooo good!"

I reached down and held his head in place, not letting him stop until I came. As soon as my legs collapsed, he reached over in the drawer for a condom and slipped it on, then positioned himself and slid inside. I was so wet I was afraid I wasn't going to feel anything, but it wasn't long before it started feeling good. I mean really, really good. I was rocking my hips with him.

"That's it. Give it to me."

I wrapped my legs around his waist and moved with him. Kenyon lifted up and plunged with deep, even strokes that had me moaning and crying out. "Yessss! Yes, Kenyon!"

"Whose pussy is it?"

"It's yours, baby." Right then, I would have said just about anything.

"Whose?"

I opened my eyes and found him staring down at me

with a look of seriousness on his face. "Yours. Ain't nobody getting this but you."

"You promise?"

"I promise."

"Good, because this dick is all yours." He rose up on his arms, and you would have thought he was doing push-ups the way his body rose and lowered on top of me, plunging deeper and deeper. I was crying out. My head was thrashing on the pillow. Kenyon was proof it was all about the way you worked it. I was seconds away from coming when he rose and pulled my hips down to the end of the bed.

"Turn over."

I immediately complied, then raised my hips in the air, ready for a deep plunge. He started pounding, and I rocked my hips back to meet each and every one of his strokes. Within seconds, I called out his name. "Kenyon . . . yes, baby. Yessss! That's my dick. That's mine. I don't want nobody getting this but me!"

"You don't have to worry. I don't want nobody but you."

I was delirious and saying shit I wasn't even conscious of saying. All I knew was, it had been too long since I'd had some. It wasn't long before I came hard, and Kenyon was seconds behind me.

"I fin to come! Here it coooooomes!" He moaned and penetrated deeply, then collapsed on top of me.

Kenyon lifted me in his arms, and I heard myself giggling like a schoolgirl. He lowered me to the center of the bed and lay beside me. "Come're, girl."

I rolled into his arms, and he held me against his slick, hard body. "Mmm, you feel so good."

"You do too." He pressed his lips to my forehead. "Nikki, I'm gonna tell you. I'm not into games. I'm feeling you. And this ain't about sex. I mean . . . I would love to see where this relationship leads."

I threw my leg over his and buried my face against his chest. "I'm feeling you too." Maybe it was just the sex, but I hadn't felt like this in years.

"Don't say that if you don't mean it. I could see myself falling in love with you," he warned.

I lifted my head and looked up into his sexy eyes. "I never say anything I don't mean."

He brought his juicy lips to mine, and I sucked on the bottom one, loving the way it felt between my own. I had found a good man who was interested in me . . . only me, and that made me feel good. Kenyon slipped his tongue inside my mouth. Next thing I knew, I was straddling him, rocking my hips back and forth, and minutes turned into hours before I finally cuddled in his arms and drifted off to sleep.

15

Trinette

I pulled my Benz onto the dealership parking lot and stepped out in a black pencil skirt that hugged every curve and a white ruffle top covered by a short suede jacket. On my feet was a pair of five hundred dollar black stiletto boots making me feel sexy as hell. Not only did I need to feel sexy but look it as well. I swung my purse over my shoulder, then browsed down the first row of luxury cars. It was important I stood close enough to the door that any salesman on the floor would see me. Because I was there to be noticed.

A short white dude quickly headed my way. I frowned. He was not at all who I was looking for.

"Good afternoon, ma'am, may I help you?" he asked.

I looked him up and down. "No, I'm just looking around."

He glanced over at my CLK 350 and saw dollar signs. "If I can be of assistance—"

"You can't"—I cut off his sales pitch with a wide, fake smile—"but thank you so much for asking."

He dropped his head, nodded, then moved on to help a fat woman with a baby on her hip. I didn't mean to embarrass the man, but there was really no point in him wasting my time or his.

"Well, well, tell me you're here to see me."

I glanced up and spotted Michael coming my way in a pink dress shirt and tie. A man after my own heart. Not every man can get away with that color, but he could. "Ohhhkay . . . I came to see you."

He smiled and I watched his eyes peruse the length of my legs before settling right at the cleavage I made sure went noticed with the low-cut blouse.

"Actually, I am thinking about trading my car in."

"Why? A woman who looks like you is supposed to drive a Benz."

Of course I am. I acknowledged his comment with a smile. "Mmm-hmm, I agree, but I'm trying to buy a new house and I don't know how I am gonna be able to afford both." I love playing the damsel in distress because there's always a man ready, willing, and, most important, *able* to rescue.

"Well, maybe I can help you with that little problem of yours. That's if . . . you want my help."

I gazed at Michael underneath my lashes while chewing on my bottom lip. "Depends on what kind of help you're offering?" I asked sweetly.

Reaching up, he grazed his thumb along my cheek. His voice was low, soft, and understanding. "Then maybe we can work something out in trade."

I moved in close and placed my hand to his chest,

enjoying the feel of his hard body against my skin. "I need three grand to put down on a house I want. You think you can help me out?" I asked, testing him.

"The question is, can *you* help me out?" A wicked gleam glistened in his eyes that said he wanted some of this caramel goodness bad enough to pay for it.

"I can help you in more ways than you could ever imagine." He gave me a long, hard look. I was making my intentions known because I was ready to add him to my list of sponsors. "You've been trying to get some of this for almost a year now. How much are you willing to pay to finally have a taste?"

He didn't hesitate, and that was a good thing. "Whatever you need, sexy. I take care of my women."

"Boo, this is the show-me state. What you need to be doing is meeting me someplace and showing me how much you want me."

Michael turned and went back inside while I returned to my car and waited. I was about to wear his ass out.

Last night was the last straw with Smooth. That man couldn't get a hard-on without his girlfriend . . . Levitra. I was getting tired of jacking him off while waiting for the pill to kick in, then I had to ride his dick because him being on top was a waste of time. His belly was in the way. Every time I was with him, I had to remind myself that looks and good dick had nothing to do with this. But I was starting to think I needed to find a substitute quick or start charging that fool for overtime. After seeing Michael the other day at the office, I knew he was someone who was willing to pay for the coochie. Watching Michael leaving with Maureen, I decided what the hell. The man . . . the money . . . and the means. I needed a new house, and nothing or no one was going to stand in my way. Even Levitra, if I had the patience for another episode.

It wasn't long before Michael came out and hopped into a silver Escalade truck with dealer plates. I followed him to a hotel on the outskirts of town. I waited for him to pay, get the key and go inside before I climbed out the car and walked to room 2A.

"So how we gonna do this?" he said as soon as I shut the door.

I tossed my jacket onto a nearby chair, then unzipped my skirt and allowed it to fall to the floor. I did the same with my shirt, then struck a pose in a red bra and matching G-string, making sure he saw he was getting well more than his money's worth. "You pay, you play," I purred, then squeezed my breasts together.

His eyes were glued to my double Ds while he reached for his wallet and pulled out several one hundred dollar bills. "Check this out . . . I've got a thousand on me, but you make it worthwhile, you'll have the rest of the money by the end of the day, plus there's plenty more where that came from." He dropped his pants and stepped toward me. I pushed him away.

"Uhhh-uhhh. Boo, this ain't store credit. I'm just like layaway. You don't get the merchandise until you pay for it." What kind of fool did he take me for? I moved over to the bed and took a seat, still wearing my boots, and waited.

"You're playing, right?" Michael asked with his hand holding his crotch.

I slipped off the G-string, then slid back on the bed with my legs spread wide and eased two fingers inside my kitty. "Do I look like I'm kidding?"

"I-I guess I . . . I could r-run to the bank." I had that fool stuttering and ready to come all over himself.

"Don't you keep a checkbook?"

His brow rose suspiciously. "Yeah . . . in the car."

"Shit, I know where you work . . . your wife too. Go get it and don't keep me waiting. Time is money." That fool buckled his pants and ran out the door so fast, he almost fell on his face.

Shit, I accept it all, cash, check and credit cards. I wasn't worried about Michael playing me, because if the check was rubber, you better believe Ms. Netta was going to clown his ass.

Michael came back, and I waited until a check was made out in my name before I reached for his zipper and lowered his pants and a pair of tighty whities. It took everything I had not to laugh. The way Maureen was always bragging, you would have thought her man was packing. That fool had barely enough to wrap my fingers around. I licked my lips. This was going to be easy. I dropped down to my knees and sucked him like it was a lollipop.

"Oooh, yeahhh, just like that . . . just like that!" He panted.

I know. He didn't have to tell me I was good. What he was about to find out was I had skills. Mad skills. I mastered the art of pleasing a man. I planned to enjoy him. Devour him completely so I became an addiction he couldn't do without.

His hips were rocking following the rhythm of my mouth. I worked him a little longer, then rose. "Lie on the bed," I ordered.

Michael looked pleased to have a woman in charge. "Damn, I've been dreaming about getting some of this for a long time."

You and hundreds of others.

My body hummed with need and my inner thighs

ached. This was strictly business, but that didn't mean I couldn't get a little satisfaction out of the afternoon just as long as I was running things. I straddled him, rubbing my clit against his hard length. Teasing him. Michael reached up and unfastened my bra and tossed it aside.

"Damn, your titties are pretty."

He felt them, tasted them. Leaning forward he closed his mouth over my nipple and sucked. I answered with a moan. Oh, did his tongue feel good. But there was no time for falling under his spell. I had to stay in control. I slid my hands along his body, stroking him down until I reached for his dick and slid my hand along his length, measuring all five inches. "You want me?"

"Hell, yeah, I want some," he replied, his voice sounding a little strained.

"How badly you want it?" I asked as I fondled him.

He moaned, then chuckled. "Three grand bad."

I had to laugh at that. He definitely wanted some of me really bad to spend that much, but I definitely wasn't complaining. And I would make sure he got his money's worth. Ms. Netta offered a money-back guarantee, and so far no one had demanded a refund.

I reached for a condom I had already slipped underneath the pillow while he was out at his car, and I eased it over the tip. Michael's breathing became short and uneven. Without missing a beat, I turned around so my ass was facing him, then eased up on my knees and lowered over his length . . . slowly, torturing him before moving to long, hard thrusts. In no time I had him saying my name.

After putting in a fabulous performance, I showered, then promised to get together again over the weekend. Smiling, I moved to my car, repaired my makeup and pulled away. Keeping Michael on retainer was definitely going to be an asset.

When I reached the strip mall, I parked, then climbed out my car and moved inside the bank with a grand in my purse and the check for two grand from Michael's personal account in hand. I moved through the door just as Maureen was coming out, swinging her hips like she was all that in a long winter white coat.

"Hey, Trinette," she sang. "Three more days before I close on my house! I had to make sure everything was in order. How was your lunch?" she called over her shoulder.

"Better than you'll ever know," I replied with a smirk as I moved up to the teller and handed her the check. "And it will only get better."

16

Nikki

I don't know what was wrong with me. It took weeks, even months, before I realized I was even interested in being more than just friends with Donovan, but with Kenyon . . . it was different. Every time he called, my heart raced like some teenager, and each time he came over, my coochie got wet just at the sight of him.

We'd been dating for a week, and already I was wondering what it would be like to share my life with him. Every date left me wanting more of his smiles, and laughter, and his lovemaking. Despite the rumors, the man was definitely skilled in the bedroom. I found myself often thinking about his naked body lying on top of me, being inside of my body. I just couldn't seem to get enough of him. What in the world was wrong with me?

"We're about to go back on the air!" yelled one of the assistants, snapping my ass out of a trance. Commercial break was over.

"Welcome back! This is Nikki and you're listening to *Truth Hurts*. Tonight we've been talking about love at first sight. And y'all came with some tripped-out stories! As I said earlier, I wanna know if it really exists. If you've felt that way about someone, please give me a call at 832-HURT." The lines were already lit up. "Caller, you're on the air."

"Yeah, I believe in love at first sight. I met my man at my friend Shawna's house. He was so fine with broad shoulders and pretty eyes—"

Uhhh-uhhh, I didn't ask how he looked. "How long did the relationship last and are the two of you still together?"

"Well, uh, it only lasted one night but it's been two years and I'm still in love with him."

Oh, brother. "Next caller."

"Yeah, Ms. Nikki, there is no such thing as love at first sight. That's just lust."

"And you don't think lust and love can be interchangeable?"

"Absolutely not. All that is are hormones running wild."

"That's an interesting concept. Lust is the body wanting what the body wants. I ain't mad. But anything worth truly having is worth working for. Hmmm, I'm going to end the evening with an e-mail from Junior. Y'all know Junior; he's been unlucky with love. Last month we hooked him up with a caller, and he sent me this e-mail.

" *'Ms. Nikki, thank you so much for the hookup. It's wonderful to know there are people out there like myself who believe in true love. You won't be hearing from me again. I think I finally got it right this time, and it's all because of you.' "*

"Well, isn't that sweet. I wish Junior all the best. And to all of you others out there who believe in love at first sight . . . you only live once, so enjoy it while it lasts. Hopefully for you, it's a lifetime. Good night."

I got off the air and slid away from my desk. Another successful night. My cell phone rang. I glanced down and smiled when I saw it was Kenyon.

"Hey, you. Got time for a drink?"

The sound of his voice made my nipples hard. "Yeah, a drink sounds fabulous."

"I'll meet you at your house in an hour."

I wrapped up the night and made it home to find Kenyon already waiting in front of the house. I frowned. There were several things I liked about Kenyon, but I forgot to mention there was one thing about him I didn't like. His promptness. I was used to a man being just a little late. I hadn't even parked yet and he was already coming around to my car and was opening the door for me.

"Hey, baby."

The second I saw his dimples, I melted. He is so sexy. In his hand was my favorite bottle of wine. I climbed out the car smiling, and he pulled me toward him and kissed me hard on the mouth. I welcomed his tongue and leaned back against the car, allowing the weight of him to rest against me. Oh, he was a magnificent kisser. But then I was an excellent teacher.

"Come on. Let's go inside before I get some of that right here in front of the house."

Laughing, I walked onto the porch and spotted a long box leaning against the screen door. "What is that?"

Kenyon's eyes sparkled with laughter as he shrugged. "I don't know. Why don't you look inside and see?"

I turned the lock, then reached for the box and stepped into the house. Kenyon followed me into the living room. After tossing my purse onto the couch, I took a seat and released the ribbon and looked inside. I gasped. Six huge red roses.

"These are gorgeous. Did you buy me these?" He must have placed them on the porch before I had arrived. No wonder he was early.

"I don't know, did I?" He tried to hide a smile, but I'd been around him long enough now to know when he was trying to stay humble. Kenyon was always doing things like that. Buying me candy and flowers and taking me out to dinner. It was as if every day he thought of some way to put a smile on my face.

I set the box aside and straddled his lap. "Thank you, Kenyon."

"You're welcome, baby."

He smelled so good I kissed and licked him along his neck, then started unbuttoning his shirt.

"Don't you want some wine first?" he murmured.

"What I want . . . tastes better than wine." I released the last button, then undid his pants and reached inside and released him.

Kenyon moaned. "Damn, baby."

"Oh, you ain't seen nothing yet." I dropped down to my knees and swallowed him between my lips. Within seconds my head was bobbing up and down at his crotch and he was moaning.

"Nikki, stop before you make me nut on myself," Kenyon warned.

I released him. "Uh-uh, not before I feel you inside of me."

I got up and quickly shed my clothes, and he dropped his pants. "Lean over the chair. I wanna get it from behind."

I assumed the position and guided him inside my body where my coochie immediately clamped around his penis.

He gave a loud moan. "Oooh-weee . . . yeah, I missed being inside of you."

I rocked my hips and met his strokes, and within minutes my juices started flowing and I was speaking in tongues.

"You like that, baby?" he asked.

"Yessss . . . oooh, I like that!"

"You love what daddy's doing to you?"

"I love it! Oooh, I love it!" He gripped my hips and pumped my ass against his dick, and I was coming so hard, I screamed out with release. It was just too good. How had I gone this long without it? "That's it! Don't stop, Puhleeeeeze don't stop!" I wanted to feel every inch he had, and since his thing was so skinny, I squeezed my muscles tightly around him.

"I ain't going nowhere. Nowhere!" he cried.

I came hard and Kenyon came right behind me. "Oooh, that was good," I panted. I was so out of breath.

"This is only the beginning." Kenyon trailed kisses down my back. "Baby, I already told you. You got me, I'm not going anywhere. This . . ." He took my hand and wrapped it around his dick. "This belongs to you." He kissed the side of my neck. I'm ticklish as hell. All I could do was thrash on the chair, laughing and screaming at the same time.

"Kenyon, stop!" I cried out. He tickled me one last time, then stopped and slapped me playfully across the butt.

"You are silly." Rising, he retrieved the bottle of wine. "I'll grab the corkscrew and meet you in the room."

"Okay." I dashed into my room and reached for a bottle of Mediterranean perfume and sprayed it in the air. I loved for my room to smell like a floral paradise. Still giggling, I went over and pulled the comforter back on the bed. I couldn't remember the last time I felt that happy and alive. It didn't even bother me that I was about to share my bed for the first time with someone other than Donovan. Until this moment, my room had been off limits. Instead we made love in the family room on the floor in front of the fireplace. But tonight was going to be different. I was ready to take our relationship a step further.

The phone rang and I was tempted not to answer it, but it was my mother. Big Mama had been home for three days. Today was her first day of physical therapy, and she was probably wondering why I hadn't dropped by before I went into the station that night. I had intended to, but I had stayed late at the bookstore, then ran out for Chinese before going on the air.

"Hey, Mama."

"Nikki."

Something about the sound of her voice made my heart still. "Mama, what's wrong?"

"S-She's gone. Big M-Mama's gone."

I froze. "What! When?"

My mama was crying now. "S-She stopped breathing a couple of hours ago, but you . . . you were on the air and . . . and I didn't want to bother you. There was no point in upsetting you."

"What do you mean? That's my grandmother! Where is she now?"

"S-She's still here. The funeral home's on their way to pick her up."

This couldn't be happening. Mama was lying. She had to be. "Don't let them touch her until I get there! I'm on my way." I hung up the phone, then looked in my closet trying to find something to wear. I had to get to Big Mama. She needed me. I needed her. "Big Mama, why didn't you wait?" I crumpled to my knees. "No!" I screamed at the top of my lungs. She couldn't be gone. "No!"

Kenyon came running down the hallway calling my name. "Nikki . . . Nikki . . . baby, where are you?" He stepped into the room and found me still down on my knees, crying my eyes out. "Baby? What happened?" he asked, and dropped on the floor beside me.

"Sssshe's gone!" I screamed. "Big Mama's gone!"

I saw the panic on his face. "Oh, no."

"Whyyyyy!" I screamed at the top of my lungs, and Kenyon tried to hold me in his arms, but I clawed and kicked and screamed, trying to get him off of me. "Let me go . . . dammit . . . let me go!"

"Nikki, I got you. Let me be there for you," he pleaded while he pinned my arms to my sides.

I finally collapsed against him and couldn't stop crying. "She's gone. My g-g-grandmother's . . . gone."

"I know, and I'm so so sorry. But she's at a better place. I know you don't wanna hear that yet. But she told us when we went to see her, she was ready to meet her Jesus."

This couldn't possibly have been happening. It was a dream. I just knew it. "I'm not ready yet. I-I should have gone to see her today. I-I should have been there after work like I had promised." I screamed again, and Kenyon covered my mouth.

"Shhh! Baby, you've got to calm down."

"Don't tell me to calm down! My grandmother is dead! You hear me. Dammit, she's dead!"

I threw punches at him, then got up from the floor and raced into the living room stark naked. Kenyon caught me before I made it into the kitchen and carried me back to my bedroom, kicking and screaming. "Get out of my house! You hear me. I want you to get the fuck out!"

"Nikki . . . no, you don't."

"Yes . . . I . . . do." I tried to punch him, but he blocked my hand and I started crying loud again.

Kenyon carried me to the bed and lay down beside me. "Baby, you'll just have to be mad at me, because I'm not leaving until I know you're gonna be okay."

I'm never going to be okay again, didn't he understand that? "I want Big Mama. Oh, my God! I need to go see her. I've got to go and see her now!" I struggled to get up, but he wouldn't let me go. "Stop it! I need to see her."

"Okay, I'll take you to her, but first you need to calm down." He wrapped his arms tightly around me. "I'm gonna be right there with you. I told you. I'm never going anywhere. I love you, girl. I love you so much."

I was hurting and I clung to him, crying my eyes out. I had just lost the most important person in my life. I looked up into his loving eyes and felt a tug at my heart. There wasn't anything he wouldn't do to make me happy, and I love him for that. "I love you too." Maybe not in the same way he thought he loved me, but I did feel love for the man he was. I was sure in time, if I opened up my heart and let go of the past, I'd be able to love Kenyon with all my heart and soul.

17

Trinette

I hate funerals and usually refuse to go to one unless it's my immediate family. The only reason why I was even there was because Nikki's my girl and Big Mama was like a grandmother to all of us.

I wasn't surprised Nikki was taking it hard. Real hard. During the funeral services she dropped to her knees and screamed at the top of her lungs. I was crying so hard myself, for a split second I was actually glad Kenyon was there to help her back to her seat. Today, he was her rock. Donovan wasn't there and she needed someone. I just wished it was someone other than that crazy mothafucka.

We were at the gravesite and they were getting ready to lower Big Mama in the ground. Kenyon was sitting in the front seat right alongside Nikki, her sister and mother like he had been a part of their family for years.

"Ashes to ashes, dust to dust . . ."

Nikki's bottom lip quivered and the tears started falling again. Kenyon was right there, pulling tissues out of his pocket, mopping her face. You would have thought he had been with Nikki for years the way he was all up under her and doing what he thought was best. When Nikki moved to put a red rose on top of her grandmother's coffin, he took her hand and moved up along with her. Just as they started to lower the coffin into the ground, Nikki collapsed. I pushed through the crowd.

"Y'all let me through!" By the time I made my way to the front, Kenyon had already scooped Nikki into his arms and was carrying her back to the limo. I followed and took the seat across from him.

"Lay her down," I ordered.

He gently lowered her head.

I moved beside Nikki and patted her gently against the cheek. "Nikki . . . girl . . . can you hear me?"

She mumbled something, then started crying softly. Kenyon instantly pulled her in his arms again and held her close. His expression looked as if he was seconds away from passing out himself.

"Are you okay?" I asked.

He started shaking his head. "Yes, but my baby isn't. She's been trying to be strong, but I knew she was gonna fall apart. That's why there was no way I couldn't be here today."

Okay, whatever. The way his bottom lip quivered, he looked like he was ready to cry. If he had, I swear I would have laughed.

I reached for a tissue and mopped her forehead. "Nikki's gonna be okay. She and Big Mama were really close. Time will heal all wounds."

"I know. . . . That's why I plan to be by her side the

whole time. I've already talked to my boss about taking some time off."

I rolled my eyes. "The last thing she needs is to be smothered."

He looked offended. "I'm not gonna smother her, but she doesn't need to be alone."

"I'll stay a few nights with her."

"You don't have to," he said quickly. "I was planning to stay with her anyway."

Damn! Ain't nothing worse than a needy man. "I'm sure, but I already planned to spend the weekend with my girl. . . . My bag is already in the car."

Kenyon looked like he was about to say something else but thought better of it. "Okay, well, if you need anything . . ."

"I won't," I replied, cutting him off with my tongue and a roll of the eyes. "Nikki, you go ahead and let it out, girl. This is your time." I started patting her back, and slowly the sobs stopped. She just sat there on Kenyon's lap with her face buried against his chest.

I wanted to talk to my girl alone, but that definitely wasn't happening with the way Kenyon was clinging to her as if his grandmother had passed away.

"Baby, it's gonna be okay," he murmured. "Everything is gonna be okay," he murmured closer to her ear.

The crowd had moved away from the gravesite, and everyone was getting in their cars, heading back to the church for dinner.

"I'll see y'all back at the church."

Kenyon gave me a smile and looked relieved I was finally leaving so he could have Nikki all to himself. Maybe it was just jealousy, but something about Kenyon rubbed me the wrong way.

I climbed out the limo and moved across the grass

to where Nikki's sister, Tamara, was heading my way. I stopped and squeezed her hand.

"How's Nikki?" she asked.

I shook my head. "Not too good."

Tamara gave me a solemn look. "Well . . . at least she has Kenyon. That man has brought a lot of joy to my sister's sad life." She squeezed my hand again, then moved inside the limo. Nikki and her sister were never close. When Tamara turned eighteen she moved west and rarely ever called or came home. At least she took the time to pay her respects.

I stood and watched as Nikki's mama and aunts climbed in, then I moved to my car and followed.

Back at the church, Nikki walked around like a zombie while Kenyon held her hand. He loved every second of her needing him, and for some reason it bothered me. Lord, forgive me, but I was sitting in a church thinking, what does this man have that makes Nikki like him so much? Rumor had it he wasn't working with much, but I know folks be hating so you can't believe everything you hear, but at the same time I wondered what she found so attractive about a clinging man.

Brushing my ill feelings aside, I went over and tried to get Nikki to eat, but she shook her head and Kenyon told me, "She'll be okay. She had toast this morning." I rolled my eyes and walked away. I mingled with her family who were all raving about the new man in poor Nikki's life. She had brought him over to her mother's for dinner and he had such manners and she deserved a good man after everything she had gone through. I agree, she did deserve a good man, but not him. Lord, please forgive me because I knew this wasn't the place. The sooner I could get rid of Kenyon for the evening, the better.

I parked my car in front of Nikki's house around seven. Kenyon had parked his in the center of the driveway, taking up both parking spaces. I moved up to the door, rang the bell and waited for what felt like forever before I rang the bell again. When no one answered, I stuck my key in the lock and walked in.

"Anyone here?" I called. I moved through the kitchen, and Kenyon came from the family room and gave me a puzzled look.

"How did you get in?"

No, he didn't. "Uh . . . unlike you . . . I do have a key." I rolled my eyes.

He held up his hands, signaling he meant no harm. "I was just wondering, because I locked the door."

I brushed past him and went into the family room where Nikki was curled up on the couch. When I stepped into the room, she gave me a sad smile. "Hey, girl. I didn't hear the doorbell."

"I rang twice, then I used my key." I took a seat beside her and reached inside my bag. As soon as I pulled out a bottle of tequila, she smiled. "I figured you could use a drink."

"Yeah. Margaritas sound really good about now."

Kenyon came into the room, hands in his pockets, looking nervous. "Nikki, I'm gonna clean the kitchen and put all that food away for you."

I stepped in. "Don't worry about it. . . . I'll do it later. We might wanna get our eat on after we start drinking."

"Oh, yeah? What are you drinking?"

"Margaritas." And before he could set his lips to

ask, I added, "We're about to have some *girlfriend* time."

The frown on his face was clear. He had heard the emphasis that he was not invited and it was time for his needy behind to go. "Well . . . I guess I'll go. You need anything? I can run up to the store and get you another bottle of ibuprofen."

"No need. I've got one in my purse . . . see." I held up the bottle and smiled.

"I'm fine, Kenyon, but thank you for everything."

"Nikki, you know I'll do anything for you and your family." He moved over and gave her a kiss. Then he headed toward the door with his hands in his pockets again. "I'll call you later and see how you're doing. Okay?"

I rose. If I didn't help him to the door, he would never leave. "Let me lock the door behind you." By the time we reached the door, he looked so sad I figured I needed to at least say something nice. "Thanks for being there today."

He smiled. "You don't have to thank me. I love Nikki and wouldn't do anything to hurt her. I know Big Mama meant the world to her. She was a nice lady and I miss her myself."

I screwed up my nose. He made it sound like he'd known Big Mama for years. "Yes, she was very important to all of us." I swung the door open.

"Take care of my baby," he said.

"Don't worry, I will."

I watched his needy ass walk down the steps, looking like he didn't have a friend in the world. Halfway down, Kenyon turned around. "You think Nikki would like it if I went and bought her some flowers?"

I couldn't believe this fool was trying to find any

excuse he could so he could come back. "Not tonight. I've got things under control. Go hang out with yo ho'ish friend Jay. Tell him to holla at a sistah."

Kenyon chuckled. "I'll do that."

I waited until he pulled off. As I shut the door a thought came to mind. I opened the screen and rang the doorbell. Nothing. No wonder she didn't hear me ring. She had one of those wireless doorbells, so I took it off the frame and carried it into the kitchen.

"Kenyon gone?" Nikki called from the family room.

"Yes." Finally. With his needy ass. "By the way, your doorbell isn't working. You got some extra batteries?"

Instead of just telling me, Nikki rose and stepped into the kitchen, then pointed to the drawer to the right of the microwave. "Yeah, there in that junk drawer on the end."

I opened the drawer and removed a small screwdriver and popped open the cover. I looked inside, frowned, then held the doorbell up for her to see. "You don't have any batteries in here."

She gave me a weird look. "That's strange. It was working just fine when my family started raiding my house this morning."

I looked at her and rolled my eyes. "That clingy-ass man of yours removed the batteries."

Nikki laughed as if what I said was ridiculous. "Why would he do that?"

"So you wouldn't hear the doorbell when I came over . . . so he could have you all to himself."

She was laughing hard now. "Why in the world would he do something that crazy?"

"Why you think? 'Cause that stalker doesn't want you with anyone but him. He's too clingy."

Nikki shook her head. "Girl, shut up and hook me up with a margarita."

I was glad she was laughing, but I wasn't done talking about her man. I waited until we both had a drink in our hands before I brought him up again.

"So what's he working with?"

Nikki gave me a strange look. "Excuse me?"

"Come on. Paint the picture. Take me there," I encouraged.

"Netta, I am not answering that question."

"Shit, I figured he threw the whoo-whoo on you the way you been acting."

Blushing, she responded, "The whoo-whoo? You a fool! Kenyon is just a really nice guy."

I cracked a smile. "So you're saying the rumors aren't true?"

"What rumors?"

"That his ding-a-ling is only this big." I held up a pinky finger.

Nikki rolled her eyes, but I could tell she was struggling to keep a straight face. "No. The rumors aren't true. I told you about listening to folks around here."

I shrugged. "Hell, you can't hate me for trying to look out for you."

Shaking her head, Nikki returned to the family room. I put the doorbell back, made sure it worked. It did. And made us some frozen margaritas using her blender. As soon as I filled two glasses, I moved into the family room where Nikki was either watching TV or staring into space. "Here you go."

"Thanks." Nikki leaned back on the couch and took a sip. "Mmm, Netta, you know you make the best margaritas."

"Thanks, girlfriend." I got comfortable on the couch and crossed my legs. "Seriously, Nikki, talk to me. I wanna know what you like about Kenyon. He just seems too needy, and you know I can't stand a needy man."

She made a face. "He isn't needy. If anything I think he's a little insecure, which is hard to believe as fine as he is."

I wouldn't have said all that.

"He is really a nice guy. We talk, I mean we talk for hours about everything, and that is something Donovan and I never did. We laugh. I haven't laughed so much in years. He has a wonderful sense of humor."

"Girl, but he seems so wimpy. He was practically crying this afternoon."

"He isn't wimpy. As soon as I found out Big Mama had passed, Kenyon was there by my side. I don't think I could have gotten through the last few days without him."

I was her best friend and I hated knowing she needed someone else more than she needed me. It wasn't like we were licking pussies, but she's my best friend. Enough! I was already sick of talking about his needy ass.

"How you feeling now that everything's over?"

She shrugged. "About as good as can be expected. Now that she's gone, I feel so alone. Empty. I feel guilty I didn't go see her the day she died. I thought I had more time." Tears streamed down her face, and I felt guilty.

"Nikki, I'm sorry for bringing her up."

"No, really. I want to talk about her. Big Mama was my world, and knowing I will never see her again makes me so sad. I miss her so much." She brushed fresh tears away.

Reaching over, I squeezed her hand. "I know, girl. I'll miss her too."

Nikki shut her eyes and slanted her face toward the ceiling, fighting damn hard to maintain control. "I wrote Donovan. He and Big . . . Big Mama were close. I know he would wanna know."

"I'm sure he would. Have you heard anything from him?"

Opening her eyes, she shook her head. "No . . . nothing."

I wished there was some way I could get the two of them back together, because I didn't care what Nikki said, something about Kenyon just wasn't right.

18

Trinette

"Where you at? I thought your plane got in at seven!" I was irritated because I had dinner reservations and it would be near impossible to get another before nine.

"My plane was delayed. What you want me to do, put a gun to the pilot's head?" Leon snapped.

"Whatever, just hurry!" I barked through the phone. "I wanna at least take you by to see the house before it gets dark."

My statement was met by intense silence.

"You still there?" I asked in a slightly softer tone.

There was another long pause, and when Leon finally spoke his voice sent a chill down my spine. "How much longer we going to live like this?"

I pulled the phone away from my ear, then back. "What?"

"You heard me, Trinette. How much longer are we going to live like this?"

Where the hell was this coming from? "I don't know. Why are we having this discussion now?"

Leon blew out a long, impatient sigh. "We'll talk when I get there." Ain't that a bitch! He hung up on me. I didn't have time to have attitude, because I was suddenly nervous as hell. What made Leon decide to ask when I was planning to move with him? I dialed Nikki and asked her. After all, she is supposed to be the expert.

"He's having second thoughts," she said the second I stopped ranting and raving.

"What do you mean he's having second thoughts? We're supposed to close on my new house next week." Uhhh-uhhh, this could not be happening.

"Obviously, Leon's had time to think."

"Well, it's too late for that. We already have a contract on a house!"

"I hate to say this, Netta, but it's never too late."

"You're supposed to be my friend." Didn't she understand I needed her on my side?

"I *am* on your side," Nikki said as if she could read my mind. "But you need to look at it his way. Leon wants to know when you're planning to move to Richmond, and I think your husband deserves an answer."

I took a deep breath and settled down on the bed. "I don't know when I'm moving to Richmond. I still need to make director at my job . . . first . . . then we can talk about it."

"So . . . you're telling me when you make director you'll be ready to go?"

I hesitated. "Not right away. Listen, I *want* this house and Leon is gonna have to realize everything else has to wait. Look, I gotta go before he gets here." I was too close to getting my house to lose everything now.

I hung up the phone, then moved into the bathroom and applied my makeup with care, then looked at myself in the mirror. I had found the House of Deréon outfit at the outlet last month. The pink sweater had a plunging neckline and showcased the twins. The black jeans hugged every luscious curve nicely. Yep, Leon was gonna be licking his lips when he saw me. I took my bottle of Sexual perfume and sprayed a little at my cleavage. The fragrance had a hint of an aphrodisiac in it, and I needed my husband begging me to give him some before the night was over. Unfortunately, a quick glance down at my watch reminded me it was Friday the thirteenth, and suddenly I didn't have a good feeling at all.

As soon as I heard his rental car pull up in the driveway, I hurried to greet Leon at the door. He stepped in rolling his suitcase, looking like he hadn't slept in days. His jeans were wrinkled. The T-shirt he had on beneath his leather jacket I had bought while we vacationed in Memphis last year. It was now dingy looking. On his feet were a pair of scuffed-up gym shoes he must have dug out of the trash, because I swore I threw them away the last time he visited. And he was in serious need of a haircut, but instead of bitching about him, making me look bad, I held my tongue and gave him a warm smile. "Hey, boo-boo."

"Hello." He tossed the greeting out, sounding casual, then brushed past me without even a kiss and headed upstairs to my—oops—I mean our bedroom. I followed and stood in the doorway as he sat on the end of the bed. I tried to appear upbeat and happy to see him. "You want something to drink?" I asked.

The expression on his face said he wasn't in the mood for games. "No."

"Okay . . . then let's talk," I said, growing impatient by every passing second. Here I was looking luscious and he hadn't even given me a peck on the cheek.

Leaning forward, Leon rested his elbows on his knees, then looked up and met my gaze. "I don't think buying another house is a good idea."

"Why? We already talked about this. . . . I thought we agreed?"

He shook his head. "It was a mistake. You had me so caught up in your excitement, I wasn't even thinking straight."

"So this is all my fault?" I asked with attitude.

"No. I didn't say that."

"Then what are you saying?"

Leon closed his eyes as if he was tired and would rather go to bed than have this discussion. "I'm saying . . . what's happening between us? When are you planning to move to Richmond with me?"

Pouting like a baby, I crossed my arms against my chest, then shrugged. "I don't know. I was hoping to move in the next two years."

"Then why do we need to buy another house?"

"Because I want to," I answered stubbornly.

Looking down at the floor, Leon shook his head. "It's always been about what you want. I'm tired of that."

And I was tired of this conversation because it was obviously not getting me anywhere fast. "Why now? Why you wait until we have a contract on another house to start having second thoughts?"

"I think now is as good a time as any."

Who was this stranger and what did he do with my

husband? I moved over and straddled his lap, then placed my hands against his cheeks and gazed deep into his eyes. "Leon, baby, we're meeting with the realtor tomorrow. It's Valentine's Day weekend." I pressed my lips to his and ground my hips against his crotch. All I had to do was give him some, then I'd have him where I wanted him. Unfortunately, Leon turned his head and pushed me away.

"Quit! That's not going to work this time."

I rose. Stunned. I had never seen Leon like this . . . stubborn . . . standing his own ground.

"I'm not meeting the realtor tomorrow. Let's just leave it alone. I think the financing falling through was a sign we need to walk away."

"No, it isn't. It's a sign we need to find a different company because the one we have is full of shit."

Leaning forward, he took my hand in his. "Right now, we need to be talking about us."

I snatched my hand away. "Uhhh-uhhh . . . not until we finish talking about my house."

"You're right. That's exactly what it is, *your* house." Leon dragged a frustrated hand across his face. "It's not like I'm going to live in it but once a month and then I still have *this* note to make as well," he added with a sweep of his arms.

I was getting madder by the second because nothing I was saying was making a difference. "I love you, Leon. I have every intention of growing old with you, but right now has to be about me. I have worked hard at the DFS office and I'm not about to give that up, moving to Richmond with you. I need time to build my career and I *deserve* to be director."

He just smiled at me sadly. "And I *deserve* the right to live in the same house with my wife."

"I wanna live with you . . . just not yet." I decided to turn the tables on him. "Why don't you come back here? If you love me and wanna be a family, then you'll come back to St. Louis. You said before you could work from home. Well, this new house will have plenty of room for a home office." I was grabbing straws, but at that point I was desperate enough to say anything.

"I've worked too hard to get to chief financial officer to give that up."

"Yeah, but you want me to give up my career! When you moved to Dallas, I gave up my career and followed. I did the same thing when you transferred to Simi Valley. Now you're in Richmond and you expect me to pack up my life again and follow you. That's not fair!"

"I'm the breadwinner."

"And what am I . . . croutons?" I stood there with my arms crossed, chest heaving. I was so upset, I couldn't find the words to explain how I was feeling.

Leon dropped his head, and when he looked up again his expression was sad. "I guess neither of us are willing to give up our career for the other."

I swallowed. "No, I guess not." I was so mad I didn't even want to look at him anymore. I swung around and went down to the kitchen, where I poured myself a glass of wine. Leon disappeared into the bathroom. When he came out, he moved and stood in the doorway.

"You wanna go and get something to eat?"

"Nope. I've lost my appetite," I said, unable to keep the sarcasm out of my voice. We had already missed our reservations. Besides, I wasn't interested in sitting across the table from him. Not after the way he had just stuck a stake through my left eye.

"I'll run and go get a pizza." He headed toward the door, but before he opened it, he turned around. "It wouldn't matter to you if we ever lived together, would it?"

I stared at him over the rim of my wineglass while I took a sip, then shrugged. "I'm fine with our marriage the way it is . . . for now. I thought we both understood each other. I thought you supported my dream."

"I do support your dreams. But I *am* a man and I get lonely sometimes. It would be nice to come home and find you there to hold . . . and talk to. Sometimes, on the weekend, I like to see a movie or go to dinner . . . and it would be great to have someone to do that with."

"We can do that this weekend."

He gave me a sad look that was easy to read. He was clearly disappointed. "You don't get it, do you?"

I slammed the glass down on the counter. "No, *you* don't get it! You just don't wait until two days before closing on a house to change your mind. I agree, maybe we do need to sit down and talk about our marriage, but we've already committed to this house. I've poured out thousands in earnest money, inspections, appraisals . . . this is crazy!"

He waved his hand in the air, dismissing me, then turned his back. "I already told you, I'm not buying the house." With that he left, slamming the door behind him.

I couldn't remember the last time I had ever seen him that stubborn, let alone disagreeing with something I wanted. And I wanted this house so bad. It looked like Trinette. It smelled like Trinette. It even spelled T-r-i-n-e-t-t-e. The house was so close I could already see myself pulling up in my circle driveway. Leon was the only thing standing in my way.

I called Nikki again. She didn't sound happy to hear from me.

"Netta, I'm getting ready to go on the air in thirty minutes."

"Okay, call me later." I hung up and dialed my cousin Peaches, who I hadn't spoken to in months. She is happily married with two kids. I allowed her a few minutes to brag about her family before I changed the subject and told her what happened.

"Peaches, Leon's never said anything to me before about being lonely and wanting someone there."

Silence met the phone.

"What, Peaches?"

"I . . . I think Leon might be seeing someone else."

"What?"

"I'm serious. That's the classic sign. Here it is Valentine's weekend and he's tripping. I bet you the female he's fooling with saw those loan papers lying around and started tripping . . . probably even gave him an ultimatum."

I took a moment to think about what she said. It had to be the answer. Just four days ago, Leon was just as excited about the new house as I was. Now he refused to even go and take a look. My stomach started to churn at the idea.

"Netta, girl, you better throw that pussy on him and save your marriage. Kayla's crying . . . I gotta go." She hung up.

I poured myself another glass of wine, thought about what Peaches had said and waited for Leon to return. It was past ten and I had already finished half the damn bottle and was lying on the couch when he walked in, looking as if he had stopped and had a few drinks himself.

I rolled my eyes at him. "I thought you were bringing a pizza."

He rested his weight against the doorjamb. "I was, but then I decided I needed a drink and went over my boy Aaron's house."

My eyes glared at him. I was sure he felt the heat. "If you came to Missouri to break my heart, why did you even bother to come? You could have done that over the phone."

"I came to see my wife. So we could talk about her living with her husband again."

I was so angry I stormed up to the bathroom and drew myself a hot bath, then climbed in. I was so mad that tears were streaming down my face. How dare Leon do this to me.

Sure, he was right, we needed to talk about our marriage, but not then. Not while everything was going the way I wanted. The perfect job was almost at my fingertips, and the house would put me where I needed to be. I had already planned a family barbecue for Memorial Day. I couldn't wait to let my family see just how good I was living. But in a matter of hours Leon had ruined everything. That night was the first time in my marriage I was scared shitless. What in the world could possibly happen next?

19

Nikki

"Oooh-weee! We're back, and if you missed the show, you've missed an evening of straight-up drama! Let me tell you . . . you've definitely missed something. This is Ms. Nikki, and caller, you're on the air."

"Ms. Nikki, this is Shaunda, and I got a problem."

I adjusted my microphone. "Go ahead, Shaunda, we're listening."

"Well . . . uh . . . I just found out last month I'm pregnant, and before I had a chance to decide what I'm gonna do, my boyfriend proposed."

"Why do I get the feeling there is more to this story?"

She sighed with exasperation. *"Because . . . there is. It's not his baby or . . . at least I don't think it is."*

I fidgeted with excitement on the seat. "Okay, you're gonna have to back up and start over. Are you saying you're pregnant by another man?"

"Yes . . . or at least I think so. See, my boyfriend and

I been together for almost two years. Well . . . three months ago we had a big fight and I ended our relationship. While we were apart, this dude started working at the Quik Trip with me. And one thing led to another and, well, we ended up sleeping together."

"Oh, boy!" Now we were getting to the juicy part. "Let me guess—you didn't use protection?"

"No. I didn't. I was hurting and wasn't thinking. And I had no idea my boyfriend was going to come back a month later and propose."

"So what are you gonna do, 'cause inquiring minds wanna know."

Shaunda hesitated. *"I planned to terminate the pregnancy, but my boyfriend found out, and I panicked and told him the baby was his."*

I smacked my lips. "Then what happened?"

"Well, Terrence confronted me at work and wanted to know if the baby was his, and I couldn't lie to him. He wants to be a part of his baby's life, and I don't know what I'm gonna do."

"What do *you* wanna do? That's the question. We're getting ready for a commercial break, then we'll be back and maybe someone out there can help Shaunda figure out what to do."

I turned off the microphone and reached for my soda. All that talking made me thirsty, and it had been one hilarious evening. I needed a good laugh.

I still hadn't returned to the store, but I needed to be on the air. I realized I needed my job and my man to help me move on.

There was still a minute before we went back on the air when Tristan came into the studio. "Nikki, you need to pick up line two."

I gave him a suspicious look. "Who is it? And it better not be Mr. Loser."

He shook his head, trying to keep a straight face. "Better." Tristan swung on his heel and headed back to his desk. I hate when he does that.

I pushed line two. "Hot 97, and you got Ms. Nikki on the line."

"Yeah, this is Darren . . . Shaunda's fiancé."

Oh, shit! This was about to get good. "Hello, Darren, welcome to the show. Don't go away, and I'll be right back." I waited until Tristan signaled we were back on the air and switched on my microphone.

"This is *Truth Hurts* and you're listening to Nikki Truth. We're on the air with Shaunda. Before commercial break she was sharing her big problem. She's pregnant and her fiancé is not the father, but he *thinks* he is. At the same time the other man knows about the baby and is planning to be a part of his child's life. Ooohweee, I got my own head spinning just thinking about it! Shaunda, does Terrence know you're back with your fiancé?"

"Yeah, he knows, and he still wants to be in his child's life."

"Sounds like a good man to me. There are a lot of men who won't stand up and be a man."

"I know, and that's what makes this so hard," she said, voice heavy with emotion.

"Answer this . . . do you love your fiancé?"

"Yes," she said without hesitation. *"I love him with all my heart, but I just don't know how to tell him the truth."*

"Hold on, we have a caller on the line who would like to speak. Caller, you still there?"

"Yes, I'm here, and I would like to say something."

Shaunda gasped. *"Darren, is that you?"*

"Yeah, Shaunda, it's me. Why couldn't you tell me the baby wasn't mine?"

"I-I didn't know how."

"It wouldn't matter, I love you regardless."

"Well, listeners, there you have it. Isn't love grand? We're outta time, so I'll allow the two of them to work out their problems off the air. In the meantime, this is Nikki Truth with Hot 97 WJPC, saying good night." I turned off the microphone and raised my arms in the air. Another fabulous night.

Twenty minutes later, I was walking out to my car when I spotted Kenyon sitting on my hood.

"I thought maybe you might wanna share a bottle of wine before you go to bed?" His large hands took my face and held it gently.

I had planned on going home and starting a new mystery novel I had bought, but spending time with Kenyon wasn't a bad exception. The man had a way of growing on you. "Sure, why not?"

"Okay, I'll meet you there." He gave me another slow, drugging kiss, then opened my car door for me and waited until my seat belt was on and my car was started before he moved and climbed into his Lincoln.

He followed me at a close distance. He was so sweet, but at times he seemed too eager to please. It's funny that a woman always wants a good man but when she gets one, there are doubts. I guess I just liked a little mystery and excitement, and with Kenyon you just didn't get that. What you see is what you get. His love was unconditional. I guess I should have felt flattered he loved me, but with so much uncertainty in my life, at times, it was just a bit too much.

I pulled into the driveway, and Kenyon pulled in

right behind me. He was out of his car before I got out, and moved beside me.

"I was listening to your show when my daughter Rachel called," he said as I put the key in the door.

"What was wrong?" I asked.

His nostrils flared as he spoke. "She had some fool over her house who wouldn't leave. I had to tell him he needed to go home."

It was amazing how he believed in talking and trying to reason. If it had been one of my cousins or Trinette's brothers, they would have acted first and asked questions later.

"I'm glad she's okay," I said, then opened the door. Kenyon immediately headed to the family room to let Rudy out his kennel. The second the door was opened, he ran to the back door so he could go out and take care of business.

While they were out back, I moved to my room and changed out of my clothes, then put on a caftan. I reached into the closet on the top shelf for a perfume I hadn't worn in years I thought Kenyon would enjoy. When I pulled the box down, something fell on my head. I stared down at the picture and collapsed on the floor. It was me holding Mimi in my arms only hours after she had been born. My lip quivered and next thing I knew, I was crying.

Kenyon stepped in the room, holding two wine-glasses. "Here you . . ." His voice trailed off. "What's wrong?"

I shook my head, trying to hold back more tears. "Nothing."

"Uh-uh. It's definitely something." He set the glasses on my dresser, then scooped me in his arms, carried me over to the bed and took a seat with me on his lap. "Now talk to me."

I buried my face against his chest. I tried to block out her precious little face and those amazing chocolate eyes she had inherited from her daddy. "Four years ago, I had a little girl."

His eyes widened. "You do? I bet she looks just like you."

"She did." Kenyon's hand stilled. My lip quivered. "Mimi died right after her second birthday."

"Oh, baby, I'm so sorry." He pulled me close, and I let my tears fall freely. "Do you feel like telling me what happened?"

"S-She . . . she was hit by a car." I started bawling as that afternoon came rushing back. "I was in the backyard with her. She was playing and somehow I . . . I had drifted off to sleep." I paused long enough to wipe my eyes. "The gate was open and s-she wandered out the yard and into the street. The sound of brakes screeching and a woman s-screaming woke me up, and I . . . I came running. I found my daughter . . . lying in the street."

"Oh, baby!"

Hot tears rolled down my cheeks. "How could a mother fall asleep when she knows her daughter is playing? I was so tired. I had worked at the bookstore all day trying to get ready for opening day and then went to the radio station. Donovan had gone to the shop, and I thought while she played in the yard, I could relax. I had no idea the gate was open."

Kenyon stroked my back with a comforting hand. "Sweetie, you can't beat yourself up about it."

"I can't help it! If I hadn't fallen asleep she . . . she would still be alive."

For a long time, he simply held me and said nothing, and I appreciated that.

"I m-miss her so much." Tears choked my voice.

"I know you do, baby." He rubbed my back soothingly. "What can I do to cheer you up?"

I wiped my eyes and offered him a small smile I wasn't at all feeling. "How about handing me a glass of that wine?"

He kissed my lips. "Anything you want." Reaching over, Kenyon grabbed a glass and handed it to me. "I told you, I'm always here for you."

"Thanks." I took a sip, soothing my dry, aching throat.

"Do you have a picture of your daughter I could see?"

I nodded. Instead of retrieving the one from the closet, I moved over to my drawer and reached inside for a five by seven I kept close. I handed it to him and took a seat cross-legged on the bed beside him.

Mimi had on a yellow dress I had found on clearance at Sears. I had styled her shoulder-length hair in a single ponytail with a matching yellow ribbon. "Tamika was two in that picture. The photographer spent almost a half hour trying to get her to smile. She was such a sweet baby."

"She's beautiful just like her mother."

I nodded. "Yes, she is." We were silent for a long time just staring down at my little girl's chubby face and beautiful dimpled cheeks. Kenyon eventually handed me the photograph back and planted a kiss on my lips.

"Thanks for sharing her with me," he said.

I was getting teary eyed again. "Thanks for being there for me."

"I'll always be there for you. If you haven't figured it out, I love you, Nichole Sharice Truth."

"And I love you." I needed him in my life. I just hadn't realized how much I needed him until now. Trinette was wrong. Kenyon was a good man, and I wanted him in my life. There was nothing psycho about him at all.

20

Trinette

I woke up the following morning around three to the sound of Leon snoring loudly on his side of the bed. How in the world could he sleep at a time like this? My carefully planned-out future was crumbling before my eyes.

After my bath I had returned to the room to find Leon already under the covers. I sprayed my body with his favorite perfume, Jo Malone's French Lime Blossom, then dropped the bath towel to the floor and slid under the covers. I had snuggled up to Leon, and when he had reached out for me I realized it was up to Ms. Netta's powerful pussy to persuade Leon.

I'd rained kisses down along his chest, stopping long enough to suckle each of his nipples. When he moaned, I had felt in control and rolled him over onto his back. My lips had traveled all the way down to his crotch, and I'd wrapped my fingers around his dick. Just as I was about to deep throat him, Leon had called my name.

"Netta?"

"Yes, baby," I purred as I licked the head.

"I'm not changing my mind 'bout the house."

Stunned, I released him. Leon had simply sighed and wasted no time going back to sleep.

Hours later I still couldn't believe my husband had rejected me. I rolled out of bed and reached for my robe from off the chaise in the corner, then moved into the living room. It was chilly, so I adjusted the thermostat to seventy-five, then took a seat across my Italian leather couch and closed my eyes.

I was not sure what I was going to do. My hands were tied. Sex wasn't even working and that had always been my most powerful weapon. Without it I was vulnerable and defenseless—two things I try never to be. I was also helpless. There was no way I could buy the house by myself. I needed Leon, but regardless of how helpless I was, there was no way in hell I was about to beg a man, even if it was something I wanted. What I couldn't understand was, why now? Why did Leon wait until two days before we were scheduled to close to change his mind? I didn't understand that.

He was being unfair. Leon had the degrees and a career most black men could only dream of having. Why couldn't I have the same? Why is it when I wanted something there was a problem?

I was so upset I started crying again and couldn't stop. All I wanted was a chance to shine. Was there another woman involved? And if so, did I really care? I'd said before, if he found someone else, then good for him. Hell, that way I wouldn't have to ride his ass the whole weekend we were together or feel guilty when I wasn't. Some other woman doing my job for me didn't matter as long as the money kept coming in.

My nose was stopped up and my eyes were swollen by the time I heard movement in the other room. I blew my nose and waited another ten minutes before Leon finally came down the hall, and my heart stopped. He had his coat on and his suitcase in his hand.

"I'm going to head back home."

My heart practically stopped. "Home? This is your home."

Leon shook his head. "No, it isn't. It's *your* home. All the decorating, furniture . . . none of my clothes are hanging in your closet. This isn't my home . . . hasn't been in a long time."

I sat up on the couch. "So what are you gonna do, just walk out and leave me to deal with the realtor and the mortgage company?"

He moved over and took a seat. "I think you can handle it."

"Why are you doing this to me? It's Valentine's Day!"

The eyes he bored on me said he wasn't at all interested in my tantrums. "What difference does it make what day it is?"

I shook my head and allowed the tears to fall again. "Why now?"

"I don't know. I mean . . . I'm just not sure what I want anymore."

This whole conversation was so damn confusing. "Since when? We've talked all week and everything was fine—at least I thought it was."

"Think about it, Trinette, what have we built together? We have no bills together except the condo. We have a joint account you barely ever deposit any money into. In the eight years we've been married we should have grown as a couple."

"We *have* grown. You're CFO of one of the biggest financial institutions in the world and I'm about to be director. If that ain't growing, I don't know what is!"

He licked his lips and sighed. "I meant how have *we* grown? What do we have?"

I couldn't think of anything, but right then that just wasn't as important as him understanding I wanted my house. "Leon, this is not the time. I think our relationship is wonderful just the way it is. When I see myself getting old I see you beside me."

"I wanted the same thing."

My brow rose. "Wanted? What, you don't think about us getting old together?"

Sadly, he shook his head. "Not if our relationship doesn't change."

My heart started beating nervously. Things were spiraling out of control. "Do you wanna be married?"

There was a long silence before Leon finally replied, "I don't know. I need some time to think."

"Think? What is there to think about?" My entire world was crumbling right before my eyes.

"I need to figure out what I want."

"What about what *I* want?" While swallowing back tears, I gave him a long, disgusted look. "We're all set to close on this house and you walk in here with your bag packed ready to run back to Richmond. What the hell's really goin' on?"

"I figured it was probably best for me to go on home. I doubt you want to be around me after I said no about the house."

He was right. The rest of the weekend would be hell, but that didn't stop my heart from breaking because he was abandoning me at the lowest point of my life. "It's Valentine's Day, dammit!"

Leon gave a small smile and shrugged. "What difference does it make what day it is?"

"It makes a big damn difference. We just celebrated our eight-year anniversary!"

"I know, and that's what makes this so hard, but I have to do what I feel in my heart."

It was final. There was no budging. I started crying my eyes out and reached for another tissue. Leon has never liked seeing me cry. Reaching over, he stroked my hair as he spoke.

"Netta, can you honestly say you're happy with our life the way it is?"

"Yes," I began between sniffles. "I am content with our life because I know it is only temporary. As soon as I reach my goal, you and I are gonna come full circle and we'll be living together again." This was fucking unbelievable. Never in a million years would I have imagined this. "It's always been about you and your career. Why is it I can never have my time?"

"Baby, you know I have always supported every decision you've made. All I have ever wanted was to make you happy."

I looked at him, not bothering to wipe away the tears running down my cheeks. "Then why are you breaking my heart now?"

"I don't mean to, but . . . I can't go on like this. I'm lonely and need you with me."

"Are you seeing someone else?" I asked with a look of skepticism.

He dropped his head. "This isn't about anyone but you and me."

The thought of Leon spending the lover's holiday

with another woman sent a fresh wave of anger through me. "You didn't answer the question."

He paused and looked directly at me. "No . . . I'm not seeing anyone else."

He was lying. I knew good and damn well a man wouldn't admit to fucking someone else. All he did was piss me the fuck off. "You know what? You're right. We've been married eight years and we haven't done shit together. We have no bills together. We already live apart. So you're right . . . we ain't got shit."

"And that doesn't bother you?"

I sighed, growing tired of the whole damn thing. "Nope, but obviously it bothers you, so I guess you better call the airline and book yourself an early flight back."

Instead of reaching for his phone, Leon just sat there looking unsure of his next move. I didn't know why he was having doubts when a few minutes before he was all set to walk out the door and leave me.

I rolled my eyes at him. "Go ahead. I agree it is probably time for us to move on. Our lives have gone in two different directions. I'm living in St. Louis and you're not coming back, so we have no choice but to get on with our lives."

He dropped his head to his hands. "Take whatever money you need out of the account and pay your debts off."

There he went throwing my credit in my face again.

I stormed out the room and moved into the bathroom and washed my face. The entire time I listened as he contacted the airline. I was crushed. He was dumping me on Valentine's Day . . . my favorite holiday, and going back to Richmond to spend the holiday with another woman. I brushed away the fresh tears because there was no way I was letting him see me fall apart as he walked out the door.

Leon came down the hall. I reached for a hair tie and pulled my hair back.

"If you want, I can stay," he said.

I surprised myself by laughing. Hell, what else could I have done at that point? "Stay? For what? Don't stay because you feel sorry for me. Go ahead and get on back to that little bitch."

He reached for me, but I pushed his hand away. "There isn't anyone. All I want is you."

"Yeah, whatever. A'ight, give me a hug. You have a safe trip back," I said, my voice dripping with sarcasm. I tried to give him a quick hug, but Leon held on tight and refused to let go. Part of me couldn't wait for him to leave, but the other part wanted to hold onto him and our life for as long as I could.

"I can stay," he said after he finally released me.

"No . . . this is probably for the best. You have a wonderful life. Don't worry about me. I'm gonna be all right."

"I know you will. I just hope you realize we could be even better together."

I didn't want to hear anything else he had to say. I moved away from him and stepped into the living room and waited for him to follow. When Leon finally walked into the room, he paused.

"You better get rolling before you miss your plane."

Leon grabbed his suitcase. As he headed to the door, I watched him reach up and start wiping his eyes. Was this man for real? Did he really expect me to believe he was crying? He was the one leaving me! It was then I looked down and for the first time noticed that Leon was carrying a small black suitcase I had never seen before. There wasn't enough to fit in that mothafucka but a change of clothes. My pulse raced. Leon never intended to stay. He never traveled with anything but that big, ugly-ass army green bag. So why didn't he bring it this time? The answer was obvious. Leon never had any intentions of spending the holiday with me. He had flown down just to end our relationship. Leon really was leaving me for another woman. My heart hurt like I never thought imaginable as I watched him walk out that door and my life forever.

21

Nikki

"Nikki."

"Huh?" I was half asleep when I answered the phone so it took me a few seconds to figure out it was Trinette crying on the other end of the line. "Trinette? What happened?"

"Leon . . . he's . . . he's gone," she managed between sniffles.

"Gone? Gone where?"

"He went back to Virginia. It's over."

"What?" I sat straight up in bed. Kenyon shifted onto his side and reached out for me.

"Baby, you okay?" he mumbled.

I put my hand over the mouthpiece. "I'm fine. Go back to sleep." I slipped out from under the cover and caught a glimpse of his chest all the way down to the patch of hair at his crotch. I had to bite my bottom lip.

Damn, he was sexy. Last night he worked my ass every which way and had me screaming his name. I had to lock Rudy out the room because he had thought Kenyon was hurting me the way I was carrying on and had jumped in the bed and bitten him on the ass. Luckily, he didn't break the skin.

"Nikki, you still there?"

Shit. I had gotten sidetracked and forgotten all about my best friend. "Sorry, girl. Let me go into the living room," I began as I moved down the hall and flopped down on the couch. "Okay, what happened?"

Trinette released a shaky breath. "He's not buying the house."

"But you close on Monday."

"It doesn't matter. He said he doesn't wanna do it."

It didn't at all sound like the Leon Montgomery I knew and loved.

"He said he is tired of living like this . . . that I need to be moving to Richmond with him, not trying to buy a house in Missouri. Can you believe that shit?"

About damn time. I thought Leon had totally wimped out. He was right. "Well, I'll have to agree with Leon, although the timing is all wrong."

"That's what I told him. I mean, why didn't he say something about this before? Why he wait until we're about to close? After I have already told everyone I'm moving, he doesn't want to buy another house. I don't understand it. Now I got to embarrass myself and let the realtor know the deal is off."

Heaven forbid, Trinette embarrassing herself. This is a kid who refused to go to the corner store with food stamps. We lived in the hood where everyone got food stamps. "Did you say Leon left?"

"Yep. Caught an early plane back. That mothafucka never had any intentions of staying. He came down with an overnight bag."

I was quiet because there was one possibility. "Do you think he's seeing someone else?" If he was, Trinette couldn't blame anyone but herself.

She sniffled. "He has to be. I even told him as much. Why else would he leave me on Valentine's Day?"

"Okay, rewind a second. You told him what?"

"To hurry back to that bitch!" she screamed in my ear.

Oh, brother. "And what did he say?"

Trinette sucked her teeth. "He said this isn't about anyone but him and me."

"So he never came out and said he was seeing anyone else?"

"No."

There was silence. I hated to say it, but it sounded to me like Leon might have met someone else. And like I said, I couldn't blame him. Anybody would get tired of living apart after a while. I kept telling Trinette, but nooo, she didn't want to listen. Leon is a damn good man and he deserves some happiness in his life . . . if not from Trinette, then definitely from someone else. "What are you gonna do about the house?"

Trinette sighed, the defeat apparent in her voice. "What else can I do except call the realtor and tell him we're pulling out of the contract. Hell, I wouldn't be surprised if the owners decided to sue us."

"Hopefully they'll just take the five grand and call it even."

"Shit, I forgot I won't be able to get my earnest money back! Not to mention all the money I spent on inspections and the home appraisal." Trinette released a strangled laugh. "This is so fucking unbelievable."

She sounded so pitiful, but I had to be honest with her . . . at least a little bit. "Yeah . . . but you knew this day would come. You said so yourself."

"I know . . . but it's different now that it's finally happened." She started crying.

"It's gonna be okay." I didn't know what else to say because I knew how she felt. I had felt the same way when Donovan told me it was over. Thank goodness I had Kenyon in my life.

"Why is it I can't have a chance to do something in my life I feel proud of? All I want is a chance to have a career of my own. He's got a pension and a 401k. Why can't I have the same thing?"

I took a deep breath. "You can, but it comes at a cost."

"That's bullshit!" she barked.

"I know it isn't fair, but life ain't fair." There was a long silence. I sat there listening to her sniffles, trying to think what I could do to make things better. I won't say Trinette got what she deserved, but I will say she got what she wanted. Her actions these last two years dictated the outcome.

"Now what am I gonna do?" she finally asked.

"You can go and get your husband back," I suggested.

"Nope. A man only gets one chance to walk out on me."

She could be so stubborn sometimes. "Then all I can say is, you're gonna be just fine because if you think about it, Trinette, how much different will your life really be? I mean . . . the two of you already live apart.

You've got your condo, a bad ride, a good-ass job, dick jumping at you from every direction. I mean . . . what's gonna be different other than Leon is no longer in your life?"

Trinette blew her nose in my ear before saying, "You know I can't make it on my own."

I released a heavy sigh. With Trinette it always had to be about money. "Yes, you can. Just pay off all them damn credit cards and you'll be just fine."

"I guess. Leon did tell me to take whatever I needed out the joint account."

"See, then you need to do just that. It's time you stopped leaning on Leon and started taking care of yourself."

"I know. You're right."

"You're gonna be all right. Give it a couple of days and try calling him."

"I ain't calling his black ass! Hell, he walked out on me so he could rush back to some bitch and spend Valentine's Day with her." She blew her nose again. "I bet she found out he was buying a house and gave him an ultimatum. It has to be, because he's never had balls like that before."

Personally, I felt his reaction was long overdue, but I was not about to tell her that. "Maybe not . . . maybe he just wants you in Richmond with him."

"I was coming . . . just not when he *said* I needed to come. I'm tired of Leon making all the decisions and deciding where we live."

I blew out a long breath. "Then I guess this is probably all for the best."

"Yeah, you're probably right." She didn't sound as convinced as she wanted me to believe. "At least now I don't have to feel guilty about messing around anymore. I can fuck whomever I wanna fuck whenever the *fuck* I want."

Okay, she was starting to sound crazy. "Girl, get some rest and we'll talk later, okay? How about dinner tonight?"

She gave a bitter laugh. "Nikki, puhleeze, it's Valentine's Day. I'm gonna find myself a date."

I should have known those tears were temporary. "Listen, don't start something outta anger. And don't go looking for revenge."

"I'm not, but I *am* gonna make sure the world knows my life doesn't stop because Leon Montgomery decides it does. I had a life before I met him and I'll damn sure have one long after he's gone." On that note, she hung up the phone. I sat there for the longest time debating if I should call her back. There was no telling what Trinette was going to do now that she had been knocked down from her pedestal. Hopefully, she'd learn something, but I wasn't about to hold my breath. If anything, things were about to get crazy.

22

Trinette

Leon had told me to take what I needed. Well, I did. I needed it *all* in order to get on my feet and start over. Unlike him, I don't have a six-figure job.

I waited until I drove over to my bank and deposited the money into my personal checking account before I called Nikki. She answered on the first ring.

"Remember when I told you Leon said for me to take whatever I needed outta the account?" I said by way of a greeting.

There was a noticeable pause. "Yeah?"

I took a moment and moistened my lips. "Well . . . I took it all."

"All?"

"Well, everything but three dollars and twenty-eight cents." I started laughing and couldn't stop. It felt good . . . damn good to be back in control.

"You are a mess." Nikki didn't sound the slightest bit amused.

"Hell, I'm not about to let him take that money and spend it on some other female."

She blew out a long breath. "Who says he has someone else? You don't know that for sure."

Sometimes my girl seemed slow. "He does. It's been a week and not a single phone call, and then he had the nerve to send me an e-mail last night."

"What did it say?"

"It said our lives had grown in two different directions and he'll always love me, but it was time for him to get on with his life and for me to take whatever I needed outta the account to clean up my credit."

Nikki cleared her throat. "Well . . . you *do* need to work on your credit."

"Whatever! I plan to do that. I just took a little extra in the meantime."

Nikki started talking to her assistant who was in the background asking about the price of a book. "Sorry about that. Now . . . how much *did* you take?"

"I *said* all of it."

"How much is *all* of it?"

Damn, she was nosy, trying to sound like somebody's mama. "A hundred grand."

Nikki gasped. I knew she wouldn't approve, but so what?

"Goodness, Trinette! The man gave you everything and you're stealing his money." I didn't miss the critical tone of her voice.

"Technically it's *our* money."

"Whatever." There was heavy sarcasm in her voice. Who was she to judge me?

"Ohhhkay . . . so tell me . . . now that you have taken the money, how do you feel?"

"It feels damn good." Actually it felt good five minutes ago. Now that it was done, it didn't feel any way at all like I thought it would feel. Instead, I still felt empty inside, but I wasn't about to tell Nikki that so she could start analyzing me.

I pulled out of the parking lot. "I'm ready to plan a trip."

"I thought you were gonna start working on fixing your credit?"

"I mean afterward." Damn, she took all the fun out of everything.

"I guess." Nikki was quiet for a moment before she finally said, "At least call or e-mail Leon and let him know you have taken the money."

"For what?" I snapped. "Leon checks his account on a regular basis."

"You should still tell him."

Maybe she was right. Leon might be trying to buy tickets for him and his woman to go on a vacation. That would definitely be one way for him to find out the money was gone. Ha-ha! Nikki makes me sick, acting like she's my mama, but she's right. The least I could do is tell him. "Okay, I'll e-mail him when I get a chance and tell him."

"Good. Look . . . I need to go. Some of us do have to work today. Enjoy the rest of your day off, and go treat yourself to a new pair of shoes."

I wasn't going to tell her that not only did I buy shoes but I bought an entire outfit and accessorized it with a fresh weave. "I might just do that. But right now I'm running late for my date."

"With who?"

Did I mention she was nosy? "Don't worry about it. It's with someone who knows how to treat a woman like me."

As soon as I got off the phone, I met Smooth at Lumière Place Casino and Hotel, where we had lunch, then tried our luck at the blackjack table with his money before going up to one of their luxurious suites.

After I rocked Smooth's world, and regained the power Leon momentarily stripped me of, I showered and left the suite first. We never arrived or left together. Smooth was married, and I wasn't trying to break up any happy homes. Besides, I didn't want him. His wife would never have to worry about sharing with me. It was bad enough she had to share her husband with Levitra.

When I reached the parking lot, I looked to make sure no one was around to see what I was doing. I liked keeping my shit private. When I got into my car, I checked my messages and was listening to one from Michael, asking if we could hook up later that evening, when I spotted Smooth coming out the casino. He moved across the parking lot looking cool and confident. He didn't notice me, and that was a good thing. That gave me a chance to check him out. Although he had a big belly, he was definitely good-looking and had confidence. Too bad his dick didn't work on command. But he had enough money to make up for what he was lacking, and that's what made him a wonderful sponsor. Not to mention the eleven hundred dollars now in my wallet. Between him and Michael, I would be able to afford a new house in no time. No matter how long it took, I was determined to show Leon that what hurts me can only make me stronger.

I pulled off and was heading out the lot, in the direction of the highway, when I noticed Smooth climb into a Navigator with personalized license plates and pull off. I couldn't believe it.

CIMON.

23

Nikki

I walked in the house and Kenyon was already calling
me. I didn't understand why the man felt the need to
call me all day. I enjoyed him, really I did, but sometimes it got to be a little much. Trinette was right about
him, only I wasn't ready yet to admit to her that she
had a point. Last thing I needed was for her to rub it in
my face that she knew more about Kenyon than I did.
But I had to agree since the dust had settled and I had
gotten past the lust, Kenyon was starting to smother
me.

I have this thing about a man being a man, and nothing is worse than a man being needy. It was Friday and
I wanted to spend the evening relaxing after a long
week—alone. After leaving the radio station, I went
home and had just put my purse down on the bed when
my cell phone rang. I didn't even have to look down at
the screen to know it was Kenyon.

"Baby, I'm gonna have a few drinks with Jay."

"Okay," I replied, taking a seat on the end of the bed and pulling off my shoes.

"I'm not gonna be out all night or get drunk, but you know my boy, he'll be drunk before ten, and someone needs to drive him home."

"Ohhhkay." I'm not his mother. I didn't know why he felt the need to tell me every step of his day.

"You sure you don't wanna come out? I would love to have you on my arm."

Closing my eyes, I tried to keep my temper in check. We had already gone through this earlier. "Kenyon . . . not tonight. I just wanna take a hot bubble bath and relax."

"Okay." There was a pause, and I knew before he spoke he wasn't ready yet to take no for an answer. "You want me to come over and wash your back?"

Kenyon had already been over that week, and I just wasn't in the mood for company. "No. I would really like to relax and catch up on a couple of Netflix movies I haven't had a chance to watch yet."

"Well, save the action movie for me for tomorrow night, okay?"

"All right," I said impatiently, wanting to get off the phone and get my weekend started.

"I love you," he finally said.

"Love you too," I said quickly, then hung up and flopped back onto the bed.

Don't get me wrong, it felt good having a man in my life. Kenyon was a little over the top at times but very attentive and knew what it meant to take care of a woman. While I bathed, I thought about my feelings for him and couldn't say for sure how I felt anymore. His behavior lately had been a little too much to digest at once. Now I was starting to wonder if I really loved him or if I was on the rebound. I just wasn't sure, and that is why I had started distancing myself from him. Kenyon was into me, and ever since Big Mama passed away, I had become dependent on him being there when I needed him. That wasn't necessarily a bad thing, but until I had a chance to sort out my feelings, it was best to keep a little distance, because I was starting to think Kenyon was in way too deep with me. The last thing I wanted to do was break his heart.

After my bath, I moved into the family room and turned on the gas fireplace. It was early March and pretty chilly out. I grabbed a book and wrapped up in a blanket on the couch and read until, at some point, I must have drifted off to sleep. In fact, I was having a good-ass dream when the phone rang.

"Hello?" I said, not sure if I was still asleep or not.

"Hey, Nikki."

It took a moment for the voice to register, and when it did, I was suddenly wide awake. "Donovan . . . uh . . . are you still in Iraq?"

"Yep. It's five in the morning here."

It felt so strange hearing his voice after almost eight months. I had never expected him to call me again. "I got your letter."

He cleared his throat. "Yeah . . . and I just got yours. I'm so sorry about Big Mama. I wish I could have been there."

A sob filled my throat. "Thanks, that means a lot. Big Mama thought the world of you." There was a long, uncomfortable silence. "Thanks for calling," I finally said.

"Nikki, listen . . . I need to talk you about the letter I sent." He paused and took a deep breath, and I could tell whatever he was trying to say was difficult. "I wrote that letter because . . . well . . . because I didn't think you cared anymore. Then yesterday I got your letters . . . all five of your letters, and I—"

"All five?" I couldn't believe what he was saying. "You're telling me you didn't receive any of my letters until yesterday?"

"Yeah . . . crazy, ain't it? I don't know what happened, but they must have been sent to the wrong unit and were just sitting there, because I got all five at the same time."

My heart was pounding heavily. "I mailed the first letter eight months ago."

"I know. I noticed the date of the letters and had to call you right away. When I didn't hear from you, I thought maybe you decided to move on."

"No, I thought that was what *you* wanted. If my memory serves me right, that's exactly what you told me in your letter. Why did you say it was time for us to move on?" I didn't even try to hide the bitterness from my voice.

"I only wrote that letter because I was hurting."

There was more silence. What did this mean? He never received my letters. Donovan never received *any* of my letters. All this time I thought he was trying to tell me our relationship was over, when in actuality he never received my letters.

"Nikki, there is so much I wanna say, but I don't wanna do it over the phone. I should have never sent you that letter. I should have waited until I got home so we could have talked in person."

"I agree." I was just as guilty. I too should have waited until he told me to my face.

"I'm coming home on leave Friday for ten days, and I would like to see you."

My heart was pounding, and I was afraid to speak. "Okay," I barely managed above a whisper. There was a long silence and I didn't know what else to say, but just knowing he was on the other end was enough for me.

"I won't keep you, but I had to speak with you and let you know I want to talk."

"Are . . . you planning to stay here?"

He gave a strangled laugh. "I guess I hadn't thought about that."

"You're welcome to stay." It was his house as well.

"No, it would probably be better if I stay in a hotel."

I felt stupid for even suggesting such a thing, especially since he was the one who said we needed to move on with our lives. "Okay."

"I need to check on the barbershop and take care of a few things. I'll call you when I get in, and then I can come out to the house so we can talk." There was another pause. "You ever get that leak under the sink fixed?"

Tears slid from the corners of my eyes. In the first letter I had written him, I told him there was a slow leak under the kitchen sink. "No."

"I'll take care of it when I come home."

I swallowed and took a deep breath. The last thing I wanted was for him to know I was crying. "Okay."

"Talk to you soon."

After I hung up, I hugged my pillow. It took a while to digest what Donovan had said. He hadn't received my letters. How in the world had that happened? But more than that, what did it mean for us? All this time I thought he had been ignoring my letters and, despite my telling him I wanted to make our marriage work, he had decided after having some time to think that he wanted a divorce. Instead, all this time, Donovan thought I didn't care. He was a soldier over in Iraq under the impression his wife wasn't the least bit interested in how her husband was holding up. I felt sad for both of us. I had already written our relationship off and had even started a new one with another man, even though I knew in my heart something wasn't right. Now I knew why. Our relationship wasn't over quite yet.

I lay there for a long time, thinking about how I would feel when I saw him standing at my door again.

Donovan was right. He didn't need to stay at the house. The situation would be awkward for both of us. This way we could talk without feeling pressured. Maybe nothing would come of us seeing each other, but it needed to be done. I didn't dare allow myself to start thinking, what if. Our marriage had grown apart long before Donovan had left, and I wasn't sure if I wanted to salvage the relationship even if we could. I lay there for the longest time wishing Big Mama was still around so I could talk to her. She always had the answer.

I didn't get much sleep, and around seven I finally got up, took a shower and started cleaning up the house. I had just shut off the vacuum when I heard the phone ring.

"Good morning. You want some breakfast?"

I smiled at the sound of Kenyon's voice. "What are you getting?"

"I'm down near Mama's House and said, you know what, let me see if my baby wants some pancakes."

"That sounds good. I'll make coffee."

"I'll be there in a bit."

I hung up, smiling. I had a new man in my life and had already started building a new life for myself. I wasn't sure if I wanted to turn back at this point.

I took a shower and was dressed in jeans and a T-shirt by the time Kenyon arrived.

"Hey," he said with that beautiful smile on his face. He gave me a kiss.

He looked good in blue jeans and a Nike sweater shirt. He shrugged out of his jacket and draped it over the end of my couch. I watched as he moved into the kitchen carrying a plastic bag of food. I smelled it and my stomach began to growl. I followed him.

"I wasn't sure what you wanted so I got everything."

"You ain't lying." There were pancakes, grits loaded with butter, hash browns, scrambled eggs and bacon. Goodness.

"Yeah, but there's nothing like Mama's House."

"You're right about that." I poured us both a cup of coffee and had a seat.

"How'd you sleep?" he asked.

"Not too good." I waited until we were both sitting at the table before I continued. I figured it was a good idea to be honest. "Donovan called." I decided the only way for us to have a relationship was to be totally honest.

"Really?" he said, then took a sip.

"Yes. He'll be home on leave this weekend and he wants to come by and talk."

Kenyon was quiet. "What do you think about that?"

"I think we need to talk."

He was quiet for a while, and I didn't miss the muscle at his jaw twitching. Donovan contacting me was not at all what he wanted to hear.

"I agree. I think you need to talk so the two of you can get this over with and move on. Like you said, the relationship is over. So yeah, you *do* need to talk. But I'm not worried, 'cause you're my baby now. Right?" He looked over at me with those gorgeous eyes, and I smiled.

"Yes, I'm your baby."

"I told you, Nikki. I love you and I'm not going anywhere." The look in his eyes told me he meant every word.

24

Trinette

"You are the bomb."

"Of course I am." I wish I could have said the same about Michael. The way Maureen raved, you would have thought her husband had mad skills in the bedroom. Instead, he barely scratched the itch. But I had to keep reminding myself, it wasn't about that. If I needed good sex, I could get that from Jay. Michael was only good for one thing. Money.

"Whose place is this?" I asked.

"You like it?" he asked with a silly grin on his face. Who wouldn't? It had mahogany wood floors, high ceilings, and a large master bath with a jetted tub. It was gorgeous. Michael reached over, then held up a set of keys. "These can be yours."

"Mine?" This place was better than the little condo I was currently living in. But I knew nothing this good came for free. "I heard an *if* at the end of your statement."

He stroked my stomach. "I don't like to share. If I can have you exclusively, then this place can be yours."

"As in my name on the title?"

"As in I let you live here for a year for free. That way you can sell your place, work on fixing your credit, and hopefully finance it on your own in a year."

I don't know what I was thinking when I told him about my financial situation, but since then he'd paid two of my credit cards.

I looked around. It was so tempting. I would have a wonderful new place, and as far as everyone knew, I had done it all on my own. "And what are you expecting outta the deal? What do you mean *not sharing?*"

"Come on, Trinette. You're not a dumb woman. Either you play by my rules or the deal's off."

The thought of living rent free for a year was definitely tempting, to say the least. But damn . . . the last thing in the world I wanted was to owe a man something. "I'll let you know."

"When?"

"When I'm ready, boo-boo." I leaned over and gave him a promising kiss. I do things on my own time. "I've got a lot to consider."

"Don't keep me waiting too long."

While rubbing my clit against his thigh, I purred, "Do I keep you waiting for this?"

He gave me that greedy little smile. I went ahead and took care of him *again,* then rolled over and decided a nap was in order. The king-size bed felt heavenly with those 500 thread count sheets.

Michael slapped me playfully on my ass. "I'm going

to shower and head back to work. There's a spare key lying on the dresser. It's yours."

"Uh-huh." I rolled over and allowed myself to fall into a deep sleep. I woke up hours later and showered and got dressed. Just as he said, a key was lying on the dresser next to a stack of hundreds. Smiling, I slipped them both in my purse. I definitely could get used to this, and I had to admit owning the condo would be nice. The best in town, but I didn't like the idea of being a kept woman.

I slipped on my shoes and made sure I had my things before I locked the door with my own key. I had to smile at that. As I was coming down the sidewalk, an old woman with wrinkled olive skin and blue hair came up the way with a small dog on a chain.

"Well, hello. Are you my new neighbor?" asked the old busybody.

I shrugged. "Maybe."

"I'm Clara, and this here is Precious."

There was absolutely nothing precious about her dog. In fact he was a straight-up mutt, but I patted his head anyway. "Aren't you precious?" I said in baby talk.

"By chance, that wouldn't be your Mercedes parked at the other end of the street?"

I gave her a curious smile, wondering how she knew that, when I realized I had my keys in my hand. Everyone knows what a Mercedes key looks like. I gave her a Juicy Fruit smile. "Why, yes, it is."

"Well, you might want to call a tow truck, because you've got a flat."

"What?"

She sniffed the air and left me standing there by myself.

I hurried off to the curb and walked around my car. What the hell! Not one but two flat tires.

With straight attitude, I reached inside my purse for my cell phone, then looked inside my wallet and removed my AAA card. As soon as I got off the phone I went on back inside the condo. I had a forty-five minute wait. I grabbed myself a bottle of water, then moved into the family room in back and had a seat. The fully furnished condo had a sixty-inch flat screen and a chocolate leather wraparound sectional. I was flipping channels when I heard the lock turn. I quickly shut the television off, then froze.

"Damn, this a nice place!" exclaimed a deep male voice.

"It belongs to my husband. It's furnished rental property he hasn't bothered to rent after the last tenant left."

Oh, my goodness! That was Maureen, and whoever that was with her sounded so familiar.

"Shit! We got our own spot to chill. I'm loving the shit outta this!"

Hell, nah! That was Chuck, the freaking security guard! Peeking from the corner of the wall, I watched as they moved down the hall to the bedroom where Michael and I been fucking. Thank God I had remembered to make the bed.

"Mmm, daddy . . . what you got in there waiting for me?" Maureen cooed.

"Why don't you look inside and find out?"

I was too through.

I heard a zipper, then Maureen cried, "Daaayum! Where the hell you get all of that?" After that, she must have dropped right down on his dick, because within minutes, I heard the bed rock and both of them moaning.

I know I should have left then, but I couldn't help it. I had to see that shit for myself. I slowly crept up to the door and peeked in. Maureen was leaning over the edge of the bed, and Chuck was doing her doggy style at the angle where neither could see me. I reached down for my phone and took a picture and made sure the original piece of African artwork hanging over the bed was in the photo. After two more shots, I moved away from the door.

I slipped out the door and walked up to my car just as the tow truck arrived. I looked over at the window to make sure Maureen wasn't looking out. She wasn't. She was too busy getting fucked by Chuck. I wasn't mad at her. With what Michael was working with, I fully understood her desperate need for a little something on the side.

The tow truck driver greeted me with a tip of his hat. "How you doing, ma'am?"

"Not too good." I would think that was obvious.

He moved over to the car and crouched down and examined the tires, then released a long whistle. "Damn."

"What?"

"Somebody slashed both your tires."

"Slashed? Who the hell would do some shit like that?"

He shrugged and rose to his full six feet. "Don't know, ma'am, but I'll tow it in."

I showed him my card and he wrote down the information, then offered me a ride. Hell, I didn't have much choice. Not while Maureen was a few feet away, getting buckwild. I was tempted to call Michael and tell him his wife was getting freaky deaky with the security guard but decided maybe I'd keep that piece of information. It might become valuable at another time.

25

Nikki

By Friday evening, I was a nervous wreck. Donovan had called the night before to say he would drop by around six. I had spent the entire day getting ready for the evening. First thing on the agenda was getting rid of Kenyon.

I didn't think I would ever get him to leave. I couldn't believe how insecure he was feeling about the entire thing. Thursday night he put his work in making sure I was satisfied, and again this morning. I tried to reassure him that all Donovan and I were planning to do was talk. We owed that much to each other. As much as I hoped, I wasn't going to even set myself up to think we might have a chance. That man was gone eight months and not one letter besides the one to say we needed to move on. I deserved better than that.

I ran to Macy's and bought myself a cute pair of low-ride jeans and a red sweater, because I always look good in red. Denise hooked up my locks and arched my eyebrows, then I hurried home and had barely enough time to shower and fix my makeup when the phone rang.

"Baby?"

Damn, it was Kenyon. "What do you want?" I didn't mean to sound annoyed, but he was getting on my nerves.

"Just checking to make sure everything is okay."

"Why wouldn't I be?" This conversation was ridiculous.

"Uh . . . I don't know." He cleared his throat. "You know I love you, right?"

"Yes, I know you do." There was a pause.

"I hope you love me at least a little?" he said with laughter in his voice, but I knew he was serious. Did he not understand how important tonight was for me? Obviously, he knew but didn't care.

"And you know I'll do anything for you. Baby . . . we complete each other. I hope you don't forget that."

"I know, Kenyon." I ground the words out between my teeth.

"Baby?"

Closing my eyes, I took a deep breath. "Yeah?"

"Remember what I said. . . . I won't let anyone come between us."

Oh, my goodness, he was pathetic. "I'll call you on Sunday."

"Okay, baby." He sounded pleased by my answer.

I hung up. I really couldn't deal with him at that point. Before he and I had a chance to see where our relationship would lead, I first had to find closure with Donovan. Why couldn't his needy ass understand that?

I checked on the shrimp jambalaya I had simmering

on the stove and removed a peach cobbler from the oven. They were both his favorite, and I figured since he'd been in the desert for eight months, he would appreciate a home-cooked meal.

I moved into my room and checked my hair and makeup to ensure both were perfect. They were. I turned to the side and smiled at how well my butt looked in the new jeans. They were definitely worth the hundred dollar price tag. I wore a red V-neck sweater that made my breasts look good. They were small, but as Donovan always said, more than a mouthful is a waste. I wanted Donovan to see and remember how beautiful I was.

The doorbell rang and my heart practically leaped out my chest. I told myself to relax. Rudy was having a fit, barking like he'd lost his mind. "Rudy, be quiet!" I yelled. Obediently, he dropped his head and moved under the coffee table.

I had to take several breaths before I finally had the nerve to open the door. Standing at five ten was Donovan, looking fine as hell. He must have spent the entire time lifting weights, because his medium build had bulked up.

"Hey." His chocolate eyes sparkled.

I couldn't stop looking at him. His light skin had bronzed beautifully. Time had done him wonders. "H-Hello . . . uh . . . come on in."

He stepped in, and I smelled him as he passed. *Wonderful.* As soon as Rudy spotted him, he raced over and started jumping up and down.

"Hey, boy! Hey . . . I missed you too."

I stood back and watched the two of them. Donovan loved Rudy as much as I did. At some point in our lives our dog had become the child we no longer had.

Donovan looked at me, then tilted his head toward the kitchen. "Is that jambalaya I smell?"

Smiling, I nodded. "I thought you might like a home-cooked meal."

"You right about that."

"Then follow me into the kitchen. I've got corn casserole and peach cobbler as well."

He smoothed a hand over his short dark waves. "Girl, what you trying to do?"

Swinging around, our eyes met. "Welcome you home."

Stepping into the kitchen, Donovan glanced around at the freshly painted cream wall. I had the house professionally painted shortly after he was first deployed. "The house looks good."

"Thanks." I moved over to the stove and turned off the eye. Dinner was ready.

As I moved over to the cabinet to retrieve a bowl, Donovan grabbed my arm. "Hey, Nikki . . ." I swung around and faced him. The expression on his face was serious. "I just needed to tell you again how sorry I am about Big Mama. I wish I had been here. You know I loved her."

"And she loved you."

He pulled me into his arms and held me tight, and the tears started and didn't stop. I held on to him.

He pressed his forehead against mine. "I spent weeks, then months, wondering why I hadn't heard from my wife, and I couldn't understand why you hadn't written me."

"But I did," I countered.

"I know that now, but I didn't then."

I was shaking my head. "Things haven't been good between us since Mimi died."

"Nikki, please. . . ." I watched him mentally shut down.

"No, Donovan. We need to talk about it. I think we've waited too long. I'm on the radio three nights a week playing therapist, yet I've never been able to do anything to help us. We need to talk about the day our daughter was killed."

"I know . . . just not yet."

Maybe I shouldn't have brought up Mimi, because the mood was suddenly lost. "Okay." I looked up into his eyes. The pain I saw mirrored the way I was feeling. "Why did you tell me it's time for us to move on?"

Donovan took my hands and led me into the family room and over to the couch where we took a seat. "Let me start by saying I wrote that letter because I was hurting. It had been months and I hadn't heard anything from you."

"Why didn't *you* write me?"

He ran a frustrated hand across his face before he spoke. "Because I was being stubborn. I was waiting to see if you wrote me first. I wanted to know if you still cared. And when you didn't . . . well . . . I—"

"But I did write you," I replied defensively. There was no way he was putting everything on me.

"I know. I know that now. For some reason I didn't get your letters until now."

"I don't know why you didn't get the letters. I mailed them from the bookstore. The same place you mailed mine."

He shook his head. "The reason why I mailed yours to the bookstore was because I wanted to make sure you got it. I know you have a tendency not to check the mailbox but once a week."

He did have a point.

Donovan cupped my hands with his. "There is no point in us getting all bent outta shape over who mailed who first. Let's just focus on us right now."

I nodded.

"Nikki, look at me. The only reason why I said it was time for us to move on was because, in my mind, I thought you already had."

"I thought you didn't want to be married anymore."

He pressed his warm lips to mine. "No. I love you, Nikki. I've always loved you."

"And I love you, but . . . we have to admit our relationship has been distant long before your deployment."

Lowering his gaze to his hands, Donovan replied, "Yeah, you're right."

"We used to talk about everything. What happened to us?"

Donovan's shoulders slumped with defeat. "I don't know."

There was a long silence before I finally spoke. "I know what happened."

Donovan knew where I was going with our conversation, because he immediately sprung from the couch and turned his back to me.

"Donovan, you've got to stop running. We have to talk about this."

"Nikki," he warned.

"No, I'm not gonna stop! We can't keep pretending it never happened." I could see he was starting to shut down, but I wasn't stopping this time. I rose and walked around and stood in front of him, forcing him to look at me. "We've got to talk about what happened to Mimi."

"Let's not." He moved into the kitchen and retrieved a bottle of beer from the fridge.

I followed him into the room. Angry tears were running down my face. He was so stubborn. This time I had to stand my ground. "Donovan, not talking about it has ruined our marriage!"

He twisted off the cap, then bored painful, sad eyes in my direction. "Okay, what would you like to talk about? Me leaving the gate open so my daughter could wander out front and into the street after you'd told me a dozen times to close it behind me?" His voice cracked at the end.

I gasped. And there was a long pause. "You . . . you think I blame you?"

"Well, don't you?"

I shook my head and brushed fresh tears away. "No. I-I blame myself. I should have been watching her. I was so tired and I thought . . . I thought if I was out in the backyard with her, at least she could play in the yard while I lay in the hammock. What kind of mother dozes off?"

Donovan lowered the bottle on the counter, then rested a comforting hand on my arm. "Sweetheart, you were tired. You had been up all night writing a business proposal after leaving the radio station. I should have been more understanding. I should have taken the morning off at the barbershop." His lip quivered, and being the man he was, he took a moment to try to pull himself together. "Do you know how many hours I spent going over that day, wishing I had taken a second to make sure I had closed that gate behind me?" He shook his head. "I've gone over it so many times I lost count."

"You can't beat yourself up."

He dropped his arms angrily. "But I do! That was my daughter! I should have been there for her. I should have been there for you." A tear slid from his eye. He tried to brush it aside, but they kept on coming. I made the first move toward him. He grabbed me tight and held me.

A sob rose to my throat. "I blamed myself, but after a while I had to let it go. I had to say good-bye to our daughter and start living again. I just thought you blamed me for her death, and I thought I lost you too."

He looked down at me and shook his head. "No way, baby. Never. I love you. I loved the both of you so much. Y'all were my whole world!" Donovan broke down, and I never heard him cry like that since his mother was found stabbed to death in an alley when he was sixteen. I cried along with him for the daughter I lost, the husband I missed and the years we could never get back. After a while I pulled away from him and stared out into the backyard. I could still see Mimi out in her sandbox playing with her blocks.

"So what do you wanna do?" he said.

I turned to face him. "I want to do whatever we need to do to make our marriage work."

The corners of his mouth curled upward. "Baby, I want the same thing."

I moved to him, and he kissed me and pushed his tongue between my lips. I moaned and met each stroke, happy to have my husband holding me again. Nothing had ever tasted or felt so good. I wrapped my arms tightly around him, wanting to never let this man go again.

Donovan kissed me once more, then scooped me into his arms and carried me back to our bedroom.

Wrapping my arms around his neck, I stared up in his eyes. "What about dinner?"

"It can wait. I've been gone a long time, and right now I need to make love to my wife."

My heart sang. Yes, I was his wife. He lowered me to my feet, and we each quickly shed our clothes and slid beneath the covers and started kissing and stroking each other. Donovan was hard. I wrapped my hand around his dick and he groaned.

"I advise you to stop or it's gonna be over before it even gets started," he warned. I definitely didn't want that. I needed to feel him inside of me bad.

Donovan rolled me onto my back, then he positioned himself between my legs and slid inside and collapsed on top of me. "Damn, baby! I forgot how good it felt to be inside you."

"So did I." I tried not to think about the fact I had been screwing someone else for two months. But no more. My relationship with Kenyon was officially over now that I had my husband back in my life.

Donovan rose and started stroking, deep and low. I wrapped my legs around his waist and rocked my hips with him. He and I had a special rhythm only we knew. We moved together slow and fast. He'd stop now and then to suckle my breasts.

"Roll over," he commanded.

I assumed the position for doggy style, my favorite. Donovan knew exactly how to hit me just right. My breasts were swinging and his balls were slapping against my butt as I drove back harder and harder to meet his strokes. He hit my G-spot, and it wasn't long before I was coming. "Oooh, baby . . . oooh-weee . . . that's it! That's my spot!" I screamed.

"Yeahhh . . . I'm about to come!" He moaned, then

howled long and hard as he came with a force that sent me lying flat on my stomach. Finishing, he drove home with three final pumps, then collapsed on top of me.

We lay there quietly together. I was so happy that tears were running down my face. Everything was going to be all right between us. I could feel it. Closing my eyes, I snuggled deeper, loving the way it felt lying against my husband once again.

In my purse, from across the room I could hear my cell phone ringing. It was Chris Brown's "Kiss Kiss," Kenyon's special ring tone. Why the hell was he calling me?

Donovan rolled on his side. I opened my eyes and smiled up at him. He kissed my lips. "I love you, Nikki. I'm willing to do whatever it takes to fix our marriage."

"So am I, sweetheart."

His expression then got serious. "If there is anything you need to tell me, now is the time."

I dropped my eyes to the bed. He was giving me the opportunity to tell him if I had been messing around on him. I knew from years of experience if a man said tell him the truth, he was lying.

"Donovan, I don't have anything to tell you except I'm willing to put everything into fixing our marriage."

I noticed his shoulders sag with relief before he kissed me again. "So am I, baby. So am I." Donovan gathered me in his arms, and I rested my head on his chest while he drifted off to sleep. I started to do the same when I heard the house phone.

I rolled over and picked up the cordless phone. The caller ID said PRIVATE. "Hello?" I spoke softly so I wouldn't disturb Donovan.

"Baby?"

I shot out of the bed. It was Kenyon. I moved out the room and down the hall. "Why the hell are you calling me?" I whispered, which wasn't easy to do considering the fool had the balls to call my house when he knew damn well my husband was home.

"Baby, before you get mad, listen to me. I-I just realized I left my underwear hanging on the back of the bathroom door."

"What?"

From the living room, I could hear Donovan moving around. Oh, my goodness! He was heading to the bathroom.

"Baby, I love you. I wouldn't do anything on purpose—"

I hung up and hurried down the hall and into our bedroom. I could hear Donovan peeing. I knocked once on the door, then stepped inside and found him standing over the toilet. Thank goodness his back was to the door, because if he had been sitting, Donovan would have been looking directly at Kenyon's white boxers. He glanced briefly over his shoulder, then focused his attention on not peeing all over the toilet seat.

"Sorry, dear, I need my robe." I snatched the underwear along with my blue robe that was hanging on the back of the door so quickly, I practically ripped off a nail. "Ouch!"

"You okay?" Donovan started to come over toward me.

"No, no! I'm fine . . . really." I ignored the pain and scrambled out the bathroom and into my room, where I stuffed Kenyon's underwear in the back of my lingerie drawer. Damn, that was close!

Taking a seat on the bed, I stared down at my hand and saw that the nail on my index finger had been ripped all the way to the meat. Kenyon was going to get a piece of my mind. Part of me wondered if maybe he had done that shit on purpose.

26

Trinette

I don't know why I had even agreed to go to Travis's house when I knew it was a mistake.

I drove over to Dellwood into the South Creek subdivision. The houses were mostly small, three-bedroom homes. Some of the houses looked well kept, but the majority had seen better days. The only whites still in the neighborhood were too old to move somewhere else. I turned onto Nashua Drive and stopped in front of a dingy white house with black trim. My brother Travis and his wife bought their first home six months ago and were excited about having guests over. I wished I could share in their excitement, but unfortunately it was going to take everything I had just to be in the same room as Mama.

I climbed out my car, taking extra care not to get dirt on the mink coat Michael bought me last week. Underneath, I had on a slamming black Antonio Melani pantsuit with smoking winter white snakeskin boots. Trust and believe, Mama was going to know I could hold my head up high and proud. I'd come a long way from being her live-in babysitter and Uncle Sonny's victim. Kim must have been watching for my car, because I had barely stepped onto her porch when the door swung open.

"Hey, Netta! I'm glad you made it." She gave me a warm smile that said she meant every word. I tried to smile but it was hard, considering who was waiting on the other side.

Darlene.

It was amazing, but for the first time in years, I could say Mama looked good. She wasn't the curvaceous beauty who, back in the day, turned the heads of men and women like I'm doing these days, but she was still pretty just the same. All traces of her crackhead days were gone. But as I always said—once a crackhead always a crackhead.

"Hello, Netta," she said, voice soft with a nervous edge. I don't know what she had to worry about. Well, maybe she was scared I might pull Leon's gun out on her again.

Ignoring Mama, I turned to Kim. "You need any help?"

She shook her head of short, sassy curls. "Nah, girl, yo mama already done did every thang."

I pursed my lips. Feeling uncomfortable standing in the same room with Darlene, I moved into the living room with my brothers and had a seat next to Cornbread. "What y'all watching?"

"Lakers and Celtics are playing." He brought a beer to his lips.

"When you gonna do something to your head?" I asked, reaching up and tugging on his hair.

"Damn, girl. Quit!" He leaned out of my reach.

"You need to let me hook you up." Back in the day I was the hair braider and the barbershop because there was no way we could afford haircuts let alone a relaxer for me. That's why I used to spend hours in the morning learning how to do my own hair. For a long time, I had dreamed of becoming a beautician, but later decided I wanted a more meaningful career that took me away from the ghetto. The joke's on me, because at my job the majority of my clients are ghetto. At least if I was doing hair I would be earning tips for my service.

"Take your coat off and stay awhile," Koolaid said, and gave me a look that said don't even think about leaving.

I rolled my eyes. "This coat is real. I'm not about to leave it lying around so one of y'all knuckleheads can spill beer on it."

"That a nice coat, Netta," Mama said, appearing in the doorway.

Again, I ignored her and focused on the game. I didn't have the slightest idea what was going on, because my mind was on the only other woman in the room.

Mama moved over beside Travis and took a seat. Out the corner of my eye, I could see her staring right at me. Feeling increasingly uncomfortable, I released a long exaggerated sigh, then rose and moved into the kitchen with Kim, who was pulling a pie out the oven.

"Netta, I spilled iced tea all over me. Can you watch that pot of greens for me while I go change?"

The front of her shirt was definitely wet. "Sure." I

moved over to the sink and cussed under my breath when I found the floor sticky. "Damn." I walked over to her laundry room and found a mop, then wet it in the sink and was mopping up the iced tea when Mama walked into the kitchen.

"Are you gonna just ignore me all evening?" she asked.

I stopped mopping and looked up at her. Fear brimmed her brown eyes and the corners of her mouth. "Yep, that's my plan."

"I-I was hoping we would have a chance to talk." Her voice was so calm, it left me on edge.

"What in the world could we possibly have to talk about?" I asked with a hand propped to my hip.

Mama tossed her hands in the air. "Me, you, the mistakes I made and what I need to do to make things right again between me and my daughter." She tried to smile. "That would be a good place to start."

I sucked my teeth. "Ohhhkay, let's see . . . you were strung out on crack. You paid bills by lying on your back, and I was left to raise my brothers. Your choices robbed me of a normal childhood. So, no, there isn't anything you can say that will make up for all the things you put me through."

She had the nerve to step into the room. "You may not believe it, but I did what I could to make sure there was food on the table and clothes on your back."

"Was that before or after your crack fix?"

Mama flinched as if I had struck her. "I was *sick,* Netta. I didn't know what I was doing. I was so depressed trying to do the best I could to provide for my five kids, and I found crack as my comfort."

I laughed even though there was nothing funny. "I guess now I'm supposed to forgive you, right?"

Shaking her head, she replied, "No. I know you probably won't ever forgive me."

"Ain't no *probably* about it. You ruined my childhood. I never had a chance to be a child because of you. Instead, I had to raise my brothers." And deal with Uncle Sonny climbing in my bed.

"I'm sorry, Netta. If I could give you those years back I would, but I can't. All I can do is try to be a better person and stay clean. Drug addiction is a disease, and every day I am fighting for my life. I'm paying for it now. If I don't get a kidney soon, then I'll be dead. Will that make you happy?"

"Maybe. I've hated you for over fifteen years. Do you really think I'm gonna change after all this time?"

There was no disguising the pain in her voice when she spoke. "I could only hope you would."

"It ain't never gonna happen." I moved into the laundry room and rinsed out the mop. Don't you know she had the nerve to follow me? "What do you want?" I asked, glancing out the corner of my eye.

"We need to have this out. I'm tired of feeling guilty for the life I once lived. Your brothers have forgiven me. Why can't you?"

Something boiled up inside of me, and I couldn't hold the pain in a second longer. I dropped the mop and swung around so fast, Mama stepped back. "You wanna know why I can't forgive you? Because you didn't believe me!"

She gave me a puzzled look. "What are you talking about?"

"When I told you Uncle Sonny was raping me, you didn't believe me."

She stood there, lip quivering with stunned reaction. "I . . . I didn't know."

"Why you wanna lie! I came to you and told you he was climbing in my bed at night and you refused to listen. You slapped me!" I would never forget that day, because it was the only time my mama had ever put her hands on me.

Travis rushed into the room. "Is everything okay?"

I gave him a smug look. "Sure, I reminded Mama what Uncle Sonny had been doing to me all them years."

Travis just stood there and said nothing, but the shame was apparent in his eyes.

Tears streamed down Mama's face. She looked sadder than I'd ever seen her. "I didn't know. I . . . I was strung out on that stuff, and maybe you told me . . . but I swear to you, I don't remember you ever telling me."

I moved all up in her face, being belligerent and shit. "Don't lie to me. You knew and you didn't believe me! You said I was lying."

Travis walked over and pulled me back away from her. "Netta, you need to calm down," he warned.

"You need to stay outta it. She wanted to know why I hate her . . . well, now she knows." I shrugged loose from his grip and stormed out the room.

"Netta, baby, please believe me . . . I didn't know!" Darlene kept calling my name, but I wasn't stopping until I was out that house. Quickly, I moved through the living room where the others were sitting, watching the game.

"I'm outta here!" I pushed past Koolaid, who tried to block my way. I pushed him so hard I don't think he even realized my strength. Slamming the door behind me, I hurried to my car before the first tear fell, then wiped my eyes and started the engine. There was no way in hell I was going to cry over that woman. There was no way I was going to think about forgiving her.

I reached for my phone and dialed Smooth's phone number and asked him to meet me at the Hilton. He agreed. I arrived at the hotel in no time. The man behind the desk knew me by now, and before I even opened my mouth, he was handing me a key. I showered and was under the covers when Smooth finally arrived. I hoped he took his little pill the minute he had gotten off the phone with me because I didn't have time to sit around and wait for Levitra to get on her j-o-b.

"I had to come up with a good one to get outta the house tonight," he explained the second he stepped into the room.

I rose from the bed and sashayed over to him wearing nothing but what the good Lord gave me. "Obviously you wanted to see me, otherwise you wouldn't be here." I removed his shirt and unbuckled his pants.

"You must want some of this—"

"Shhh! No talking." Some men just don't know when to shut up.

It didn't take me but a few seconds to completely undress him. Thank goodness he was already hard. I retrieved a condom from my purse and rode him like a horse. For a few moments, I just needed to forget about my jacked-up life and think about how far I have come. And how men like him had made it all possible. When I was done, I rolled over and closed my eyes, hoping when I woke up, the pain would be gone.

At some point I must have dozed off. The next thing I knew, Smooth slapped me across my ass, startling the mess out of me. "Damn, girl! You definitely give a man his money's worth." He rose, reached into his wallet, tossed several hundreds on the bed and headed into the bathroom.

I lay there for the longest time staring over at that money, and for the first time, I had a sick feeling inside. I felt cheap and used. What I was doing was no better than what my mother did for all those years. In fact, it was worse. Mama did it to put food on the table for her children. I was sleeping with men for my own selfish needs.

Smooth came out the bathroom, fastening his pants. "That was so good, I'm tempted to stay here a little longer just so I can feel those juicy lips of yours wrapped around my dick!" He gripped his crotch, then chuckled.

Tears stung the backs of my eyes, but I would be damned if that mothafucka saw me break down.

"Go ahead and enjoy the room. Matter of fact, why don't you stay here tonight, and if I can get away long enough, I'll be back."

Leaning forward, I scooped the money in a big pile and started counting out the bills. "Nah, I got things to do, but thanks for the offer."

He looked a little disappointed. Too damn bad. He already managed to make me feel like a two-dollar ho.

"I'll call you," he said just as his cell phone rang. Smooth hurried out the room and waited until he was in the hall before he answered it.

Eight hundred dollars.

That was what an hour of my time was worth. I had the money to hit the mall and buy myself that Prada bag I was dying to have. But shopping just didn't feel as exciting as it used to. Before, messing around was fun and challenging. It was all about me showing who really had the power. Pussy, that's who. But when it was all said and done I went back home to my life as Mrs. Leon Montgomery. That was something no one could take away from me. At least that's what I thought. Now I had nothing but a wet ass and a deep feeling of emptiness, the same way I felt all those years when Uncle Sonny was crawling between my thighs.

Last year, he died of cirrhosis of the liver. When I heard Uncle Sonny was sick, I had made it my business to go to the hospital to finally give him a piece of my mind and spit on his ass. I had hoped to feel a sense of satisfaction to find him lying there only hours away from joining the devil. Instead, I'd walked in the room and had gasped at what I saw. Uncle Sonny had been so thin, he looked as if the life had been sucked out of him. There were tubes everywhere. I had moved up beside the bed, and he had opened up his eyelids, staring up at me. Tears had flooded his eyes, and he had whispered, "I'm sorry." Shaking my head, I had run from the room and out to my car. Later, Koolaid had called to tell me Uncle Sonny had passed away only minutes after I had left.

I put the money Smooth gave me in my wallet and tried to smile. *At least now I'm getting something other than a sore coochie.*

I showered and got dressed, feeling worse than when I had arrived. When I reached my car, I gasped when I saw SKANK written in red lipstick across my windshield.

27

Nikki

Kenyon was on his way over. I had barely been in the house five minutes, and the instant I hit the bedroom, my phone rang. It was as if he had a camera and knew the exact second I stepped through the door. I glanced around the room, then shook my head. I was being ridiculous. There weren't any cameras around here.

I kept trying to go over everything that had happened over the weekend. I was so happy, my heart was racing. I was going to save my marriage, but to do so I needed to end my relationship with Kenyon. I wasn't at all looking forward to breaking his heart. He cared about me. I cared about him. I almost thought myself in love with him and would have probably stayed with Kenyon if Donovan and I hadn't decided to make our marriage work. I knew deep in my heart I wanted that more than anything. I loved Donovan, and we had too many years to simply just walk away. He was working at the shop that evening, which gave me the perfect chance to talk to Kenyon.

I heard a car pull into my driveway. I moved nervously to the door just as Kenyon knocked once, then stepped inside.

"Hi." He had a wide grin on his face, and damn did he look good. I tore my eyes from him and focused on Rudy, who came racing into the house and jumped onto me. "Hey, handsome, you ready to come in already?" I cooed as he bounced around the room.

"Can I get some love too?" Kenyon moved up beside me, lowered his head and kissed me passionately on the mouth. I returned the kiss, then pulled back feeling guilty. While Rudy raced off to find his toys, Kenyon and I took a seat on the couch. He draped an arm around me, but I moved to the other end of the couch.

"We need to talk."

I saw the uncertainty in his eyes. Kenyon was such a good man. He didn't deserve to be caught up in the middle of my mess. "What's wrong?" he asked.

I rose from the couch, needing a little space between us while I gathered my thoughts. "Donovan and I talked. We really, really talked, and we're gonna try to work our marriage out."

Kenyon sat there for the longest time, saying nothing, even though I saw the muscle at his jaw twitch.

"I'm really sorry." I didn't know what else to say.

Shaking his head, he finally said, "I can't believe this. I thought the weekend was supposed to be about finding closure."

"Kenyon, it was, but when I saw him, I realized I still have feelings for my husband."

"You have feelings for me!"

"I do . . . but not the same feelings I . . . I have for him."

"Baby, we're good together." He was pleading with his eyes.

Lowering my eyelids, I shook my head. "It doesn't matter how good we are together. I need to do this. If I don't, I'm always gonna wonder what if. Please understand."

Kenyon was quiet for a long time. "Okay, I understand. You need to see, otherwise, you'll always wonder. I'm okay with that as long as I'm still in your life. If I have to be second for a while, then I can deal with that."

Oh, God. Did he really think I was going to keep him on the side? "Kenyon, there can't be any *us,* because if there is I'm not giving my marriage a real try."

He leaned back and pouted, crossing his arms at his chest. "So you're saying we can't see each other anymore?"

What part of that did he not understand? Rising from the couch, I shook my head. "Kenyon, I can't be emotionally involved with two men."

He rose and moved over and stood in front of me. I inhaled and wasn't sure what I was going to miss most. His smile or his smell.

"I love you," he said.

"And I love you, but I love my husband more. Please understand."

Completely ignoring what I said, Kenyon lowered his head and brought his lips to mine, and we started kissing. I loved the way he made me feel, but I owed it to Donovan to give our marriage a serious try.

"You know he can't make you feel as good as I can," he whispered against my lips, and ground his hips against mine for emphasis. "Let me make love to you."

Oh, how easy it would have been to have let him carry me off to my bedroom and make love to me, but I couldn't have done that no matter how wet he was making my panties. I pushed him away. "Kenyon, I can't."

He stood there shaking his head as if I was making the biggest mistake, and part of me felt I was. What if things didn't work out this time with me and Donovan?

"I thought your husband was just home for ten days?"

"He is. Donovan doesn't officially get back in the states until June."

A lightbulb must have went off in his head, because Kenyon's lips curled upward into this weird smile. "You know what? I'm not going nowhere. Wait! Let me finish. What I'm saying is . . . I'll be right here when you're ready. Think about it, Nikki. Until your husband gets home you'll need someone to come over and handle his business, and when you do, you let me know." He turned on his heel and headed toward the door. Rudy came running after him and jumped on his leg. Kenyon stopped, turned and looked at me for the longest time, and my skin began to crawl.

"See, even Rudy knows who daddy is." He gave me a silly grin. "Call me tonight after you get under the covers."

I stood there long after he had gone out the door.

28

Trinette

"Trinette, I think Donovan and I are getting back together." Joy bubbled in her voice and shone in her eyes.

"That's good."

Nikki smiled. "I know. We finally realized after all these years we have a serious communication problem in our marriage. We've talked, but we've never *really* talked about us, and then when Mimi died . . . we just totally shut down. But I think we've finally got it figured out," she said while eating homemade chips and salsa.

I know I should have been happy for my girl, but it was hard when my own life was in shambles. But it's always been like that, Nikki having all the fucking luck. For some reason things just come naturally for her. She had a man first. She got her degree. She started her own business. Things just happened for her

while my ass had to scuffle and scrape to get ahead.
That's part of the reason why I act the way I do. When
it comes to men, Nikki knew who she wanted and got
him, and Donovan stood by her no matter what. The
situation with their marriage falling apart was sad, especially for me because I've known the two of them
most of my life and they are my family. Knowing they
were getting back together, I felt happy and jealous as
hell. Why couldn't shit happen like that for me and
Leon?

"What about Kenyon?" I asked after our waitress
arrived with our margaritas.

Her smile dropped. In all her happiness, she forgot all about that needy mothafucka she'd been screwing.

"Trinette, I told Kenyon it was over and I was
gonna save my marriage, but I really think that at the
back of his mind he's hoping he'll be able to convince
me to keep messing around with him."

"Can he?" The selfish side of me wanted things between her and Donovan to not be as perfect as it
seemed.

Nikki shook her head. "No way. I like Kenyon."
She gave me a painful look. "I even told him I loved
him."

"Love him? Do you?"

She looked me straight in the eyes and didn't blink.
"I love him, but I'm not in love with him." Leaning forward, she rested her elbows on the table and continued.
"Kenyon's a good man with a good heart, but he's not
strong enough for me. I need someone with a lot more
confidence than he has."

I couldn't help but laugh. "I told you his ass was

needy. That's why my girl Brittany wouldn't date his ass. She said just by talking to him over the phone, she was turned off, plus he used to blow up her phone."

Nikki blew out a heavy breath. "He does the same thing with me. And I can't understand why he's acting so desperate. He's a good-looking man with a good job with a lot going for him, but all he wants is to be with me."

"Girl, 'cause he's crazy! Crazy men don't know what the word *no* means. He wants you, and nothing is gonna change that except him finding another woman to fill your shoes. Until then you're stuck with his ass."

She gave me a worried look. "When Donovan gets home I can't have Kenyon still hanging around."

I shrugged as if it was no big deal. "Then let Donovan handle him."

She was quiet. "You know how jealous Donovan is. I didn't dare tell him I had been involved with someone."

Oooh, this was definitely getting good. All I needed was a bowl of popcorn. "What? Ms. Goody Two-Shoes wasn't honest? I can't believe that. Usually guilt gets the best of you."

"I know, and I feel terrible lying to my husband but I don't want him to think about that while he's all the way in Iraq. If I have to, I'll tell him later."

"If Kenyon has his way, he's gonna tell him."

"That's what I'm afraid of. Although deep down I really don't believe he would tell."

"Girl, I couldn't put anything past a psycho." I couldn't believe she was taking up for his crazy ass.

"The reason why I say that is because if he tells my

husband, he knows he won't have any chance of being with me."

"Yeah, but with your husband outta the way, he has a chance of wearing you down and finding his way back in your life. He's too scared of losing you. Girl, this is like an episode of *Truth Hurts*."

She gave a strangled laugh. "Right!"

"Damn . . . what *real* man acts like that? Doesn't he know begging and acting needy is a turnoff?"

Nikki gave me a defeated look. "I told him, but it doesn't seem to do any good."

I took a sip before I spoke. "What you need to do is go ahead and put an ex parte on his crazy ass."

She shook her head. "I don't think it's that serious. I'm sure I'll work everything out pretty soon."

"Well, you better figure it out, because Donovan is gonna be home in three months and you know good and damn well he don't believe in sharing."

"I know. We're flying to Vegas for a little quality time together before he goes back over."

"That's nice."

"I've already asked Annette to cover for me at the station, and I'll get Karen to run the store. I'm hoping with me gone for four days Kenyon will start to realize it's really over between us."

"Let's hope so, but I'm not putting too much into that idea. Men like him don't know what *it's over* means. This is one time when you can't be nice." I reached for a chip and dipped it in salsa.

"Is that a new bracelet?" Nikki asked.

I smiled and held out my wrist so she could take a closer look at the diamonds and rubies. "Yep. Michael gave it to me."

Nikki pursed her lips to prevent from saying what she really wanted to say. "Have you heard from Leon?"

"Nope." I tried to act like it didn't bother me he hadn't called, but it hurt. I still couldn't get that morning out of my head. His walking out on me still hurt.

She gave me a sympathetic look. The last thing I wanted was her sympathy. "I thought he would have at least called you by now."

"So did I." I brought the napkin to my mouth. "But I guess he's occupied." I knew I sounded bitter. My husband spoiled me for years, and just the thought of him doing all the things he's done for some other woman bothered me.

"Have you thought about at least calling him?" Nikki asked between sips.

I rolled my eyes and looked at my best friend as if she lost her mind. "You know me better than that."

She took a moment, and I could tell she was choosing her words carefully. "Trinette, I don't know how to say this except to say you need to start looking at yourself."

"What's that supposed to mean?"

"It means you've taken Leon for granted for years. Nothing he did was ever good enough. The man made sacrifices and tried for years to do things your way, but at some point you have to be willing to give up something as well or the marriage will never work."

"For years I had things taken from me. So now I'm not willing to give up shit."

Nikki gave me a sad look. She knew what I was talking about. There was no need for me to spell it out.

"Trinette, you can't let the past dictate the future. I

made that mistake with Donovan and I almost lost him. I know your husband loves you. Regardless if he's found someone else, the two of you have too many years together, and I am ninety-five percent certain he would give you another chance if you asked him."

"That five percent is the reason why I'm not willing to put myself out there."

"You need to finally be honest with your husband. Tell him how you feel. Share with him your past so together you can have a future."

My cell phone rang, and I was glad. Nikki was crazy if she thought I was about to have my husband all in my business and feeling sorry for me. The last thing I wanted was for him or any man to think Ms. Netta is weak.

"Hello."

"Hey, sexy. I need to see you."

I could tell by the desperation in his voice that *seeing* me was the last thing on his mind. He was more interested in having a piece of me. But for the first time, the thought of spending the evening with my legs up in the air made me sick to my stomach. Unfortunately, I was on a mission. "I've got a busy schedule today and time is money," I heard myself say.

"Whatever you need, I got you."

I knew he would agree. "I'll meet you in an hour at the condo." I put my phone down, reached for my drink and took a sip.

"Who was that?"

Damn, she was nosy. "That was Michael."

She tsked me. "Don't you ever feel guilty messing around with someone else's husband?"

Oh, no, she wasn't trying to go there with me. "Some ho in Richmond didn't feel guilty messing around with mine! I figure if she was doing her job then there would be no need for women like me."

"I guess that's what happened with you and Leon. . . . You weren't doing your job." Nikki rolled her eyes, then took a sip of her drink.

I sipped my margarita and stared at her through lowered lids. "Puhleeze, I could get Leon back tomorrow if I wanted him."

"Prove it."

I pointed a French manicured nail in her direction. "I'm not one of your listeners on the radio, so quit trying to analyze me. What you need to be doing is worrying about your own marriage and getting rid of that psycho before he fucks up everything." I reached inside my purse and tossed a twenty on the table. "Look . . . I gotta date. I'll holla at you when you get back." I turned and walked to the ladies' room before she had a chance to comment. Some days Nikki pissed me off. How dare she judge my actions? My husband left me and yet she wants me to beg his ass to take me back. Nikki had known me long enough to know I don't beg nobody.

I moved into the stall and pulled out a vaginal wipe I always kept in my purse for just such emergencies. I needed to make sure I was fresh. On the way out, I checked my face and reapplied my lipstick, then forced a smile. It wasn't at all how I was feeling, but I was going to be a few hundred dollars richer by the end of the evening, and that was enough to make any sistah smile.

As I moved through the restaurant I noticed someone at the bar staring at me. Ugh! Cory's big-headed
ass. He waved, but I rolled my eyes and headed out the
door. The last thing I wanted to do was to make him
think I was still interested. The only thing that had my
attention was money.

29

Trinette

"Trinette?"

I didn't recognize the voice. "Who is this?"

"This is Kenyon," he said with a chuckle that made my skin crawl.

"Kenyon?" What the hell was he doing calling me? "Whassup?"

"Trinette, can you please tell Nikki I need to talk to her?"

I looked down at the clock on my desk. It was barely nine o'clock in the morning. "About what?"

"None of your business!" he yelled into the phone. Then he apologized and started stuttering before I could cuss his ass out. "I-I'm sorry for yelling. I-I just need to talk to her. . . . It's important."

"Well, I'm sorry. She and her *husband* are outta town, spending some time alone."

"Do you know where she went?" It was sad how pitiful he sounded.

"Nope. And if I did I wouldn't tell you. Nikki's *married,* Kenyon, and you need to get that in your head. She's *m-a-r-r-i-e-d.*"

"Trinette, I know that she's *married,* but my baby and I are good for each other and you know we are. Don't you? Don't you know we're good together?" He sounded desperate for me to agree with him.

"She's happier with her husband." Crazy fool. "I thought you went to church every Sunday."

"I do."

"Then you know all about the Ten Commandments and wanting your neighbor's wife, or however it goes." Hell, my ass has been sinning for years.

"I don't care what anyone says, I know the Lord put us together. I just know it."

Okay, this mothafucka had not only flown over but had the nerve to land on the damn cuckoo's nest. I hung up on his ass. Nikki can listen to that shit, because I was not. What I am going to do is have a long talk with Jay about his boy, because something definitely was wrong with him.

"Trinette, you're wanted in the conference room," Claudette called from the front desk.

Oh, shit! This is it! I got all excited and rushed into the ladies' room to freshen up. Last week I had interviewed in front of a board of five for Yolanda's position. I answered every question that came my way with confidence and sophistication. Those members were impressed with my knowledge and dedication to the organization. I can be ghetto, but trust and believe, Ms.

Netta knows when to turn that shit off and play the game, and last week I played it well.

While I powdered myself I thought about the chances of my being offered the director's position. One hundred percent. At the end of the interview I was told it was going to be at least six weeks before they made a decision, and possibly a second interview, but apparently they knew a good thing when they saw it. I freshened my lipstick and tried to think of my acceptance. The best way would be to act as if I had no idea when I knew all along that job was mine.

With my purse under my arm, I sashayed to the conference room, knocked once, put on a smile and entered. The second I stepped in, I stopped when I saw who was sitting at the table with Yolanda. There weren't any board members. The only other person in the room was Cimon.

Yolanda signaled me over to the table. "Trinette, come on in and take a seat."

Cimon rolled her eyes at me. I gave her my infamous smirk that dripped with confidence about who I am and what I do as I took a seat.

"Cimon came in to see me about you suspending her case, and since you're her case manager, I felt it was only fair you sat in on the meeting."

"I agree." That bitch thought she was going to be able to go behind my back and dog me.

Rolling her eyes, Cimon replied, "Well, like I told her, I can't feed my kids without my stamps."

Yolanda glanced briefly at her file as she spoke. "Yes, I understand, but there are a few flags in your file."

"What kinda flags?"

No, this bitch ain't sitting here acting like she had

no idea what we've been talking about. Uh-uh, she wasn't about to make me look bad. "As I told you, *Cimon,* I needed to see proof of income to cover your car note."

"My daddy pays it," she replied with a smirk I was tempted to slap from her face.

"And that's fine. We just need to know that." Yolanda hand wrote a couple of notes in her case file. "Please understand, we're not here to point the finger. We provide a service. Getting benefits is not a privilege."

"Nor is it a way of life," I added, making sure that hood rat knew my director had my back. "That's why we have programs in place for job training, which so far you don't seem the least bit interested in."

She pouted her lips with attitude. "Am I gonna get my food stamps or what?"

Yolanda nodded. "I'll reinstate you for three months."

Cimon turned and gave me a smug look. "I would also like a new worker."

Yolanda's eyes traveled nervously from Cimon to me and back to Cimon. "Everyone has a heavy caseload."

Cimon sucked her teeth. "I think working with her is a conflict of my interest."

"Why's that?" Yolanda's brow rose.

" 'Cause she's screwing my daddy."

It took everything I had to keep a straight face. How in the hell had she found that out? Yolanda looked confused and at a loss for words. So I decided to help her out. "Sleeping with your daddy? I have no idea who your father is."

"Everyone knows my daddy. Simon Clark a.k.a.

Smooth." She said his name like he was a celebrity or some shit instead of a brotha with a limp dick.

"Sure, I've heard of him," I explained smoothly and shrugged like it was no big deal.

"Well, I don't want her handling my case." She blew out a long breath.

I got ready to speak, but Yolanda held up a hand, halting any further discussion. "Fine. I'll reassign you, but the same rules apply." She rose, marking the end of our meeting, and headed out the conference room. I watched that hood rat get up and I cringed. Her low-rider jeans were so low, I could see the crack of her ass. Cimon glared in my direction as she headed to the door.

"What the hell you looking at?" I asked. I might have class and style, but I'm from Englewood Park and I would go toe-to-toe with her ass.

She stopped and propped a hand at her bony waist. "You just make sure you stay away from my daddy," she warned.

"Or what?"

A sinister smile curled her lips. "Or you'll be sorry."

Rising, I sashayed over in her direction, until I was standing a few feet away. "Little girl, I don't scare that easy. So unless you want to lose your food stamps for real for real, I advise you to get outta my face."

Cowardly, she backed away, then started laughing. At least she had sense enough to turn on her heel and leave. As I watched her move down the hall, I wondered if she was the one who had left that message on my windshield.

30

Nikki

I spent a lovely week in Las Vegas with my husband, then kissed him good-bye and watched him board his plane, heading back to join his unit in Iraq. I cried most of the flight home. It had been two days and I was missing him like crazy and counting the days until his return.

To help pass the time, I buried myself in my work at the bookstore. It had been a considerably long day and I couldn't wait to get home and take a hot bubble bath and relax before Donovan called me around nine.

I pulled into the driveway, then moved up the porch and put the key in the lock. The second I opened the door, Rudy came to greet me. What in the world? He was supposed to be in the kennel. I grabbed an umbrella from the closet close to the door and carried it through the house, as I followed the smell of pork chops into the kitchen. I stepped cautiously into the room and found Kenyon standing at the stove with a spatula in his hand. As soon as he spotted me, he gave me a warm, welcoming smile.

"Hey, baby. Dinner will be ready as soon as the potatoes are done."

I looked at Kenyon as if he was crazy. "How the hell you get in here?"

"I used my key," he replied with a shrug. "When I drove by the bookstore and saw you were still there, I thought maybe you'd be getting in late and I wanted to make sure my baby had a good hot meal after a long day." He was smiling and looking like his cooking in *my* kitchen was the most natural thing in the world.

I couldn't believe this shit. "Kenyon, we're not together anymore."

"Sweetheart, listen." He paused and took a deep breath. "I know you're confused, but I'm here for you. . . . That's never gonna change. Soooo . . . why don't you run upstairs? A bubble bath is waiting for you." He walked over and had the nerve to try to kiss me. I jumped away from him.

"I want you to leave *now*!"

"No, you don't," he said, then turned and moved back to the stove. "I'm not finished cooking yet." Rudy ran over to Kenyon and jumped on his leg. "See? Rudy wants me here."

I was so mad, I could hardly speak. "I don't care what Rudy wants. I want you outta here!"

At first he looked surprised by my behavior, then Kenyon dropped the spatula and came over and put his hands on my shoulders. "Baby, why are you acting like this?"

I jerked away from his touch. "Quit calling me baby! I'm not your baby!"

Holding up his hands in surrender, he replied, "Okay, okay. I'm sorry. It's gonna take me a while to get used to calling you Nikki."

"Rudy, come over here," I called, but my dog didn't budge. "I said come here!" He still didn't move. I rolled my eyes at Kenyon. "Listen . . . I've already told you Donovan and I are saving our marriage."

He turned his nose up. "I don't know why you're wasting your time when you know it's not gonna work. You love me."

"I *love* my husband." Talking to him was like speaking to a brick wall.

Kenyon shook his head. "But you love me too."

It took everything I had to control my voice when what I wanted to do was scream at the top of my lungs. "Kenyon, I care about you, but what we had is nothing like my relationship with Donovan. We've been together most of my life. That means more to me than our two-month relationship."

He moved toward me. "Where was he when Big Mama died? Huh? I was here by your side doing everything I could to support you. You opened up your home and your family to me, and now you wanna take it all away."

I couldn't believe it. He looked as if he was seconds away from crying. What was even worse was I actually felt sorry for him. "I really appreciate everything you've done for me, and I'll never forget it, but my husband will be home soon and we plan to make our marriage work."

Moving closer, he forced a weak smile. "I understand, but in the meantime until he gets back, I wanna be with you. We're good together. I don't wanna make love to any woman but you."

Why did he have to bring up sex? True, our connection was powerful and explosive, and nothing like I have experienced with any other man. But with him whining, the last thing in the world I would want was for him to touch me. "I'm not gonna ask you again to get outta my house. If I do, I'm calling the police."

"Baby, why? You know I would never do anything to hurt you. All I want is the best for you."

I propped a hand to my hip. "Then leave me alone so my husband and I can work out our marriage."

His smile was sad as he shook his head. "I can't do that, because I love you too, and I already know it isn't gonna work between the two of you. You and I talked about everything together, things you couldn't talk to him about . . . and our sex life is wonderful. We fit perfectly together and you know it."

Did he realize his begging was such a turnoff? "All I know is you better get out my house. I don't care how things were between us. That's the past. Our relationship is over." From the puzzled look on his face, I could see talking to him was a big waste of time. He was totally clueless.

"Let's just sit down and eat, and when we're done if you still want me to leave I will."

"I don't want your food!"

He flinched at the tone of my voice. "Nikki, I haven't done anything to you. I was there for you when you wanted me. I haven't tried to do anything but love you. So why do you suddenly hate me so much?"

"I don't hate you," I cried defensively.

"Then why do you act like you do? I've done nothing but love you."

I just stood there unsure what to say. He was right. I didn't have a reason to hate him. He was the victim here, and instead I was acting like I was. It never dawned on me how he was feeling. "I'm sorry. I really don't hate you, Kenyon. I hope when the dust settles we can at least be friends."

Grinning slightly, he replied, "Well . . . how about we start with you having a seat and eating? Woman, I slaved over that hot stove for you," he teased.

Kenyon looked so pitiful and the food looked so good. I released a heavy sigh, then went ahead and slipped off my jacket and took a seat at the kitchen table. My desire for a bath would have to wait until after he'd gone. As soon as I was seated, his smile returned. Probably because I let his needy ass have his way.

Kenyon reached inside my refrigerator and pulled out a bottle of wine, then reached for a corkscrew. "I bought your favorite. I was at the store and I said, 'My baby has had a hard day at work. Let me get her a bottle of wine.' "

I released a heavy sigh. I hate when he talks to himself like that. The sooner I get this over with the better. The second he filled my glass, I brought it to my lips. The way I was feeling, I'd have the rest of that bottle finished in no time.

"Baby, how was your day?"

My eyes rolled in the direction of his smiling face. "My *name* is Nikki, and my day was long and eventful like every Tuesday."

"I'm sorry to hear that." Reaching inside the cabinet over the sink, he removed two plates and stepped over to the stove. "If you want I can give you a massage after your bath."

I shut my eyes to keep from screaming. I saw why he hadn't had a woman, because who in their right mind would want him? "No, I'll be fine. After I eat I'll take a bath and relax."

"But I already ran your water," he insisted. "Go ahead and take your bath, then we can eat. I'll wait."

See . . . this is what I got for feeling sorry for him. "No! The only reason why I'm not putting you out is because you cooked. So, let's just eat."

"Okay . . . okay." He carried over the plates and took a seat across from me. I looked down at the food and had to admit it looked as good as it smelled. "I spoke to my sister Paulette today. She told me to tell you hello."

"Next time you speak to her, tell her I said hello." I hated to say it, but I was going to miss his family more than I was going to miss him.

Kenyon tried talking with his mouth full. "She planning a surprise birthday party for my oldest sister next month and she wanted to invite you."

I shot him a hard look.

"Baby, please, just think about it. You know how my family feels about you, and Paulette would like to have you there."

I shook my head. "I can't."

He stared at me for a moment before he finally spoke. "Just . . . just think about it, okay? I'm not going without you."

I took a bite of my pork chop. It was pretty good. "Why not? That's *your* family."

"But I can't show up without you. They've never been there for me like you have. I'm serious. My sister's more interested in you being there than me."

I finished eating relatively in silence while he rattled on and on about his day at the office. He was an insurance agent and a natural-born salesman. As soon as I was finished, I carried my plate over to the sink.

Kenyon sprung from his chair. "Let me have that. Go on and take your bath while I clean the kitchen," he insisted.

I shook my head. This dude just didn't know when to quit. I guess that's why he works in sales. "Don't worry about it. I appreciate you cooking."

"You know my mama raised me better than that. I believe in cleaning up my mess." He was too damn persistent.

Suddenly I felt a migraine coming on. "No, I don't want you to clean up. I just want you to go."

"Why are you treating me like this? I thought we were enjoying dinner as two friends."

I'd had more than enough. I held out my hand. "Give me my key."

He reluctantly reached inside his pocket and handed it to me. "Will you call me later?"

"Kenyon, I'm not promising you anything." Raw hurt glittered in his eyes, but there was no way in hell I was feeling sorry for him.

"Well, I'll . . . uh . . . I'll just wait and maybe I'll hear from you later."

I walked to the front door and held it open. "Goodbye, Kenyon."

He stepped out onto the porch, then turned around. "If you call and I'm in the shower, just leave a message and I'll call you right back."

I shut the door in Kenyon's face. He'd be waiting a long time for that call.

31

Trinette

"Daaayum! Who did this?"

"That's what I want to know." I just had my car towed over to Michael's dealership because I had come out at lunch to discover someone had thrown a brick through my windshield.

"Do you have any enemies?" he asked.

"What beautiful woman doesn't?" People either loved Netta or hated her. That's just the way it had always been for me.

"I'll take care of it. Don't worry about it." Michael signaled for me to follow him to his office, and as soon as the door was shut he was all over me. Hell, I know how the game is played. He take care of me. I take care of him. "Damn, I missed you," he murmured between kisses.

I rolled my eyes toward the ceiling. I just saw his ass

yesterday. He stuck his thick tongue inside my mouth and slobbered me down, but when his hand cupped my breast, I pulled away from his grasp.

"Michael, come on. This is a place of business. Anyone can walk in."

He shrugged. "No, they won't. . . . I'm the boss."

I wasn't the least bit impressed and moved out of his reach. "I need to ask a question," I said as I took a seat on a leather couch he kept in the corner of his plush office.

"Sure, baby, what's on your mind, because I definitely know what's on mine." For the first time I felt naked under his lustful gaze.

"This is serious," I snapped. That was a man for you. Always got coochie on the brain.

"Okay . . . whassup?"

Okay, now that I had his attention I wasn't sure how to start. One thing I needed to do was to choose my words carefully. "Does Maureen have access to the cars on your lot?"

"No, why?"

"Because someone has been following me. Once in an Altima and just yesterday it was a Jeep. Never the same car, but it always has dealer plates."

Michael gave me a weird look. "Why in the world would my wife be following you?"

Men can be so stupid sometimes. "Why do you think? Maybe she found out we're messing around." He started laughing as if it was the most ridiculous thing he had ever heard. All that did was piss me off more. I then went on to tell him about the slashed tires and the lipstick on my windshield.

"So, let me get this straight . . . you think my wife slashed your tires, wrote on your windshield and borrowed cars from my lot just so she can follow you around without you knowing it her?"

"People have done worse things before."

"Trinette, my wife is clueless. She knows nothing about you and me. I've told you before . . . my game is tight." Just like a man to think he's smarter than a woman. I gave him a look that said I wasn't convinced. "Serious, if Maureen knew, I would be the first person she would confront."

I crossed my legs and didn't bother to respond.

"What did you decide about the condo?" he asked, changing the subject. Apparently, he didn't like me accusing his wife of harassing me. "You want to make it our little home for the next year?"

For what? So Maureen and Chuck could use it while I'm at work? "What would Maureen say about you 'renting' the place to me?"

"She could care less about that place. It's mine. Not hers."

Yeah, like I said, he didn't know his wife as well as he thought he did. "I'll pass, but thanks for the offer."

"Just think about it, okay? Trinette, baby, you wouldn't have to want for anything."

Probably not, but I would have to be at his beck and call. Available and willing each and every time he was ready. I wasn't having any of that. "My condo is still on the market. If and when it's sold, then I will think about it."

"Sounds good to me. Now come and give your man some love."

I slowly rose from the couch and swayed my hips over to where he was standing. He captured my lips against his, then reached for the buttons of my blouse and unfastened them. "Damn, you got some pretty titties," he moaned. He unfastened the front clasps, and my breasts sprung free. While he suckled and played, I reached for his belt buckle. Michael knew how to work his magic on my nipples. They were hard, and my body was dying for what he had to offer, although I don't know why, since he wasn't working with much.

As soon as his pants were down, he reached under my skirt and ripped the tights from around my waist.

"Hey, those cost me fifty dollars!"

"I'll buy you another pair," he murmured against my neck, and slipped my panties down around my ankles. The second I kicked them away, he lay me back against his desk. "Wrap your legs around my waist."

Michael slid inside and rocked his hips against me. I looked up at the ceiling, anxious for him to get done, and for some reason my mind wandered to Leon. The last several days I wondered what he was doing. More than anything I wanted him to be happy. Why hadn't his happiness ever mattered to me before?

"I'm almost there!" Michael moaned, and then he howled long and hard, and I cried out on cue.

"Oh, yes, big daddy! That's it!"

A few short strokes and he was crying out my name and collapsed on top of me. Michael rained kisses along my neck and shoulder. "Oooh-weee . . . you got some good shit!"

I gave a weak smirk. All I wanted was for him to get up so I could clean off and go home. I opened my eyes and looked over at the window in time to see two of his sales team peering in the window, grinning.

"What the hell . . . ?" I pushed Michael off of me.

"What's wrong?" he asked as he rose.

Sitting up, I pulled my shirt closed. "Your employees are in the window watching us!"

He chuckled and reached for his pants. "So . . . let them look."

He might as well have slapped me in the face because his words stung just as hard. I pushed him aside. "I gotta go."

"Where are you going? You can't drive your car."

"Don't worry about it. I'll catch a cab."

He reached for his wallet. "I guess you can afford it."

I looked over at the window to see if the two men were still watching when Michael handed me several bills. They weren't, but just knowing they had been watching had cheapened the encounter. I couldn't even look Michael in the eyes. All I wanted was to go home. After stuffing the money in my purse, I quickly fixed my clothes.

"Baby, I should have a new windshield for you tomorrow," he reassured me with a kiss.

Nodding, I walked out his office and headed straight for the bathroom to clean myself up and repair my makeup. When I looked into the mirror, I didn't at all like what I saw.

I didn't even bother calling a cab. Instead I started walking and thinking about my life and all the mistakes I had made. Men loved me, but all they ever wanted was sex, and I gave it to them. Most of the time I didn't even know their last names. As I thought about it, it made me so sick to my stomach I barely made it to a bush before I vomited the contents of my stomach. What in the world had I done? I had taken a gamble, and in the process I had lost the best thing that had ever happened to me.

32

Nikki

I rang the doorbell again, then peeked through the window and frowned. I knew she was at home because her Mercedes was in the driveway.

I was worried about Trinette. I'd been calling her for the previous three days with no answer. Her job said she had been calling in sick. Said she had some kind of flu bug. I wasn't buying it. If Trinette was sick, she would have called me whining like a baby until I agreed to bring her spoiled ass some soup. Tristan said he spotted Trinette in the mall last weekend shopping her tail off, but as far as I knew no one else had seen her since.

"Trinette, I'm not leaving, so you might as well open this door!" I screamed and banged on the door at the same time. If she was asleep, then her ass needed to wake up. Knowing her, she probably had some man in there, but I didn't care. Dammit! A couple of years ago, she had given me a key, but for the life of me I didn't know where it was.

I knocked again and hoped she hadn't done anything stupid. As quickly as I thought about it, I pushed that ridiculous thought aside. Trinette loved herself too much to try anything stupid, but that didn't mean she wasn't thinking about it.

For the last couple of weeks, she had been trying to act like her breakup with Leon didn't bother her, but I knew better. That girl was hurting, and I don't care how much dick she tried to ride, that wasn't going to change the fact that Leon walked out on her. Trinette had this hard exterior wall she had put around her heart years ago to keep from getting hurt, but like I told her, money and sex didn't make up for what her life was missing. At some point, she was going to have to face her demon and let her guard down in order to love and be loved.

I was preparing to walk around back and break a window or something when I finally heard the lock turn. I flinched when I saw her. Trinette was standing there with her weave matted to her head.

"Damn, bitch! Quit ringing my doorbell," she barked, then turned and walked back through the house. I followed.

"If you'd answer my phone calls I wouldn't have to be ringing your damn doorbell." I followed her inside. Eeew! It was funky. It stunk like old food. I glanced around the house, which was a complete mess. Photo albums and pictures were all over the living room floor. I moved into the kitchen and discovered the smell. A package of catfish nuggets was in the sink thawed out. On touch the package was warm; there was no telling how many days it had been sitting there, stinking. I turned my nose up and went up the stairs to Trinette's bedroom. At the door, I had to take a step back. Her room was also a disaster. Clothes were everywhere. Dresser drawers sitting open. Closet doors as well.

"Girl, what's up with you? Why haven't you been answering my calls?"

Trinette climbed back in bed and curled into a fetal position, staring off in the opposite direction. "I don't want to talk to anyone."

I moved over to the side of her bed and took a seat. "Why not? What's going on with you?"

She wouldn't look at me. "I miss him."

"Who? Leon?"

Pinning me with a hard look, she spat, "Who else?"

"Shit, I don't know. You said you were seeing someone else."

Trinette looked away, and I could tell she was trying to fight tears. "I fucked up, Nikki. I really fucked up. How could I have been so stupid?"

I placed a comforting hand at her back. "Have you talked to him since you took all his money?"

She shook her head.

"Well, why don't you start with a phone call?"

"I can't call him, because if I hear the rejection in his voice, I-I'm gonna lose it." She practically choked on a sob.

It was nothing worse than seeing my best friend behaving as if she had no reason to live. Some people could handle the pressure. Unfortunately, Trinette wasn't one of them. "How about sending an e-mail and telling him how you feel?" I suggested. The sooner she talked to Leon, the sooner she would get back to her normal vain and self-centered self, because I couldn't stand the pitiful Netta.

Trinette rolled onto her back. "I don't want to put myself out there so I can be rejected."

"That's your problem. You're always worried about looking bad. You've got to let your guard down and quit trying to be so hard."

"Nikki, I don't know how to be anything other than the way I am."

"I'm not saying change who you are. Hell, for some reason Leon fell in love with your crazy ass just the way you are."

"Forget you," she mumbled.

I laughed, trying to lighten the mood a little. "Seriously, though . . . you've got to start understanding that marriage requires hard work and dedication. You've got to quit taking Leon for granted."

She blinked but didn't comment because she knew good and well I was telling the truth. "You can't think *me;* in a marriage it's *we.* Marriage is a partnership and a commitment to each other. I'm definitely not one to talk, because after Mimi was killed I gave up caring about my marriage and all I thought about was how I felt. I didn't even consider what Donovan was feeling. And because of it, we disconnected and our marriage was hanging by a thread, but I have woken up, and I know I love Donovan and there's no other man I would rather be with."

"Not even Kenyon," Trinette teased as she brushed tears from her eyes.

"*Especially* not him. Donovan is my soul mate just like Leon is yours, but I gotta be honest with you. . . ." I purposely allowed my voice to trail off.

She rolled her eyes and groaned, "Oh, Lord, what else is new?"

"Whatever. . . . I wouldn't be a real friend if I wasn't. If you're gonna make your relationship with your husband work, you've got to stop fucking around."

Trinette blew out a long breath. Hey, as I say all the time on my show, the truth hurts. She finally nodded her head and said, "I know."

"I'm serious. Are you ready to give up your other life in order to save your marriage?" I looked her dead in the eyes because I wanted to make sure she really understood what I was saying.

She started bawling again. That was not at all the reaction I was expecting. "Yes, I-I want m-m-my husband back. I-I didn't know it then, b-but I know it now." She sniffled and reached for a tissue from the nightstand. "I guess it took Leon dumping me for me to finally realize I don't want to live without him."

"Praise the Lord!" I murmured, and glanced up at the ceiling. It was definitely a miracle if Trinette was talking about realizing and not wanting to live without someone other than "me, myself and I." I leaned over and hugged my best friend. She had a traumatic childhood that she somehow allowed to dictate her life.

"I'm not gonna beg him to take me back. Part of me feels it's too late, and I can't blame anyone but myself for that. But I would like for him to know how I feel."

I stared down into her sad eyes and tried to reassure her. "You can do it."

"I don't know. . . . Where do I start?"

"Girl, you can start by doing something about your breath, 'cause you're killing me," I replied, frowning.

"Forget you." Playfully, she punched me in the leg.

I struggled to keep a straight face. "I'm serious. You

also smell as bad as your kitchen. Get your butt in the shower while I go put out your trash."

Trinette gave me a big hug. "Nikki, I don't know what I would do without you, girl."

I held my nose. "Smell like that again and you're gonna find out."

She laughed for the first time, and I smiled and left the room, heading for the kitchen.

I didn't know what to think about that girl. If she didn't get it together, she was going to lose Leon for good. Not that I was one to talk. Kenyon was still blowing up my phone and popping up at the bookstore. I was starting to wonder if he was ever going to get the hint.

33

Trinette

"I'm calling about an old credit card that was sent to collections."

"What's the account number?"

I rattled off the number I found from an old bill. I could hear her typing on a keyboard.

"Is this Trinette Montgomery?"

"Yes, it is," I replied.

"I must inform you this call may be monitored or recorded. The information I am about to discuss is in an attempt to collect a debt. Ms. Montgomery, we've been trying to reach you for almost two years since the bill turned over to us for collections."

Yeah, whatever. "How much do I owe you?" I already knew, but I wanted to hear what she had to say.

"$932."

I leaned back on the chair. "Hmmm . . . don't have

it. I don't even have a job, but I just got my taxes and want to spend it paying this bill. I'll give you half."

"Half? I'm sorry, but I only can go down thirty percent."

She was lying. I had spent all day the day before reading this enlightening book called *Debt Cures* that educated me on paying debts. Ms. Netta got up this morning, knowing exactly how to play the game of debt relief. "I *only* have half. Either you take it or I'll spend it at the mall, buying a new pair of shoes."

There was a three-second pause before she replied, "Hold on while I talk to my supervisor."

My lips curled in a smile. Her mama obviously ain't raised no fool. I held the phone and stared out my kitchen window and thought about the past few days.

The last week was hell for me. After Michael made me feel like a ho, I just shut down. No phone calls or personal appearances. I was so ashamed I didn't want anyone around me. Michael personally delivered my car to the house, but when he knocked at the door I pretended I wasn't at home, and he left the key in the mailbox.

The rest of the week, I hung out at home by myself, and I realized I didn't like the person I had become. I had everything, but in reality nothing I had was worth having. I had said to my clients so many times, "No one can change the way you're living your life but you," and that's what I was trying to do. Make over Netta into someone I was proud to be. Today, I had negotiated five debts, and it felt good. Damn good. Two more debts and I will have covered every derogatory item on my credit report. In the process, I had put a dent in the money I took from the joint account, but that didn't matter. Not anymore. It was time for me to start living on my own two feet.

"Ms. Montgomery?" The customer service representative returned to the phone. "You still on the line?"

"Yes."

"Well, I have good news! I spoke with my supervisor and she has agreed to $466 *if* you can pay that today."

I smiled. Not for a moment did I doubt they would accept my offer. "Sure . . . as long as you agree to remove this debt from my credit report as well."

"T-That shouldn't be a problem." I guess my request caught her off guard. What's the point of giving them what they want if they can't do something for me in return?

Crossing my arms, I strolled across the room as I spoke. "Wonderful. Fax me a copy of the agreement and I'll give you my bank information." I gave her the number to my personal fax and agreed to call her after I received the information.

I hung up my phone and was heading toward my office when the doorbell rang. "Who the hell could that be?" I wondered as I moved through the house. No one knew I had taken time off from work except my job and Nikki. As soon as I peeked through the peephole, I swung the door open and asked, "What do you want?"

Darlene had the nerve to be standing on my doorstep with her hands buried deep inside the pockets of a navy blue trench coat that as far as I was concerned had seen its better days. Her shoulder-length hair was pulled back in a bun that looked too severe for her thin face, not that I really cared.

"I came to talk."

Out the corner of my eye, I saw Travis's Escalade

parked in front of my neighbor's house. I rolled my eyes in Mama's direction and spat, "We don't have anything to talk about."

"Yes, we do." She then had the nerve to walk in my house and move over to the couch and take a seat. It was obvious she wasn't leaving until she had a chance to say whatever was on her mind. I thought I might as well get this shit over with.

I slammed the door shut, then moved over and stood in front of her with my arms folded against my breasts. "Okay, so talk."

Darlene unfastened the button of her coat and slipped her arms through. She was wearing a yellow short-sleeved blouse. I gasped at the sight of her arms. She's light brown like me so the purple bruising was apparent.

"What happened to you?"

She followed the direction of my gaze, then held her arms out so I could get a closer look. "Dialysis. I think they've stuck me in every place possible."

Thinking about what she went through on a weekly basis deflated some of my anger. I lowered onto the love seat across from her. "How often do you go? Once a week?"

Shaking her head, Mama gave me a sad smile. "Try three times a week."

I forced my eyes away. I didn't want to care, and the fact I was feeling sorry for her only made me madder. "What is it that you want?"

She shrugged and looked nervous again. "I want to clear the air between us and give you a gift." I hadn't noticed the book in her hand that she now held out for me to take. I stared down at it as if it were cursed.

"What's that?"

"Something I want you to have." I made no attempt to take the book. Darlene eventually gave a defeated sigh and placed it on the couch beside her.

I sat there for what felt like forever waiting for her to speak. Taking in her features, noticing the dark rings around her eyes. She looked tired . . . and weak.

"I wanted to talk to you about your father."

I leaned back against the seat, heart pounding with anticipation. Since I was a little girl, I had asked my mother about my father, but she always said he was a one-night stand whose name she couldn't remember. Even then I knew she was lying.

"I met Darren Austin when I was barely eighteen years old and he was thirty. I'll never forget the day I brought him home to meet my mama. Jean had a fit . . . cussing . . . going off. She told me to either end the relationship or get out and never set foot at her door again. Darren was my first, and I was so in love, I moved in with him. There wasn't anything I wouldn't do for that man and he knew it. Eventually he started putting his hands on me. If I refused to do what he said, he kicked my ass. I tried going home, but Mama refused to let me come back so I had no choice but to stay with Darren. He knew he had the control and no one could help me, and it wasn't long before he started pimpin' me to his friends." Mama wrung her hands nervously in her lap as she drew in a shaky breath. "Afterward, he wanted all the intimate details, then he would beat me for not resisting."

"Why didn't you just leave?"

"Where would I have gone? Times weren't like they are now. I had no money, no education and nowhere to go." Her eyes pleaded with me to understand, but I didn't. "By this time, he had already introduced me to cocaine, and I was thankful for anything to take my mind away from the pain."

I pursed my lips at the mention of her first drug of choice.

"Then one night I was gang-raped. Darren tied me down to the bed, and while three of his friends took turns on top of me, he sat in a chair smoking a cigarette and watched."

I sprung from the love seat. "I don't want to hear anymore!" This story was just too painful and reminded me too much of what I had gone through. I could feel her pain and her feelings of helplessness because I had been there as well.

"Netta, let me finish!" Mama shouted, and I froze. She hadn't raised her voice to me in a long time. "Please," she pleaded, her voice softer now. Tears pooled in her eyes, and I felt that traitorous tug at my heart. "Please just let me talk, and I promise I will never bother you again."

"Fine . . . go ahead and finish." I flopped back down on the seat.

Mama wiped her eyes. "After they left, Darren beat me so bad he fractured my ribs. He said I should have resisted. I knew at that point if I wanted to live I had to get away from him. I waited until he went to the club, and I went to Mama with one eye swollen shut and begged for her to let me in. And don't you know she slammed the door in my face." Mama gave a laugh that lacked humor and lowered her gaze to the floor. Tears dampened her lap.

"I made it to the hospital, and a nurse there gave me the address to a battered women's shelter. I was still living there when I found out I was pregnant with you."

I closed my eyes, trying not to think about the fact

that my father could have been Darren or any of the men who had raped her. No wonder my life was so fucked up.

"I was determined to get my life together. The shelter helped me get a job and a place to live, and when you were born it didn't matter to me who your daddy was. One thing for sure, y-you were my b-baby." Her voice cracked. Tears burned at the back of my eyes, but I willed them away. "You were four when I started dating Travis's father. All I had ever wanted for you was a family. I thought Trey loved me, but I found out he was married. After that I started looking for love wherever I could find it, but it was always the same thing, men taking and tossing me aside when I was all used up. Before long I had five kids and no man and a job that barely put food on the table. I started working nights and leaving y'all at home alone. You were eleven at the time and responsible enough to take care of your brothers if they needed something. Someone must have hotlined me, because I came home to find all of you gone. Social services had taken y'all away!" She sniffled. "I was willing to do whatever I had to do to keep my kids together. I worked during the day as a cashier and turned tricks at night to hire a lawyer to get y'all back. There was no way I was turning my back on my kids like my mama did."

I couldn't stay quiet any longer. "But you did turn your back. You left me with Uncle Sonny!"

She pressed her palms together and closed her eyes like she had taken a moment to pray. "Netta . . . I'm so sorry about that. Back then I had no idea, I swear to you." She dropped her eyes. "I didn't find out until later."

I was confused. "Later?"

Mama nodded and looked at me. "When I lost my job, I let my brother move in with us. By then I had gotten turned on to crack, and before long that was the only way I could get the pain to go away. I was sick, Netta. I know that's hard for you to believe, but I didn't know what I was doing from one day to the next. All I wanted was that good feeling. Sonny paid the bills and supported my drug habit." She placed a shaky hand to her head and smoothed it across her hair. "I saw you in the hospital that day you came to see Sonny. I was standing on the other side of the door. You never did care for him, so I was surprised to see you run outta his room crying. After you left, I went in Sonny's room and demanded he tell me what happened. That's when he broke down and confessed everything. I was so angry, I reached for a pillow . . . and smothered him with it."

"What?" My eyes snapped to hers, and I knew she was telling me the truth.

Mama stared at the ceiling and looked as if she was trying to find the right words. "I blamed myself for what happened to you, and if I couldn't do anything else I wanted to make sure he experienced what it felt like to be helpless."

Sitting across from her, I couldn't find the words to bridge the silence between us. There wasn't anything I could say. My mother had killed my uncle.

She sniffled. "All I had ever wanted to do was to protect my children and keep them together. Instead, I failed all of you." With a sigh, Mama put back on her coat, then rose from the couch. I got up as well. "Thank you for listening. I felt it was time you knew." She reached out and touched my arm, and something inside of me cracked. Before Mama could turn away from me, I reached for her and wrapped my arms around her waist. Mama grabbed hold of me and the two of us held each other and cried.

"Thank you," I said.

She looked up into my eyes. "A mother is supposed to protect her own. I'm just sorry it took me so long." Her smile was sad as she released me and walked out the door.

34

Nikki

"Hey, Nikki, Kenyon called. He said, 'Tell her I love her, and I always will.' " Trinette did a good job of sounding like him and then started laughing hysterically over the phone. I was glad she was at least back to work and in a good mood.

I groaned. "He is soooo sad."

Trinette was right. Kenyon was nuts, or maybe a better way of describing it was by saying the dude was obsessed. The crazy dude was calling my phone every hour on the hour and had the nerve to leave a message with every call. I eventually had to turn my cell phone off, but all that did was make him start calling my house. I had to contact the phone company about getting a new phone number. It was easy to ignore calls to my cell phone, but the house was another story all together. With Donovan coming home, the thought of Kenyon just happening to call in six months was not worth the risk. I had to make up a lie and tell Donovan I changed my number because I was getting too many hang-up calls. Since I was ignoring his calls, Kenyon started texting, and each text was more persistent than the last.

"Hey, I told you something wasn't right with that dude."

I removed several old copies of *Ebony* off the shelves and filled the rack with May's edition as I spoke. "Netta, I don't understand him. Ever since I told him it was over between us, he's been acting psycho." I couldn't even bring myself to tell Trinette how psycho he was acting, because I would never hear the end of it. "I had to change my home number."

"I don't understand it either. What man begs a woman to stay with him? That's such a turnoff! I still don't know how you were with him in the first place. Nikki, you sure know how to pick 'em." Hearing her laugh was so much better than all that crying she had done last week.

"You got some nerve. Don't forget you've dated some doozies in your day."

"True that," she admitted.

"Remember Mr. Stutter?"

"Y-Y-Yes. I used to hang up the phone long before he could get the words out."

I was cracking up. "And let's not forget Cory."

"Eeew! Girl, don't remind me. He's still calling my job, but ain't anything like *your* Kenyon."

I let out a long, aggravated sigh. "Yeah, thanks." Glancing at the door, I noticed a florist moving into the bookstore. I was anxious to find out if the beautiful bouquet in his hands was for me. "Trinette, let me get back to work. I'll holla at you later." I put the phone in my pocket and moved out into the aisle and down toward the front of the store to greet the delivery guy. "Aren't those beautiful! Please tell me those are for me."

He gave me a warm smile. "Well, if your name is Nikki Truth, they are."

"That would be me." I grinned as I took the vase filled with a dozen long-stemmed pink roses from his hands. I set it on the table, then signed my name on a clipboard and returned it to him. "Let me get you a tip."

While holding up his hands, he shook his head. "Don't worry about it. It's already been taken care of."

I watched him leave, then reached inside for the card. *I thank God for second chances. I luv u Donovan.* Damn, I had a good man, and obviously he recognized he had a fabulous woman, because he had ordered his boo flowers. Smiling, I carried the bouquet over to the counter.

"Oooh! Those are gorgeous," Karen complimented. I could see the envy in her eyes. From the way she talked, all a man seemed to bring her was heartache and pain.

"Yes, they are. Thank you. My husband bought them for me. I'm gonna leave them here on the desk for both of us to enjoy."

Nodding, she agreed. "Looking at them will definitely brighten up the day."

I looked outside and frowned. It was definitely March because it had been raining all morning. Business in the store had been slow. On mornings like this, I spent the majority of time restocking the shelves.

After taking a final sniff, I returned to the magazine section and was cracking open another box when I spotted Kenyon browsing the discount books to my left. When the hell did he get here?

Holding the box cutter in my hand, I moved over to where he was standing. "Can I help you with something?" I asked with a hand at my hip. This dude was really trying to push my buttons.

He cocked his head to the right and smiled. "Hello, Nikki. I'm in the mood for a good mystery. Got any suggestions?"

"Yeah, I suggest you get the hell outta my store!" Thank goodness no one else was there, because I hated to act ugly in public. Karen came around the counter and gave me a concerned look. I waved my hand, indicating I had everything under control.

Kenyon glanced down at the box cutter and looked nervous. "Why are you acting like I've done something to you? All I am trying to do is come in here and buy a book from a black-owned bookstore instead of giving my money to Barnes and Noble. That's it."

Blowing out a long breath I replied, "Okay, then go ahead and find something, then please leave." I swung on my heel and returned to the box of magazines and was putting them on the shelves when I felt someone standing over me. I didn't even have to look to know it was Kenyon.

His eyes were lit up with excitement. "Baby, I found something that sounds really good."

I looked past the latest James Patterson to glare at him. "How many times I gotta tell you to stop calling me baby?"

He brought a hand to his mouth. "I'm sorry. I just wanted to let you know I found something. Have a good day." Without another word, he moved to the desk, where Karen was more than happy to help him. Out behind the cabinet, I watched him smile as he spoke. The confident man had returned, and he was gorgeous standing there in black slacks and a pinstripe shirt. While I watched him I couldn't help but remember how good we had been together in bed. Even now I lay awake at night and relived him being inside of me, stroking me deep, making me come like no other man has ever been able to do, including my husband. And that's part of the reason why I needed him to stay away from me. I resented that I still thought about him, when the only man who should feel my mind is Donovan. I forced myself to turn away. Kenyon was the past, and maybe some of our time together was memorable. However, the only man I wanted in my life, lying between my thighs at night, was Donovan.

I buried myself in my work until my stomach started to growl. Glancing down at my watch, I saw that it was almost noon.

"Karen, I'm gonna run out and grab some lunch."

"Okay, I'll go when you get back."

I reached for my purse behind the counter and swung it over my shoulder. It was rare when I got a chance to go out and eat, but today I was feeling just too good. "Can you pick up some stamps while you're out?"

"Sure," Karen said, then frowned. "By the way, I . . . uh . . . been meaning to tell you this last month while I was cleaning out the desk drawers, I found a bunch a letters. I assumed your last assistant *forgot* to mail them so I stuck them in the mailbox. It wasn't until your flowers came in today and I . . . uh . . . looked at the card I realized the letters were to your husband."

I cocked my head to the side, looking up at her. "What? Wait a minute. You're telling me you found a bunch of letters in the drawer that were never mailed?"

She nodded. "At first I thought maybe you had stuck them in the drawer for me to send out, but yesterday I found an electric bill that hadn't been mailed either."

"What?" I knew why it had taken so long for Donovan to get my letters.

"I'm sorry."

"No, it's not your fault. It's that stupid chick I had working here in the office. No wonder they threatened to disconnect my electricity in November. I went down there arguing with them like a damn fool for nothing. Damn! No wonder my husband never got his letters." I was tempted to call Tiara and cuss her out. Knowing her, she probably had done that shit on purpose. She was always a little too happy when Donovan came into the office, and he said she brought her son in every week to his shop just so he would cut his hair. I was so pissed, I was halfway to my car before I realized Kenyon was leaning on the hood.

"What do you want?" I definitely was not in the mood for him.

He rose and moved toward me. "Baby, please, I just wanna talk to you."

I pressed the remote on my key, starting my car. "Talk to me about what!"

His answer was pitiful. "Why . . . why do you act like you hate me? I've never done anything to you."

"Except stalk me."

Kenyon swallowed hard. "I just . . . I just wanted to see you."

"Okay, you're seeing me, now leave me alone."

"Baby, baby, please, just hear me out," Kenyon pleaded.

"Quit calling me baby!" This man was so pathetic. Didn't he realize I didn't want to hear shit he had to say.

I must have looked like a lunatic, because he backed up a bit. "Baby, I-I mean Nikki, please . . . just listen and don't interrupt."

I rolled my eyes, crossed my arms and leaned against my Lexus. "What? I don't have all day."

"Sweetie, we fell in love," he began with a shrug. "You fell in love with me and I fell in love with you. We have something special, and that's not going to easily go away. Please, don't interrupt. I-I care about you and I can't just turn off my feelings like that."

I was quickly getting impatient. "Well, you're gonna have to."

"You're my best friend."

Oh, goodness. His lips quivered and he looked like he was about to cry. Damn! The last thing I wanted to do was to feel sorry for him. "Kenyon, listen, you're a really nice guy. Really, you are, and there is a woman out there who is gonna love you, but I already have someone to love me."

"He can never love you like I do."

"You're right. He loves me more. Now get outta my way." I pushed him aside and hopped into my car as fast as I could. I was sick of hearing all that whining. I couldn't even feel sorry for him anymore.

"Wait!" He started knocking on my glass. "Baby, please, let's just go out to lunch and talk."

"Kenyon, I don't want to go out with you! Do you know how pathetic you sound begging?"

"I'm just fighting for what I want. My sister told me I needed to start standing up for myself. Well, baby, I'm standing up. I want you and I'll take you any way I can get you."

Talking to him was a big waste of time. I'd had callers with issues, but his ass took the biggest cupcake. I put the key in the ignition, and thank goodness Kenyon had sense enough to get out of the way when he did, otherwise I would have run over his feet.

I peeled away from the lot cussing under my breath. Kenyon was pathetic. As I hit the corner, my cell phone rang and I tapped my earpiece.

"Hello?"

"Baby, please, just give me another chance."

You've got to be kidding. "Why are you calling me?"

"Baby, please . . . I miss you."

"Well, I don't miss you. You drove me crazy, smothering me all the time."

"Baby, I've never done anything but try to love you." The desperation in his voice was sickening.

"Kenyon. You need some help. You really need to go and see a therapist."

"Nikki, there's nothing wrong with me." This was so ridiculous I felt like laughing.

"There is something definitely wrong with you. You drive a woman to drink."

"Baby!" he squawked, and had the nerve to sound offended.

I gave a strangled laugh. "I'm serious. You're so damn worrisome. Stop calling me." I was really laughing.

"Okay, okay. Call me later if you wanna talk." He sounded so sad.

"Kenyon, I'm . . . not . . . calling you."

"Baby . . . just call me later."

"Uh-huh." I had no intentions of calling him, but I knew it was the only way I could get him off the phone.

He ended the call before I could. Kenyon had some serious issues far worse than I could deal with.

35

Trinette

I waited until Thursday after I got home from work, showered and changed into a white gown and robe that made me feel sexy and confident before I took a seat in front of my computer. For the longest time I just stared at a blank e-mail before I finally took a deep breath. "Just do the damn thang," I mumbled to myself.

> Dear Leon,
> I come to you with a humble heart to thank you for changing your mind about the house. Buying it would have been a ridiculous move on both our parts. Also, by saying no, you forced me to finally take a good look at my life, and I've realized you were right. How have we grown together? As painful as it is to finally admit, we haven't. Instead, all I have been doing these last eight years is ride

on your coattail. I have done nothing to stand on my own two feet. And because of it, I finally started working on fixing my credit with the money you gave me. Can you believe it? In one week I paid off every creditor I owed and disputed the debts that weren't mine. What I can't understand is why did it take me so long to do something that was so easy to fix? It just shows me that I depended on you too much and took our marriage for granted for so long, and I don't blame you for finding another woman who was more deserving of your love. It's my loss.

I also want to apologize for my behavior all these years. I don't care what you say, I loved you in my own selfish way, and I do know one thing for sure, no woman will ever love you the way I have. I know your habits and I know your behaviors. I love you and I will always love you and regret the mistakes that I made to pull us apart. I understand your reason for wanting a divorce, and you will not get any resistance from me. In fact I went to see a lawyer yesterday, and I was bawling so hard in her office she asked me to give it a week to think about it and come back. She would then file the papers for me. I just wanted to let you know I am trying to move forward with my life no matter how painful it is. I am hurting and will always regret the way I treated you. I hope in time you can forgive me. You will always hold a place in my heart. I love you, and that will never change. I wish you all the best in your future endeavors. I hope your girl knows she has a good man and appreciates you. You deserve it. Take care.

I read over the e-mail twice, then walked away from it and thought about what I had written. The last thing I wanted was to sound like I was begging him to take me back. That wasn't it. I had messed up and needed to admit my mistakes in order for me to get on in my life. But I'm not going to lie. Part of me still hoped there was a chance for the two of us.

I read it out loud one last time, added a paragraph about taking all the money and then I clicked SEND. Immediately, I felt like a weight had been lifted. With a smile I hurried into the spare room and stuck in an old Billy Blanks tape. For the first time in weeks, I felt like working out. I kicked and punched through the entire tape, then went to the bathroom and took another shower. By the time I got out of the shower, I felt so relaxed, I slipped into a velour running suit and decided to treat myself to a steak. I was slipping on my shoes when the phone rang. I moved to my nightstand and almost choked when I looked down at the caller ID. It was Leon. Oh, my God! Oh, my God! I took a deep breath and a seat on the bed, then picked up the receiver before the last ring.

"Hello?" My voice was shaking so hard I hoped he didn't notice.

"Hey," he began in that deep robust voice I missed so much. "I got your e-mail."

"Oh . . . okay. I, uh, just wanted to let you know I took the money outta the account."

There was a pause. "How come you never said those things to me before?"

I leaned back on the mattress and lowered my eyelids. "I don't know. But I had to get everything off my chest. It's the only way I'll ever find closure." I paused, trying to gather my thoughts. He didn't say anything, just waited. "I just needed to tell you I was sorry. I really needed you to know that."

"Why?"

Damn, was he really going to make me say it? "Because I was a fool. I took our marriage for granted. I stopped putting in the work. I put you and I on the back burner and was so busy focusing on what I wanted instead of what we needed that I allowed our marriage to fall apart. That was so unfair. And it might be hard for you to believe it, but I'm hurting. I didn't think our marriage ending would matter all that much to me, but it does." I slipped a pillow under my head and got comfortable. "Regardless of how selfish I had been, one thing I could always say . . . was my husband loved me. It was one thing I . . . I had always been confident about, but you dumping me on Valentine's Day is something I'll never understand."

"I didn't dump you on Valentine's Day," he denied.

"Yes, you did!" I couldn't keep the anger out of my voice. "You flew down here on Friday the thirteenth, told me you weren't buying the house, then waited till Valentine's Day to tell me it was over."

"I never said it was over. I just said I needed time to figure out what it was I wanted."

I couldn't hold back the tears from my voice. "You left me . . . on my favorite holiday to spend it with a-another woman."

"Netta, there's no other woman."

I wanted so badly to believe him, but I just couldn't

make myself do it. "I-I can't do this. This was why I haven't called."

"Why did you e-mail me?"

"Dammit, because I'm hurting!" I screamed at him. "I needed to get everything off my chest so for the first time in weeks I can finally get some sleep and start seriously planning my new life."

There was silence. I was already regretting sending the e-mail. Marriage was too hard, and I just don't think I was ever any good at it. "Listen, we're past this and there is really no point in us bringing up what happened. I don't hate you. I never can. I will always love you and want only the best for you. These last few weeks have been a learning experience for me. I can't believe it, but it took you deciding not to buy the house for me to finally get my shit together, and I thank you for that. I finally will have control over my own life, and that's something I've never had."

"Are you saying I never allowed you to be your own woman?"

"No, you did, but you also allowed me to lean too much on you . . . to depend too much on you, and that was a mistake."

"What's wrong with a man wanting to take care of his wife?"

"Nothing. Absolutely nothing, but I got too comfortable, and because of it I started taking you for granted." I was getting emotional again. Damn, what was wrong with me? "Anyway, I finally feel like I'm actually doing something for me. I'm looking forward to graduating in May and planning the next six months of my life. I'm gonna work on paying off one credit card at a time until they are all paid off and cut up. The money you gave me will make that possible. So, thank you."

There was a pause, then Leon released a heavy sigh. "I told you eight years is too long to just move on that quickly. It's gonna take time for both of us, but I want this transition to go as smoothly as possible because I care about you."

"I appreciate that." I took a deep breath. I needed to end the call before he did. "Well, thanks for calling. Talking to you made me feel more at peace, and I appreciate that."

He hesitated as if he wanted to say something else but didn't. "Thanks for e-mailing me."

"No problem. You take care." I hung up the phone before he had a chance to say anything else. I reached for my purse and keys and headed out the door and into my Mercedes. Once behind the wheel I got ready to put the key in the ignition, when I dropped my head onto the steering wheel and started bawling my head off. I lied. I didn't feel closure. I felt lonely and so damn empty. And I missed my husband sharing my life with me.

After my phone call with Leon, I felt so sad, and the feeling followed me through the next couple of days. I felt empty. Can you believe that shit? Me, Trinette Montgomery, feeling lonely. But it wasn't a regular kind of lonely. There was suddenly a void in my life I needed to somehow find a way to fill. Another man was definitely not the answer, nor was shopping. Somehow I had no desire, and that's rare for me. No, what I needed to do first was find some kind of inner peace, and that meant for the first time in my life I needed to open up my heart and let everything out I had been holding inside all these years. That one e-mail just wasn't enough. There were so many other things I needed to tell Leon. There was no way I could open up my heart to him over the phone or in person. It had to be the chicken way—in a letter, because then I couldn't see his face or his reaction. I don't know why it was important to open up to him, because it wasn't like I was trying to get him back, but a part of me felt like I needed to let him finally meet the woman he had married. Maybe then I would have a better understanding of the person I had become and maybe it would give us both some peace in the process.

I fixed myself an apple martini, then moved into my office and took a seat in front of my computer. I had never been much of a writer, but I kept a journal for many years. It was just a way for me to find peace in my own mind.

For the longest time I just sat there sipping my drink and staring at the keyboard. *Just open your heart.* It took three martinis before I finally took a deep breath and started typing.

> You're probably amazed to hear from me again since in all the years we've been together I've barely e-mailed you at all, but there are some things I need for you to know about me. Maybe then it would make some sense as to why our marriage was doomed from the beginning.
> I'm a hateful bitch. I know it. Hell, my family all know it. But my past made me the way I am. I've always tried to be someone I wasn't, trying to compete with the Joneses, as my cousins used to say with their hating asses.

Remember when you used to ask me why I hated my uncle Sonny so much and didn't want to have anything to do with him? Well, it's because Uncle Sonny sexually molested me for almost four years. A week after my twelfth birthday my period started. He came to me one evening when we were at home alone and said, "I heard you're a woman now." I couldn't believe my mama had told him. He walked up to me and gave me a hug, then brought his lips to mine and said, "I'm going to show you what women do." Mama was somewhere out in the street, chasing a rock, while he led me back to his bedroom, shut the door and climbed on top of me. I screamed and fought, but he didn't stop until he was finished. After that he used to sneak in my room whenever Mama was out. I wanted to tell someone, but he threatened to kill Koolaid and for the longest time I believed him. He started giving me money and thought that made it all right. By the time I was fifteen, I finally found the courage to say no. I tried to bite his dick off when he forced me to go down on him. After that he never touched me again.

I was determined to get out of Englewood Park and discovered I could use sex to get whatever I wanted, so I used it to my advantage. That's how I paid for my apartment and had the money to cover what grants wouldn't so I could afford to go to college. Men saw me and all they were interested in was getting between my legs. I let them for a small price. There were times when I didn't feel I was any better than my mother, when she was fucking for a rock. But I was determined that if I needed to use someone it had to be to my benefit. My determination to have a better life was what kept me warm at night.

Then you came in my life, and for once a man didn't want anything from me but me. I wasn't used to that and I kept my guard up. I realize now I always have because I just didn't know how to trust a man. You were a good man, but you married a woman who's fucked up in the head. It wasn't you. It was me.

I hit SEND and released a heavy sigh. A tear slid down my cheek, but I didn't bother to brush it away. That life seemed so long ago, yet the pain I felt growing up felt as raw as if it had been just yesterday. No young girl should have to go through what I had gone through. My mother should have protected me.

I didn't have time to be sitting there feeling sorry for that lost little girl. I had a lot to be thankful for. Moving into the kitchen, I fixed myself another martini and was walking to my room when I looked over at the bookshelf on the wall and noticed the book Mama had left me. I had stuck it there when she left but never bothered to look inside.

I carried the book over to the table and took a seat, then looked inside.

The pages were filled with the first ten years of my life. Pictures only minutes after delivery all the way up to the spelling bee I won in the fifth grade. On these pages were the happiest accounts of my life. Things I had forgotten about like my dog Spencer I had at six, my favorite pink frilly dress, and the birthday party I had at Chuck E. Cheese's. Somehow through all Mama's years of living on drugs, she had held on to this book and the memories, and had given them back to me.

As promised, Mama hadn't contacted me since she'd come to the house. The ball was now in my court. I no longer hated her. I just wasn't sure yet if I was ready to reach out to her.

A bell sounded, indicating I had a message. I went back into my office, clicked the mouse and my heart pounded when I noticed it was from Leon. My hand was shaking as I opened his e-mail.

I wish you had trusted me enough to have told me about your childhood. As your husband it's my job to protect my wife, and I feel frustrated I hadn't known. I really feel like I understand why you behaved the way you did. I couldn't begin to admit I know the pain you went through, but my heart hurts knowing it happened to you. You are one of the strongest women I've ever known, and that's one thing I've always admired about you. The other is your determination to succeed at anything you set your mind to. I truly hate that I only knew only a piece of Trinette. I feel robbed and cheated because you were never the wife you could have been. I know deep inside there is a loving and vulnerable woman because in the eight years of our marriage, I witnessed glimpses of her. I just wish you had trusted me enough to have let your guard down and allowed your husband to love you. In a way, I feel I never allowed you to know the real me because I too feel like I also held on to a piece of myself. In the back of my mind, I was always prepared for our relationship to end. I had a backup plan so when, not if, you decided not to come to Richmond there would be no real loss. I loved you, but I don't feel as if I totally opened up my heart to you.

A sob rose to my throat. I felt as if Leon were standing in the room talking to me. It may sound crazy, but I could hear his deep robust voice and felt the warmth of his large hands holding mine.

I hit REPLY and allowed my fingers to fly across the keyboard again.

Why is it now when we're no longer together we both realize the mistakes we made? I know I guarded my heart, refusing to allow myself to be vulnerable again. I was a scary ass growing up and that's why Uncle Sonny hurt me for so long. In high school I was looking for love in all the wrong places and had my heart broken one time too many. By the time I met you, I had already put my heart under lock and key, and I just couldn't see risking everything. Now I know that was a big mistake.

I wrote a few more lines, then sent the message and found myself sitting there sipping my drink as I waited for him to reply. We went back and forth for almost two hours before I finally decided it was time for me to go to bed.

The next morning, I hurried to work before the other case managers arrived. Something was heavy on my mind and I needed to share it with Leon before I lost the nerve. I booted up my computer and typed a quick e-mail.

> Do you think it's possible to get together and talk in person?

I hit SEND before I could chicken out and change my mind. But after ten minutes of nothing back from him, I started to panic. If he said no, I would feel like a fool. If he didn't respond, I would feel like an even bigger fool. What in the world was I thinking? I immediately e-mailed him again.

> Ignore my e-mail and please don't respond. Seeing each other is not a good idea. It's best to leave things alone.

I quickly hit SEND, then released a deep breath just as Maureen came waltzing in wearing a black suit with a candy apple red shirt and matching shoes. Ever since I had fallen apart, I hadn't been taking as much time to get ready in the morning. Don't get me wrong, I'm going to always look good, I just didn't feel fabulous.

"Good morning, everyone," Maureen said as she moved to her desk and then turned to me. "Hey, girl, you know what today is?"

I gave her a weak smile, then returned to my case

files. This afternoon she and I would be going through a second and final round of interviews for the director's position. All other candidates had been eliminated.

My computer chimed, indicating I had received an e-mail. One click of my mouse and my heart pounded. It was from Leon.

> I think meeting is a good idea. If nothing else we'll both find closure.

My heart hurt. It sounded to me like he had already moved on with his life. But deep down I needed to see him. Part of me wanted him to see me and think about all he was giving up so he would have second thoughts and beg me back. It was crazy. I know. I wanted Leon more than I wanted anything else, including the director's position, but I was too proud to put my pride aside to admit I still loved this man and didn't want him with anyone else. I never thought him being with another woman would bother me, but I was wrong.

I reached for my mouse, hit REPLY and typed a simple message.

> OK. When would you like to meet?

36

Trinette

That Friday, I could barely focus at work so I took the rest of the afternoon off and jetted to the mall to find something sexy to wear. I needed Leon to see everything he was giving up and desperately needed him to want me.

After an hour of shopping, I packed up my overnight bag and hit the highway. I couldn't get to the airport fast enough. My hands were shaking, and the entire time my mind was racing. Listening to music didn't help, so I called Nikki.

"Hey, girl, you on your way?"

I released a long, shaky breath. "Yes . . . Nikki, I'm so nervous."

"I know how you feel. I felt the exact same way when Donovan came home."

That was at least a relief to hear. "I keep thinking,

what if I see him and feel nothing for him or, even worse, he no longer feels anything for me?"

"That's just nerves. The two of you have spent a lot of time e-mailing the last two weeks and getting things off your chest."

"We have. I can't believe how much. It's scary. I've never allowed myself to be this vulnerable before." I was crying now because I was nervous and the unknown was driving me insane.

Nikki tried to comfort me. "Big baby, quit crying. The two of you are gonna be just fine. Just open up your heart and love that man, and the rest will be easy."

"I sure hope so, Nikki. I love my husband so much. I don't know what in the world I was thinking all these years."

"Don't worry about that. At least you finally got it right."

"I hope so. . . . I sure hope so. Thanks, Nikki. Please pray for us."

"Girl, the person who needs prayer is me." She chuckled. "If that fool pops up at the store one more time I'm going to scream."

It felt good to laugh. "You need to just get an order of protection against that crazy mothafucka. It don't make sense for someone to be stalking you like that after you already told him it was over."

"Yeah, but I don't think it's that serious. I'm hoping eventually it will start to sink in."

"It better, 'cause I know Donovan ain't having it."

"Don't I know it. Anyway, I'm getting ready to lock up the store. Enjoy the weekend and we'll talk on Sunday. I've got my fingers crossed."

I hung up and felt so much better as I continued down Highway 40. "Please, Lord. Please let my relationship with my husband work itself out." I believed in prayer, and I've been doing quite a lot of praying lately. If I didn't have anything else, at least I had my faith in God to pull me through.

Growing up, we rarely went to church, but prayer was always a big part of our daily life. I remember Mama sitting on the side of the bed while I knelt down and said my prayers. Afterward, she'd tuck me in and tell me how much she loved me. Those were some of the rare memories I had of the woman she used to be. As much as I hated to admit it, I saw a glimpse of that beautiful yet humble woman when she had visited my house. I frowned. The last thing I wanted to do was think about my mama.

I pulled into the hotel parking lot shortly after nine and checked into my room. Leon and I agreed we needed to meet at a neutral location. I barely had a chance to look around the luxurious suite when my cell phone rang. My pulse raced. It was Leon.

"My plane just landed," he announced.

"Already!" Oh, shit.

His laughter sounded forced. "Yeah, already. You don't sound like you're looking forward to seeing me."

"No, definitely not that. I just thought I . . . I would have a chance to shower before you got here."

"Well, get showered. I'll be there shortly."

I hung up and took the quickest shower ever, then sprayed on some smell good and slipped into a pair of Baby Phat jeans and a pink blouse. One thing I loved about Leon is that he always noticed how good I looked. Tonight, I wanted his eyes to be all over me. I wanted him to remember how good it used to be between us.

I sat there on the couch with my legs crossed and

waited for what felt like forever for him to arrive. All I could think about was the way I had treated that man all these years. How I had taken his love for granted. I had been a straight-up fool. I would never get over the pain I felt when I realized he was gone from my life. Leon was a good man and there was no way I wanted to lose him to another woman.

Knock! Knock!

I jumped off the couch. My heart was pumping like crazy as I moved to the door. "W-Who is it?" I asked. Nervousness was definitely apparent in my voice.

"It's your husband."

I opened the door and he barely got inside before I was in his arms holding him, and he held me back tightly. "Hey, Netta," he cooed.

Leon moved over to the couch with me and took a seat. I couldn't let go. The tears started coming and kept on falling. I didn't care if he saw me cry over him. I loved this man. He leaned back and I saw he had a few tears of his own. He pulled me to him again, and I held on. And for the first time I felt like things were going to be all right.

"Why are you shaking?" he asked.

"Because I was scared. I-I didn't know. I didn't know if you would still feel the same way about me."

"Baby, I can't get over eight years that quickly." Leon leaned in and kissed me, and I kissed him back. "You are my soul mate."

"I-I missed you so much." I started bawling, and he hugged and rocked me like a baby.

"Come on, let's lay down," he suggested. "I've been up since five and that was a long flight."

I nodded and we got undressed and slid under the

covers. He rolled beside me and held me in his arms and for the longest time we just kissed.

Leon was the first to break the silence. "I can't believe you're here with me. I thought I'd never see you again."

I tried to smile but my lips quivered. "Boo, I . . . I thought the same thing."

We continued to kiss and express our feelings, and we fell asleep in each other's arms. Everything was going to be all right between us. I could feel it.

37

Nikki

"You're listening to *Truth Hurts,* and I am your host, Nikki Truth. I've got another hot show lined up. Tonight we're gonna kick off the evening with a story I saw earlier this morning on ABC News. This female got her tail beat over a no-good man. Apparently this woman who owned a beauty shop was messing around with this other female's husband. Instead of the wife confronting her husband, she and her friends went to the female's shop and beat her butt. Not only that, while they took turns whooping on her, one of the stupid friends filmed the whole thing and like a fool placed it on the Internet. Just dumb. Now they're going to jail. I saw the entire video, and it was so sad. The female didn't even fight back. Instead, she allowed them to whoop her. Ladies, when will we learn? It is not that serious. The phones are open. I want to hear what you think." Before I was even done, the phone lines lit up like Times Square. I took a few calls, then Tristan signaled for me to pick up line two. "Caller, you're on the air."

"Hi, Ms. Nikki, this is Jennifer, and well . . . I disagree. I do believe some women deserve a beat down for knowingly messing with someone else's man."

I adjusted my microphone as I spoke. "Jennifer, I get the impression your husband messed around on you."

"Well, uh, I—"

"And I guess you confronted the female instead of confronting your man."

"Yes, because she knew he was married."

"And so did he, but that didn't stop him, did it?"

There was a brief pause before she finally answered, *"No."*

"Just what I thought. Wake up, girlfriend." I depressed the button. "Next caller."

"Hi, Ms. Nikki, this is Keisha, and I saw that video myself. My heart went out to that female. That was so totally uncalled for. I couldn't believe they locked her in her shop and whooped her tail. I was embarrassed for black women."

"Keisha, I agree. Next caller."

"Hi, Ms. Nikki, this is Tracy. When will women learn no man is worth all that drama. If he is cheating on you, most likely he did it to the woman before you, and when he gets tired he will do the same to the next. Let that good for nothing man go on about his business and be someone else's headache."

"Well said, Tracy. If he loved you, he wouldn't cheat. Women, we need to grow up and act our age. Is it really worth going to jail and being away from your kids for a man? Trust and believe, while you're locked up, he has moved on to the next."

The rest of the night was wild. We were flooded with phone calls and I read a few crazy e-mails, and by midnight I was happy to sign off for the night.

I climbed into my car, then reached down for my cell phone. I had a couple of missed calls, including one from an unknown number. On the drive home, I checked my messages and was actually surprised to find that one was from Kenyon. For the last week, he had been good about just e-mailing and calling me in the morning. The evening calls had stopped.

"Baby, I'm sorry to bother you b-but my daughter was in a bad car accident. Her car is totaled. They're taking her into surgery." I could hear the fear and uncertainty in his voice. He was scared for his daughter's life.

I put the phone aside and drove home with the radio off, deep in my thoughts. The memories of Mimi's last day came flooding back. I remembered riding in the back of the ambulance with her and waiting outside the operating room while they tried to save her life. Unfortunately, the internal injuries were too severe. Kenyon had been there for me when I needed someone most. He held my hand and allowed me to cry in his arms when Big Mama passed. Part of me felt like turning the car around and joining him at the hospital. He was probably scared out of his mind. Already, he had lost his wife. The only thing he had left of her was the child they had created. But as much as I wanted to be there for him, I knew if I went down to the hospital, he would confuse my support for something else.

Once home, I parked in the driveway, headed inside and let Rudy out in the backyard. He hated being confined inside the privacy fence, but too bad.

I reached for my cordless phone and curled up on the couch in the family room while I made the phone call.

"Hello? Baby?"

I groaned inwardly. Was he ever going to stop calling me baby? Just let it slide, I thought. "Hey, I got your message."

"Thanks . . . thanks for calling me back." His voice was shaky, and it was easy to figure out he was nervous. "They just took Rachel into surgery."

I glanced out at Rudy, peeing on my rose bush. "What happened?"

"She was in a car accident. The officer said she ran a red light and an oncoming truck hit her from the side."

"I'm so sorry."

"I didn't even recognize her car. It was so smashed I . . . I don't know how she survived." He sounded so sad, and my heart went out to him.

"Don't think like that. You've got to think positive. Is she conscious?"

"Barely . . . in and out. They gave her something that knocked her out before they wheeled her into surgery."

"Did they say what was wrong with her?" I asked.

"An arm is broken and there are some internal injuries."

Just like Mimi. "I'm so sorry. Everything is gonna be fine. . . . Wait and see."

He released a long breath. "I sure hope so. My daughter is all I got left."

"She's gonna be fine. Watch."

There was silence on the phone, and that was rare for Kenyon. That man didn't know when to shut up. But I could understand he was worried about Rachel.

"Tell me something about your daughter."

"Well . . . she's stubborn as hell."

I chuckled and moved over to the door and let Rudy in. "Most women are."

"But she's always been stubborn. I remember when I was trying to potty train her. She refused to let me dump her pot. She had to do it herself."

"Really?" I said with amusement.

"Yep, she was the same way when she started walking. She used to push my hand away, wanted to do it all on her own. Now that she's grown, she hasn't changed."

"Sounds like my kinda woman."

"Yeah, she gets that independent spirit from her mother," he replied, sounding slightly amused.

"Were they close?"

He took a moment to think about his answer. "I guess about as close as a mother and daughter can be. She took her mother's death hard, but Rachel mourned in her own way."

"How so?"

Kenyon gave a defeated sigh. "Drinking . . . a lot of drinking and partying. I've picked her up from the club a couple of times because she was too drunk to drive."

I curled one leg beneath me on the couch, getting comfortable. "At least she had sense enough to call you."

"Yeah, but I can't help but wonder if she was drunk when she ran through that light."

I nibbled on my lips, considering what he said. "Have they taken her blood?"

"Yeah . . . but the tox screen isn't back."

"Try not to think about that right now. Just focus on being there for your daughter. Stubborn or not, she's gonna need you." A thought came to mind. "Who's at the hospital with you?"

"No one. I didn't want to call and worry my sisters. I figured I'd call them after surgery." He cleared his throat. "I told you I don't have too many friends."

"What about Jay?"

He chuckled. "Uh . . . Jay and I are club buddies. We go out drinking and talk about women, but outside of that we don't hang out much."

"That's too bad. I thought you were closer than that. I'm glad I've got Trinette. We've been friends forever."

"You're lucky."

I smiled. "I know." There was silence, and I figured it was time to get off the phone and get ready for bed before Donovan called. "Hey, I've gotta go. Please keep me posted, okay?"

"You know I will," he answered urgently.

"Yes, I know," I whispered, and hung up the phone.

38

Trinette

"Trinette."

I could tell by the tone of Nikki's voice something was bothering her. "Hey, whassup?"

"Have you heard from Kenyon?"

Oh, my goodness. "Why in the world would I hear from him?"

"I don't know. I thought maybe Jay had mentioned him."

Reaching inside my desk drawer, I removed a fingernail file. "I stopped messing with Jay, remember?"

"Good for you." There was a pause. "Do me a favor and send Kenyon an e-mail."

"For what?"

"To make sure he's okay. I'm worried about him. Last time we spoke was two nights ago. He was throwing up and his stomach was all in knots."

Rudely, I sucked my teeth. "Maybe he ate some bad Mexican."

"No. He only acts like that when he's upset. His daughter's accident and our breakup really has him upset."

I don't know why my girl thought she's all that. Kenyon would be okay. He had a woman before her, and he'd find another.

"Just do me this favor. Send him one of your daily jokes or tell him you were just e-mailing to see how he was doing."

"Nikki, just leave him alone. Donovan will be home soon, and the two of you can live happily ever after." I tried not to sound like I didn't care, but the truth of the matter was, I didn't.

"Trinette, even though it's over between us, I do care about him. The last week we have worked on just being friends."

I blew out a long breath because she wasn't going to quit until I agreed. "All right, send me his e-mail and I'll send him something, but you're gonna owe me big time for this one."

"Thanks. I just wanna make sure he's all right."

"Yeah, yeah."

I went to meet with another client, and by the time I got back to my desk, Nikki had sent me his address. I opened a new message and tried to think of what to say to him. He was psycho—I didn't care what Nikki said—and smothering and desperate, and needed to get a life.

Hey, Kenyon, sorry to hear about you and Nikki. If you ever need an ear I'm here. When you see your boy tell him he owes me dinner.

At least that way I was able to get a plug in for myself. Maybe I was no longer messing around, but Jay still meant a lot to me.

It had been two weeks since Leon and I spent a wonderful weekend together and nothing or no one was going to ruin what we now had. If Jay no longer wanted to be friends, then fuck him. Smooth and Michael had been blowing up my phone, but I told them both I was no longer interested. Since then nobody has messed with my car. I still think the tires were a random act of violence, but the message in lipstick was pointed directly at me. And like I told Smooth, he better have a talk with Cimon and warn her to stay the fuck away from me.

I worked on my cases for the rest of the morning. Two of my clients lost their EBT cards, so I had to go in and issue new ones. I didn't know how they could lose them. It was just like having a credit card. More than likely they sold their food stamps to someone and let them use their cards and never had them returned. People were always trying to beat the system.

"Trinette, you have a call on line three. Whoever it is talks so low you can barely hear him," Patricia added with an exaggerated frown.

I reached for the phone and pushed the blinking button. "Trinette, may I help you?"

"Trinette, thank you so much for e-mailing me! I really need a friend right now."

I didn't recognize the voice. "Who is this?"

"Kenyon."

I groaned inwardly. I was gonna kill Nikki when I saw her.

"Trinette, I love her so much."

"I thought y'all were working on being friends?"

"I was, but I can no longer hide my feelings. I had hoped by not calling her for a few days she would start to miss me and want me back in her life."

I half listened while I searched the Internet. "Kenyon, Nikki loves her husband."

"I *know* she loves me too."

I had to laugh at his attempt at confidence. "It doesn't matter. She's married to Donovan and committed to him."

"There isn't anything I wouldn't do for her."

"I know," I mumbled.

"I'll take whatever she'll give me. One afternoon a week is better than nothing at all, because none of the women in this city compare to her."

Oh, my goodness. Is this dude for real? "Kenyon, please. You need to move on."

"I'm not ready to move on. A year from now I won't be ready. I told her all she has to do is call me and I'll be there for her."

I was trying hard not to laugh at his simple ass. How in the world had Nikki been screwing this pathetic negro?

"Can you please ask her to give me another chance?"

I slapped a frustrated palm against my forehead. This fool was worse than Cory's worrisome ass. "I'm not doing that. Just let it go, Kenyon." My friendly advice was met by silence. "Kenyon, you still there?"

"You know . . . my mom told me the same thing last night . . . to let her go because if she's mine, she'll come back to me."

I frowned, remembering something Nikki had told me. "Isn't your mother dead?"

"Yeah, but she still talks to me."

"Ohhhkay, you know what, I've got to go." I started to hang up, but Kenyon called out my name.

"Trinette, wait! I-I appreciate you talking to me. Can you please give Nikki a message for me?"

He was wearing my nerves. "What?"

"Tell her I-I love her and if she needs anything, and I mean *anything,* she knows I-I got her back."

I hit the dial tone, because there was no way in the world I was going to listen to another second of that shit. What in the world was Nikki thinking even letting that fool crawl up between her thighs?

Maureen came strolling into the office. She had taken the morning off. I watched her sashay across the room. Someone was still following my car. Part of me suspected it was her, but if she knew about me and Michael, I couldn't tell. Since she'd moved into her new house, she'd been smiling in my face. Today she wasn't.

"Trinette, I need to talk to you." She grabbed my hand and led me into the break room and shut the door. I had a bad feeling about whatever was on her mind.

"Whassup?" I asked, crossing my arms.

"Have you ever thought your husband was messing around?"

I looked at her face, trying to see if she was running game. The pain I saw looked genuine, which I thought was strange since she was fucking around as well. Relaxing a little, I nodded. "Yep. Once."

"What did you do?"

"Girl, I followed his ass." I don't know why I was telling her that, but I guess since I was done fucking Michael I didn't have to worry about her finding him with me. Michael must be screwing someone else.

"That's a good idea. I'll try that and I guarantee when I find out who the bitch is, she's going to regret fucking with my man." She rolled her eyes, then opened the door and walked back to her desk. I didn't know if she was playing dumb or what. I knew I just needed to watch my back. You keep your enemies close and your so-called friends closer.

39

Nikki

Okay. This shit was no longer funny.

Kenyon had officially reached stalker mode. After Trinette called to let me know nothing was wrong with Kenyon except that he was crazy, I decided maybe it was best he wasn't calling me. Then I went to the grocery store after work and spotted Kenyon at the end of the aisle, watching me. As soon as he spotted me, he waved and moved my way. I'd be blind to say he didn't look good in chocolate dress slacks and a cream button-down shirt and blazer.

"Don't you look nice," I complimented. Hey, there is nothing wrong with giving a man his props.

"Thank you. I just dropped in to grab some chips." He was smiling so hard you would have thought he was auditioning for a toothpaste commercial.

I leaned against my cart. "How's your daughter getting along?"

"Much better. She's getting around and learning how to write with her left hand."

"Good for her." She had broken her right arm in two places, and lacerated her liver.

"Just bought that new Jet Li movie. You wanna watch it together?"

Immediately, I shook my head. "No. That's not a good idea."

He frowned. "What's wrong with two friends watching a movie together?"

"Nah . . . I'll pass." He didn't say anything. He just stood there, his eyes traveling my length appreciatively, and for the first time I felt uncomfortable. "Well, good seeing you. I better get going." I pushed past him and was halfway down the aisle when I glanced over my shoulder and found him still standing there, watching me.

While I finished shopping, I kept spotting him somewhere not too far away. When I finally got in line, Kenyon moved in the line beside me. I reached for a magazine and ignored him.

"You look beautiful as ever."

"Thank you," I replied without even bothering to look his way.

I couldn't get out of the store fast enough. Out in the parking lot, I quickly loaded my backseat and was anxious to be long gone before he came out. I put the car in reverse and was backing out of the spot when he tapped on the glass.

I flinched and rolled down my window. "You scared the shit outta me!"

"Sorry," he replied with a sympathetic smirk. "I wasn't sure if you noticed but you have a flat."

"You got to be kidding me." I put the car in park

and climbed out. Sure enough, my left front tire was flat.

"You must have run over something." Kenyon slipped out of his blazer and laid it across my front seat, then popped my trunk. I stood back and watched as he reached for the tire iron. "It's a good thing I was around." He gave me a silly smirk, then went to work on changing my tire. "You really should reconsider watching the movie with me. I can bring over the popcorn and your favorite wine." He pulled the flat tire off and examined it. "Look at that . . . you ran over a nail." He pulled out the spare and placed the flat tire in my trunk,

The entire time I stared at his back. Even though I had driven through a new construction area on the way to the store, I had a gut feeling Kenyon was responsible for the flat.

He glanced over his shoulder. "So you want to watch the movie tonight?"

"I said no."

"Come on, Nikki. Just think about it," he insisted.

I gazed down at the tire iron, wanting to smash him across his head. He was never going to change. He had no intentions of moving on. That was now painfully clear. I couldn't be his friend. No longer could I accept any of his phone calls, because as long as I was in his life he was always going to think he had a chance.

"There, you're all set." He rose and dusted off his slacks.

"Thanks." I tossed the jack and tire iron in the trunk and slammed it shut.

"So, we on for tonight?"

I swung around. "I said no!"

He flinched and stepped back as if I had struck him. "Okay, you don't have to yell."

"Yes, I do, because that seems to be the only thing you understand." I handed him his blazer and climbed into my car.

Kenyon walked over to my window. "How about we go and get some catfish instead?"

I backed out of the parking spot, put the car in drive and started to pull off. That fool was still holding on.

"Wait! Baby, please talk to me. Why do you hate me so much?"

Ignoring him, I started driving across the lot. Folks were pointing and laughing. "Leave me the fuck alone!" I screamed. He kept holding on, running alongside the car.

"Baby, please. I love you!"

I put my foot on the gas and took off faster than allowed in a parking lot. This time he let go. Glancing out my rearview mirror, I watched him standing in the middle of the lot, calling my name.

40

Trinette

I strolled into work feeling like a new woman. Hair and nails done. New spring outfit and shoes. It had been three weeks since Leon had flown down, and I was looking forward to flying to Richmond to spend the upcoming weekend together. I gave everyone a bright smile, then moved to my desk and took a seat. I had a huge caseload for the day and several actions that needed to be taken care of. I had another client who still hadn't brought me her check stubs. I had no choice but to cut off her stamps. I was preparing to call her when my phone rang.

"DFS, Trinette speaking."

"Hey, beautiful."

At the sound of Michael's voice I rolled my eyes. "What do you want?"

"I need to see you."

"I told you it was over," I said, trying to whisper.

"Come on, Netta. One more time for old times' sake. I've got a surprise for you."

I wasn't the least bit curious about his surprise. But I was tired of him calling my house, cell and office phone. "You've got to stop calling me."

"I will when you come and see me. I promise."

I'd been ignoring his calls for weeks because I was trying for once in my life to be faithful to my husband. But this mothafucka, no matter how many times I ignored his phone calls, he kept calling me. I must have fallen on my head when I let his ass con me into giving him my house phone number. Now the fool called me at least three times a week from different numbers. I was starting to worry, because Leon was coming down next month and the last thing I needed was this psycho mothafucka calling my house. There was no telling what he was capable of doing. His wife was only two cubicles away and he was crazy enough to call me.

I looked over the partition wall to make sure Patricia's nosy ass wasn't listening. "Michael, I already told you, I'm trying to be faithful to my husband."

"Be faithful tomorrow, I need to see you tonight."

"What part of no don't you understand . . . the *n* or the *o*?"

"Damn, sexy, I got a surprise for you. Something you left at the condo."

I couldn't help it. Now I was curious. "What?"

"Come and find out."

I wasn't in the mood for games. "I'll pass."

"You dropped one of your diamond earrings at the condo."

Oh, shit! The one-carat diamond earrings had belonged to Leon's mother. I thought I had lost it forever. "I'll drop by the dealership tomorrow and pick it up."

"Please, Trinette, I need some of you," he whined. "I haven't had any good pussy in a month."

I could believe that.

"My dick is hard. If I have to pay for some, I will."

I thought about this Coach purse I had seen at Macy's. I also thought about planning a fabulous weekend for Leon and me at a five-star hotel with a Jacuzzi in the room. "How much you willing to pay?"

"Name your price."

"A thousand."

"You got it."

Damn, I should have asked for two. "What time, and I don't have all day?"

"I'll take whatever I can get. Maureen has aerobics class at seven, so why don't you meet me then at our spot?"

There was no way I was meeting him at the condo. I mentioned the first place we met, a low-budget motel off the highway. It was clean but cheap. He agreed.

I went home, showered, douched, then put on a blue jean skirt and heels. When I pulled into the parking lot shortly after seven, his SUV was already parked in front of room 3B. I knocked twice, then waited. He opened the door and smiled at me with those pretty teeth of his, and I found myself smiling as well. Michael was definitely something to look at. I wished I could say the same about his dick.

"I'm glad you came."

I stepped into the room and took a seat on the bed. He moved and took a seat beside me, then leaned in and kissed me. "Damn, girl, you're fine."

I grinned at the compliment. "So, where's my earring?"

He rose and moved to the nightstand and handed me a small box. "Open it."

Smiling, I felt like a kid on Christmas as I removed the beautiful bow and opened the box. I gasped. Not only was my earring inside but also a matching tennis bracelet. "It's beautiful."

"I saw it and had to buy it for you."

I smiled up at him. "Thank you."

"Hopefully you'll change your mind about us. " The next thing I knew his hands were all over me. I pushed his horny ass away, shaking my head.

"Uh-uh, negro, you know you pay before you play."

He looked pissed. "Damn, I thought the bracelet would be enough."

"Well, you thought wrong. We already had an agreement."

Michael reached inside his pocket and peeled off ten crisp Ben Franklins and handed them to me. I stuck them in my purse, then turned to him. "Now, where were we?"

He started kissing and petting and taking off his clothes. "Let me get a condom." He rose from the bed and moved over to his pants.

I reached for the zipper of my skirt, then suddenly I paused. What in the world was I doing? I had a good-ass man and we were on the verge of having a wonderful life together, and here I was about to jeopardize everything for a thousand dollars.

By the time Michael had slipped the condom on and was on his way back, I was already putting my shoes back on.

"Trinette, what's wrong?"

"I can't do it. I love my husband too much." I

reached inside my purse and tossed his money and the bracelet onto the bed.

"You're playing, right?" he asked with a chuckle.

"Do I look like I'm playing?" I swung the purse over my shoulder and moved toward the door. He had the nerve to come after me.

"You ain't going nowhere." He grabbed my arm.

"Mothafucka, unless you want me to kick you in the nuts and scream rape, I advise you to let my arm go."

I guess his naked ass thought twice, because he released me. I swung around. "And if you ever call me again, I'm telling your wife." I swung open the door and moved across the parking lot to my car, smiling at my decision. I loved my husband more than money. Can you believe that shit? I wasn't about to jeopardize my marriage for anyone.

I was almost to my car when I heard tires squeal and spotted a dark vehicle come flying in my direction so fast I had to dive between two cars.

"What the fuck?" I got up and looked both ways. The driver was long gone, and I barely had a look at the car. It had been traveling way too fast for me to see who was behind the wheel, but one name came to mind. Maureen. Thanks to my advice, she had found out I was screwing her husband.

41

Nikki

"This is Nikki Truth and you're on the air."

"Hello, Ms. Nikki."

The male voice sounded vaguely familiar. "Hello, who am I speaking to?"

"This is Junior."

Mr. Loser. Ain't this some shit. "Well, well, well . . . long time, no hear. That must have been some woman!" I said with dramatic emphasis.

"She was . . . or rather, she still is." He took a deep breath. *"What do you do when you love a woman with all your heart and she doesn't love you back?"*

I took a moment to think about an answer. "You open up your heart to that person, and if they don't love you back, then you find the strength to move on. There is someone out there for everyone, and if she doesn't feel the same way, then maybe the two of you aren't meant to be together."

"I don't agree. We fit so good together. I love her with everything I have, and if her husband wasn't standing in the way, we would have been perfect together, I know we would."

Oh, my God! I choked on my spit. Nobody talks like that but . . . "Kenyon, is that you?"

There was silence on the air, and then I heard that eerie laugh. *"Yes, baby, it's me."*

It took everything I had not to cuss him out over the air. "I thought you said your name was Junior?"

Suddenly his voice changed to the one I had grown accustomed to hearing. *"I am a junior. I'm named after my father."* He started laughing as if it were the funniest thing in the world. "I just didn't want everybody in my business."

I looked across the glass at Tristan, who was up out of his chair with his hand cupping his mouth, eyes bugging out of his head. I was on the air, and there was no way I was about to fall apart. I just needed to hold it together and play along.

"Junior . . . did you say she's married?"

"Yes, but she isn't happy with him," he replied. I was surprised he was playing along with me.

"You knew when you first got involved with a married woman, chances were the relationship couldn't be anything but temporary." I was so pissed I could have screamed, but this was probably my last chance at talking sense to this dude.

"B-but she wasn't happy. Now that he's back from the war he's got her mind all confused and she's feeling guilty about no longer loving him."

This dude was crazier than I thought. "Did you tell you she loved her husband?"

"Yes, b-but I know s-she loves me." Kenyon always stutters when he gets nervous.

"Yes, maybe she does, but it sounds to me like she loves her husband more. I'm assuming the two of you got involved while her husband was over in Iraq, is that correct?"

His voice softened. *"Yes, and we fell in love."*

"But what did she tell you?"

He released a heavy sigh. *"That she owed it to her husband and her marriage to try."*

"And why can't you respect that?"

"B-because I know s-she's confused."

"Doesn't sound like she's confused to me. Instead it sounds like you refuse to accept that our . . . I mean, your relationship is over."

"I believe in fighting for what is mine!"

"But she isn't yours. Legally she belongs to another man. There's a saying—let her go and if she's yours, she'll come back to you."

"Wow! My mother told me the same thing."

Damn, that fool's mama is dead. "Then you need to listen to her. Marriage is a sacred union. Are you a Christian?"

"Yes. I've been praying to the Lord."

"Then you know what she's doing is right. How about praying to the Lord to give you the strength to move on?"

"Because she's mine!"

"If she's married, she was never yours in the first place."

"There's nothing wrong with having hope."

"Then keep hope alive." I hung up. "Sorry, but that's one brotha who refuses to believe it over. We're about to take a commercial break, and when we get back we're gonna switch gears and discuss why women mess with married men."

I took the headset off and was clearly shaking. I had been involved with Mr. Loser. Kenyon Monroe and Mr. Loser were one and the same. It was so crazy I started laughing. Many times I had said, what woman in her right mind would want to date that dude? And now I was one of those women. By the time Tristan had come to my office, I had tears in my eyes.

"Are you okay?"

Shaking my head, I reached for a tissue. "Hell, nah, I'm not okay."

Tristan took a seat beside me, eyes bugged out. "Oh, my goodness, girl. You were dating that loser."

I took a few seconds to think about it, then took one look at Tristan. The two of us exploded with laughter. What could possibly happen next?

42

Trinette

"Well, what do you think?"

I looked at Leon totally in shock. "What I think is . . . I've got to be dreaming."

I stood in the living room of a forty-two-hundred square foot home with twelve-foot ceilings, a spiral staircase and more room than my current furniture would fill.

"I love it!" I threw myself into his arms. "Thank you so much."

Leon kissed me, then stared down in my eyes. "You're my wife, and there isn't anything I wouldn't do for you. All I ask is you love me in return."

I started crying. I couldn't help it. I didn't deserve this man. I knew that now. "I still can't believe I almost lost you."

"You got me now."

What he did next made my jaw drop. Leon got down on one knee and reached for my hand.

"Leon . . . w-what are you doing?"

He grinned. "What does it look like I'm doing? I'm getting ready to propose to your sexy behind, again. Now hush."

It took everything I had to hold it together when he began to speak.

"Netta, I knew from the first time I set eyes on you, you would be the woman I would spend the rest of my life with. And nothing has changed. My heart still beats heavily every time you're around. My body craves your touch when you're gone. My life isn't complete without you in it, and you would make me the happiest man in the world if you would marry me again."

I was bawling because I was so happy. I had almost lost this man until God had given me a second chance, and there was no way in hell I was going to ever take him for granted again. Trust and believe. "Yes, yes, I wanna marry you again."

He rose and dipped down and captured me in a kiss. It was by far the best I'd ever had. I held on tight and didn't want to let him go. There was no telling how long we would have stood there kissing if we hadn't heard someone clear her throat. I turned around.

"I'm sorry to interrupt, but does that mean you decided to take the house?"

I looked from the realtor to my husband and started laughing. I forgot she was even there. I nodded. "Yes, we'll take it."

We spent a fabulous weekend together, and on Monday I climbed out my car with the biggest smile on my face. Who could believe marriage could be so grand?

After putting an offer on the house, Leon took me to a fabulous Thai restaurant where we had spicy noodles and meat, then we spent the evening in bed hugging and holding each other and simply talking. It was amazing how much the two of us had to talk about. Eight years' worth.

I strolled into the building, waving at Chuck, then swung my hips as I moved toward my desk.

"Good morning, everyone," I sang merrily.

"Good morning, Trinette," Patricia said with her brow up inquisitively. "How was your weekend?" I already knew her nosy behind wanted all the details.

"Fabulous. We spent a great deal of time talking, put an offer on a house and we went shopping for this little thing." I swung my hand out.

Patricia took one look at the diamond glittering on my finger and jumped from her seat and came over. "Let me see your hand." She practically yanked my arm out the socket. "Is that a yellow diamond?"

I nodded. "It's a canary yellow diamond. A ten thousand dollar diamond." I made sure I said it loud enough for Maureen to hear me as she strolled in late as usual. She tried to act like she wasn't interested in what we were talking about, but I knew better.

The day after being at the motel with Michael, I had come in prepared to fight. Trust and believe, I left the hoop earrings at home and a small jar of Vaseline was still in my purse. Luckily, Maureen's behavior in the office hadn't changed. She came in talking about her house and husband as usual, so I was no longer sure it was her who tried to run me down in the parking lot.

I looked at Patricia, but I spoke loud and clear for the whole office to hear. "Leon said he wants to renew our vows. Girl, he dropped down on one knee and proposed to me all over again, then said he wanted to buy me a new ring." I held out my hand for the others who crowded around to see. "I knew this was the ring the moment I saw it."

"I guess so at that price," Maureen mumbled under her breath. She walked over and took a look and tried not to look impressed. I couldn't help but glance down at her finger. Her diamond didn't in any way compare to mine. And to think I thought her man was everything. "It's nice," she said with a shrug. "I don't really care for colored stones."

I pursed my lips. "That's funny, 'cause a month ago you were talking about getting a chocolate diamond."

She rolled her eyes and returned to her seat. "Actually Michael's planning to buy me a pink diamond."

I just bet he is. She was hating, and I wasn't in the mood for her shit. This was my time to shine, and no one was going to take that from me.

As soon as everyone had a chance to look and compliment, I walked up to my supervisor's door and knocked.

Yolanda smiled. "Hey, Trinette. Come on in."

I stepped in swinging my hand, making sure she saw my finger. "I would like to talk to you in private if that's okay."

"Sure, close the door." I pulled the door behind me and moved over and took a seat across from her.

Her brow rose curiously. "What's going on?"

I couldn't believe I was about to do this. "I would like to let you know I will be joining my husband in Richmond in June."

She removed her glasses from her eyes as if she needed to look at me closer. "Are you saying you're leaving?"

I swallowed. "Yes, I'm moving to Richmond shortly after I graduate."

Yolanda steepled her fingers and was quiet for a few seconds. "I'm not supposed to say this, but I hope my telling you this will help you to change your mind. You were getting the director's position."

My mouth dropped, and then my heart started pounding. This was the moment I had been preparing for, for the last year, but the job in no way compared to my marriage. "Thank you so much for considering me, but I'm gonna have to pass." I rose and walked back to my desk and started my day, but it was hard to concentrate. All I could do was think about my new house. Of course I had photos to pass around the office.

Nikki wanted me to meet her for lunch. I told her I'd meet her at the St. Louis Bread Factory at noon. I walked in and got us a table in the corner and waited. The whole time I stared down at my ring. It was beautiful, and I felt like the luckiest woman in the world.

I spotted Nikki moving across the restaurant looking fabulous in a khaki skirt, white shirt and brown flats.

She flopped down on the bench across from me. "Girl, I am about to pull my hair out! At first it was funny, but now Kenyon is so got-damn worrisome."

I pointed a finger in her direction. "I told you something wasn't right with him. You should have listened to me and left his ass alone a long time ago."

"I don't understand it. I tell him Donovan and I are working things out, but he keeps saying there's nothing wrong with having hope. What the hell is wrong with him?"

I started laughing. "Yeah, your radio show was hi-

larious. I heard the end of it just as I made a mad dash
to catch my plane."

"Netta, I've never been so embarrassed in my life.
I can't wait to leave for the book expo in New York,
just so I can have a break from his worrisome ass."

I reached across the table and squeezed Nikki's
hand. "Hey, don't let anything or anyone stand in the
way of your happiness."

Her brow rose. "What's gotten into you?"

I gave her a dismissive wave. "Leon. Leon's what's
gotten to me. Nikki, I have never been so happy before
in my life."

She gave me a weird look, as if she didn't believe a
word I said. Any other time I could care less if my best
friend believed me, but now it was important for her to
know I have changed. "In the last several weeks I have
realized that I have a good man I've taken for granted
for so long. I almost lost him, but now I've got a second chance and I'm so grateful."

Her eyes grew wide. "Trinette, girl, are you crying?"

I nodded. "Yes, because I'm so happy. Look." I
held out my hand, and she took one look at my ring and
started screaming.

"Oh, my goodness!"

A woman at the next table rolled her eyes, and I
heard her mumble "ghetto" under her breath.

"Bitch, I can show you ghetto!" I snapped, and she
quickly turned and looked down at her menu.

"It's beautiful." Nikki had tears in her eyes.

"We're renewing our vows in July, and we would
love for you and Donovan to be there."

"I'd love it, too." She locked her eyes with mine.
"Are you sure this time?"

I was nodding and wiping tears at the same time. "More sure than I have been about anything in a long time." I know my girl was skeptical, but I was for real. "I'm serious, Nikki. I have taken Leon for granted for so long and I can't understand why, because he is such a good man and he has been nothing but good to me. And when I think about all the things I have done to him over the years, I feel so sad I want to cry be . . . because he didn't deserve to be treated like that, and if he didn't love me soooo much he would have left me a long time ago, but I am soooo thankful he hasn't. I'm . . . so thankful." I was crying again. Nikki reached for a couple of napkins and handed them to me. "Thanks, girl. I'm acting like a crybaby."

"And you look a mess. Netta, your mascara is running all down your cheeks." She was crying and laughing at the same time. I started laughing, and I reached inside my purse and removed my compact and started laughing even harder when I saw how horrible I looked.

"Girl, I look like somebody just beat my ass or something." I wiped away the mess the best I could.

Nikki chuckled. "I am so happy for you. Really, I am."

I snapped the compact closed and returned it to my purse. "Thanks, girl. I knew if anyone would have my back it would be you."

"Always. I only want the best for you, and I'm glad your ass finally came to your senses. You know I love Leon like a brother."

"And I love my man with everything I have. Now . . ." I began, reaching for a menu. "What are you gonna do about Kenyon?"

Nikki gave me a worried look. "I don't know."

"Well, do like I did with Cory. Threaten to tell his mother."

She gave me a confused look. "Netta, his mama is dead."

"Exactly." For the first time since she'd taken a seat at the table, Nikki breathed a sigh of relief. All I could think was, she better do something fast because Donovan was due home in a month.

43

Nikki

I love attending BookExpo America. It's always a fabulous opportunity to get a lot of free books, meet a lot of the popular authors, pass out business cards and encourage authors to add my bookstore to their tour.

I had two rolling suitcases filled with books and catalogs from several of the big houses. I always made it my business to visit the Kensington Publishing booth as well as several others before heading down to the African-American Pavilion.

Physically drained, I made it back to my hotel and moved down the hall to my room. I was ready to take a hot shower and get room service. I slipped out of my clothes, called downstairs and ordered a salad, then jumped in the shower. Twenty more days and Donovan would be back in the states. I couldn't wait to wake up beside him every morning. This time our marriage was going to work, I was confident of that.

I climbed out the shower just as I heard a knock at the door. Damn, room service was quick. I slipped into a hotel robe and padded across the room. The moment I swung the door open, I was swept up in a kiss. I was so shocked it took me a second to react and push him away.

"What the hell are you doing?"

"Showing my baby how much I missed her." Kenyon was smiling as he moved over to a table in the corner, carrying a bag. "I brought your favorite wine and some fruit."

Okay, this mothafucker was definitely stalking me. "How in the world did you know I was in New York?"

He gave me a puzzled look. "Baby, don't you remember? You invited me to go to New York with you?" He shook his head, then reached for the corkscrew.

"I didn't . . ." I paused, suddenly remembering I'd not only told him in detail about the exposition but had also said it would be fun if he attended. "Fool, that was when we were still together!"

"Sweetie, I understand," he said with a reassuring smile.

"Understand what?"

"That you had to pretend we weren't together so your husband wouldn't know. I understand. But I had this day circled and my ticket bought, and I knew you still wanted me to come so we could spend this time together. By the way, something is wrong with your cell phone. I tried calling you to see if you wanted to share a cab from the airport, but I wasn't able to get through to you." Kenyon swung around and carried over a glass of wine. "Baby, here you go."

I slapped the glass away, splashing wine all over his

shoes and the carpet. Kenyon frowned, then moved into the bathroom and came out wiping himself off. "Why are you angry?"

"Why do you think I'm angry? Because we . . . are . . . not . . . together . . . anymore." I spaced out each word evenly.

He looked up and gave me that sexy smile of his, and I ain't gonna even lie, my nipples hardened in response. "Baby, I told you we would always be together. Nothing or nobody is ever gonna change that."

"Either you get outta my room or I'm calling hotel security!"

The smile slipped from his face. "Baby, we love each other. Why are you playing games and trying to act like you didn't want me here?"

"Because I don't!"

"Room service!" called a voice from out in the hall.

I moved toward the door quickly and opened it. I looked down at the name tag. "Charlie, come on in, because this fool is leaving."

The short white dude with blond hair and blue eyes had to be in his twenties. He looked from me to Kenyon, then pushed the cart inside. I held the door open. "Kenyon, you need to leave."

He looked confused at first, then turned angry. "Oh, so that's whassup! You're trying to get rid of me so you can spend time with him."

This dude had really lost it. "What are you talking about?"

"Don't play dumb! I fly all the way up here to spend a romantic week with you and then you try to play me with this short butterball. So tell me, did the two of you meet in the elevator?"

Charlie held up his hands. "Sir, I don't know what you're talking about. I just came to deliver the food."

"Sure you did, and my woman just happens to be sitting in her room half naked waiting for you."

He turned to me. I frowned and tightened the belt on my robe. "Ignore him. He's crazy. Kenyon, get the hell outta my room!"

That damn muscle at his jaw twitched, and the next thing I knew he flipped the food cart over and charged the delivery guy. "That's my woman! She's mine!"

I tried to pull Kenyon off him. My belt kept coming loose and my robe flapping wide open. I ended up reaching for the bottle of Moscato wine and breaking it across Kenyon's head. He crumpled onto the carpet, and Charlie scrambled to his feet.

"What the hell just happened?" he asked. His blue eyes were wide with fear.

I shook my head. "I'm sorry, but I have no idea. That man is crazy."

"Obviously." He looked down at Kenyon, who groaned and rolled to his side. Charlie balled his fist ready to go another round. He had just gotten his ass kicked, so he would want to go sit down somewhere before Kenyon dusted the floor with him again. I quickly moved to the phone, called the front desk and asked them to send up security.

Rubbing his head, Kenyon slowly rose to his feet. Charlie's punk ass suddenly chickened out and dashed from the room, leaving me alone with that psycho.

"Security's on the way," I warned, just in case he was even thinking about trying anything.

Kenyon gave me a disappointed look. "Nikki, you were wrong for hitting me. All I ever done is try to make you happy, and this is the thanks I get. Mark my word, you're gonna regret taking my love for granted." He hurried out of the room and down the hall.

If that wasn't proof that dude was crazy, then nothing is. The second I got back to St. Louis, I would get an ex parte.

44

Trinette

It was Saturday and I was sitting at my kitchen table studying for a big test when my cell phone rang. I looked down and smiled when I realized it was Leon. Every time I saw his picture flash across the screen I felt all funny inside. "Hey, baby. Missing me already?"

Leon cleared his throat. "I was just out to my mailbox, and guess what I found?"

"What?" Like I didn't already know.

"A letter." He sounded surprised.

I was smiling because my letter had arrived. I knew it would make his day. Monday, I had taken the time to send him a personal handwritten letter just to let him know I was thinking about him. I truly needed to start doing that more often. "Really now? From who?"

There was a pause. "I don't know. There is no return address."

Leon is such a kidder. I decided to play along. "Wow, a mystery letter."

"Yeah . . . let me read it to you."

I moved over to the refrigerator for a bottle of water while I listened.

" 'Dear Leon, I don't know if you're the right Leon Montgomery who's married to Trinette Montgomery, the case worker who lives in St. Louis. If not, please disregard. If this is the right Leon, I feel it's my duty to tell you about your wife. The adulteress . . .' "

What? I dropped the water onto the floor. That wasn't the letter I sent him. My pulse was racing and I didn't dare breathe while I waited for him to continue.

" 'Your wife is not the woman you think she is. She has no intentions of moving to Richmond. She doesn't really want you. The only reason why she is still with you is because of the money, and without you she can't afford to live the life she has grown accustomed to. She spends her time at work bragging about how she got her man wrapped around her finger while she has a different man in her bed every week. She's been sleeping with men in Ft. Leonard Wood, St. Louis, Chicago and Dallas. In fact she has been messing with the husband of one of her clients for some time now. What she's doing is not right, and I felt you should know. You deserve better than that. Trinette has been this way all her life, and she's not going to change for you or anyone else, because all she truly cares about is herself.' "

There was a long silence. All I could hear was my heart pounding heavily against my chest.

"Well . . . is that true?"

I moistened my mouth so I could speak. "No, Leon. It isn't true."

"Which part isn't true? That you've been messing around on me or the part about you only wanting me for my money." I could tell by the tone of his voice he was hurt. That was one thing I never wanted to do to him.

"Both."

"Now I know you're lying, because all you've ever cared about, Netta, is money. Why would someone be lying on you?"

"Because folks be hating on me."

"No, it sounds to me like someone decided to tell on you." He released a frustrated breath while I tried to think fast as to what to say. "Is this why you didn't want to come to Richmond and live with me, because you were messing around?"

"No, that isn't why! I told you, I was trying to live for me. Get my degree and a promotion so I could be more than just your wife. Why's it so hard for you to understand?"

"It's not. I told you before I'll support you in every way, but I get the feeling there is a lot more to this story."

"Why you say that? Because someone sent you a letter and now you're gonna believe what someone else said?" My knees threatened to give out. I managed to make it to the table and take a seat.

"Trinette, I asked you before to put everything on the table, and you said you had, so I'm going to ask you again. Have you been messing around?"

I learned a long time ago you can't admit everything. "I didn't start seeing anyone until after you dumped me on Valentine's Day."

"I *didn't* dump you on Valentine's Day."

"Look, let's not go there again."

There was a pause. "Are you and this man still to-gether?"

I quickly answered. "No, I ended it right after it got started. I was hurting."

"So because you were hurting you found comfort with another man?"

"What was I supposed to do . . . sit around and hope you changed your mind and took me back? You dumped me on Valentine's Day!" I was yelling now be-cause I was angry. I had put everything into making our marriage work and this was how he wanted to treat me. I deserved better. "I thought we were past this. I thought we were leaving the past behind and starting fresh."

"We are, but we can't do that until we put everything out there on the table. Honesty is important. If I can't trust you, then we don't have anything."

My heart was pounding so hard my chest hurt. "What makes you think I'm not being honest with you now?"

He sighed. "I just don't know. I'll probably never know."

"Leon, I've changed since we've gotten back to-gether."

"How do I know that? How do I know you're still not messing around with that dude? Do you know how it makes me feel to know some other man has been fucking my wife?"

"I know good and damn well the way you like to screw you haven't always been faithful!"

He forced a laugh. "That's the difference between you and me. I take my marriage vows seriously."

I gripped the receiver and dropped my head. "Baby, I made a mistake. I'm sorry."

"And what about the men in Chicago and Dallas?"

"I don't know where that shit came from, because that's definitely a lie." Hell, this was one time I wasn't lying. I used to date a dude in Chicago, but that was many moons ago. There was a long silence, and the hairs at the nape of my neck curled. I don't think I'd ever been so scared in my life. "So now what do we do?" I asked.

"I don't know. Knowing you slept with someone else, I need some time to think."

I wasn't going to beg. I couldn't. I had given everything I had to my marriage. I just didn't have anything left to give. "Okay. But before you hang up I just want you to know I love you. I never realized how much until after we split up, but I know now and I am willing . . ." My voice broke. I took a breath trying to hold on. "I'm willing to do whatever it takes to make things work." I didn't even wait to see if he told me he loved me. I couldn't handle it if he hadn't. I hung up the phone and fell to the floor and cried like a baby. Someone was out to get me, and I was determined to find out who it was.

45

Nikki

Trinette came barging into my office at the back of the store. I had just gotten back from New York yesterday and hadn't even called to tell her I was back. I was ready to cuss her ass out when I saw the look of panic on her face. "What happen to you?"

She flopped down on the couch, and it was several seconds before she finally found the words to speak. "Leon dumped me."

"Again! I mean . . . why? Why did he dump you this time?"

Her eyes snapped to me and I saw the pain. "Someone from St. Louis took the time to find his address and send him a letter telling him about everything I've been doing."

"What?" I couldn't believe that shit. Someone had finally told on her. "How did you find out?"

"Leon called and read the letter to me, then he told me it was over."

"Oh, no! Who would do something like that?"

She shook her head. "It could be anyone. It could be Jay's girlfriend. It could be this girl named Cimon. I was messing with her daddy."

"You had you a big daddy, huh?"

She ignored my attempt to make light of the situation. "I wouldn't be surprised if it was Maureen. I think she caught me coming out of the motel with her husband a couple of weeks ago. Whoever the bitch was, she tried to run me over."

"Whoa! Slow your roll! You were at a motel with her husband?"

"Yeah, but—"

"Uh-uh. No buts. I thought you said you were committed to your marriage and you were gonna do everything in your power to make your marriage work."

"I am."

"Then why the fuck were you in a motel room with someone else's husband?"

She knew she was wrong. I could tell by the look on her face. "I don't know why I went, but once I got there I changed my mind and left."

Did she really think I was stupid enough to believe her? "You are so full of crap."

"Nikki, I'm serious. I had no intentions of screwing, but he said he had a surprise for me and I was curious what it was."

"Well, let's see . . . if you were meeting him at a motel, it's quite obvious what his surprise was. How about some dick!"

She shook her head. "It wasn't like that."

I rose. "You know what, I am so sick of your shit! You have me feeling sorry for your ass, but you haven't changed. You're never gonna change. I've got enough problems dealing with Kenyon." I turned around and walked out my office. Trinette came to the wrong place if she was looking for sympathy.

"Nikki, you tripping," she called after me.

Swinging around, I faced her. "No, you tripped. Leon is a damn good man, and he doesn't deserve this. You're my girl, but I'm tired of your shit and I'm not gonna lie to you. The only person who can help you is yourself. You got yourself in this mess and you'll have to get yourself out."

Trinette looked so lost sitting there on my couch. "I don't know how."

I'd never heard her sound so defeated before, but I wasn't about to feel sorry for her. I'd humored her enough over the years. "You'll have to figure that out yourself. Oh, and one more thing, watch your back. Someone is out to get you, and it's probably someone close to you."

46

Trinette

Lying in bed at night, all I could think about was Leon and how lonely I was. It wasn't fair. I tried to do everything right, and what had it gotten me—heartache.

Someone was out to get me. They had slashed my tires. Wrote on my glass. Thrown a brick through my windshield and followed my ass around town. But the worst thing of all was the letter to my husband.

Someone wanted revenge, and I needed to find out who that person was. One thing for sure, whoever it was knew enough about me to share my past with Leon. The only person I told my personal business to was Nikki, but I knew she wouldn't do no shit like that. There were my brothers, but they would never hate on me either.

I forced myself to go to work when what I wanted to do was lie in bed and never get up. I buried myself in my work. Then four days after my heartbreak, Yolanda moved out onto the floor and asked for everyone's attention.

"I would like to announce the name of our new director. Let's give a round of applause to Maureen."

Everyone started clapping. Several looked over in my direction, waiting to see my reaction. I thought it was going to hurt, hearing she got the job that was supposed to have been mine, but it didn't. That job didn't even matter to me anymore. Even though Leon and I were no longer together, I still didn't want it.

Maureen looked over at me and gave me a triumphant smile. That bitch had no idea the only reason why she had gotten the job was because I had turned it down. I waited until Patricia had gone to lunch before I went over to Maureen and congratulated her.

She looked surprised. "Uh . . . thanks."

I leaned against her desk, arms crossed, watching her eyes as I asked, "How's things with you and Michael?"

"Fabulous. Why?"

I shrugged. "Well, a couple of weeks ago, you were worried about him mess—"

"I've taken care of that problem," she replied, quickly cutting me off.

My brow rose. "Oh, really, and how's that?"

"That's personal and none of your business."

"Come on, tell me. What did you do, slash her tires? Send her husband a letter?"

Her eyes widened. "She has a husband? Do you know something I don't?" she added with a confused look.

I laughed and moved toward her. "I don't know. You

tell me." It finally dawned on me, Maureen was too dumb to do any of those things. She wasn't anywhere near as smart as I had originally thought.

"Trinette, I have no idea what you're talking about. If I'm going to be your boss, you're going to have to understand I can't share my personal life with you anymore. What would it look like, me hanging with the support staff?"

Leaning forward, I whispered for her ears only, "I guess that means you won't be hanging out with Chuck anymore either." Maureen's eyes grew wide with fear. All I could do was smile. "Don't get the shit twisted. The only reason why you got the promotion was because I turned it down. If you don't believe me . . . ask Yolanda." Smiling, I moved over to my desk and retrieved my purse. "I'm going to lunch."

On the ride over to Harry's Chicken & Seafood, I thought about Maureen's behavior. If Michael was messing with someone, it definitely wasn't me. I thought she was too dumb to be stalking me, but I wasn't quite ready to take her off my list of suspects.

I parked and walked into the restaurant and spotted Nikki sitting at a booth in back. "Hey," I said as I flopped down in the seat across from her.

"Hello," she mumbled. She avoided eye contact, so I could tell she was still angry at me. "I went ahead and ordered."

"Thanks." I cleared my throat. "Look . . . I asked you here because I wanted to apologize. I'm really sorry, Nikki. You're right. All I've ever done is fuck around on Leon, and no, I don't deserve to get my husband back."

Her eyes met mine. "I wouldn't take it that far."

I shook my head. "No, it's true. I used up all my chances living dangerously on the edge. I love having power over men. I like knowing I can be the richest bitch in St. Louis by using the power of my own pussy. It's sad but true."

"I heard your coochie ain't all that," she teased.

"Then whoever you were talking to lied. 'Cause this shit is dripping in gold."

She laughed, and despite my jacked-up life I joined in. "Listen, I've lost everything else in my life, but I can't lose you, too. You're my best friend, and I don't know how you have put up with me all these years, but one thing I know is your friendship means the world to me."

"I love you too, Netta. I've learned a long time ago, you are who you are. And I can either be one of those people who loves you or one of those who hates you. I decided just to let most of your shit go in one ear and out the other, and I love you regardless."

I stuck my tongue out at her, but inside I felt so good. Nikki was a sister to me, and whenever everything else in my life was going wrong, it was a relief to know she was still there.

As soon as the waitress left after delivering our drinks, Nikki looked over at me and asked, "Have you found out yet if that man's wife is stalking you?"

Shaking my head, I took a sip of my drink. "Nope. I think she might be a little too naive to step to me like that. What's even worse is, she's now my new boss."

"Ouch! I guess that means she got the director's position." When I nodded she added, "How do you feel about that?"

"I really feel better than I thought. I hate the fact she

got it and that seems to be the only thing that pisses me off, but other than that, I would take Leon over that job any day."

"I sure hope the two of you can get back together."

I shrugged and wasn't about to put much stock in that thought at that point. "Maybe one of these days, but I need to get my head on right first."

Nikki gave me a weird look, then reached across the table and placed her palm to my forehead. "You feeling okay?"

Laughing, I slapped her hand away. "I'm feeling fine. Probably better than I have in a long time. Graduation is right around the corner, and after that . . . well . . . I don't know, but at least I have options, and it's definitely time for me to try doing things a little different."

Nikki nodded, then reached for her glass.

"Have you heard from Kenyon?" I asked. Her stalker cracked me up.

She frowned at the mention of his name. "No, not even an e-mail in over a week, thank God. Hopefully, the ex parte scared his ass."

"I can't believe he showed up in New York! Maybe that psycho has found him someone else."

"Let's hope so." She took another sip, then smiled over at me. "I've got some good news."

"What?" Whatever it was had her eyes dancing with excitement.

"Donovan's coming home in two weeks."

"You're serious?"

She started nodding her head as a tear rolled down her cheek. "I'm so happy."

I winked at her. "I'm happy for you."

"This will be our time to start over fresh. I want us to work. I'm ready to have another baby."

My eyes grew wide. "What?"

Nikki drew in a shaky breath. "I'm serious, Trinette. I think I've mourned over Mimi long enough. She's gone, but I'm not, and I need to start living again."

"Good for you," I said, giving her a high five.

"I've already stopped taking my birth control pills." Something over my shoulder grabbed her attention. Nikki leaned in close. "Netta, there's Jay."

I swung around on my seat and sure enough, there his fine ass was. "I'll be right back." I rose and sashayed my hips in a slamming Vera Wang dress up to the cashier and tapped him lightly on the shoulder. He looked surprised to see me.

"Hey, Netta . . . uh . . . whassup?" His eyes darted all around, acting nervous as hell.

"I should be asking you that."

"I've . . . uh, been meaning to call and talk to you," he shot back.

I quirked a perfectly arched eyebrow. "Oh, really, about what?"

Just then his baby mama Ronnie came over and pushed up close to her man. "Hey, Trinette. Whassup, girl?"

I looked her dead in the eye to see if there was any indication she knew about me and Jay. To my relief, her smile looked genuine. Jay looked relieved as well.

"I should be asking you," I replied, pointing to her stomach. She had to be at least five or six months pregnant. So that's what Jay been meaning to talk to me about.

" 'Bout to have another baby by this fool here," she said, smiling as she spoke. "But at least he finally made it official." She held out her hand, wiggling her ring. I glanced up at Jay with my brow raised with a look of amusement. I guessed he'd been meaning to talk to me about that as well. He finally decided to marry Ronnie.

"Wow!" Her ring was maybe a half carat at its best. Jay is such a cheap ass! "It's gorgeous," I lied. Then I couldn't help it. "Look what my hubby got me." I held out my hand and showed her mine.

"Daaayum! Now *that's* a ring," she replied, then rolled her eyes in Jay's direction. I guaranteed he'd be back at the jewelry store the next day.

I winked at him. "I'm happy for both of you." And I was. I thought I would be hurt to know Jay had chosen another woman over me, but the truth of the matter is, I never wanted Jay, but I didn't used to want him with anyone else either. But now I no longer felt that way.

He looked relieved. I guess he was expecting me to show my ass. "Thanks, Netta," he replied, then glanced over to my booth. "Is that Nikki sitting with you?"

I nodded. "Yep."

"Do you know if she's heard from Kenyon? I've been trying to reach him all week and he hasn't been answering his phone or been at work."

"Puhleeze, she put an ex parte on that stalker! Ever since his daughter's car accident, he started acting crazy."

Jay gave me a weird look. "Daughter? Kenyon's daughter died of crib death when she was three months old."

Hell, nah! My mouth was wide open. This story got better every day. All of a sudden I started laughing hysterically and dragging Jay over to Nikki at the same time. "Nikki, giiirrrl, you've got to hear this."

41

Nikki

"I am so happy for you," Trinette replied. I knew it was hard for her to be happy for me when her marriage was in a shambles, but it showed she was a true friend. "We need to go out and get you new luggage. Something pink."

I frowned. "You know I'm not about to go to the airport with some loud-ass pink suitcases." I started laughing and she joined in. At least she was laughing.

Trinette suggested meeting for lunch when I had called her that morning to tell her Donovan was back in the states and I was flying to meet him in Miami on Friday. We'd decided to go on a second honeymoon and start our new life off fresh. I had no problem with that. I definitely needed to get away. It had been two weeks since I discovered the truth about Kenyon's daughter. He was still acting psycho, calling my phone all hours of the night. Anonymously, of course. Otherwise he'd have been violating the terms of his ex parte and I'd have him arrested. The man wasn't stupid. Just psycho.

I glanced down at my watch. "I guess we better get outta here. You've been gone for lunch long enough."

"Nikki, I am not worried about Maureen, trust me." She gave me a look that said there was a lot more to that story. I decided to save that tale for another day when I'd time to spare.

"I really wanna get to JCPenney and do some shopping," I suggested.

"Okay, I'll go with you."

My head whipped around. "Are you feeling well?"

Trinette gave me a weird look and laughed. "Why you say that?"

"Because you don't shop at Penney's, remember?"

She shrugged. "I guess it's time for me to accept I'm not rich and the clothes at JCPenney are cute and at least it's affordable."

I punched her playfully in the arm. "Looka here. My girl's tryna change! She's finally bringing her head out from the clouds."

She gave me a sad look. "Yeah, I just wish I did it while Leon and I were still together."

"It's not too late," I reassured her.

She rose and tossed down enough money to cover the bill. "I'm not so sure."

I got up from the chair, shaking my head. "I don't care what you say, Leon loves you and I *know* he'll take you back."

"I hope you're right, but I need to make sure I am ready this time. Come on, let's ride in my car. I'll bring you back after we get done shopping."

"Cool." I loved her Benz. It was so smooth, I see why people spend the money to own one.

We got into her car and had gone three blocks when I looked into the side view mirror and noticed a black car was riding on her ass. "You see that car on your bumper?"

Trinette glanced up into her rearview mirror and nodded. "I see her. That's the same bitch who tried to run me over."

"What?" This was the first I'd heard of that, or maybe I hadn't been listening.

"I bet you it's the same female who sent Leon that letter." She made a quick left at the next light, and the black car turned as well. "Hold on." Trinette made a U-turn at the corner, and sure enough the car followed. "Told you that crazy bitch is following me!"

She wasn't lying, the car was coming up behind her and riding on her ass again. I tugged on my seat belt to make sure it was secure, then gave her a side-long glance. Trinette had the look in her eye that she was ready to fuck somebody up.

"I bet you that bitch is the one who also slit my tires."

I looked over at her, mouth wide open. "When did that happen?"

Shaking her head, she spat, "You don't wanna know, but I've got a sneaky feeling it really is Maureen riding my ass."

"That *is* a strong possibility, considering you were screwing her husband."

Trinette briefly took her eyes off the road. "I also caught her screwing the security guard."

Damn. DFS was a regular soap opera.

When Trinette stopped at the next red light, I swung around on the seat and looked inside the car behind us, trying to catch a glimpse of who was behind the wheel, but the windshield was tinted too dark.

"Can you tell who it is?" she asked.

I stared a little longer, then turned back around. "Nope. I can't even tell if it's a male or female."

Trinette released a crazed laugh. "Oh, it's definitely a female. Trust me." She peeled away the second the light turned green, and the car was close behind. "What the hell does she want with me?" she screamed.

I'd be lying if I didn't say I was worried about how it was gonna turn out. "I guess she wants you to leave her man alone."

"I stopped fooling with Michael a while back," Trinette barked as she turned on the main road toward the mall. "I wasn't lying when I said I was committing to my marriage." She glanced out her side view mirror. "Why's she playing? Don't she know I will whup her ass?" She stopped at another red light.

"I guess she doesn't think you'll go there."

"Then I'ma have to show her. Hold on!"

I braced myself. The light turned green, and Trinette started to pull away when she suddenly slammed on her brakes so hard the car behind her crashed into hers, throwing me forward in my seat.

"You okay?"

Thank goodness I was wearing my seat belt. "I'm fine but your airbag doesn't seem to be working."

Trinette released her seat belt. "I'll worry about that later." We climbed out the car just as the woman in the car behind us took off running. "Oh, no, you don't, bitch!" Trinette reached for something on the floor in the back of her car, then took off after her.

"Netta, where you going with that hammer?"

"I'm about to get my life back!"

Traffic had stalled in both directions, but there was no way I was letting Trinette go after that woman without a witness. As angry as she was, there was no telling what she was liable to do. I turned off the car, locked our purses inside and headed in the direction I saw her heading.

The female was tripping over her heels while Trinette was too stubborn to leave her fifteen hundred dollar Jimmy Choos in the street. Whoever the woman was, she had long dark hair, and from what I could tell she was thick. Before Trinette went back to school, we used to jog three evenings a week, so running was not that big of a deal, although we hadn't done so in months.

"Netta, wait up!" She looked like a damn fool running down the street swinging a hammer in the air. I tried to run as fast as I could because there was no telling what my girl was bound to do when she caught that female. Trinette's life was a mess. She had lost Leon because the woman she was chasing had sent her husband a damaging letter. There was no telling what Trinette would do to her if I wasn't there to stop her.

As soon as I turned the corner, I spotted Trinette heading down an alley. I increased my speed and started gaining on her, which wasn't hard to do, considering she had on designer pumps and I was wearing flats.

"Trinette, wait up!"

She ignored me and kept on going. I have to say that stalker chick was running for her life. Someone must have given her the memo and told her Trinette was not to be fucked with.

Then everything happened so fast. That female dodged between two cars, and another car was backing out of his garage and tried to stop but wasn't quick enough, and that chick went flying over into some trash cans near a fence.

"Oh, shit!" I screamed, and whizzed my way down the long alley, because I didn't need to get hit, and grabbed Trinette just as she was prepared to pounce on the woman.

"Let me go so I can beat that fuckin' bitch's ass!" she cried, and tried to break free of my grasp while swinging the hammer in the air.

"Uh-uh, she's already laid out. What more do you want?" Holding onto her, I moved up closer. "Who the hell is that?"

"If you let me go, I can find out!" Trinette replied, then pulled free, but not before I snatched the hammer from her.

The black man who had been backing out of his garage was standing over the woman, and his fat stomach was blocking our view. "Ma'am, are you okay?" He looked scared to death. So was I. Luckily, we were in an alley and there was no one else around.

Trinette and I moved in closer just as the female sat up, leaving the long black wig lying in the grass. My mouth dropped and I heard Trinette suck in air. That wasn't a female. It was a damn man!

"Who the hell is that?" I looked to Trinette for answers. Her eyes grew large, and then she dove on top of him.

"Cory . . . you bastard!" she screamed, and started clawing at his ass, kicking and punching. It took the man and I both to pull her off him.

Cory sprung to his feet and started laughing hysterically while Trinette continued to kick and scream. *This* was Mr. Lottery winner?

"Gotcha!" he cried.

"You mothafucka! You ruined my life!" Trinette screamed, and balled up both fists. Just as she was about to lunge at him, I stepped in between them.

Cory quickly sobered. "And you ruined mine! You can't be playing with people's emotions. You told me to get rid of that bitch car, so I did. I test drove a different car every week, trying to get your attention, but you were too busy messing with all them other dudes to notice. Then I finally found out who the man was in the photo I found in your drawer . . . your husband. I was so mad, I flattened your tires, tossed a brick through your window and left you a lovely message on your windshield." He shrugged. "And when none of those things worked, I felt it was time Mr. Leon knew who his wife *really* was. Doesn't feel so good, does it?" he added with a smile. "That will teach you not to call my mama!"

Cory started laughing again, and I didn't even try to stop Trinette when she reached down, grabbed the hammer off the ground and threw it straight at his forehead, knocking him flat on his ass.

The driver of the car and I looked at each other at the same time.

"You see anything? I didn't see nothing," he said.

"Neither did I."

"Me neither." Trinette and I replied at the same time.

All three of us turned around and got the hell out of there.

48

Trinette

"Trinette, Maureen wants to see you," Patricia said the second I returned from lunch.

I looked over at my coworker and rolled my eyes. My lunch hour wasn't even officially over for another five minutes. "What's she want?"

"What does she ever want? Something to complain about."

I took a seat and reached for my compact. There was no way I was stepping into her office with a hair out of place. Ever since Maureen got the director's position she had been in my ass every chance she got, that is, when she wasn't rubbing it in my face. Let me just say, working under Maureen had been a chore. She did everything she could to piss me off, hoping at some point I'd simply just go off on her ass and quit, but I had other plans.

After what Cory put me through, I was a changed

woman. I drove by the gym the day before. He was back at work with two big knots on his forehead and way too embarrassed to tell anyone what really happened. And that was fine with me. The last thing I needed was to go to jail for clocking that fool with a hammer. In no way did those knots compare to the damage he had done to my life. However, while his ass stayed in the hospital overnight for observation, I paid a visit to his mama and told her everything her son had done to me. I think that's where the second knot on his head had come from.

Nikki left that morning to join her husband in Miami, leaving me in St. Louis with all the psychos. I was so fucking jealous. If only it could have been me and Leon. Trust and believe, Ms. Netta hadn't given up hope just yet.

I fixed my lipstick, and as soon as I was certain I looked my best, I walked to her office, knocking once, then entered. Maureen frowned at the sight of me.

"There you are. I was wondering when you were getting back."

I glanced down at my watch, then back at her. "Last I checked my lunch hour ended at one."

She sneered her lips up and then leaned forward in her chair. "There seems to be a bit of a problem."

I took a seat in the chair across from her. "What kind of problem?"

"Cimon Clark filed a complaint against you."

That gutter bitch just didn't know when to quit. I leaned back in the chair. "What kind of complaint?"

Maureen gave me a hard, penetrating look. I didn't know who she was trying to scare, because it definitely wasn't me. "Said you were dating her father and because she disapproved you cut off her benefits."

I laughed. "She's lying and not even my client anymore, so you can deal with her."

"She's still your problem. I'm endorsing the complaint, and it will be up to the board to decide how to handle it. I guarantee you're going to be terminated. In the future, if you want to screw a client's father, then keep it out of my office."

"You know, I am really getting sick of working with you," I spat.

Maureen cocked her head to the side. "Well, guess what? I'm the boss. Either you get it together or I'm going to have to find someone who wants a job. I don't know if you heard . . . but times are hard." She gave me a phony smile.

"Really now?" I was so sick of her ass. "You know what . . . hold that thought." I rose and walked back out to my desk.

"What she say?"

I ignored Patricia and reached inside my desk drawer for an envelope, then returned to Maureen's office and took my seat. The smirk on my face must have scared Maureen because she gave me a curious look.

"Can I help you?"

I tossed the envelope across the desk.

"What is this?" She flinched and stared down at it as if it were anthrax.

"Go ahead . . . open it up and see," I encouraged.

Maureen cracked open the seal and reached inside. I watched her face drop as she looked at the photos of her and Chuck getting their freak on at the condo. "W-Where did y-you get these?"

I pointed a chastising finger at her. "Don't worry about that. All that matters is I got them and there are plenty more where they come from. In fact, I already have an envelope addressed and ready to mail to Michael the next time you fuck with me."

She didn't say shit.

"Now . . . I want you to make the complaint go away and reassign that hood rat back to my caseload. It's time Cimon started looking for a job."

I left her ass sitting there speechless as I moved back out to my desk long enough to log off my computer. I think I just earned the rest of the day off.

Patricia was staring me all in my grill. "What happened?"

"Girl, quit being so damn nosy!" I didn't mean to yell, but damn!

She sucked her teeth like a horse and had the nerve to roll her eyes. "Whatever . . . you gotta call holding on line one."

I wasn't even in the mood for another client complaining about not getting enough money to support them and their bad-ass kids. "This is Trinette."

"Trinette, this is Donovan."

Something in his voice scared me. "Hey, what are you doing calling me?"

He gave a nervous laugh. "I was wondering if you'd seen my wife."

"What do you mean? Aren't you meeting her in Miami?"

"I *am* in Miami. I'm at the airport, but she didn't get on her plane."

My heart started pounding and I started to get scared. When I talked to her the previous night, she was so excited about her second honeymoon. Nothing would have stopped Nikki from getting on that plane. "Did you check the airline?"

"Yes, and they said she didn't get on the plane. I've

tried calling her cell phone, but it goes straight to voice mail."

"Okay, okay. Maybe she got on a later flight."

"Maybe." Donovan didn't sound convinced.

"Okay. I'll go over to her house and see if she's there."

"Thanks, Trinette. I'm trying to think positive, but I have this feeling something isn't right."

I had the same feeling. And it wasn't about something but someone. A certain nutty mothafucka who came to mind.

"I'll call you back as soon as I hear something." I hung up and reached for my purse.

"Trinette, what's wrong?" Patricia asked.

"I gotta go." I hurried out the building and out to my dented Mercedes and peeled out the lot. While I drove to Nikki's house, I called all her numbers including the bookstore, and even Karen hadn't heard from her. Something wasn't right, but I didn't want to believe it just yet. Nikki's cell phone went straight to voice mail, so I had to believe she had shut it off before boarding a plane.

I pulled in front of her house. Her driveway was empty, and I frowned. I swore she told me she was taking a shuttle to the airport, but maybe she decided at the last minute to drive and left her car in long-term parking. Maybe the shuttle was late, so at the last minute she had to drive herself and park, and by the time she did all that, she missed her plane and had to catch the next one. I tried to think of every possible scenario. Yep, that was probably what had happened. So then why didn't she call Donovan and tell him?

I rang the doorbell twice, and when I didn't get an

answer I put my key in the lock and went inside. "Nikki, you in here?"

There was no answer, so I moved through the house, looking for anything that seemed out of place. Everything was perfect as usual. The dishes were all dried and put away. I went into her bedroom. Her bed was made and the timer was running on her lamp in the corner. I checked her closet for the red luggage we found at JCPenney, and all three pieces were gone. Her prescription allergy medicine was missing as well. There was no sign of her being there.

She had to have gone to the airport. I was so confident, I went over to the long-term parking lot she always used to see if I could find her car. After driving up and down the aisles, I spotted her Lexus with personalized plates TRUTH and released a sigh of relief. Just what I thought. She had caught a later plane to Miami. I immediately called Donovan and told him I had found her car.

"Thank goodness. Thank you, Trinette."

"No problem. I'm sure she'll be calling you shortly. Just have a good time."

"I will. Hey, Trinette . . . Nikki told me about you and Leon. I'm sorry. If you want, I can call and talk to him for you."

No, this was one battle I needed to fight on my own. "No, don't do that. I got myself in this mess. I'll have to figure it out myself."

"Can I give you a piece of advice?" His voice held a degree of concern.

I sighed. "Yes . . . anything."

"Prayer helps. I did a lot of that while I was in Iraq."

"Thanks, Donovan. I'll try that." At this point I was desperate enough to do anything.

"I'll make sure to say a prayer for the both of you as well."

"I appreciate that."

I went home, showered and had just fixed a cup of hot tea when Jay called. "What do you want? You know I'm still mad at you for not telling me about you and Ronnie."

He blew out a deep breath. "I'm sorry. I just didn't know how to tell you."

"Easy . . . just move your lips."

There was a pause. "I guess . . . I like having you in my life. If I told you I had decided to marry my baby mama, I figured all that would change and . . . well . . . I was afraid of losing you."

His words brought a smile to my lips. "You'll never lose me. Friends for life, right?"

"Absolutely." I could hear his smile. "Ronnie's gone to Belleville to her mother's. I thought maybe you wanted to go to happy hour tonight and talk."

"Don't you and your boy Kenyon kick it for the Juneteenth celebration?"

"Yeah, but he said he's spending the evening with his baby."

I brought the mug to my lips. "His baby? He must have another baby, because Nikki's in Miami with her husband."

"Nah, there's no one else. The only woman he ever talks about is Nikki. In fact, he said they were spending the weekend together, then going on a trip. He even said he might not be back, but I know better than that."

Oh, shit! I dropped my mug and rose from the

chair. "Jay, do me a favor. Try reaching Kenyon and call me back. But first, give me his address."

I hung up and grabbed my keys and headed out the door. On the drive over, I called Nikki's cell phone, and again it went straight to voice mail. It had been three hours. She should have been in Miami by now. I then called the police, which was a fucking waste of time. Nikki had to officially be missing forty-eight hours before they would get involved.

Halfway to North County, Donovan started calling my phone, but I ignored his calls because I knew what he was going to tell me. Nikki hadn't gotten on another plane. I tried Kenyon's cell phone and didn't get an answer, so I drove straight to his town house. On the ride over, I thought about what I would say and how I would say it. I didn't want to make him suspicious.

His Lincoln MKS was in the driveway. I moved up to the door and rang the doorbell, then before he had a chance to answer, I started knocking on the door. I waited for what felt like forever. What the hell! I knew he was in there. I got mad and started banging on his door.

Kenyon finally swung it open. "What the . . . oh . . . uh, hi, Trinette." His frown changed to that creepy smile of his.

I forced one of my own. For some strange reason his crazy ass was wearing a tuxedo. "Hey, Kenyon, have you heard from Nikki?"

His eyes darted around. "No . . . why?"

I was still standing at the door. He hadn't even invited me in. Something was definitely not right, but I continued. "I think something has happened to Nikki."

I watched the expression on his face. "Why do you think that?"

"Because she hasn't made it to Miami."

"Miami? Why is she going to Miami?" he asked like he didn't already know.

"To see her husband."

"Maybe she caught a later flight." He shrugged and was just too damn calm. Kenyon is never calm. If he didn't know where she was, he would be hysterical at this point.

"Nope. I've already checked. Something happened to her before she got on the plane." I tried to look behind him, but Kenyon blocked my view.

"Is her car at the house?"

He knew damn well it was not. "No, it's not."

Kenyon shrugged like it was no big deal. "I'm sure her car's at Park Express."

I propped a hand at my hip and gave him a look that said I was onto his ass. "How would you know where she parked?"

He looked nervous for a moment, then his smile returned. "Isn't that where everyone parks?"

"No, it isn't." I heard a crash inside, and Kenyon looked nervously over his shoulder, then down at his feet, and there was Rudy. Kenyon's eyes practically bulged out his head.

"What's Rudy doing here?"

He answered without hesitation. "Nikki . . . uh . . . asked me to watch him."

"No, she didn't. Let me in!" I tried to push past his crazy ass, but he blocked the entrance.

"Listen, I've got a date and don't have time for this! If you find her give me a call." He slammed the door in my face, almost breaking the hand I used to try to stop him. For a skinny mothafucka he was strong.

I knew for a fact Nikki was putting Rudy in the

kennel for the week. Kenyon would have been the last person she would have left her dog with.

I hopped in my car and looked over at the house and spotted Kenyon peeping out between the blinds at me. *Psycho ass*. Either Nikki was in there or he knew where she was. Either way I wasn't leaving. My phone rang. It was Jay.

"He didn't answer."

"That crazy mothafucka is at home! I just knocked at his door." I was so pissed I was pounding my fist against the steering wheel.

"Netta . . . what's going on?"

"I think he kidnapped Nikki." I quickly brought him up to speed, then there was silence on the line. "Jay, you owe me."

He sighed. "This shit is crazy as hell. What do you need me to do?"

"Try to get inside his house. I'm gonna drive around back. This time I'm getting in even if I have to break in." Jay was yelling something, but I hung up. I didn't need anyone trying to talk me out of helping my best friend.

I rode around the block and parked in front of a house with a FOR SALE sign in the yard, then got out and ran through the alley. Thank goodness it was casual Friday and I was wearing Deréon jeans and a pair of mules. I walked until I found his house, then tried the gate. Damn. It was locked. I was going to have to hop the fence. Double damn! I had just gotten my nails done. It took three tries before I managed to get my big ass over the fence, then I walked slowly across the lawn and moved toward the building.

49

Nikki

Trinette, please come back.

Tears were running down my cheeks the second I heard her Benz pull off. Help had only been a few feet away, and now she was gone. But I wasn't ready to give up hope just yet. I knew Trinette well enough to know she wasn't going to give up that easily. I just hoped it didn't take her long to figure out I was inside.

Kenyon strolled into the dining room. And to think I once thought his swagger was sexy.

"Well . . . I wanna apologize for that interruption. Trinette just doesn't understand *we* wanna to be alone."

I screamed, "You crazy fuck!" Only underneath the duct tape strapped across my mouth, it came out sounding like gibberish.

"Baby, did you say something?" he asked, then leaned over and kissed my forehead. I wanted so badly to punch his ass, but it was impossible with my wrists tied to the arms of the chair. "Let me go warm our food again so we can eat."

I watched him carry the plates into the kitchen. As soon as he was gone I started squirming around in the chair, trying to loosen the ropes around my wrists and around my midsection.

This was a nightmare. The last thing I remember was Kenyon knocking at my door and holding a rag to my mouth. When I woke up, I was dressed in this stupid-looking wedding gown, with a tiara on my head. I cussed him every which way, and when that didn't work, I tried pleading with him. He seemed almost sympathetic and prepared to free my hands when Trinette came onto the porch. The second I tried to scream, he covered my mouth with tape.

"Here we go, baby. Nice and hot." Kenyon stepped back into the room, grinning proudly as he placed a plate of food in front of me, then took a seat.

"I'm not your baby," I mumbled, knowing good and damn well he couldn't understand me.

"Oh, I'm sorry. You can't eat with tape over your mouth. Promise to be good?"

You sick fuck! I nodded.

He gently removed the tape, then smiled. I immediately spit in his face and watched the slobber slide down his cheek.

Kenyon reached for a napkin and wiped his face and gave me a saccharine smile. "I thought you promised to be good."

I looked at him and wailed. "Why are you doing this to me?"

"Because you're confused and I'm trying to help you," he said, like the answer should be obvious.

"I don't need your help. I need you to let me the fuck outta here!" I yelled.

"I'm sorry, but I can't. You're my wife," he explained, like I would believe anything that came out of his mouth.

"Your wife?"

He nodded. "Yes, baby . . . we were married last night."

Ohhhkay, instead of checking to see if this fool had been arrested, what I should have been doing was checking Fulton State Hospital to see if any of their patients had escaped, because he definitely needed to be in a straitjacket.

I decided to humor him. "How were we married last night?"

He chuckled. "Quit playing, you remember. It was a beautiful ceremony. My mother and our daughters were there, and everyone was laughing and having such a good time."

Okay, he truly was cuckoo for Cocoa Puffs. "Kenyon, you need help."

He reached up and cupped my face. "Baby, quit saying that! Nothing's wrong with me. The only person who needs to understand we're together is Trinette. You need to watch your friend. She's hating on us. Next thing you know, she gonna start rumors." Nothing they taught me in college could have prepared me for this crazy fool.

"Now hush so I can feed you. I spent all afternoon slaving over the stove for you."

He put peas on a spoon and tried feeding them to me. I turned my head. "I'm not a baby! Free my hands so I can feed myself."

"Yes, you are. You're my baby," he cooed.

"Kenyon, I don't want you. Now or ever. Please, get that in your sick head!"

He didn't seem to be the least bit disturbed by my outburst. Instead he reached for a knife and started to cut into his steak. "Nikki, baby . . . you're gonna love me again even if it takes all summer. I've closed my office for the week and rented a little house for the two of us at the lake. We leave tomorrow. I think time away from everyone and everything will help you to remember what we had before Donovan came and screwed with your head."

Reasoning with this moron wasn't getting me anywhere but to a secluded location down in southern Missouri where no one would be able to find me. I had to think of some way to get away from him before it was too late.

There was another knock at the door. Kenyon flinched, then tried to pretend like he didn't hear it.

"Aren't you gonna get that?" I asked, hoping it was Trinette and she had brought the police.

"Just ignore it and they'll go away." He cut another piece of meat and brought it to my lips. Instantly, I turned my head.

"I'm not hungry."

"Yo, Kenyon, man, I know you're in there!" It was Jay banging heavily at the door.

Kenyon hissed and rose from the chair. He must have done one of those exorcist moves because when he swung around, his eyes lit on fire. "Not a peep outta you," he warned. "Otherwise, I'll have to kill Rudy."

I felt his anger from where I was sitting and knew that was no idle threat. There was no way I was letting anything happen to my dog. I nodded and sat there listening as he moved to the door and opened it.

"Yo, man, whassup? It's Juneteenth and we got a table reserved for all the fellas at the club," I heard Jay say.

"I already told you I-I was spending the weekend with my girl."

Kenyon was stuttering, so Jay definitely made him nervous. While I continued to listen, I swore I heard a noise coming from the kitchen and focused my attention, waiting to see what could possibly happen next. After a few seconds, I decided . . . nothing. Kenyon must have stepped out onto the porch to talk to Jay, because I couldn't hear any more of their conversation. Without wasting another second, I struggled in the seat, trying to loosen the ropes around my wrists, when I heard someone calling my name.

"Nikki," whispered a familiar female voice.

I whipped my head to the right and spotted Trinette standing in the doorway to the kitchen. I cried out with joy. "How the hell you get in here?" It didn't really matter as long as she was here. I don't think I'd ever been so happy to see her.

"Through the window." Her eyes darted around. "Is he still on the porch?"

I nodded. "Hurry up and untie me."

"You owe me a manicure." At that point Trinette could have had anything she wanted. She moved around the table and started loosening the knots at my wrists. "What the hell happened?"

"That crazy fool drugged me and brought me here." I was talking soft and fast because I knew we didn't have a lot of time before Kenyon returned.

"Well, I just called the police and told them I spotted him dragging a body from the house." Reaching for the steak knife, she cut the ropes from one wrist and then the other. She was working on the rope strapping me to the back of the chair, when the front door opened.

"Hide before he sees you!" I cried, and Trinette dashed into the kitchen. Seconds later, I heard a scuffle at the front door and a crash, then Jay was calling my name.

"Nikki . . . Nikki . . . you in here?"

"Help! I'm in the dining room!" I screamed.

Jay dashed into the room and did a double take when he saw me. "What the hell . . . ?" He moved behind me and cut away the last rope. "Let me get you outta here. Where's Netta?"

"I think she went out the back door." Rising, I glanced over my shoulder. "Where's Kenyon?"

"On the floor. I hit him in the mouth." We both headed for the door, but before we reached the foyer, Kenyon came around the corner. I noticed the gun in his hand and froze.

"Where do you think you're going?" He took two steps toward me, and I shook my head and dropped down on the sofa.

"Nowhere." He didn't have to ask me twice.

Jay held up his hands and tried to reason with a crazy man. "Kenyon, man . . . let us go before someone gets hurt."

"The only one who's gonna get hurt is you for trying to steal my woman." He pointed the gun at Jay and the look in his eye said he would kill him if I didn't do something—quick. "We've been friends for years. I can't believe you would try to take my woman from me. She's my wife, man!" He was waving the gun around and looking like a lunatic.

Crossing my legs, I leaned back on the cushions. "Baby, Jay ain't even my type. You know you're the only man for me." I had to play like we were really a couple. It was the only way we were going to get out of this thing alive. Kenyon looked confused and shook his head.

"I saw him trying to take you away with him!" He looked at me, then swung back and pointed the gun at Jay's head.

"N-No, he wasn't! He was . . . uh . . . taking me to look for you," I stammered. "I would never leave you. You're my husband. Tomorrow we leave for the lake with our children." Jay had sense enough to lower onto a nearby chair.

Kenyon's body stiffened. "Our children?" He smiled, wearing a glazed, far-off look. "I thought you were mad at me."

I shook my head. "Just 'cause I get mad at you doesn't mean I don't still love you. That's just part of being married."

He lowered the gun slightly, then raised it back to Jay's head. "No! You're just trying to trick me!"

"No! I'm not." Out the corner of my eye, I saw Trinette with her finger pressed to her lips. Kenyon's back was turned so he didn't see her cautiously moving across the dining room floor.

"Kenyon, man, listen to your girl!" Jay cried desperately.

"Shut the fuck up! That's my wife you're talking about!" he shouted, then started scratching his head with the butt of the gun and looking totally confused as he paced across the room.

"Sweetie, let's just leave tonight for the lake. How about it?" I suggested.

A slight smile curled his lips. "You're serious?"

I nodded. "Yes, baby. Let's go." I rose and slowly moved toward him. "Just put the gun down."

He nodded. "Okay ... but not before I shoot this nigga here." He raised the gun and pointed it at Jay. "Sorry, dude. I never liked your pretty-boy ass anyway." Just as he started to pull the trigger, Trinette came up from behind and slammed him across the skull with a cast iron skillet. The gun went off, and a bullet hit a painting on the wall. I screamed, we all ducked and Kenyon fell to the floor. Sirens could be heard in the background.

"About damn time," Trinette muttered under her breath. "You okay?"

I nodded and breathed a sigh of relief. For a second there I didn't think I would make it or ever see Donovan again. "Give me your phone." Trinette reached in her pocket and handed it over.

"Come're, Netta." Jay pulled Trinette to him and seared her with a wet, juicy kiss. "Thanks for saving a nigga's life."

She pursed her lips. "Just remember, I get to be that baby's godmama."

He grinned. "You're on."

While we waited for the police, I dialed Donovan's number, and as soon as I heard his voice I started sobbing. It was going to hurt him, but if he and I were going to have a future together, I had to tell my husband the truth. And hope for the best.

50

Trinette

My heart was pounding so hard I had a headache. The last several weeks, I'd barely had any sleep and wouldn't be able to rest until I did what I had to do.

I pulled into Cedar Ridge subdivision and drove around a bit trying to remember where my husband lived. It's sad. I visited him so infrequently I seriously didn't know which townhouse complex was his. I was not going to cry. Nope. I'd been doing way too much crying the last few weeks, ever since I saved Nikki from that psycho.

Kenyon was presently in a mental health facility awaiting trial. We were hoping he finally got the help his crazy ass deserved. Otherwise, he'd be back on the street and ready to stalk his next victim. Men like him will make a woman run back home and appreciate what she already has.

Nikki and Donovan came back from Florida, looking so happy together. Watching and listening to the two of them gave me a lot to think about. You had to fight for what you wanted because absolutely nothing came easy. And that's why I decided it was time for me to get my husband back.

I packed up my home and put everything in storage, then handed the condo over to the real estate agency. The afternoon before, I gassed up my Mercedes and headed down the highway. My backseat was piled high with stuff. I didn't stop except to sleep, get gas and pee.

I finally spotted my husband's white Chevy Avalanche in a parking spot on the left and moved to an empty space not too far away. I turned off the car and sat there for the longest time before I dialed Nikki.

"Are you there yet?" she asked.

I tried to keep the fear from my voice. "I just pulled up in front of his building."

"Did you call him?"

"Yes, but as soon as I heard his voice, I hung up." What if he rejected me before I even got there? "If it's over, I want him to tell me to my face."

Nikki took a deep breath. "Good luck, Netta."

"Thanks, I truly need it."

"You'll be fine. Just open up your heart and let him know how you truly feel. It's too late to be proud."

I gave a rude snort. "My pride went out the door weeks ago." I knew I had one shot and if I fucked this up I'd lose my husband forever.

I climbed out the car, then I moved up the walkway to the townhouse with 2511 over the door and rang the doorbell. My heart was beating so hard, I don't think I'd ever been that scared in my life.

After a few seconds, I rang the bell again. I knew he

was there. Just before pulling into the subdivision, I had stopped at a gas station and called the house. As soon as I heard him say hello, I hung up.

I decided to knock on the door, then suddenly heard movement. I held my breath and almost fainted when a female answered the door.

"Hello?" she said.

She was beautiful with a caramel complexion like mine, and hair so fine and straight I wouldn't have been able to find a brand of weave that looked as good.

"Can I help you?" she asked with growing curiosity.

I shook my head and slowly backed away from the door. What a fool I had been to think we possibly still had a chance.

Before I could make it back to my car, she called after me. "Excuse me? Are you looking for Leon?"

Damn! Why didn't she just leave me the fuck alone? I was already humiliated enough as it was.

"No!" I called over my shoulder.

"Oh . . . well . . . then it's my mistake, because I swear you look just like the woman whose pictures he has all over his house."

I turned around and gave her a hard look. "Then who the hell are you?"

She dropped a hand to her hip. "I'm his partner Aaron Smart's wife."

"Ohhhkay . . . and what are you doing answering my husband's door?"

"My husband and I were on our way to dinner when Leon called and said he needed to see him immediately. Your husband and mine are in his office on an overseas conference call. Leon asked me to get the door." She had attitude in her voice and had every right to.

I dropped my shoulders. "I'm sorry. I just assumed . . ."

She held up a hand. "No need to explain. I would have done the same thing if some woman had answered my door." She smiled. "Come on in. There's no telling how long they are going to be on the phone. At least I'll have someone to keep me company. By the way, I'm Deja."

Almost an hour passed before the door to Leon's office opened and a tall, dark man came out followed by Leon. As soon as Leon saw me he frowned. I didn't care how angry he was. I was so happy to see him, I felt like crying. It had been two months since I'd last seen him, and if I had my way I would never go another day without seeing him again.

Leon took a step forward and forced a smile to his lips. "Aaron, this is my wife, Trinette."

He held out his hand. "I've heard so much about you. It's nice to finally meet you."

"The same here." I shook his hand, then looked to my husband, who was avoiding eye contact.

Deja rose and moved beside her husband. "Sweetie, I hope everything went okay?"

He pressed a kiss to her forehead. "Everything went great. Leon, man, we're going to get out of here." He took his wife's hand and waved over to me. "Nice meeting you again. Maybe one evening the four of us can get together for dinner."

"I would like that." More than you'd ever know. I waved goodbye to both of them. While Leon walked his guests to the door, I stood there shaking in my shoes, trying to find my courage. The door finally closed and Leon strolled back into the room.

"Hey," I said, trying to break the ice.

"Hello, Trinette. What are you doing here?" Leon only called me Trinette when he was pissed with me.

"I . . . I needed to talk to you."

Leon shook his head. "I don't think there is anything left for us to talk about." He started to turn away, but I grabbed his hand, halting him from leaving.

"Please, just hear me out," I pleaded.

He looked down at me, his face expressionless. "All right . . . talk." Leon moved over to a leather couch and took a seat.

"Okay . . . ." I nodded, then started wringing my hands nervously in front of me. I was so scared. I felt as if I were on the witness stand. Whatever happened in the next few minutes would dictate my future.

"I want . . ." I stopped and cleared my throat. It was so dry I thought I was going to choke. "I want my marriage . . . I . . . want you."

"You should have thought about that before you fucked those other dudes," he countered coldly. The look in his eyes said he was still hurting.

Shaking my head, I began to plead my case. "I didn't *sleep* with all those men. I'm not gonna stand here and lie and tell you I've never messed around on you, because I would be lying."

"Finally! We're getting to the truth," he replied sarcastically.

If I wanted to save my marriage, for once I had to be honest. "But I'm not lying when I tell you after our Valentine's breakup, I changed. I swear to you, Leon, I don't want nobody but you."

He laughed. "Now, how do I know you won't mess around on me again?"

" 'Cause, I've learned my lesson."

Leon didn't look convinced. "I'm sorry. . . . I don't know if I am willing to take that risk."

My chances were looking slim to none, and it was time for me to put aside what little pride I had left and throw myself at the mercy of the court. "Leon, please . . . please give me another chance and I swear I'll be the best wife ever." My eyes were misty, but I stood there waiting for him to say something, and for a second I saw his expression soften and I thought I had his attention.

"I don't think so." He rose, and I started crying hard. My entire world had just walked out the room. Leon groaned and turned around and placed a comforting hand to my shoulder. "Netta, quit crying."

"I'm sorry. I'm so sorry . . . and scared." I pushed away from his grasp, needing space to think.

"Netta—"

I held up a hand. "Please . . . I'm not finished."

Nodding, Leon crossed his arms and waited.

"I'm having surgery on Monday."

"Surgery?" I could tell he wanted to say something, but he simply nodded and waited for me to continue.

"I'm giving Mama one of my kidneys, but I had to come and see you first." My voice cracked and I took a moment to clear my throat, then took a deep breath. "Leon, I've made a lot of mistakes in my life, but you were never one of them. You have always been my rock. I love being with you. I miss your laugh. I miss your smell. I miss the way you complain about me spending way too much money." I was crying and wiping my nose, but nothing was going to stop me from what I had to say. "I've always imagined us growing old together, two wrinkled old folks, holding hands and sitting out on our front porch in rocking chairs. I don't want those things with anyone else, and I'm willing to do whatever it takes to have those things with you." I took a deep breath, trying to slow down the tears, and pushed on. "All the material things in the world mean nothing without you. The condo is still on the market. I sold most of our furniture and some of my clothes. Everything I have left is in my car. I've come to you with nothing but my heart." My voice cracked and my head was pounding. But I couldn't stop just yet. "Baby, I know I've fucked up. I know I've taken your love for granted, but if you give me another chance I'll be a wonderful wife and mother to your children." I was eating snot but I didn't care.

For the longest time Leon said nothing. My pulse raced, and any second now, I was sure I was going to pass out. I put my heart on the line. There was nothing more I could do or say. The phone rang, and when Leon rose and went to answer it, I knew I had lost him.

Picking up what was left of my pride, I moved into the bathroom and blew my nose and started bawling. There was nothing I could do. I had nothing left. Trying to pull myself together, I splashed cold water on my face and patted my face dry. I looked a complete mess, but that was nothing compared to the way I felt.

Swinging my purse strap onto my shoulder, I headed to the door and had just turned the knob when Leon spoke.

"Where you going?" he asked.

I glanced over my shoulder. "Back home," I replied between sniffles.

"This is your home."

I whipped around, too scared to speak.

Leon moved toward me. "Did you mean what you said about having a baby?"

While I nodded my head, fresh tears streamed down my face. "One, two, five like mama. Whatever you want and long as I'm with you." My purse fell to the floor.

"Come're."

I started walking toward him, not wanting to get ahead of myself, but when he pulled me into his arms and kissed my lips, for the first time in months I relaxed. "I love you so much," I said, and started bawling again.

"I love you too . . . crybaby," he teased, and then I was laughing and crying at the same time because everything was going to be all right. The truth hurt, but that was one time the truth had set me free.

Catch up with Nikki and Trinette's latest escapades in

Consequences

In stores April 2013

Turn the page for an excerpt from *Consequences* . . .

1

Nikki

"Nikki?"

"Trinette? Why are you whispering?" Even though I had asked the question, I had a sneaky suspicion I wasn't going to like the answer.

"I'm out in the garage, sitting in my Mercedes."

I dropped my pen onto the desk, then leaned back in the large leather chair and closed my eyes. By the tone of my best friend's voice, I knew this conversation was going to be a long one. "Trinette, why are you sitting out in your car?" The sooner we got to the point, the better. Talking to her sometimes was like pulling teeth.

"'Cause I didn't want to take a chance of Leon hearing what I'm about to tell you," she whispered.

I groaned into the mouthpiece. "Hell, I'm not sure I want to hear this myself. What did you do now?"

Don't you know she had the nerve to sound offended?

"Me? Why does it always have to be me?" she argued.

I gave an impatient sigh. Sometimes she can be so damn dramatic. I had enough problems of my own and really didn't have time for her bullshit. "Trinette, c'mon, just get to it."

"Okay . . . okay . . . but you've gotta promise not to get mad," she pleaded.

I shook my head, then glanced over at the clock. It was almost six o'clock. I still had boxes of books to inventory and a millions other things to do before heading to the radio station tonight.

"Netta, I am five seconds from hanging up on you. Five . . . four . . . three . . ."

"Okay, okay!" she blurted in a rush of words. "I think I'm pregnant."

It took several seconds before her announcement registered. Trust me, anyone who knew Trinette Meyers-Montgomery would understand my surprise.

"*Ohmygoodness* . . . that's wonderful! And about damn time!" I laughed because I never, and I mean never, expected this day to happen. "I'm finally going to be Aunt Nikki. What'd Leon say? I know he's happy!" There was a long pause and I knew then the shoe was about to drop.

"Um . . . I'm not sure if this baby's Leon's."

"What?" There was no way I heard her right. "Trinette, please tell me you haven't been doing what I think you've been doing?" Especially since she'd promised to never do it again.

"Nikki . . . I've been having an affair."

2

Trinette

I knew I was going to regret calling Nikki. Trust me, she may be my girl, but she's not one to talk. Don't judge Ms. Netta, not when you have skeletons in your own closet. And Nichole Sharice Truth definitely had secrets that she better hope were never revealed.

But despite her being a hypocrite, she's my best friend—hell, my only friend—and I needed someone to talk to about my latest dilemma.

Ever since I moved to Richmond with my husband of ten years, I have been trying to make new friends, but women were too critical and catty. I know because I'm one of them. I am clearly a dime piece, and no offense, but women have always felt threatened by me. Especially since I've always had a thing for stealing someone else's man. Anyway, since I didn't have anywhere else to turn, I had no choice but to call Nikki, who lives in St. Louis. It was times like this that I wished I still lived close by.

"Trinette, *ohmygoodness!* How could you?"

See, didn't I tell you she was going to judge me? I could hear the disappointment in her voice. Hell, she had no idea how guilty I already felt about this situation, because I didn't set out to sleep around on my husband . . . again. It just sort of happened.

Before I moved to Richmond, I fucked around on a regular basis. Once, twice, three times a week, it didn't even matter. It wasn't even about the money, because my husband had plenty of that. It was the thrill of the chase and knowing I could get away with it. That is, until Leon got sick of my shit and asked for a divorce. Trust me, I wasn't used to being dumped and it hit hard. I was so devastated I begged him to take me back and vowed I would be forever faithful.

We renewed our vows and everything was going so well until a year ago when I started having an itch that I needed another man to scratch. I love my husband, really I do, but sex hasn't always been the best between us. Meaning, on most nights, he's gotten his long before I get mine; then I'm sneaking off to the bathroom to finish the job with my vibrator.

No, don't get me wrong. Despite the sex, Leon's a good man who has spoiled me rotten to the point that nothing is good enough unless it's the best. And I think that is the only reason why I have stayed with him as long as I have—because he allows me to be me.

When I attended college, it was with one plan, and that was to find myself a husband. The second I saw Leon pulling into the parking lot in a new car, I knew I was going to be his wife. What I hadn't realized was that he was a financial genius who had been recruited by several major banks. For a girl from the projects, I was mesmerized and so caught up in the life he could offer me that there was no way I could say no when he asked me to marry him. Even though I knew deep down in my heart I didn't love him the way a man truly deserved to be loved, because Ms. Netta didn't have time for the "L" word. I was more interested in being provided for. And it ain't been easy. For so many years all people did was take and I never received. But with Leon, it was my time to get everything I felt I deserved.

I settled in as the corporate wife and satisfied my husband's needs. I provided Leon with a home he was proud to return to every night and a bed where I rocked his mothafuckin' world. In exchange, he gave me a hefty allowance that most women could only dream of having.

But over the last year, I realized that money just wasn't everything. Can you believe it? Me? Trinette Meyers-Montgomery saying money isn't everything. Well, it's true. At thirty-three, I finally discovered that no amount of money would fill that empty void in my heart. Something was truly missing in my marriage and I wanted something more. And when I met Jrue Jarmon, I finally figured it out. I needed to love somebody.

Don't get me wrong. After Leon and I renewed our vows, I had every intention of finally being committed to our marriage. That's saying a lot for a woman who'd been messing around on her husband since before the ink had dried on our marriage license.

I used to think something was wrong with me when it came to men and relationships. I had even started blaming it on my Uncle Sonny, who had climbed in my bed at age twelve, robbed me of my virginity, and continued raping me until I was sixteen. For years, every time I crawled into bed with a man and made him pay for some ass in cash, I blamed him and my crackhead mama, Darlene, for making me the woman I had become.

Leon saved me from a life that I never wanted to look back upon, and part of me stayed with him as long as I have because I felt I owed him. I tried to make it work. Lord knows I did, but I craved something more than my husband. Leon is a brilliant man with simple needs who never could challenge me sexually. A lot of that has to do with the fact that I'm a beast in and out of the bedroom.

"What do you mean, it sorta happened?"

Sometimes Nikki's worse than having a mama. "What I mean is . . . I'm in love."

Nikki started laughing in my ear. "Netta, puh-leeze! The Tin Man's gotta have a heart to fall in love."

I don't know why she thought I was heartless. Sure, I've used people along the way and stepped on the backs of anyone who stood in the path of me getting what I wanted, but I am far from cold.

"Nikki, I'm being serious. I'm in love."

I heard a heavy sigh and I knew she was probably rubbing her forehead. Hell, I know I stressed my girl out with some of the crazy shit I do, but she had no choice but to listen, because I didn't have anyone else I could talk to.

"So who is this guy?" she finally asked.

I closed my eyes, suddenly feeling so ashamed as I said, "My boss."

"Oh, God, Netta! This is getting worse. And you think you're pregnant by your boss? Have you really lost your damn mind?"

"I think I have. For the first time in my life I've met a man who touches me in more ways than just sex, and it feels so good." I was shaking from simply expressing my feelings. "Nikki, listen . . . I love Jrue."

"Jrue?" She gave a rude snort. "Is he rich?"

I already knew what she was getting at. "Yes, but it has nothing to do with his family's money."

"Mmm-hmm." She didn't at all sound convinced. I told you Nikki is always quick to judge me.

She thinks since she's the host of the popular radio talk show *Truth Hurts*, where she gives relationship advice to thousands of listeners, that that made her an expert. I am the one with degrees in counseling and social work.

"Netta, girl, what you're feeling is lust, not love," she said, trying to diagnose me.

"How the hell you gonna tell me what I'm feeling? I know what love is! I can't sleep. I can't think of nothing but him and having him hold me in his arms. Hell, I can't get enough of the way his skin smells."

"What?" Nikki gasped, then chuckled. "The way his skin smells. Are you serious? You got it that bad?"

See, I knew it was going to be hard for her to believe me.

I was afraid to answer. Should I deny how I feel or just keep admitting my feelings? Expressing myself was something I had never been good at doing, but I was so desperate I was willing to give it a try.

"Yes, dammit! That's what I'm trying to tell you. I am so in love with this man that my head hurts!" I still couldn't believe I had let my guard down and let someone get in, but I had. Now I couldn't go a minute without thinking about that fine-ass man sliding between my thighs.

"Oh, Trinette! This is a big mess. I can't believe you weren't using condoms!" Okay, so she was back to treating me like a kid again.

I shifted uncomfortably on the front seat of my car. "For your information, we *did* use condoms. They just broke once . . . or twice." That's what I get for buying that *barely there* brand.

Nikki breathed heavily and mumbled something under her breath that I couldn't make out, and that was probably a good thing because I was three seconds away from going off.

"So when will you know for sure if you're pregnant?"

"My period's already a week late. You know how I feel about taking an at-home pregnancy test, so I'm going into the clinic on my way to work tomorrow." The last time I trusted one of those over-the-counter tests, it gave me a false positive. I had spent almost a week hiding out in my dorm room, wondering who the daddy was, before I'd finally made an appointment down at the free clinic and discovered all that anxiety had been for nothing. After that I never trusted self-testing again.

Nikki gave another heavy sigh. "I just pray that you're not pregnant. It's really going to complicate things if you are. Especially when we both know how badly Leon's been wanting a baby."

It was one of the reasons why Leon had agreed to give our marriage one last try. Because I had promised to get off the birth control and finally have a baby. Me? Ms. Netta pregnant? You gotta be crazy. I admit, I thought I was too selfish to be a mother because everything always has to be about me. With a child, I would come second, and that wasn't even an option. So I kept taking my birth control pills that Leon knew nothing about. However, once I started having an affair with Jrue, I started losing my focus and got so wrapped up emotionally I was forgetting appointments and, most importantly, forgetting to take my birth control pills.

"I know, Nikki. Don't you know I've been sitting out in this car thinking about how I've made a mess of my life? A baby complicates things."

"Ya think! Goodness." She groaned into the phone. "So what are you going to do *if* you're pregnant?"

I answered without hesitation, "I'm going to get an abortion." Silently I pleaded for her to understand. Nikki was quiet and I knew why. She doesn't believe in abortions. She gave birth to her first child even when she and her husband had barely been able to take care of themselves. "Nikki, I don't have a choice."

"Look, why don't we cross that bridge when you get there? I . . . I just hate to see you make a hasty decision before you have a chance to think it through."

"What's there to think about? I can't have this baby!" I screamed, then panicked when I realized I was talking loud enough for Leon to have accidently heard me. Dammit. There was no way in hell I wanted him to know or even suspect that I was pregnant. "I just can't and I won't," I added in a low voice.

Instead of arguing with me, Nikki did like she always does and changed the subject. "So what's the deal with you and this Jrue? How does he feel about you?"

I smiled at the mention of his name and felt my juices flowing below. Goodness. He had that type of effect on me. "He told me he loves me."

There was silence and I could just see Nikki at her desk shaking her damn head, sending those honey-brown dreadlocks flying in every direction.

"You know I don't approve of half the shit you do, but if you're certain that you're in love, then . . . I'm sure together we can come up with a solution."

"Hey, at least that's something," I replied with a soft laugh.

"So, then, what's the plan? Is this guy pressuring you to divorce Leon so that the two of you can be together?"

I glanced over at the door to make sure it was still closed, then leaned in close and whispered into the phone, "Well . . . there *is* one more thing I forgot to tell."

"And what's that?" Nikki groaned.

I wet my lips and mumbled, "Jrue's married."

Also by Sasha Campbell

Suspicions

As the owner of *Situations,* the hottest beauty salon on the south side of Chicago, Noelle Gordon has a direct line to the private lives of her clients. But when an abandoned baby girl appears on her doorstep, Noelle finds herself at the center of a personal drama. Could the baby be her husband's? Or maybe her grown son's? Both men deny it—but Noelle is sure one of them is lying . . .

Scandals

Newly divorced single mom Monica Houston needs to find a job. When her best friend suggests she answer an ad seeking exotic dancers, they both laugh. But with no work in sight, it's no joke. Soon, Monica is dancing at Scandalous, and the money is flowing. But to hold on to her children, and her heart, she'll have to keep it a secret from both her ex and her new man. Too bad someone in her life has other ideas. . . .

In stores now!

Sizzling Fiction from
Dafina Books

The Hottest African American Fiction
from
Dafina Books

Check out bestselling author
Mary B. Morrison!